D0112272

A SAVAGE WISDOM

Norman German

Thunder Rain Publishing Corp.
Thibodaux, LA

Printed in the United States of America

FIRST EDITION, 2008

Cover Design: Pattie Steib
Cover Background, rubbing of Toni Jo Henry's tombstone,
by Raejean Clark

Author's Photo: Pattie Steib

Chapter 2 was published in *The Louisiana Review* as
"The Smallness of Her Life."

Chapter 7 was published in *Xavier Review* as
"Deceit Street."

Requests for Permission to reproduce material from this work
should be sent to:

Thunder Rain Publishing Corp.
Thibodaux, LA
rhi@thunder-rain.com
www.thunder-rain.com

ISBN: 978-0-9654569-6-8
ISBN: 0-9654569-6-X

Also by Norman German:

NO OTHER WORLD

THE LIBERATION OF BONNER CHILD

CONTROLLED BURN

A Savage Wisdom was inspired by
the life, crimes, and legends of
Annie Beatrice McQuiston,
also known as Toni Jo Henry,
the only woman executed in Louisiana's electric chair.

A Savage Wisdom
is an imaginative reconstruction
of Toni Jo Henry's legend.

However, the author uses the actual names and aliases
of the murderess and the fact that the killing took place on
Valentine's Day, 1940.

All other names and incidents are either fictional
or are used fictionally.

A Savage Wisdom is dedicated to
the daughter of Toni Jo Henry

. . .

if she exists

and
to my mother
for her gentle wisdom

PART ONE

"No man is clever enough to know all the evil he does."

La Rochefoucauld

But never met this Fellow
Attended, or alone
Without a tighter breathing
And Zero at the Bone—

Emily Dickinson

Prologue

(From the article reporting Annie McQuiston's execution, November 28, 1942)

VALENTINE'S DAY MURDERESS FINALLY HAS DATE WITH ELECTRIC CHAIR

Mrs. Annie Beatrice McQuiston, smiling but silent to the end, paid with her life early this afternoon in the electric chair for the brutal slaying three years ago of Joseph P. Calloway, 43-year-old Houston salesman.

At exactly 12:12, the big switch was thrown home to send 20,000 volts of current flowing through her body, making her the only woman executed in Louisiana's electric chair.

She died in the dim corridor of the parish jail house where "Little Sizzler," the state's portable electric chair, had been set up.

The executioner quickly set about the job of fastening the electrodes about her body. The brine-soaked cap was placed on her head.

"Goodbye, father," she said, looking up at Father Richard. "You'll be here, won't you?"

"Yes, I'll be right here," the priest answered.

McQuiston joked with the executioner as he fastened buckles that clamped her arms and legs to the big oaken chair. Finally, he completed his job.

"Do you have anything to say," Deputy Sheriff Reid asked her.

"No, I haven't," she answered in a low steady voice, still smiling.

Her face was thinner than three years ago when she was arrested. Her eyes were somewhat sunken from a sleepless night. Her lips were painted and her eyebrows distinct.

At 12:11, a big leather mask covering all her face save her nose was fastened to her head. The executioner stepped quickly aside and pushed in the switch that sent the current surging through her body.

Her body trembled slightly, and her fists clenched tightly, a small handkerchief crammed into one of them.

McQuiston had little sleep Friday night, officers reported. Saturday morning she ate a light breakfast as her last meal and donned her freshly cleaned dress, a simple black garment with gold buttons down the front.

At 11:25, Athas Coe, a Lake Charles barber, was taken to her cell. She protested when told that all the hair on her head would be clipped off, but submitted peaceably as Coe quickly performed his job.

When she left her cell at 12:05, she had covered her head with a gay red, white, and green bandanna. Not until the leg and arm bands were fastened and it was time to put on the brine-soaked cap was it removed. She appeared interested in every move the executioner made as he prepared to take her life in the name of the state.

Exactly at twelve, the big generators on the truck outside were turned on and at the same instant the bells of the nearby church began ringing.

Early in the evening of February 14, 1940, Joseph P. Calloway was driving from Houston to Lake Charles. At home in Houston were his wife and nine-year-old daughter. At Orange, Texas, he stopped to pick up two hitchhikers, a man and a woman. The woman was Annie McQuiston.

Holding a gun to Calloway's head, McQuiston told him to stop beside a barren rice field with a haystack. Calloway was taken into the field and he either took off his clothes at their orders or he was stripped. He begged for his life. He got down on his bare knees in the frozen earth and asked to pray.

Four days later, his body was found, his legs still drawn under him, just as they had been when he pitched forward on his face, with a hole, made by a .32 bullet, between his eyes.

No motive was ever established for the murder.

1

Valentine's Day, 1940

To make up for what he had done, Arkie Burk took his wife to see *Gone With the Wind* at the Presidio in Houston, Texas. For the first hour of the drive home, Toni Jo excitedly reviewed the movie's scenes, jumping back and forth in the movie's time, confusing actors with characters, speaking of Scarlett O'Hara, Clark Gable, Ashley Wilkes, and Olivia de Havilland.

As they drove through Liberty, Toni Jo said, "Wouldn't it have been grand to live back then, Arkie?" She didn't expect her husband to reply and didn't allow him the opportunity as she went on to talk about the burning-of-Atlanta scene, wondering how they had made it so realistic, "and those poor horses, you know *they* weren't acting, they were really afraid of the fire, do you think that's cruel, Arkie," and she didn't give him a chance to answer that question, either.

Toni Jo tensely recounted the scene where Scarlett shoots a Yankee deserter, then imitated Butterfly McQueen's squeaky voice saying, "I don't know nothing 'bout birthing babies."

By the time Arkie reached Beaumont, the emotional ups and downs of Scarlett and Rhett's story finally took their toll on his wife's nerves and she wound down to a happily fatigued mood. Slowly, Toni Jo slumped in the seat and fell asleep ten miles from Orange, leaving Arkie alone with his thoughts and the humming of tires on blacktop.

Arkie Burk could hardly believe his good fortune. While he watched sporadic lightning fulminating in the northeast, he took an inventory of his life. He had a successful business, a beautiful wife, and would have children in no time. What more could a man want? The Germans were kicking up a stir in Europe, but that was a world away, and when Hitler went too far, they'd spank him back to the hinterlands in a minute. The country was finally climbing out of the Great Depression, and those boys in Washington were making sure it would never happen again. Earlier in the decade, J. Edgar Hoover's G-men had taken care of public enemies like Capone, Dillinger, Pretty Boy Floyd, and Baby Face Nelson, and the New Deal would take care of this problem. They weren't so dumb after all.

Burk caught himself smiling into the night and laughed at himself. He checked his wife to see if he had disturbed her slumber. She looked like a dark-haired angel. The lightning crackled across the sky like a spider web.

On the Texas side of the Sabine River, a lone man stood with a thumb in the air, holding his hat down against the wind. Burk had picked up speed to charge the steep bridge when his headlights revealed the hitchhiker. He let up on the accelerator and moved his foot toward the brake, then put it back on the accelerator. Suddenly, he felt sorry for the drifter about to get soaked. He had never been so content, and his happiness transformed into a feeling of generosity and compassion. He braked hard and passed the hitchhiker, then eased back until he came even with the man, who climbed into the back seat.

Burk stayed in second gear to the top of the bridge, where he shifted into third as he crossed the state line. He was going seventy when the car hit level ground with a bump, then settled into a dreamy float just as a pregnant cloud's water broke.

Burk adjusted the rearview mirror.

"You're a lucky man if I ever saw one."

"Guess so," the hitchhiker said as he took off his hat and ran his fingers through thinning hair. "Thanks for the ride."

"Don't mention it. I'm just going to Lake Charles."

"That's fine," the stranger said. "Much obliged."

"From around here?"

"Hereabouts."

When the lightning flashed, Arkie glanced in the mirror. The man didn't look too clean, but he was friendly enough. He had a week's growth of whiskers about to call itself a beard, and despite a gaunt face, his eyes seemed alert.

"Smoke?"

"Thanks, no."

"Don't feel obliged to talk," Arkie said. "Some don't like to. I can respect that."

The man nodded. "Thanks. I'm a man of few words."

Burk drove silently for fifteen minutes.

Toni Jo stretched and yawned. She gazed at her husband and smiled.

"Are we getting close yet? I have to pee."

"Shh," Burk said, signaling over his shoulder with his thumb. "We got company."

Toni Jo peered over the back seat.

"Oh, sorry. No offense."

"Don't mention it," the stranger said.

She looked at Burk, who explained, "He's a man of few words."

"Oh." Toni Jo turned the radio on and skimmed around for a station. Even though the storm was behind them now, each lightning flash sparked through the speaker. She stopped at a song she liked, "Address Unknown," by The Ink Spots, then grew irritated at the bad reception. Finally she turned the radio off. She leaned back and rested her head. A sign read, "Lake Charles 5 mi." Toni Jo closed her eyes and resigned herself to the wait. She had almost drifted off when the stranger drew her back with a song. Toni Jo's eyes lifted in horror.

He was humming "Rock of Ages."

Her heart pounded. She locked her head straight forward, telling herself it couldn't be him. A lump of anxiety rose in her throat.

She swallowed and tried to think what the stranger had looked like. Scruffy beard, thinning hair, skinny. It couldn't be him. The stranger continued to hum, distracting her thoughts. The tone was familiar, with a difference.

Toni Jo looked at the glove box. She convinced herself it was him. They were approaching Lake Charles. She would have to do something fast.

"Arkie, take this road up here on the right." Her voice trembled.

"Toni, we're almost there. Can't you wait?"

"Take it!" she screamed.

The stranger quit humming. Burk knew something was dreadfully wrong. It had been nearly a year since he had seen his wife in such a state. He turned onto the shell road.

"Where?" he said.

Toni Jo scanned until she saw a drive leading into a rice field.

"There! Stop by that tractor."

The car halted and she leapt from her door. Arkie had barely shut his when she clutched him by the shirt.

"It's him. The hitchhiker. It's Harold."

"Harold?" Burk squinted at the dark windows. "Don't be absurd, Baby. It couldn't–."

"Listen to me!" She yanked his shirt with the strength of a man. "I know him. I'm telling you, it's him." In a loud whisper, Toni Jo said, "Do something!"

"First, we've got to find out if it's him. What do you want me to do?"

"Kill him! I want you to kill the lousy bastard." It was the first time Burk had ever heard his wife curse.

"Don't be ridiculous," he said.

"Get him out here so we can look at him," Toni Jo ordered. Burk opened his door. He reached in and pulled the keys from the ignition.

"Say, buddy, sorry for the trouble, but would you mind stepping out for a minute? It seems we got a little problem."

The stranger opened his door and stepped into the night.

"Come around here," Burk directed him. "Okay, stop there."

The stranger stood in the floodlight of the car's far beam. A fine mist drifted in the yellow cone. The man was stooped and haggard, his hair much thinner than it had seemed inside the car. His suit was clean but ill-fitting.

Burk spoke quietly to Toni Jo. "It's too short for him. And his hair was thicker than that."

"I don't care. It's him. Tell him to take off his shirt. He's got tattoos."

Burk answered softly in a high pitch. "Are you out of your mind? He's just an old bum."

"Harold," she accused. "Take off your shirt!"

The man looked across the light. He glanced down at his shirt and back at the woman. Leaving his coat on, he unbuttoned the shirt.

"Open it!" Toni Jo called.

The stranger flared one side of the shirt out. Toni Jo squinted across the lights. His chest was dark and sickly looking.

Toni Jo glanced up at her husband. "I don't care," she said. "It's him. I know it's him."

"Toni, come to your senses."

Her anger revived. "Come here!" she commanded the stranger. The man moved through the light. "It's you, isn't it?"

"Ma'am–."

"Don't ma'am me, you bastard con man. Open your shirt." The stranger looked down. He opened his shirt and looked at Toni Jo. His chest was crisscrossed with ridges of scars.

Burk winced. "Toni, there's no tattoo there."

"You idiot! He took it off." She glared at the stranger. "Not this time, you swine. You're tricky, but not this time. Take off your coat. *And* your shirt."

The man pulled them off simultaneously. The coat dropped to the muddy ground. One side of the shirt remained in his trousers.

"Turn around!"

The man stared at her placidly, as if he would never harm a soul, then pivoted slowly, moving one foot, then the other, deliberately, like an old man. His back was a field of swollen scars.

"Why did you take them off?"

The stranger turned around and gazed calmly into Toni Jo's eyes.

"Because it was an abomination in the sight of the Lord."

"What–? What do you think I am, an idiot?"

"Harold," Burk said, "is it really you?"

Without moving his head, the man shifted his eyes to Burk. "Much obliged for the ride, Arkie. I'll be moving along now." He stooped to gather his coat.

"No!" Toni Jo said. "You're not getting away this time. Stay right there."

Careful to avoid him, she walked around the back of the car and opened her door. She popped the glove compartment, reached past the papers, and grabbed the pistol by its barrel.

When she reached Burk, she held the grip towards him.

"Here. Kill him."

"Hey–. Watch–. Give me that thing. Are you out of your mind?" He took the gun from her.

"Yes, I'm out of my mind. I want you to kill the slimy bastard for what he did to me. Now!"

Burk pointed the revolver away from his body at the ground. He realized his wife was too disturbed to reason with. "Don't be a fool, Toni.

Get in the car."

She shook her head. "He's not getting away. Not this time."

"And I'm not shooting him, so get ahold of yourself." He reached for her. She tried to evade his grasp.

"Let go!" she yelled.

He gripped her tighter and pleaded, "Let's talk, okay? Let's just talk."

Toni Jo was breathing hard. She seemed to calm down. "Okay, what do you want to talk about?"

"Let me just ask him a few questions." He looked at Harold Nevers. "Okay?" She nodded. "Harold, what are you doing here? How'd you get like that?" Burk pointed at the scars with the pistol.

Nevers looked at his chest. "I erased them with a soldering iron."

Arkie's head jerked and he whispered, "God." Nevers smiled. "What you did to Toni was wrong. You know that." Arkie's words were part question, part accusation.

"Yes. I've asked God's forgiveness."

Toni Jo stepped forward. "He's conning you, don't you see that?"

Burk held Toni Jo back with his arm and glared at her. "Let me handle this, all right?" He looked at Nevers. "That right, Harold? This a con job?"

"No con job," he said. "It's the truth. Jesus is the Truth. He saved me from myself."

"Liar!" Toni Jo said.

Burk held her back. "All right, Toni, just hold on. Let's move away and talk about this awhile."

"He'll run off," she said. "He's conning you just long enough to get a jump. You turn around, and he'll be gone in a flash."

"All right," Burk said. "Let me think a minute."

Lightning flashed feebly in the south.

"We can tie his hands while we talk. Okay? Will that suit you?"

"No! He'll run. Make him take his clothes off, then tie him to the car."

"Toni–."

"Make him!"

Arkie glanced from Nevers to Toni Jo and back to Nevers. "Harold," he said, half plea, half command.

Nevers bent over and unlaced his shoes. He pulled one off. Balancing on one leg, he pulled the sock off and put it in the shoe, then stepped carefully into the cold mire. He took off the other shoe and sock, then unfastened his belt and trousers. Nevers looked at Burk and Toni Jo. He turned around and let the trousers fall to his ankles.

"Pick them up and put them in the trunk," Toni Jo said to Arkie. She kept an eye on the naked man while Burk did her bidding and returned with a rope. "Tie him up," she ordered.

His back to Toni Jo, Nevers spoke for the first time of his own accord. "I'm not the same man you knew, Annie. I'm a new man."

She went into a frenzy. "Liar! You're exactly the same. And my name is Toni Jo, you bastard. Annie was your whore."

The man turned.

In the fog-clouded lights, his heavy genitals looked out of proportion to the rest of his emaciated body. Burk was enraged at this man who had been with his wife. He felt diminished in her eyes. Humiliated.

Seeing the naked man who had let others watch while he used his equipment on her, Toni Jo lost her senses.

"You maggot, slime, shit, goddamn bastard shit sonofabitch sliming whoremaker!" She turned on her husband. "Kill him! Kill him now!"

Burk raised the gun and pointed it at Harold Nevers' chest. He pulled the hammer back and held his breath.

"Don't do this, Arkie," Nevers said. "I'm not worth it."

Toni Jo moved towards her husband.

"He's a con man, Arkie. Don't let him fool you. Shoot him." Burk continued to aim at Nevers. Toni Jo lost her patience. "Kill him. If you love me, kill him. Do it."

Do it—the phrase reminded her of what Nevers had tried to make her say. It triggered a savage vengeance in her.

"Do it!" she screamed. "Do it!" She reached for the pistol. It fired.

Shocked, afraid he had hit Nevers, Burk loosened his hold on the pistol. Toni Jo wrenched it from his hand. She aimed the heavy piece at the man's bare chest.

"This is the only thing you ever deserved," she said.

"Annie," Nevers said.

"Toni Jo! Goddamn you, my name is Toni Jo Henry."

"Toni Jo, don't do this. You're a better person than this. Don't let me do this to you."

Toni Jo wanted Nevers to fear her, but he was calm. For a moment, she thought his conversion might be real. It was an irony she could not tolerate, that he was forgiven and free.

"Down!" she yelled. "Get down on your knees."

"Toni," Burk said.

She turned the pistol on her husband. "Stay back, or I swear to God I'll shoot you, too."

"Toni," he repeated.

"Toni Jo! Can't anybody get that right? My name is Toni! Jo! Henry!"

Burk moved back a step. His wife was obviously deranged.

Toni Jo swung the pistol back to Nevers and trained it on his chest.

"Get down in the mud," she commanded.

Nevers knelt down.

Toni Jo stared at him. "Harold Nevers," she began.

Toni Jo forced herself to walk slowly towards him, as if she were sneaking up on an especially large cockroach for a disgusting but necessary extermination.

The man, naked, kneeled before her in the misty yellow light.

When she reached him, she pressed the snub-nosed .38 against his forehead and pulled the trigger, spattering his last thoughts, grey and warm, onto her face and dress.

The man fell back in the mud with a wet slap.

Burk screamed, "Jesus God, Toni Jo!"

2

April 1938

He appeared suddenly, as if from nowhere, like angels and cockroaches tend to do.

. . .

It was a clean, still April afternoon at the Time-Out Cafe. Arriving at the paper mill in early morning darkness, the workers labored for six relentless hours at their posts: the barking drums, chippers, digesters, and Fourdrinier machine. It was sweaty, dirty, dangerous work, and the men proudly wore the scars to prove it—nasty looking burns at various stages of healing on their arms and faces from working with caustic soda, bleaching, and acid solutions; twisted, knotted, or missing fingers damaged by or donated to the winders and slitters; waxy palms with large splinters enshrined in calluses from feeding the conveyor belts for thirty years.

At noon, a turbulent mass of tattooed, potbellied men invaded the diner, ringing the copper bell on the front door like a herd of stampeding cows. Laughing and mock boxing, feinting and punching, they shouted friendly curses when someone hit too hard. The same men occupied the same tables every day. Big Jake, the short-order cook, knew how many Blue Plate specials to prepare, how many corned-beef sandwiches and hash browns, how many burgers and fries. Toni Jo's job was to pour from the triple urn and then deliver fifty cups of black coffee while taking orders, personal compliments, and life's complaints from boys and men she had known for most of her twenty years.

"T.J.! What's cooking?" said R.O., a red-cheeked man of fifty who looked seventy, a lifetime of soot compressed in the large pores of his bulbous nose. While he spoke, Toni Jo studied the tuft of red and gray hair bursting from the open collar of his blue plaid shirt like a small but menacing animal. "What do I want, beautiful girl?"

"Grilled ham and cheese, don't toast the bread, heavy on the mayo. Pickles and chips on the side. Bottle o' Coca-Cola, punch a hole in the top with an ice pick."

"Not only is she pretty," R.O. said, tilting his sweat-stained fedora back and looking around the table, "but she's smart, too."

Rolling a smoke, the cinched bag of Avalon in his teeth, T-Bob, who would have graduated with Toni Jo from DeRidder High in 1936 if he hadn't gotten Tammy Sue pregnant, quipped, "O' course she can recite yer order. You been ordering the same thang for three years. A slope-headed mo-ron could recite the Pledge Allegiance if you said it to him a thousand times."

This was C.T.'s cue to take off his tired khaki cap and "whup T-Bob upside the head" until he apologized for talking like that "in front a lady." This time, the metal button thwacked T-Bob good, so he hit C.T.'s forearm, hard, with a pointed knuckle.

C.T. held his arm out so everyone could admire the muscular contortion. Beneath the taut skin, an egg-sized knot rose and subsided like a monstrous parasite rolling over after a long nap.

Toni Jo didn't mind the good-natured roughness of the men, whose kidding signaled that they knew she was way out of their league. These were men whose girlfriends had missing teeth or gold teeth, whose wives had false teeth or none at all, men with no opinions to express, whose beliefs had been the same, back three generations to the Civil War.

Halfway into their shift, these men spent an hour in the Time-Out Cafe for food and recreation. Then, like a furious wave fizzling into harmless bubbles on a sandy shore, the noon rush from the paper mill receded, leaving only the vinegary odor of evaporated sweat lingering in the air to remind Toni Jo of their presence.

After their departure, from each tabletop Toni Jo shot the collective nickel or dime tip into an apron pocket. Two terms of F.D.R.'s good words, good will, and Works Projects had done much for the morale but little for the pocketbooks of America. Just last year, the stock market had fallen faster than it had on Black Tuesday in '29 and now the country was languishing in the Roosevelt recession. The President's fireside chats warmed hearts, though few stomachs were nourished by his alphabet soup: the WPA, PWA, NRA, FCA, NIRA, FDIC, ICC . . .

Toni Jo had bussed the silver and stoneware into the kitchen and was wiping down the last table, back in the corner by the jukebox, thinking, "In four months, I'll have enough money to attend the Normal School in Natchitoches. Then I can teach anywhere in Louisiana I want. Then . . ." She had never reached that far in her daydreaming. "Then what?" She had spent most of her mental energy just getting to Natchitoches. "Get married, I suppose. Have four or five kids . . . And then what?"

The kitchen humidity drew beads from Toni Jo's forehead and upper lip. "Tomorrow, I'll turn on the fans," she was thinking when she heard the sneeze. A waitress who prided herself on missing nothing in the Time-Out Cafe, Toni Jo twitched and glanced up to see the man who seemed to have appeared from nowhere.

He wore a dusty-blue seersucker suit and a tie with a poker hand painted on it. On the gray fedora parked in front of him, he was tapping a rhythm out of time with the tune coming from the jukebox, Glenn Miller's "At Your Beck and Call"—a song he had perhaps composed or was just composing and which only he could hear.

"Bless you," she called spontaneously from across the room with a smile.

Toni Jo walked briskly towards him, apologizing while reaching into her apron pocket for the ticket book, then apologizing again for not having it and starting towards the counter. The man laughed congenially, showing a row of perfectly formed teeth.

"I'm sure you can remember my order between here and there. What's that, fifteen feet?"

"Right," Toni Jo said, nervously pushing an unruly curl back into the tiara-like cardboard cap. "What'll you have?"

The man looked at her with an unhurried smile. Feeling self-conscious under his gaze, Toni Jo spoke to fill the vacuum.

"Um, a menu. You need a menu." She pivoted on both feet without moving from her spot.

She was nervous, not because the man was handsome—though he was plenty that, she thought—but because he was unfamiliar. When she realized she was acting jumpy, she became more anxious and tried to regain her composure by focusing between his eyes, her body still twisted halfway towards the order window, her face directed at the intriguing scar, an elongated, four-cornered star, like a miniature kite someone had sailed up the bridge of his nose.

"A steak. You must have a steak back there somewhere."

"Chicken fried," Toni Jo said. The man burst out laughing, and Toni Jo blushed at the small-town crassness of the entrée.

"That's fine," he said. "And mashed potatoes and gravy—that's what folks up here eat, isn't it? And two or three vegetables. Whatever you can pick from the kitchen patch out back."

Again he laughed, but this time with a timbre that put Toni Jo at ease, as if this small town were a bad joke they had both made up.

"And tea," he called out as she disappeared into the kitchen.

While waiting for the water to boil, Toni Jo passed by the order window to peek at the Time-Out Cafe's newest patron. His left arm over the chairback, he was twisted toward the order window, twirling his hat on the index finger of his left hand while whistling "Rock of Ages." Waiting for her to do exactly what she had done, he chortled softly at his private prediction come true.

Toni Jo delivered the order. Careful not to appear too solicitous, she simply asked, "Anything else?" The man held up his hand, palm facing her, to indicate everything was fine. She pivoted and walked towards the kitchen.

"Hey!" he said. Toni Jo spun around. "How about some—how do y'all say it?—catch up?" Toni Jo laughed. "What the heck, right? When in Rome, order a caesar salad."

In the back, after tallying the lunch receipts, Toni Jo checked through the order window to discover that the man had vanished. Her heart felt like Big Jake had laid it on the chopping block and hit it emphatically, once, with a meat-tenderizing mallet.

Retrieving the stranger's plate, she found half a dozen small coins—the price of the meal and the tip, a brilliantly shiny silver dollar. Toni Jo wiped her hands on her apron and carefully lifted the heavy medallion from the table. She turned it slowly in both hands, inspecting it—the spiked crown and flowing hair, the slender neck and aquiline profile of Liberty, her lips sensuously parted—finally noticing the date, 1935, the last year the Peace Dollar was struck, the year saved by everyone lucky enough to spare a buck for the sake of sentimentality. Toni Jo wrapped the coin in a Kleenex and slipped it into the side pocket of her purse.

* * *

Thirty minutes later, the afternoon crowd began to slink and hobble in. Lenny first, then Joe Bob, then C.R., Sam T, Little Mack. They weren't knotty muscled hoodlums or dropouts, nor were they tobacco-spitting old timers, that leisure class of worn-out citizens who alternated between the courthouse steps and Woody's Barbershop from ten to four ever since there had been a town square. They were heroes, one-armed or one-legged veterans from the Great War: not even old forty, forty-five—their still-good bodies awkward with the curious subtractions—the arm that threw a baseball, the foot that kicked the can—now buried in France or blown to bits across the countryside, long since obscene compost for the first crop of postwar grapes or peacetime olives.

Unlike their boisterous, able-bodied counterparts, they talked quietly with Toni Jo, asked how her mother was doing, what she thought of Benny Goodman's new swing sound, or whether Howard Hughes was a kook, thinking he could fly around the world, pausing now and then to make sure the slack sleeve was still neatly tucked in a trouser pocket.

For her part, she attended to them, did not patronize, felt no need to overdo it. They knew she respected what they had done. Her father had died with them, his body even now lying with their fragments there in Europe while the believers among them waited over here for some kind of apocalyptic reunion with their missing parts and the rest hoped for an adequate conclusion to their broken lives.

As Toni Jo served them, she thought of the man with the kite scar and painted tie, his eyes as green as coke bottle glass. Until he walked in, she hadn't realized she had been waiting for him—though she had begun to notice a vague, nagging discontent she tossed off as mere irritation at the slow grind of her necessary job.

Her life had been small—much too small for where she thought she'd be by this time in her life, for Toni Jo Henry was beautiful and she had proof. Most Attractive, Class of 1936. Most Popular, 1936. Class Belle, 1935. Miss Congeniality, 1934. And so on, as far back as she could remember. Little Miss DeRidder, 1924. Set in a face of unblemished baby skin, her eyes, as shiny dark as varnished buckeye seeds, peered out of school yearbooks in innocent surprise.

Natural kindness she had, too, even before she realized the effect on men of her skin, eyes, and burnished-brown, not-quite-auburn hair. It was this quality that enabled her to deflect the quick hands of John Paul, star running back of the DeRidder Bulldogs in 1935 when they went to State, and just last week to gently rebuff a butt-pat from the mayor and not even make him feel ashamed—and he a married deacon at her own church.

Toni Jo was attractive and good and was beginning to chafe under the smallness of her life. Then, there he was, her first chance to make a quick, tidy escape, and she had been too guileless to flirt, to drop a suggestive word or leading hint that might result in a simple date and later marriage. Such things were not unheard of. She would have cursed her luck or stupidity if she had been given to cursing.

Frustration from long work hours, the tedium of waiting for better times, the plain energy-drain of constantly thinking of others first had been building in Toni Jo for the past few weeks. The veterans, even, were starting to grate on her nerves. When they had said their too-pleasant goodbyes and she had wiped the tables clean for the third time that day and was sitting by the jukebox looking at the fashion drawings in Wednesday's paper, a large housefly landed on the rounded corner of the table.

Toni Jo Henry was a sweet girl who wouldn't hurt a fly—except that as a waitress she was duty-bound to eliminate the pests. Thoughtfully, without taking her eyes off the insect, she doubled, then redoubled the newspaper, and in a swift, vindictive movement of displaced and long-suppressed anger, squashed the fly into a wingéd blot of red-black goo and erased him from the table with a single swipe of an ammoniaed rag.

*　*　*

At six o'clock it was C.T., R.O., T-Bob, and that crew again, only much dirtier and more rank this time. The same jokes. The same compliments and complaints. The same responses on Toni Jo's part.

Toni Jo served the men hurriedly, anxious to escape the cafe and get out the door in the early evening. She wanted to enjoy the cool walk home, smell the azaleas and give her thoughts over to the future, perhaps a change of plans, and what she could say to engage the new man should he reappear. Freshening C.T.'s coffee, she glanced out the window at a dark cloud and mentally crossed her fingers against the rain.

At day's end, while scraping down the griddle with a spatula, Big Jake furtively monitored Toni Jo, who threw utensils about, slammed drawers, and stacked papers with noisy haste. When she dropped a heavy glass mug that broke with the sound of a rifle shot, Jake stopped her.

"Hey, slow down. You clock out early, you just th'owing good money away."

Emitting a weary sigh in answer, Toni Jo stooped and began to gather the largest shards.

"Leave it," the cook ordered in a firm but friendly manner. "Go. Git. I'll see you're paid till seven o'clock. Go catch a picture show. Relax."

Toni Jo rose with a feeble smile, her cheeks flushed from the day's exertion. Big Jake, tired and greasy faced, gazed at Toni Jo with rheumy eyes. Holding the grillbrick up in one hand, he wore the stunned look of a bull just after a sledgehammer smashes its forehead with the meaning of life. Toni Jo finally saw how tired he was. She approached Jake, reached up to his cheek with a gathered edge of her apron, then planted a kiss on the spot she had cleared for her lips.

"Thanks, Jake," she said. "You're a life saver."

When she grabbed the strap of her purse and slid it off the desk, the tug reminded Toni Jo of the dollar, the largest tip she had ever received. Instantly, she became mildly happy and faintly melancholic.

She stepped out the door, then, head down, turned left automatically, oblivious to her surroundings. Halfway across the lot, someone called to her.

"Say, angel," the voice said. Toni Jo wheeled about. It was the new man, leaning on the ample and curvaceous body of a cream-colored Studebaker. Propped up stork-like, the heel of his right shoe hooked on the chrome bumper, he waved.

"Hey!" she said, paralyzed in her tracks. He smiled at her for several seconds, then, as if she were across a field instead of ten yards away, invited her over into talking range with two sweeping waves of his hand. She stopped five feet away, the distance country people keep when talking to strangers. Neither said anything for a few moments. Focusing on the kite scar between the man's eyes, Toni Jo swung the purse around her thighs, its weight reminding her.

"Say, thanks for the tip." She looked up, one eye squinted against the setting sun.

The new man suppressed a smile, took a last drag from his cigarette, then snapped it across the lot. They watched the tumbling white bullet hit and roll to a stop, sending up a languid spiral of smoke.

"It wasn't meant for a tip," he said, looking squarely at her. "It was a gift. A beautiful lady for a beautiful lady." His foot dropped to the pavement. "What's your name?"

"Toni Jo." The man tilted his face skyward and let out a laugh, full-bodied and long. "What's so funny about that?"

"Toni Jo? Are you kidding me? It sounds like the name of a poodle."

Embarrassed, slightly offended, Toni Jo dug at a bottle cap embedded in the packed, oily dirt with the toe of her shoe. She tucked a long lock of auburn-brown hair behind her ear.

"It's my name," she said matter-of-factly, looking at his neck, searching there for some indicator of the man's age: thirty, she guessed, though his skin revealed he never worked a day in his life. "What's yours?"

He looked at her as if he were going down a list to pick out one she would like.

"Harold," he said.

"Harold," she repeated blankly. "Harold what?"

"Harold Harold," he said. "What difference does it make?"

Toni Jo shrugged her right shoulder slightly and ticked her head to that side.

"Nice car," she said. The man stepped away from the vehicle and put his hands deep in the pockets of his slacks. They admired the automobile. The man lightly kicked a tire. He rattled his keys in one pocket and some change in the other.

Toni Jo said, "What kind of business you in, anyway?" *Way* glided into two syllables, way-ee.

The man who called himself Harold thought for a moment. "The money-making kind. What other kind is there? The only thing wrong with money is that you and I don't have enough of it."

"You can say that again," Toni Jo replied.

"And I'll bet if you had five hundred dollars you wouldn't be working at that two-rat cafe."

Toni Jo examined the cafe, a large crack in the window patched with tape.

"I been eatin' here since I was a kid. It's a nice place."

"To you, it's a nice place. To anyone else, it's a joint. You ever been to a real restaurant?"

"I was in Shreveport once, the Andalusia."

"I know it," Harold said. "It's okay."

"Okay?" Toni Jo said. "What's your idea of a nice restaurant?"

"Antoine's, New Orleans. Bord du Lac, Baton Rouge. Vic's in Lake Charles. There's good barbecue at the White Kitchen in Slidell. They're on my route. I'm in new territory this week, terra incognita."

"Where's that?" Toni Jo asked, thinking it was the name of a restaurant she hadn't heard about.

"That's a good one," the man chuckled. "Terra Incognita. If I ever open a restaurant, I'll call it that."

Toni Jo blushed at her ignorance. "Beautiful girls should be smart, too," her mother used to tell her. Now she knew why.

"Listen," the man said, "I'll be back this way in a couple of weeks. Would you mind–. Could I see you again?"

Toni Jo tried to read his expressionless face. Disappointed, she nodded mechanically. "A couple of weeks."

"Well, maybe two or three," the man said. They both looked off in the distance.

Toni Jo thought for a while. "I don't think I'm planning any long vacations."

The man walked around to the driver's side of his car and said across the rooftop, "Well, keep your chin up. With a face like that"—his eyes followed the outline of her body down to her ankles—"you'd be surprised where you could go."

Toni Jo, who had heard such statements her entire life, was convinced that, unlike her other admirers, this man knew what he was talking about.

"Thanks," she said.

The man slid into the seat and started the car. He ducked his head and called through the open passenger window. "Just stating a fact."

"Thanks all the same," Toni Jo said. Harold dropped the car into gear and let up on the clutch, easing the Studebaker onto the highway.

"Hey!" she yelled. He slowed and craned his neck out the window. She held her purse up. "Thanks for the gift!"

He pointed at her as the sedan moved onto the blacktop, his face quaking with laughter that Toni Jo couldn't hear for the roar of the engine taking him away.

3

April 1938

"Dollface," Ray Boy called. "Hey, Toni Jo, wake up." He put two fingers to his lips and whistled sharply. "Hey, *hey!*"

She finally snapped to. "Sorry, Ray, I guess I was somewhere else."

"Well, wherever it was, I probbly been there a few times myself. How 'bout a slice of that lemon pie?"

A week had passed since the new man had stolen away. Deliriously happy, Toni Jo felt certain somehow that he was the man she had been destined to meet, to live and die with. She had written a long entry in her diary on the night they met, the sameness of the previous month represented by blank pages.

Then she reread passages about her old boyfriends. She always had dates to the major events at school and church—banquets, homecomings, proms—but most of her escorts she thought of as brothers. She had known the boys all their lives. On the porch, Toni Jo let them kiss her good night, and she returned a kiss so short and obligatory that the boys felt they had in fact been kissed by their sister, and though they continued to remark on her beauty, they never asked her out again.

Then there was Rusty: Walter Thomas Lewis. A three-sport man. Toni Jo loved the way he looked in his uniforms and letter sweater. When most guys wore their hair slicked back over their ears with Wildroot, he kept his dry and let the brick red waves fall naturally on his forehead. Rusty went through half a dozen girls per year like an impatient, hard-to-fit man trying on shirts.

No one called Walter Thomas Lewis by his given names. An only son, he was referred to as "the Lewis boy" by other parents and "Wally Tom" by his three older sisters.

Rusty was a year older than Toni Jo. She had been watching him since moving to the high school. On the first day of her junior year, he walked into Mr. Jones's geometry class. Toni Jo's heart bolted when his eyes locked onto her and he walked straight for the empty seat behind hers. When he kissed Toni Jo at her door two Friday nights later, she felt a pleasurable pain in her chest, as if it were a balloon someone had blown up too tight.

After Rusty and Toni Jo had been dating for three months, Mrs. Henry complimented her daughter on her choice but cautioned that, although she might believe Rusty to be special, he was like all young fellows and might press her too far. Her mother never told her, but Toni Jo was an eight-month baby, and that constant reminder was Mrs. Henry's secret diploma confirming her infallible knowledge regarding the ways of boys and men.

Toni Jo sat in obedient and total humiliation before her mother. It was expected of her. Still, she felt disappointed by, almost resented, her mother's lack of trust. Weeks back, Toni Jo had promised her she would never let Rusty take her into the Star Theater's balcony, traditionally the colored section. Mother and daughter never exchanged specific words, but their eyes, in unspoken, intimate rapport, communicated that each knew of the compromised reputation of girls who did such things.

So Toni Jo could not have explained to her own, much less to her mother's satisfaction why the next Saturday she and Rusty ascended the carpeted stairs and entered the dark, mysterious realm the locals called Nigger Heaven. It was the first showing of *It Happened One Night*, starring Clark Gable and Claudette Colbert. Lit by the dusty blue cone of light spraying from the projector, Rusty waved to a couple of guys and their girlfriends as he and Toni Jo passed them on their way to the highest tier. Occupying a love seat, Toni Jo wedged her purse into the folded chair to her right while Rusty pulled something from his letter sweater.

"Psst!" he said in order to get the attention of a knot of colored boys five rows down. "Psst!" When one of them glanced back, Rusty waved him towards the love seat. The boy pointed to his chest with a frightened look on his face. Rusty nodded and waved more forcefully as if to say, "Come on up, I won't bite you."

The boy began briskly and slowed as he neared, coming to a full stop three steps from the couple. Swiveled around in their seats, the boy's friends watched and giggled at him. One made a farting noise, and they all disappeared from view laughing uproariously.

"Here," Rusty said, holding up his Coke cup. "Want some of this?" The boy nodded quickly. "Get a cup."

The boy ducked between two rows of seats and hunted around on the floor until he spied a discarded cup and retrieved it. At what he considered a safe distance from the white man, he reached the cup as far as he could. Without touching the boy's cup, Rusty poured half of his Coke into the crumpled, dirty container.

Mock gruffly, Rusty said, "You know who I am, boy?"

"Yassur. You Rusty Lewis. That plays football at the high school. You a right fast runner."

"Damn straight. Now get your tiny butt down there with your friends and I don't want to hear a peep outta y'all for the rest of the night, you hear?"

The boy grinned big, correctly reading Rusty's tone, which implied that the two were now buddies. The boy turned to his friends and stuck his tongue out at them.

Toni Jo was puzzled by all the activity until Rusty brought a half-pint of Old Crow into full view and topped off his cup with the amber contents of the bottle.

Rusty amused himself during slow scenes by throwing peanut hulls at the smaller colored boys who stayed for two or three features, getting their money's worth of entertainment and air conditioning. To get back at Rusty, they made loud smooching noises when he and Toni Jo kissed. During scenes when they weren't kissing and the boys weren't looking, Rusty brushed his fingers against the thin cotton fabric near Toni Jo's left breast and, in the silent agreement teenagers employ to salve their consciences and still feel good, she pretended not to know what he was doing.

By the middle of *It Happened One Night*, Rusty was rubbing the side of Toni Jo's breast. When Clark Gable and Claudette Colbert started bedding down in a haystack for the night, Rusty's hand boldly moved over his date's shoulder to the front of her dress and began a clumsy massage. Toni Jo pretended total ignorance, hazily thinking that if she refused to acknowledge it, it couldn't be bad. The two kissed while the credits scrolled into the darkness above the screen, ignoring the colored boys making noises at a safe distance.

Ten minutes later, the projector off, the boys chased out by an usher, the empty theater filled with the haunting quiet of a mausoleum, Rusty snaked his finger between the third and fourth buttons of Toni Jo's dress and was trying to sneak it under her brassiere for a feel of secret flesh when the illusion burst. With nothing to disguise the blatant move—no metallic human voice from the staticky speakers, no moving light on the screen, no lapful of popcorn and candy to serve as excuses not to fend away an errant hand—the impetuous ploy degenerated into a crude and obvious maneuver. Wordlessly, Toni Jo made her objection by returning Rusty's hand to the front of her dress, implying that *that* was plenty liberal of her already. His crooning pleas obviously affected Toni Jo, as he judged by her heavy breathing and humid skin, but she held her ground and told him that certain things would have to wait for their engagement.

Toni Jo did not think the actions of the evening especially significant until at school two days later, when Rusty moved to another seat in their geometry class. Wednesday, she saw him in the hall holding hands with Jeanna Rae. Until Rusty graduated and left for LSU on a football scholarship, he never spoke another word to her.

* * *

The new man had been absent two weeks when Toni Jo's mood shifted from elation to anxiety. He said two weeks, she reminded herself. Or three, Toni Jo remembered.

At night, after a warm bath to cleanse her flawless skin of the day's sweat and grease, she lay in bed under the cool sheets thinking of him—his Crosby smooth voice, the scar on his nose, a perfect set of teeth—conjuring up her most intimate physical encounter with Rusty, replacing the boy in her bedtime imaginings with Harold, quickly getting to the part when Harold would slip his hand under her brassiere with suave dexterity, then, after she resisted a bit, touch her there—over the cotton nightgown where her hand now moved, pressing, squeezing, massaging all around, until she would think, there, there where her hand, suddenly become his, ventured quickly under the cloth to touch the darker, puckered flesh and, frustrated, her conscience throwing a little tantrum, Toni Jo would fling her arms outward on the bed and finally, in the breathless higher regions near tortured ecstasy, gasp, "Oh, God, what am I going to do if he doesn't come back?"

4

May 1938

The third week of the new man's absence, Toni Jo grew despondent. She began to deride herself for her girlish optimism and obtuse naïveté. The man had merely engaged her in a harmless flirtation to entertain himself while on a boring sales route. She almost despised herself for being duped by the charming stranger.

Still, she thought she could be wrong. In the back of her mind, about where her father would return limping but alive after twenty years, she saw Harold's cream and silver Studebaker swing onto the parking lot of the Time-Out Cafe, its passenger door flinging open invitingly to sweep her up and carry her away.

By Monday of the fourth week, Toni Jo dove deep into her depression to feel its full effect and get it over with. She rebuked her pride and, in mini-sermons between waves of customers, reminded herself that she was no better than R.O., T-Boy, Big Jake, and C.T.

By the end of the week, resigned to the old grind and determined to resurrect her plan to attend the Normal School, Toni Jo had practiced serving the men with such humility and enthusiasm that she caught the contagion of the role she was playing and her old self began to revive.

Then, when she least expected him, the new man reappeared.

Toni Jo clocked out at seven that Friday evening. As she swung through the door onto the lot, a man, his face obscured by the shadow of his hat brim, waved at her from a dark blue Packard. She smiled and flipped toward him the politely indifferent wave of one stranger to another and continued walking.

"Say, angel face," he called. She stopped and turned. "I haven't seen you in a month and this is the welcome I get?" He doffed his hat and said, "It's me. Harold."

Half an hour later, the two sat eating Mrs. Henry's Friday evening meal of veal cutlets, carrots in white sauce, and mashed potatoes. Taking the new man's sudden appearance in stride, as if the last interesting thing that would ever happen to her had occurred years ago, Mrs. Henry laid out an extra setting for him.

The tea poured and helpings doled, the small talk began. Will the country ever get out of this depression? Would Joe Louis beat Max Schmeling this summer? Had there been a conspiracy behind Huey Long's assassination?

"What line of work you in?" Mrs. Henry asked at length. That's what she really wanted to know.

"The restaurant business," Harold said, and when that didn't satisfy Toni Jo's mother, he added, "I'm starting a small chain of restaurants. They say we'll be out of this depression any time now. When people have money, they like to eat out. I want to get the property cheap and be ready when the boom hits."

This seemed reasonable enough to Mrs. Henry, who went on to the next question.

"And where are you from, Mr.—?"

"Nevers," the handsome man said softly.

"Nevers. What an unusual name," Mrs. Henry sang, putting down her fork, truly interested for the first time that evening.

"I don't think–. No, wait. Wasn't there a famous Nevers who played football out west somewhere?"

Nevers had been nodding agreement, as if he were used to this line of questioning.

"Ernie Nevers," he said. "Stanford. No relation."

"That's right," Mrs. Henry said. "I remember, now that you mention it. Well, then. Where are your folks from?"

"They passed on a long time ago," he said, his eyes calmly meeting hers.

"Oh," Mrs. Henry said, trying to recover from what she perceived as a social blunder. Then, solicitous, all three talked at once:

—"I'm so sorry, there was no way for me to know."

—"Harold, I had no idea."

—"Think nothing of it. It's not important."

Harold Nevers went on to tell of his earliest memories at Boys' Village, an orphanage in Kilgore, Texas, winning Mrs. Henry's approval with humorous anecdotes about school and dorm life.

Toni Jo's mother slapped her on the arm. "Ain't he a deal? He's a card, all right."

Mrs. Henry cleared the table and announced her retirement, saying she had to rise early and open the drugstore for Mr. Vincent. An awkward silence followed her departure.

"Well," Toni Jo attempted, rising. "I guess I'd better wash these dishes. They've been gathering for two days."

"Here." The man pushed his chair back without standing. "I'll help."

"No," Toni Jo objected. "I wouldn't think of it. You can talk while I work. I wash dishes all day at the cafe, so it's nothing. Really. What shall we talk about?"

"Nothing too serious, I hope," Nevers jested. "How about the most important event of my life?" He chuckled.

Toni Jo turned sideways to see him while he talked and she worked. His eyes looked quickly up into hers, and Toni Jo wondered what he had been inspecting—her back? legs? behind?

Nevers began melodramatically, "Long ago, in a small but booming Texas town—oil, you understand—there was a boy nobody paid attention to. He was an orphan. Yes," he said, holding up his hand, as if fending off sympathy, "it's a sad story but true. One by one the boys, some of them his best friends, were adopted by parents with shiny cars and mink stoles. He was a neat, well-mannered lad of middling good looks. Year by year, on into high school, he made the best grades in his class."

Nevers had been peeling the red strip from a pack of Lucky Strikes. He paused to tack a cigarette to his lips and scrape a match on his shoe sole. When he resumed talking, the white stick bobbed up and down in his mouth.

"That's when he noticed that girls didn't care a hoot about eggheads. They went for the lettermen, especially football players." Nevers took a drag at the cigarette, then parked it on the edge of the carnival-glass ashtray. "He wasn't a big fellow, mind you. Even smaller than myself, I'd say. But he was determined to make the varsity by his sophomore year and spent the summer doing wind sprints and hoisting feed sacks at the general store. By his senior year, he was the star player. I'm skipping over the minor details, you see."

Her hands occupied, Toni Jo gave a big smile and a series of exaggerated nods.

"Seriously, now," Nevers resumed, "I . . . I mean he—he was a local hero, enshrined in the pantheon of his alma mater's trophy case, apotheosized in glass. Don't laugh, Toni Jo, this is true." Nevers tapped the cigarette on the tray and, pinching it between his thumb and forefinger, took a long pull. "Know what a pantheon is? Doesn't matter. He was a man among boys, among heroes a god. The girls gathered 'round the display case to admire his photographs. He was throwing the javelin, jumping hurdles, swinging a bat, driving for a layup in the playoffs. Suddenly, it was the last football game of the 1926 season. Two thirds of the starters from the previous year's championship team had graduated. Halfway through the season, the boy no one paid any mind to three years earlier was the sensation. He played both ways. He intercepted passes, dropkicked and returned punts, ran for touchdowns.

"The team was six and one, tied for first with Tyler. It was a crisp Saturday in mid-November. Perfect football weather. The Kilgore Diablos had home-field advantage. The teams worked back and forth like two armies of equal power. On a sweep, the boy body blocked a safety and a tackle at the end of the half to let his quarterback score. Then the kicker missed the extra point. Down seven to six, they retired to the dressing room. During the third quarter, the sensational flanker couldn't seem to get open. He had a worthy opponent, the state's hundred-yard-dash champ. With forty-five seconds left in the game, the Diablos returned a punt to mid-field. Three running plays later, they were two yards farther back. The officials informed the coach and quarterback there were six seconds left on the clock."

Nevers took a final puff and stubbed out the butt. He observed the lace hem of Toni Jo's slip peeking from under her dress.

"Go on with the dishes," Nevers teased Toni Jo, who held a plate suspended in midair. "Win or lose, that plate's gotta get washed."

Nevers noticed a rack of soap suds floating on her breast.

"In the huddle, the quarterback panted heavily, a drop of sweat and blood about to fall from the end of his nose. He straightened his old leather helmet and looked around. 'Any ideas?' he asked.

"The boy spoke up. 'Dial my number. I been setting this sucker up the whole second half. I'll fake left, fake right, and go left. Or fake right, fake left, and go right. I got him trained like a hound dog. You throw me the ball and I'll run that son of a bitch all the way to the state line.'"

The sarcastic tone of Nevers' voice had disappeared.

"The quarterback called his number. The boy faked right, feinted left, and stayed left. He ran for the scoreboard as fast as he could. He knew he might have gained only a split second on the safety. With half a field, the defender could close the gap if he lost a step by glancing behind him. He was on the ten-yard line when the whistle blew. He looked back. The live ball was spiraling down over his head. He jumped and tipped it with one hand and it floated just out of reach. Two more strides and he snagged the pigskin just before it hit the ground. He dashed into the end zone, touched the ball down on the run, made a J, and looked at his quarterback, then the hometown fans.

"It was a moment frozen in time, the quarterback's arms thrust in the air, the steady roar of the crowd filling his ears, a blizzard of confetti snowing down from the bleachers.

"He had reached that pure, calm height only a few reach and almost none survive because they keep trying to recapture that moment and then, failing, try again and again until their spirits are crushed. He had seen it happen before. Washed up sports heroes, Titans gone down in defeat to midgets. He ran to the back of the end zone, where the boys working the scoreboard hung the numbers. 12 to 7. He continued onto the track, then through the open gate and into the fading sunset."

Nevers pulled another cigarette from the pack in his pocket. He struck a match with his thumbnail and touched the flame to the end of the tube, inhaling deeply. With utter boredom, he lifted his eyes to Toni Jo, who was astonished into photographic stillness. He blew a cloud of smoke across the room, judging the effect of his story on Toni Jo by a rising nipple where the cloud of suds had melted into a damp spot.

"Then what?" Toni Jo said.

"Then nothing. He had finished his life at the school. He died. What would *you* do for an encore after a season like that?"

"He killed himself?" Then Toni Jo remembered the story was about Harold Nevers, the man sitting at her kitchen table.

"You couldn't have killed yourself, you're right here."

"In a manner of speaking, I did," he said. "This kid hid . . . I hid in the bushes till everyone went home and the stadium was dark. I walked to my dorm and waited for lights-out. Then I went up to my room, changed into my street clothes, took what I needed, and walked away from that part of my life. That night, I slept in the train station until the morning paper arrived. Headlines. Can you imagine that?" Nevers stretched his hands out as if unfolding a banner six feet long. "'NEVERS BOY SNAGS TD PASS, KEEPS GOING.'"

Toni Jo stared at him in disbelief, trying to imagine anyone doing such a thing, wondering if she would have the courage to leave her life behind without knowing what lay ahead.

"Hell, it's just a game, Toni Jo. I finally got smart enough to realize that. In an instant, watching the confetti drift onto the field in the dying light, I realized it was all nothing. Football. A game somebody made up. You run up and down a field chasing some inflated cowhide while bare-legged girls cheer." He crushed another cigarette butt in the ashtray. "I mean, what's the point?"

He looked up at her.

"War. Now *there's* something. Men die. They lose arms and legs. Their eyes. I'll tell you something. I was nine when the Great War ended. I saw the veterans coming home on crutches or riding wheelchairs, bloody bandages on stumps, their heads wrapped in gauze. I watched them for weeks, looking for defeat. Slowly, they gathered at the barbershops, the post office, the store fronts. They began to talk. They chanted the names of places I had never heard: Versailles, Verdun, the Marne, Kemmel Hill, the Argonne forest, Flanders. Then they talked of what they did and what it meant and worked on through that to how they felt, the anticipation before combat, writing last letters in the trenches, two and three and four battles, their nauseous fear. Finally they got down to it, each in a different way, searching for the right words. Then one said it and they all looked at him, knowing they would never have to say it again. 'The euphoria of battle.'

"I went home that night and prayed. That night and the next three years, I prayed for war. I still remember it. I got down on my knees, thinking that might help, and I put my hands together, gazing up at the picture on my dorm wall—Jesus in the Garden, sweating blood. 'Please, God,' I prayed, 'bring us war in my time.' When I was twelve and war hadn't come, I was exhausted, plumb tired of repeating those words for months of years."

For several minutes, Toni Jo had been standing transfixed, facing

Nevers, listening to him talk while observing his fingers as they handled cigarettes and matches. Her arms were bent at the elbows, her hands in the air like a surgeon's just scrubbed.

"You keep standing there like that," Nevers said, "and those dishes'll never get done."

Toni Jo apologized and went back to work. Nevers noted the curvature of her calf muscle as it tapered to her ankle. Neither said anything for a while. Toni Jo finished washing and rinsing the dishes and started on the silverware.

"If you don't mind me asking, Harold, what—you don't have to talk about it if it pains you—what happened to your parents?" Nevers looked at her, in no hurry to tell the story. "Or do you know?"

"I know what I was told," Harold said. "I don't know whether it's true. What I mean is, there's no way for me to find out if it's true."

Toni Jo continued to wash the forks, knives, spoons, her ear turned in his direction.

"I asked when I was around six years old or so," Nevers began. "Mr. Johnson, the owner of the Village, he told me I was too young to understand, to ask later. Every year on my birthday I asked until he finally told me. I was thirteen or so by then. He said my father had been a farmer. They lived ten miles outside of Kilgore. The doctor instructed my father not to wait until the last minute to bring my mother into town. Eight months along, she went into labor after pumping water at the well. Screaming for him to hurry, she grabbed a blanket and climbed into the wagon bed while he hitched the horses. He pressed the team to its limit, not daring to look back and check on her. At the doctor's house, he hollered as he reined in the horses at the porch. The doctor came running out with his bag. When he tossed the blanket back, he knew immediately my mother was dead."

Nevers looked at Toni Jo.

"My head was out of her body and I was struggling for breath. Strange as it sounds, my mother died before I was born. The doctor's job was simple, I was told. All he had to do was pull very hard. At least that's what Mr. Johnson said. Later, I suspected it might have involved more than that."

Toni Jo was focused on the forks and spoons, rinsing and placing the pieces in the rack three and four at a time. Without looking at Nevers, her silence indicated she was waiting for an explanation.

"I have scars on the back of my neck, but I don't remember ever getting cut there," Nevers said.

After giving this some thought, Toni Jo said, "And your father?"

Harold's eyes were steady on her face, studying the effect of each statement. "Drank himself to death in six months. That's what Johnson said. No aunts, no uncles. No grandparents." He stopped. "Can you believe that?"

Toni Jo looked up, momentarily forgetting her task, and slid her finger across a knife blade. She gave a brief, sharp cry, dropping utensils into the porcelain basin with a ringing clatter. Nevers jumped to her aid. Toni Jo clutched the finger with her hand, his hands enclosing hers, the blood running over the tip of her finger and mingling with the dish water to form a rivulet that trickled down her forearm and dribbled off the point of her elbow as the two looked first at the wound and then at each other.

"It's nothing," Toni Jo said dismissively. Just a little paper cut. These things always bleed more when you're washing dishes. It's the warm water, I guess."

Toni Jo's eyes glanced skittishly about his shoulders, chin, ears, and hair, her heart beating stronger. Finally, their eyes met. Nevers reached down and kissed her on the forehead, then softly on the nose, then her lips, Toni Jo lifting her face up to his and returning the kiss. He let her hands drop and moved his around her waist, pulling her closer. She reached to the back of his neck and touched him gently, forgetting the cut, feeling gingerly for the scars necessary to bring the rest of this living man into the world.

Her eyes closed, he kissed her deeply several times as she explored his face tenderly with her fingers. Lazily, in the light-headed swoon of first caress, desiring to see the passion on her lover's face as well, Toni Jo opened her eyes and withdrew in horror at the handsome, blood spattered-visage so close to hers.

She let out a whimper of fright, then, realizing what had happened, a short laugh of relief that sounded like the squeak of a mouse stepped on in the dark. They both laughed at Toni Jo's laugh, Nevers still not comprehending the cause of her fear. After explaining, Toni Jo worked on his face with a dishcloth, then dabbed at his collar, diluting the blood before it set. Then she sent him out to the porch swing to cool off while she tended her injured finger.

* * *

Toni Jo approached the front door ten minutes later. In the dark living room, she paused at the screen to watch the new man in her life. Lighted by a bare bulb, he was rocking on the swing, smoking and humming, one hand pocketed. *Rock of Ages, cleft for me, let me hide myself in Thee.* It was the song he had whistled in the cafe a month earlier, she remembered. Toni Jo stepped onto the porch. Nevers continued humming as she took her place on the far side of the swing. For a while, they pushed the swing gently back and forth with their feet.

"Are you a religious man, Mr. Nevers?"

Harold laughed. "Not exactly." He withdrew a knife from his pocket, cleaned under a fingernail, and returned it to the pocket. "I like that song, though. We sang it at the Village services every Sunday. I guess I don't think about the words."

He began to move his side of the swing in a motion opposite that of Toni Jo's side. She smiled at the sensation.

"Most of my experiences with church have been comic." He tapped the ash from his cigarette and, with the glowing cone, extinguished a mosquito parked on his wrist. "Comic or outrageous." He thumped the cigarette out into the yard. "Want to hear a couple of stories?"

Toni Jo smiled. "Sure. You tell good stories."

"Okay, let's see." He stopped rocking and leaned forward, placing his elbows on his knees. "Mr. Johnson—remember him?—he owned the boys' home. Johnson was also a Presbyterian minister. He conducted a chapel service every evening at six. He read scripture and talked calmly from the pulpit, and by my tenth year I was beginning to think God was a pretty dull guy. Oh, sure, there was Noah's flood, a burning bush, plagues of locusts and all that, but that was a long time ago. I guessed God was getting tired in His old age and had run out of all the really good stuff.

"During services, I sat with this guy named Horace. One day, Horace's long lost aunt or somebody came to take him away. He had already packed his things—they fit in a small cardboard suitcase—and was ready to leave after the Sunday evening service. Horace sat in the middle, between me and his aunt. Near the end of the sermon, this aunt reached down to get something out of her purse. Whatever it was, she couldn't find it. Horace jabbed me with an elbow, then jerked his head to the right. His aunt was bent over digging around in this big purse the size of a trunk—you know, moving the canned goods to another aisle and letting the dog out to play. It was like an entire world in there."

Toni Jo giggled and slapped Harold on the arm.

"So there she was, bending over, her dress splayed open at the neckline, bare-bosomed as Eve on Creation Day. Not even a slip on. And there *they* were, hanging like forbidden fruit just out of our reach. Full and round, tapering to warm pink points. I thought they were the most beautiful breasts I had ever seen. And I was right, of course, since I had never seen any before then. As her hands darted in and out of the purse, her breasts worked up and down like alternating pistons. For some reason, Horace thought this was funny. He kept glancing back and forth from me to them, like he didn't know which to look at. Then he reached over and cupped his hand to my ear. The message started as a whisper, then spasmed into a laugh and came out loud, like an emotional proclamation of faith. 'There really is a God,' he fairly shouted. Mr. Johnson paused in his sermon, his eyes falling directly on Horace. I was fighting back my laughter and doing a good job of it until Mr. Johnson, either seeing what we saw or thinking he had finally reached some poor benighted soul, said enthusiastically, 'Amen, brother Horace. Amen.'"

Toni Jo, her palms over her face like the Praying Hands, had for some time been suppressing her response in order to hear the story out. Then the dam burst and she howled with laughter, running her shoes on the wooden porch.

Suddenly, she put her bandaged finger to her lips. "Shhh! You'll wake Mama."

"Me?" Nevers said. "You could raise the dead with that chicken cackle." For a while, the two rocked the swing in synchronized or alternating rhythm, Toni Jo or Harold breaking into laughter that the other contagiously echoed, each batting at a variety of insects beginning to gather around the light bulb on the porch ceiling.

"Why don't you kill that bug magnet," Nevers suggested.

Toni Jo stood up, leaned halfway into the house, and smacked the button switch on the wall.

"That was a funny story," she said, reaching for the swing with both hands like a blind woman, her eyes not yet adjusted to the dark. "You said you had another one?"

"Yes, but this one's not funny. It's outrageous." Nevers paused to think. "One week, a bunch of the guys heard about a tent revival coming to town and wanted to go. At the public school we attended, some of the holy roller kids invited us. We'd heard all the rumors about snake handling and speaking in tongues and drinking strychnine. Hell, compared to Episcopalian services, this sounded like a circus to us. So we figured we'd have us a good time and–."

"I thought you said Johnson was Presbyterian."

Nevers stopped as if caught in a lie.

"Presbyterian, Episcopalian—what's the difference?" he chuckled.

"Okay, okay." Toni Jo made whisking motions with her hand. "Go on."

"This was just after corn-shucking and hay-baling time. We walked the mile up over and down the hill to the tent, which was lit up by kerosene lamps on six foot posts. At the edge of the field, a yellow canvas banner announced, 'T. Van Mahorn, Doctor of Divinity and Revivalist.'

"A couple of the churches sponsoring the camp meeting had tables outside loaded with corn on the cob and hotdogs. The older kids were sparking—you know, courting. Flirting and such. The children played hide-and-seek, barking dogs chasing after them and giving away their positions. The adults gathered in groups of five or six, talking ominously of the weather and war. The cool air had an amber glow. The ground was covered with pinestraw and hay and cornshucks. People were still arriving by buggy or wagon. Some of the horses wore feedsacks and their bodies were giving off steam in the autumn dusk.

"Us boys from the Village schemed and laughed in our own little knot. Lawrence had brought a frog that he planned to do something with, he hadn't decided what yet, but he told us he'd know when the opportunity struck. Rex showed us three firecrackers he'd saved all the way from Fourth of July. We stuffed as many hotdogs as we could down our gullets, talking, as we ate, about the girls in *their* clusters, which ones had real breasts and which stuffed—they in turn looking at and talking about us. Andy called to a barefoot girl with blue ribbons in her sandy hair.

"'Hey, why don't ch'all come sit in back wid us? We'll show you a good time.' The girl put a hand on one hip and made a smacking noise with her mouth, indicating her disgust at his crudeness.

"'She'll be sitting wid us in five minutes, you watch,' Andy bragged. 'Say, baby, how about I buy you a Co-Cola, hanh? How 'bout it?' The girl turned and tittered into the circle of faces.

"Then ushers started calling for the people to gather inside the tent. A portable out-of-tune organ labored with a hymn. A haze of dust rose as the throng shuffled inside. Before the entrance was a large, painted sign:

Enter, Ye Troubled and Weak of Spirit.
EXPECT A MIRACLE

Inside the tent, deacons distributed tambourines and fans with a mountain scene on one side and a funeral-home ad on the other. Just as Lawrence had predicted, the girls worked their way to our seats and sat in front of us on a long plank resting on nail kegs.

"Up front, the organist played 'Shall We Gather at the River.' A man in a yellow suit and red tie, presumably the Reverend T. Van Mahorn himself, sat in a lone chair on a small stage elevated by cement blocks stacked three high. The girls kept turning around as Lawrence pulled at the bows in their hair. The low roar of the crowd prevented the girls from hearing Rex strike a match against the board they were sitting on. The report of the firecracker drew a hatchet-faced usher to the aisle by our seats. He reached over to Rex with an offering plate attached to an eight-foot rod and rapped him on the head with it.

"'A word with you outside, young man,' Hatchet-face said. He had a red nose and only two front teeth, one yellow and one black.

"'Kiss one for me if I don't come back,' Rex whispered as he fumbled past our feet and made the sign of the cross.

"Finally, the evangelist approached the pulpit. His eyes cast down, he gripped the heavy podium for a few seconds. The assembly grew quiet. He looked up. They looked back, expectant, hopeful, hurting for someone to ease their lives. For half a minute he stared at them, his expressionless face growing a frown. Then he paced heavily back and forth across the stage. He stopped behind the lectern, his frown now a scowl.

"'Are you waiting for me!?' he shouted. 'Do you think I can bring happiness to your hard lives?—your hard liiives?' He derided the crowd, his voice a mallet beating, pounding their average souls into feeling worthless. '*I* can't bring God to you. You should be ashamed.' Many hung their heads. He looked down at them like a disappointed parent on a bad child. Then, his voice growing cheerful, his face brightening, he gave them back their lives. 'I can't bring God to you. God is already here. Where two or three are gathered in His name, He is among them. He's the Alpha and Omega, the beginning and the end—Revelation 1:8.'

"'Testify!' someone shouted from the back. The evangelist shook his head as if awakened from a trance.

"'The fields. Are alive. With the harvest. Of the Lord,' he resumed in a rich baritone. 'And God, as you know, will rip the tares from the wheat and burn them in eternal hell fire—Matthew 13:24 and following.'

"Shouts sprang up from the congregation:

—'Amen, brother.'

—'Tell us more.'

"'You will reap just what you sow.'

—'Just what you sow,' a chorus sang out.

"'Judgment Day. What a dreadful day it will be. To the unbeliever. To the believer, what a joyful day! In the twinkling of an eye, the Good Book says, we'll be changed. Oh! I almost forgot. You must be born again—John 3:7.'

"The crowd was getting worked up. They started shaking and beating the tambourines. Some of them stood up, shouting and throwing their arms fitfully skyward.

"'Yes, you must be born again. You know what I'm talking about, and yet–. Orphans! I've heard there's orphans among us. But don't forget, dear friends, we are *all* orphans! Lost in this mean old world. Without father, without mother but WAIT! God is everywhere. He did not abandon us. We abandoned Him! He made us, listen to me!'—and he whispered loudly with awe—'a little lower than the angels. Oh, Jesus, thank you.'

"Tears streamed from his eyes. He said, 'Forgive me, friends, but when I think of what God has prepared for us in heaven, why, my heart feels like it's being wranched by Jesus and the tears fill up my chest and overflow thew my eyes.'

"'Jesus, squeeze my heart,' one woman pleaded, and we laughed at that. There was something catching about the enthusiasm. It got me so worked up, I reached forward and grabbed the girl's shoulder in front of me.

"'Squeeze my heart, Susie,' I begged. Laughing, she slapped my hand from her shoulder in such a coquettish way that I wanted to take her in my arms right there and kiss her full on the mouth.

"The Reverend T. Van Mahorn had been preaching for twenty minutes when suddenly a retarded-looking girl with purple pimples started up the aisle, garbling out something about a tongue of fire licking her belly. When she reached the front, the evangelist lodged himself behind the sturdy lectern, using it like a blocker. The girl, running at full speed now, planted one foot on the stage and ran two steps straight up the pulpit, losing her momentum seven feet off the ground, then fell slap dab on her back with enough force to knock the breath from a heifer. The shocked people watched the girl writhing around in the hay and cornshucks, her mouth bubbling like a crab's. Several of the ushers finally took the initiative and ran to help her.

"'STOP!' the revivalist shouted. 'Don't touch her! Leave her there where Jesus flang her!' The preacher kept up his delivery while the girl rolled moaning on the ground. After a while, she sat up, her hair decorated with straw, and an usher helped her to the front pew while Mahorn continued to exhort his congregation.

"Then things got boring for a while. After everybody sang a hymn, an offering was taken to support what Mahorn called his I-tinerant ministry.' Then they gave the invitation–. What church you go to?"

"Methodist," Toni Jo said.

"You get the picture, then. Lots of crying and neck-hugging while deacons handed out nubby pencils and helped the new converts fill in little cards. I was figuring out what to say after the service to Susie-in-front-of-me when Mahorn starts up again.

"'Many of you tonight are here because you want to see a miracle. exPECT a miracle. That's what the sign said. Well, let me tell you something, people! God. Is not. A magician. Do you hear me? No-sir! God. Is a fearful God. The God of Moses. That same God who sent a consuming fire, a con-fla-GRA-tion, a sacred flame to eat up the unholy sacrifice to Baal. Who parted the Red Sea and destroyed an army with an easy sweep of His mighty hand. And you think He's going to heal your matchstick arms and legs tonight? He who made the heavens and earth?

"'You, in the front row, on crutches, Don't! Mock! God!' Mahorn brushed his hair back. 'You, in the wheelchair, Don't Mock God! If your broken bodies are restored, how will you repay God? If you died, you'd go to live with Him, and you *don't* want to die?' Mahorn put both hands on his hips. 'Faithless people. O-h-h-h-h-h,' he shuddered, 'I quake when I think that in the twinkling of an eye, God could consume this entire tent, this field, this largest state in the union. This world. With fire. Or what He will. The God of Abraham's burning bush. Of Jonah's whale.

'"You people. You want, to see, a miracle?' Some in the crowd cried *Yes*, begged for God's mercy on their pain. 'FAITHLESS! Do you think if God wanted bones that didn't break He would have made them of clay? So. All you with lame legs and withered hands, of hurt hearts and feeble minds, do you want to see a miracle? Then step away from the platform. Go on! Do you want to see a demonstration of God's power or not?' Many whimpers of protest reached his ears. 'Then move away from the platform, I tell you. Make way for the sound of body and mind, the strong of heart. Move back, I say!' Discouraged, confused, some angry, the people began to limp and skulk and wheel or be pushed away. 'Now,' he said, scanning across the crowd as if for someone hiding. 'Who wants to see a miracle?' A hand shot up. Three hands. A dozen.

'"Not a healing!' the man said. 'Not a trick to impress children and old women. No-sir! I'm talking about a bona-fide miracle.' He paused and drew a handkerchief from inside his coat and wiped his face. 'HYP-OCRITES!' he yelled, bending over the platform, veins popping from his forehead. A woman fainted. A child began to cry. 'DON'T MOCK GOD!' He staggered back from the effort and panted. Then softly, 'Do you want to see a miracle? Don't say yes unless your body means nothing to you. Who is willing to be *crippled* for Christ? God could easily heal this man over here with arthritis. Or this woman's child.' He paused to gather himself.

'"SELFISH! What you really want to see is proof of God's power only if it *helps* you.' The man gazed heavenward. 'How many times, Lord, have charlatans stood where I'm standing and fooled your people with a few man-made tricks?' He eyed the congregation. 'You know what I'm talking about. Fakery. Planting people in the audience with crutches so they can throw them down and shout and bamboozle the rest of the poor suckers into a frenzy that will heal rheumatism and gout and even some forms of blindness. For a while. Tem-po-rarily,' he tick-tocked his head back and forth. He looked into the bewildered faces of the believers, making them doubt. 'Long enough for him to get out of town with his traveling show and the good people's money. And then, miraculously, they begin to hurt again, begin to see hazily. BLIND! Every *one* of them blind! Yes, people, *blind* to God's *real* power.'

"'So then. If you want to see a *real* miracle, forget being healed. Is there anyone here willing to be blinded by God? He did it to Saul. Who became Paul. Who was not afraid of taking a new name and a new call. Who was made blind to see more clearly. So, who among you, WHOLE, is willing to be made lame in a mighty demonstration of the awesome power of Jehovah God, the Ruler of Seven Heavens, nine circles of hell, and all the starry universe? Elohim. El Shaddai. Adonai. Eloi Eloi, lama sabachthani.' The man extended both arms skyward, his coat fanned out, and he looked as if he might fly away. 'Praise God, the Spirit is upon me.'

"The man's eyes grew unnaturally large, and let me tell you, Toni Jo, I was afraid, *really* afraid, for the first time in my life. It was the fear you get when someone familiar does something very strange, out of a sick fever maybe, and you know they're not the person you knew.

"'Even should you die,' he said. 'Won't you die someday, someway, anyway? The Lord cometh, I can feel Him among us. Let's get down to it, then. Who, whole, is willing to become UN-whole? Who, living, is willing to die?'"

Nevers stood and turned toward Toni Jo to dramatize the scene.

"The preacher stopped, turned his back to the congregation, then whirled suddenly.

"'YOU! It might be you!'

"'Jesus, help me,' a woman gasped, clutching her chest.

"'YOU! It might be you!'

"'Glory, take me Jesus, I'm ready,' an old man said, raising his palms heavenward.

"'FAITH! This man has the faith only God can give. No, my good friend, God has not chosen you tonight. Go home and live another day. But someone,' the Reverend Mahorn said, aiming his finger around the audience like a pointer in a game of chance. 'Someone will die tonight. God will take him to demonstrate that He will not be mocked. Remember, He allowed she-bears to rip apart two and forty children who mocked Elisha's bald head—Second Kings, chapter two. So. Come now. Make way down front. Jesus is tugging at your heart strings. Be MAIMED to show the power of God. Be LAME, in the NAME, of the LORD. What a privilege, ladies and gentlemen. I wish it were me. Strike me, Jesus. I'm praying now. Jesus, strike me down.' His face skyward, eyes asquint, arms lifted, he prayed.

"'NO!' he gasped finally, exhausted. 'It's not to be, not tonight. Not me. So who *will* it be?' He glanced at his watch. 'God is a patient God. But He won't wait forever. I'll extend this invitation for one minute longer. Think about what a great witness for the Lord you'll miss if you delay. Oh, friend, don't do it. Don't spurn God.' The man, his face now contorted, sounded as if he were about to cry.

"Heads began to turn toward the back. The crowd parted as a man made his way down front. The man broke through the mass of new believers near the podium. It was Mr. Thompson, owner of the biggest hardware store in town. Although a church goer, he wasn't known to be especially religious. He walked to the front with determination, as if he were going to tell the revivalist the gag was over and expose him as a fraud. Calmly, as he neared the platform, he raised his hands. 'Strike me, Jesus,' he said.

"'The power of God!' Mahorn said. 'Climb on stage with gladness, brother, for it will be the last time you ever use your legs. Praise God. Fear Him. Come on up.'

"Mr. Thompson placed his hands on the platform and catapulted himself onto the planks, landing in a crouching position. As he stood, the Reverend Mahorn ran to him and touched him lightly on the chest with his palm.

"'Strike him, Jesus!' he said, and the man fell like a boneless scarecrow at his feet. Then, from everywhere:

—'Praise God, it's His will.'

—'Hallelujah, Thine the glory.'

"The congregation took up the song.

Hallelujah, Thine the glory.
Hallelujah, Ah-men.
Hallelujah, Thine the glory.
Re-vive us a-gain.

"'Oh, Jesus!' a shout came from the front. 'I SEE,' an old man began, 'I see heaven opening before me. The hands of Jesus descending. The nail scars.' He reached up. 'Take me, Jesus—oh, Jesus, take me home,' and he, too, fell in the dust like an empty pillowcase blown from a clothesline.

"'He's dead!' the woman beside him shouted. 'My husband is gone to *glo*-ree. Blesséd be the name of the Lord.' Her bright face was burning with joyful tears, and I was afraid for us all. I felt the Spirit sweeping through the tent and thought it would leave a path of destruction like a tornado and go out the tent onto the streets, through the town into the world, and either change every heart or kill every man, woman, and child in the attempt. Suddenly I found it hard to breathe. Something wrapped around my neck like a velvet snake and squeezed until everything turned black. The hand of God had reached down and taken me by the throat."

Harold Nevers stood spellbound before Toni Jo, his eyes unblinking.

"Harold, you're scaring me," she said, giving him a shake. "Harold, are you all right?"

Nevers shook his head to clear it of the memories and gave out a two-syllable snicker, then a three-syllable chuckle that segued into full-bodied, uncontrollable laughter.

"Yes," he said after composing himself. "I'm fine. Now. But I wasn't then. When I awoke, a beautiful girlchild stood over me, my head in her lap, her hair draped over my face. It was like shredded yellow silk and smelled of honeysuckle. Sitting up, I saw the carnage around me—chairs broken, pews overturned, people lying in all the postures of battlefield death. Everyone was either crying or praising God. An arm's length away, Lawrence's frog was squashed under a heavy bench board, its guts hanging out of its mouth."

Nevers took two steps and sat in the swing by Toni Jo.

"I discovered that only the one man had died, the one who started the chain reaction. I don't remember much after that until I was sitting on a small bridge over a dry creekbed, the smell of fresh creosote in the air. The girlchild was holding my hand in one of hers while caressing it with the other. A half moon was high in the clear sky. It was the tenderest moment of my life. She reached up and kissed my cheek and I reawakened to my body.

"And I was glad that God had made woman. I thought I must have been in love and would surely marry this beautiful girlchild. I could see into our future. For years, she and I would meet secretly and pray and plan good but anonymous deeds to perform for the needy. I was so overwhelmed with love for this angelic creature that I began to return her kisses. I kissed her on the cheek and neck and mouth. And as I kissed, I thought, *I don't even know your name. I don't even care who you are. I only know that I love you.* Her hands were all over my chest, kneading me. Then they were behind my back, pulling me closer to her as she kissed me harder. She pushed me over and rolled on top of me, her thin golden hair falling in my face, the odor of honeysuckle invading my nostrils, my heart resonating inside my chest and I was in love, drunkenly floating, and then she straddled me and moved back and forth against me like she was riding a horse maddeningly across an open field, driving it faster and faster, crying, 'Oh, oh,' and then, 'Oh God, oh-oh, God God *God!*' and I exploded and pushed her off, hard, onto the planks and I pounded the bridge with my fist and said, 'No, *No!* Not this. Not you! I don't even know who you are. You're beautiful and I love you and you're just a child.' I began to strike her with my palms about her arms and chest until her shouts brought me to my senses. Her hands protected her face and she was sobbing.

"The girl's dress was dusty and her hair was matted with sweat and tears. I began to slap at her dress to beat the dust out of it. Then we stood up and both swatted at it, laughing hysterically at the sounds of the slaps and the dirtiness of us both that would never come clean. She gazed up at me sweetly and took my face in her palms.

"'You're a nice boy,' she said.

"'And you're a nice girl,' I said. 'You're so young and beautiful, and I love you.'

"She laughed. 'What's your name, silly boy?' I told her my name and asked hers.

"'Julie,' she said. 'Julie Mahorn.'

"'No,' I gasped, shocked first by the behavior of a holy man's daughter, then at the sudden realization that she would leave the next day and I would never see her again. 'You can't be. You love me. Those things you did with me, they prove it and I can't live without you. Stay here and marry me.' I kept repeating the idiotic phrases of a desperate fourteen-year-old. Finally, I wound down like a tightly sprung clock. Understanding, she reached up and touched my face.

"'Such a sweet, innocent boy.' Then she began to pat my face lightly. 'Such a sweet, innocent boy to be soooo . . . stupid. Don't you know what happened to you tonight?'

"Shamed by the revivalist's daughter, my new faith tarnished an hour after its birth, humiliated before God, I said, 'I was saved.'

"Her laughs cut into my heart like shrapnel. 'You silly, innocent boy. You complete little fool,' she said. 'You were manipulated.'

"'What?'

"'Duped. Fooled.'

"'No,' I said, my facing growing hot. 'Mr. Thompson. I know him. God crippled him. God struck him down tonight in a mighty display of His power.'

"'Wait,' the girl said.

"'And that man that died. I don't know him, but . . . he's dead. I saw him, he's *dead*.'

"'Oh, yes,' she said, 'he's dead all right. That was real enough. But not by the power of God. Or, as Daddy would put it, not taken by God, but killed by the power of suggestion. A suicide. That man *wanted* to die.'

"I looked at Julie Mahorn's prematurely desirable silhouette in the moonlight. I felt sick to my stomach. The faint odor of musty urine penetrated my nostrils and suddenly she was nothing but a country girl with a huckster father, wearing cheap perfume that reeked of sour honeysuckle.

"I wanted to feel some deep, enduring hurt that would never leave me, that would torture me for the rest of my days and make me welcome the relief of death. Instead, I felt like a tired circus balloon, barely buoyant, its helium half escaped. The girl started up the hill towards the illuminated tent, then turned.

"'Oh, about Mr. Thompson,' she called. 'Don't worry about him. He'll be walking inside of a week. In fact, after the town gives us a good part of their savings tomorrow night, he might even be running to catch up with us before we get to the next town.' Then she raced up the hill, her giggles receding much too slowly for me, while in the distance the whistle of the Kansas City Southern announced the train's ten o'clock stop."

Nevers paused.

Toni Jo said, "Wow, that's some story."

"It's outrageous," Nevers said. "It changed my life. T. Van Mahorn. If his own daughter hadn't told me he was a fake, I would never have believed it. Still, he taught me some valuable lessons: things aren't always what they seem; you never really know somebody—that sort of thing. But one thing he said I'll never forget. He said that I could be born again. Even after the embarrassment of that other stuff wore off, weeks and weeks later, I realized that what he had said was true. And then I was born again, only this time for real. Remember that football story I told you?"

Toni Jo nodded.

"I said I went out for football because girls didn't like eggheads, remember? What I didn't give you were the details. I was a bookworm but became an athlete because I saw a cheerleader I wanted as my girl. Irene. From an egghead, I was born again as an athlete, though it took some doing. Three years. And I got Irene."

"Was it worth it?"

Nevers threw his hands up.

"Irene. That's another story. Sure, I think so."

The two rocked for a while.

"You're an interesting man, Harold Nevers," Toni Jo said to fill the silence.

"Then, of course, I was born again, *again*. After the state playoff game, when I ran out of the stadium into a new world. That's the ultimate lesson I learned from Reverend T. Van Mahorn—that when everything's gone sour and your whole life's shot, you can always pick up and start a brand new life, anywhere you want. Isn't that amazing? It really is like being born again."

Nevers reached for the pack of cigarettes in his shirt pocket.

"Don't get me wrong. It's not necessarily easy. There were hard times after that. Hell, I was just a kid. What did I know?"

Nevers smacked the Luckies against his palm and extracted a cigarette from the box.

"You can do it too, you know. Remake your entire life starting right now or any time you want. Let me ask you a question, Toni Jo. What are your plans for the next few years?"

"Well, I'd like to make enough money to go to the Normal School and then teach."

"Those are respectable ambitions." Nevers rocked the swing. "But way beneath your potential." Toni Jo jerked as if slapped in the face. "Now, let me ask you a question that could change your life, depending on how you answer it." He took a match from its box. "Would you be willing to relocate if I tripled your salary?"

"I don't know," Toni Jo said, doing some quick math. "I guess it would depend on how far I'd have to move."

"What if I could increase your wages five times?"

"Mr. Nevers, surely you jest. What kind of work–."

"What would it take to get a yes from you? Tenfold?"

Toni Jo stared at him in disbelief.

"I've been thinking about opening a restaurant on the south shore of Lake Pontchartrain. I'm looking for someone to manage it. I don't mean to misrepresent the job. It's true I'll start you at triple what you make at the Two-Rat Cafe, but it may take a while to reach that tenfold plateau." Nevers examined the cigarette in his hand. "And don't be deceived. It'll be hard work."

"Even threefold sounds too good to be true," Toni Jo said. "But, just out of curiosity, how long are you talking about with—well, with the fivefold, let's say."

"I've seen it done in a year," Nevers said. "And you *know* you'll never earn that much money as a teacher. Give it some thought. I'll be back this way in a month. If you think you're up to making that kind of clover, have a suitcase packed."

They sat quietly in the dark. Nevers scratched the match on the swing's armrest and lit a Lucky. As he inhaled the flame into the cigarette, Toni Jo heard the faint crackling of tobacco shreds igniting. He held the stick out to her in a gesture of offering.

"Thanks, I don't smoke," she said.

"Toni Jo."

"Yes?"

"Toni Jo," he repeated musingly, blowing smoke from his nostrils. "That'll never do." His dark profile turned towards her. "Come over here." He patted the spot beside him. "I'm not going to bite you." Sliding over, she smelled the blended odor of sweat and cologne. He reached an arm around her and pulled her closer. He kissed her cheek, then, briefly, her lips.

"Don't get me wrong. It's a fine name." Nevers took a lock of her hair and slipped it through his fingers. "For a waitress in a country cafe. But you'll want something more exotic in New Orleans. Something catchy. Did you ever think about what you would have named yourself if the choice had been yours?"

"Annie," Toni Jo said without hesitation. "I always liked that name. It sounds simple, but clean and pretty."

Nevers laughed. "That might be one notch above Toni Jo." Like an infernal firefly, a red glow appeared in front of his mouth as he drew on the cigarette. "Tell you what. I'll give it some thought and try to conjure up a new name that suits you. Annie's too common for a pretty-face like yourself." He tilted his head back and blew a cloud of smoke.

They kissed for a while.

5

June 1938

"I don't know," Mrs. Henry said. "Who is this man, really? You don't even know him."

Toni Jo had come in from the cafe at seven to find her mother at the kitchen table listening to Amos and Andy on the radio while working a worn-out jigsaw puzzle of a New Hampshire snow scene. Toni Jo had worked the puzzle four or five times, her mother at least twice that many.

"It's not like he's asking me to marry him, Mama." Mrs. Henry looked up at her daughter. "And he's certainly not kidnapping me. He said I'd be living in a room attached to the restaurant."

"I'd feel better if he did ask to marry you. It just don't sit right. He comes into town a couple of times, he barely knows you, and he offers you a big job. Why? Can you answer me that?"

"He likes me, Mama. And it's not a big job. He wants to open a restaurant so he won't have to travel all the time. He claims he can't go wrong with this site. It's right on a lake, beside an Amusement Park set to open next spring. There's a military base nearby, too."

Mrs. Henry tried a puzzle piece that didn't fit.

"It sounds like your mind's set on this."

"It is," Toni Jo said. "But I wanted your blessing."

Mrs. Henry looked at her daughter. At thirty-eight, Toni Jo's mother had permanent dark circles under her eyes. When she was twenty, she was already the widowed mother of a two-year-old. Her life had closed around her like a suffocating pillow.

"Go," she said. "You have my blessing. Go off with your Errol Flynn and kill pirates or whatever he does. Find some treasure. It beats the stuffings out of this dreary little town." There was no cheer in her voice, only resignation.

Toni Jo stood and hugged her mother without enthusiasm. She didn't want to appear too happy to be leaving.

* * *

Nevers had wired his arrival for eight o'clock the next morning. At nine, Toni Jo had been sitting in the porch swing for over an hour.

"Sorry," Harold called from the street. "Caught a train down the road. Liked to never seen the end of it. Might mean prosperity's around that corner F.D.R.'s been talking about."

"That's all right," Toni Jo called. "We're used to it. It happens all the time." She hefted a large suitcase in one hand and a smaller grip in the other.

Nevers met her halfway down the walk.

"Good Lord," he said, taking the larger bag from her, "you got the kitchen sink in here?"

At the car, Nevers situated the luggage among some bundles in the back seat and pulled out a camera.

"To commemorate the first day of your new life," he said. "No, no. No objections. Look, lean right here. Against the fender." Nevers peered into the viewfinder. He saw his shadow on the car and glanced up and around to locate the sun. He moved until his shadow slid off the fender. Looking through the camera again, he said, "Guess what I found on the drive over."

"What?" Toni Jo was holding very still so the picture wouldn't blur.

"Your new name I promised."

"That right? Is it a good one?" She raised her hand to cut the sun's glare. "Olivia de Havilland? Something like that?"

"Better. Drop your hand." A breeze lifted a finger curl off her face. "Can you say *Beatrice*? *Annie Beatrice*?"

"Annie Beatrice." She smiled until her teeth showed. "I like that." Harold shot the picture. "Is Beatrice a middle name or a last name?"

"Does it matter? It's like a stage name. You won't have to really change it. Now, put your hand on your head."

"I'm a little teapot," she sang, touching her head.

Nevers took the picture.

"That's it," he said. They started to get in the car.

"Wait!" Toni Jo shouted, making for the house. "Mama fixed us a basket before she left for work. Fried chicken and boiled eggs. Even a disposable salt shaker."

"Which came first?" Harold asked.

"What?"

"Which came first, the fried chicken or the boiled egg?"

From the safety of the porch, Toni Jo whirled and taunted him. "You're a strange man, Harold Nevers."

* * *

After driving south for an hour, they made their first stop in Lake Charles. Nevers pulled next to a green Chevrolet truck on a shell parking lot that ran off into a bayou. VIC's, the sign said. Only one other car, an old beat up Model A, was on the lot. The morning crew, Toni Jo guessed.

Swinging his door out, Harold asked, "Need to make a rest stop?"

"No, I'll just walk a bit and stretch my legs."

"Suit yourself."

Nevers stepped out and made for the trunk while Toni Jo walked to the edge of the bayou. The color of heavily-creamed coffee, the sluggish water moved slowly to her right. She turned around to see Nevers hoist a string-tied bundle wrapped in white paper. He disappeared around the side of the building. Just when she was thinking the muddy water could not sustain life, a prehistoric armored fish slashed the surface by a cypress knee and startled her. She laughed at her skittishness, but stepped away from the bank to avoid other surprises.

They were on Highway 90 East now. Nevers did most of the talking while Toni Jo read the small, two-toned signs and occasional billboards: Sanka, Hiram Walker Gin, Bromo-Seltzer, Havoline, Milk of Magnesia. They saw drifters hitchhiking their way north and south, east and west, seeking work or food, some of them fruit tramps following the harvest band as it moved with the seasons.

DRINK TANGEE

*

Pure Orange Drink

They passed five Burma Shave ads within thirty minutes.

In this world, through thick and thin,
Man grows bald but not his chin.

Toni Jo laughed. They had been silent for a while.

"What you giggling about?"

"That Burma Shave ad. Didn't you see it?"

"God, no. I hate those things. You read them a couple of times and you can't get the jingle out of your head. I learned a long time ago not to even look at them."

A mile before the next exit, a crudely painted sign warned them, "You're Going To Hell."

Nevers said, "I was wondering where we were going."

The next sign commanded, "Repent Now, Be Baptized Next Exit."

"Sounds good to me," Harold said as he turned south. "I could use a bath."

Ten minutes later, Nevers parked in front of the Shorebird Club in Lake Arthur.

"I'll just be a sec," he said. After a short visit with the owner, he stepped out the club's door. In the car, he pulled a yellow envelope from the inside pocket of his suit jacket and threw it onto the back seat. It hit with an emphatic thump. "Hungry yet?" he said.

"Getting there. You want a boiled egg?"

"Let's wait'll we stop for gas. I'll get us some Dr. Peppers and we can wash them down with that."

"Not me," Toni Jo said. "I never touch the stuff."

"Prune juice is for old folks, huh? You're one of those types."

"Right you are, Harry Nevers."

"Harold. Harold, okay? I hate Harry."

She poked his ribs three times. "Harry-Harry-Harry."

Toni Jo counted five Burma Shave ads before Nevers stopped at a Gulf station. Made of bright blue, orange, and white painted tin panels, it reminded her of a large toy. Three attendants in sharply ironed green uniforms swarmed around the car.

"Fill 'er up with Ethyl and clean the windows. Forget the oil. Checked it yesterday." Nevers stepped inside to buy the drinks. As the men moved busily around the car, Toni Jo watched a little girl sitting on a down-turned Coke crate beside the garage door. Her knees high in the air, her panties exposed, she was plugging her shoelaces into their eyelets.

"This is the operator. Can I help you, please? Number five? I'll connect you." She pulled a lace tip from one shoe and plugged it into the other.

"Sir? A bad connection? Sorry you're having trouble. I'll try another line."

The girl was tireless in her efforts to please the callers. When Toni Jo and Harold pulled away five minutes later, she was still at it.

"No, there's been no reported trouble with the Greenfield exchange. I'll try again. Thank you for holding."

In Lafayette, the travelers stopped at the Side-by-Side Lounge, a combination grocery and package liquor store. Nevers hauled another white bundle into the building. Toni Jo heard him and a man laughing through the open door. The heat and glare from the sun made her feel queasy. Her dress stuck to her thighs. She leaned her cheek against the cool metal and roll of windlace on the car's doorjamb. Hundreds of rusting bottle caps embedded in the blacktop resembled a coded message to the future. Coca-Cola, Jumbo, 7-UP, Hires Root Beer, Tangee.

Toni Jo imagined someone digging them up in a thousand years. A mosaic commentary. Cryptic. How would they decipher this hot, dying culture with smiling women holding coke bottles shaking them with a bad taste of salty egg yolks in their mouth?

"Beatrice, wake up!" Harold was shaking her and laughing. Toni Jo sat up and pulled a compact from her purse. A large braided crease was impressed on her cheek, and her eyes were out of focus.

"Blah!" she said. "What a horrible taste in my mouth. And I was dreaming crazy. I hate that."

Nevers headed the car south.

"We'll stop in New Iberia. You can brush your teeth at the Take-Five Cafe. I have some business there."

"What is it you do, anyway?"

"There's some Juicy Fruit in the glove box. That should tide you over till then. Do? I deliver things. Haven't you noticed?"

"Yeah, but what?"

"Bundles." Harold laughed. "Restaurant stuff. Whatever they order."

When Toni Jo opened the glove compartment and moved some papers aside to look for the gum, she saw a heavy silver pistol and her heart surged. She closed the metal door immediately.

Passing through the Lafayette neighborhoods, Toni Jo watched black men pushing mowers in ninety degree heat. On the outskirts of town, guinea fowl roamed free on the roads.

"The feathery cattle of the poor," Nevers said. As he eased his way through a large flock, dust rose, boiling sluggishly around the car. He sang along with the tune on the radio, "Why'd Ya Make Me Fall in Love?"

The two ate lunch at the Take-Five an hour later. Back on the highway, Toni Jo asked Harold if he ever picked up hitchhikers. He said he did, when the mood hit him.

They had been driving through sugarcane fields for a while. The monotony of the terrain was getting on Toni Jo's nerves. She was glad when Nevers pulled over for a hitchhiker.

"Hi ya Mack," Harold called to the drifter through Toni Jo's window. "Where ya headin'?"

The bristly faced man took off his hat and peered inside.

"Anywhere but where I'm standing." He opened the back door and threw in his bag.

"Not from these parts?" Harold asked, pulling onto the highway again.

"Nawp. Oklahoma. Little place called Stillwater."

"Too still for you, huh?" Nevers quipped.

"Too still and too dry."

"Shouldn't put *water* in a dry town's name."

"It ain't fair," the man agreed.

The men talked for ten minutes. Their steady droning about land and weather, politics and sports—combined with the heat and a full stomach—lulled Toni Jo into an uncomfortable slumber as her mind borrowed their words and weaved them into her dreams.

When she awakened, the hitchhiker was gone.

"Well, if it ain't Sleeping Beatrice." Toni Jo raised up and looked around. She groaned at the rows of young sugar cane spoking by the window. "Being a new traveler like yourself, you shouldn't fall asleep. No telling what kinds of interesting things you're liable to miss."

"Yeah?" she said. "Like what?"

"Well, let's see. One armadillo, a family of raccoons, two snakes, and a rabbit. Almost hit the rabbit."

"Exciting," Toni Jo said.

"It was. Especially for the rabbit. You also missed Franklin."

"I slept through the stop?"

"Yep. You don't think I made old Mr. Austin jump out the car going sixty, do you?"

"That his name?"

"Uh-huh. Interesting man."

"Lucky you."

Nevers laughed. "I'm beginning to like you."

A new song came on the radio and Harold sang along, making silly pantomime gestures to entertain Toni Jo—"Jeepers creepers, where'd ya get them peepers!"—bugging his eyes out at *peepers*.

The land went through a slow transformation between Franklin and Morgan City, the cane fields giving way to prairie, then a boggy-looking mass. Bayous, sloughs, coulees, and canals slashed the terrain into amorphous portions of marshland whose rancid emissions reminded Toni Jo of a pulp mill inside an outhouse.

"Before Huey Long," Harold explained, "you had to get from Franklin to Morgan City by way of Philadelphia."

Toni Jo started a laugh that died from lack of conviction.

Then, more fecund wasteland: roadkill that supported hordes of flying and footed scavengers, saw grass, tires, bicycle and automobile skeletons, half a boat up in a tree, the jettisoned detritus of the shiftless, the pests and vermin of the weed world, stagnant sloughs and ditches and more. Anything could grow from this land, and it did.

On her second ferry crossing, Toni Jo got the idea of throwing pieces of fried-chicken skin to the squawking seagulls that trailed the barge begging for supper. As one bird caught a strip, the others chased it around the sky until it dropped the meal and there was a mad, fluttering, diving race for the morsel before it hit the water.

After Toni Jo had flensed the chicken parts of their crusty skin, she and Nevers leaned on the rails, gazing into the water. Suddenly at their feet a large grey fin rose and sank at the menacingly leisure pace of creatures afraid of no living thing.

"A shark!" Toni Jo screamed. She tugged at Harold's sleeve, thrilled at the nearby danger. "Did you see that?"

Nevers grabbed Toni Jo and picked her up as if to throw her overboard. She screamed.

"Settle down," he laughed. "It was just a porpoise."

"A porpoise! Ohhh," Toni Jo said in a falling, disappointed voice. "Oh well, it was still scary."

Near the opposite shore, the two were pestered into the car by one, two, a dozen, then a cloud of mosquitoes and deerflies. Toni Jo frantically rolled up her window, aimlessly swatting the air around her.

At sunset, the car rolled noisily onto the shell parking lot of the Red Barn Diner, an old railroad club car with a roof and paint job added to suggest a red barn. Beside it, a group of children was climbing a mountain of oyster shells that stank in the dying evening. As Nevers went about his business inside, Toni Jo sat in the car listening to the somber questionings of a bullfrog and wondered for the first time where she was and what she was doing there with a strange man.

When Nevers switched on the car beams to leave, Toni Jo sucked in her breath with fright.

"Look at the size of that rat!" Beside the oystershell mountain where the children had been playing, the animal was raised up on its hind legs, licking the front of its half-wet coat of shabby brown fur, a snakelike black tail looping about its webbed feet. The rodent halted its grooming to gaze indifferently into the headlights. "It looks like it could tear up a good-sized dog."

"About like that shark could jump up and take you off the ferry," Harold said. "That's a nutria."

"A nutria? What's a nutria?"

"Good question. It's sort of like a big rat that lives around the bayous and marshes. The locals trap them for their fur. The poor man's mink, you might say. Louisiana's excuse for a beaver."

As they drove onto the highway atop a levee, the car ahead of them weaved erratically, speeding up and slowing down. Nevers flashed his high beams to get the driver's attention. When he passed, Toni Jo looked into the car, its interior lit by a dome light. In the back seat, a woman was changing her baby's diaper. Several unhappy children sat motionless while their father yelled at their mother, who was crying profusely.

Nevers said, "That's why you don't want to have kids."

A cypress swamp rose from the morass and swallowed them as darkness drew on. Toni Jo was lazily happy, heavy with sleep as Harold turned the radio dial across uninspired nasal readings of farm prices—sugar cane, cotton, hog bellies, and rice; a commercial for Community Coffee; news about Hitler's movements in Europe; a few notes of classical music; then a blues song. Toni Jo drifted away on the husky moaning of a saxophone.

At two in the morning Harold shook her awake. Toni Jo felt like she had been semiconscious during the latter part of the trip, never completely asleep, always aware of the tires rumbling on the roadway as if she were falling in slow motion down a noisy well. Nevers had already taken her luggage in.

As he coaxed her out of the front seat, Toni Jo was torn between staying there forever and escaping the thick, greasy smell of chicken engulfing her inside the car.

Harold was much too lively for her.

"Wait, now. Don't move," he said. "Stay right there and look up in that direction."

Toni Jo looked to where Nevers pointed. She saw the dark rectangular outline of what she assumed was yet another restaurant in the interminably long line stretching from DeRidder to New Orleans. As Nevers vanished into the darkness, she heard the sound of waves washing ashore. A few seconds later, through a drifting banner of fog, a phosphorescent sign blinked to life on the roof of the building.

In a jazzy pink neon script, the name of the restaurant wrote itself across the sky:

TERRA INCOGNITA

Toni Jo burst out laughing, only then realizing she had a splitting headache. In the purgatorial luminosity of the sign, she made out a red barrel-tile roof over arched windows covered by black grilles.

The radiant interior was furnished as simply as a hospital. Against a backdrop of light pink stucco was arranged an assortment of jade plants, burro's tails, and ornamental cacti. The tables and countertop were made of imitation-marble Formica. Booth benches, separated by walls of thick bullseye glass, were upholstered in pillowy red leather. Against the wall by each table, circular blue mirrors were set in spider-web frames of silver wire. Across the back wall leapt a giant blue marlin, his terrified eye staring unbelievably at the lure impaled in his gaping mouth.

What wasn't glass was chrome or tile, and the entire effect was an airy, otherworldly atmosphere deserving of a place called Terra Incognita.

Nevers showed Toni Jo around, explaining that the restaurant was situated on the east bank of the mouth of Bayou St. John, which ran north into Lake Pontchartrain. In the spring of 1939, Pontchartrain Beach, an amusement park located on the west side of the bayou, would complete its move to the east side, just down the shore from the restaurant.

"And that's how you and I will become rich," Harold concluded. "Now let me show you your room."

He walked Toni Jo to the back of the restaurant and led her through a door that opened onto an elegantly furnished room. The bed's headboard was crafted of waterfall walnut. On the mahogany table beside it stood a lamp with a blue porcelain trophy-cup base with gold-leaf handles. Under the lavender ruffles bordering the bottom of a cream lampshade sat a bisque baby with outstretched arms. Next to the doll was a cut glass jewelry box. An oval mirror hung behind a bench and vanity. On it sat a Crosley radio of molded plastic in a cathedral design. A full-length mirror occupied one door of an armoire, the other door fashioned of inlaid wood in angular designs.

Nevers took his leave of Toni Jo, telling her to sleep as late as she wanted. He said he'd check on her around noon.

Toni Jo pulled her diary from the large suitcase and, sitting in bed, spent thirty minutes on the longest entry she had ever written. In a single day, her world had changed dramatically. Drifting off to sleep under the cool sheets, she wondered what surprises the next day would bring.

6

July 1938

Interesting drudgery. That's what Toni Jo thought of the next week while Harold and Djurgis taught her New Orleans cuisine. They boiled big blue crabs, claws clacking furiously as Nevers dumped them into the seething caldron while Djurgis set aside the soft-shelled crabs for frying or barbecuing. Toni Jo had never seen anything as disgusting as a limp crab, but one sampling off the grill made her appreciate the local inhabitants' craving for the rubbery creatures.

Nevers introduced Toni Jo to Djurgis as Annie Beatrice.

"Pleezed to meet you, Meez Beetrice," he responded indifferently. Djurgis was a lean, sleepy-eyed chef of vague extraction, Mediterranean perhaps, and acted as if he had seen so much of this world that he was going through the motions of living just to have something to do on his way to the next. A black, downturned mustache entirely covering his mouth added to his dour expression.

"Never trust a skinny chef," Harold said with a smile.

Djurgis rarely spoke, and he approached every task with the dolor of a professional mourner. His method of teaching involved a few choice gestures and phrases.

"Watch thees," he would say as he dashed a precise amount of garlic onto catfish fillets or pulled tendons from a frogleg. Then he would peer at Annie as if over glasses, though he wore none, and say, "Zo. See dat? Now, you do de next one."

Squeamish at first, Annie learned quickly and pulled tendons from the frogmeat with the alacrity of a schoolboy. Dangling a tendon in front of her like a tapeworm, Djurgis said, "*Why?* you say? Look. Zo."

He took an unprepared frogleg and threw it into an iron skillet half-filled with sizzling grease. The leg contracted, ricocheted around the pan, then shot halfway across the kitchen and landed quivering on the floor in an eerie post-mortem death throe.

"Zo," Djurgis said without expression. "Pull de teen-dons out de froglegs, no?"

By the afternoons, Annie was drenched to her skin with sweat. A paste of oils, spices, and flour glued the cotton dress to her body so that it made a sucking noise when she peeled it off in the early evening. Just looking out the raised windows at the breeze kicking up waves on Lake Pontchartrain seemed to intensify the cooling effect of the overhead fans as their blades stirred the humidity into an airy roux that eddied around the room, unable to escape through the grease-clogged mesh of the screens.

Annie had no idea shrimp could be prepared in so many ways: boiled and served hot or cold in half a dozen ways; fried, barbecued, or blackened; shrimp Creole, scampi, pilaf, casserole, salad, or cocktail. Djurgis prepared the other entrées with just as many ruses to tease their distinctive flavors in a variety of directions: redfish, speckled trout, flounder, snapper, swordfish, alligator, crawfish, oysters, andouille, calamari, and boudin.

* * *

Harold's promise to take Annie to a picture show Friday night helped her through the week. All Annie had seen of the great city was a lake, a bayou, and, from a distance, two amusement parks.

"Wear your best," Nevers said as he stepped out of the kitchen Friday afternoon. "I'll pick you up at eight."

Annie mistook the Imperial Theater for a modern church. Its monolithic front divided triptych-like, the middle panel in high relief topped by a discus with a Gothic crown centered over three stars. Fleurs-de-lis, in delicate or bold motifs, adorned the side panels, all of which came to rest on a cantilevered cement awning whose facade blinked red and blue neon chevrons-and-bars. Overall, the structure gave the impression that three architects—Egyptian, Navaho, and Third Reich— had argued the design to a hybrid conclusion. As they walked through the heavy double doors, Mr. Rene Brunet, the owner, greeted them with a toothy smile.

"Good to see you, Mr. Nevers," he said, shaking his hand. "And another pretty lady, I see." He bowed slightly to Annie.

In the lobby, a Tiffany lamp hovered over the candy counter, which the patrons approached like an altar. On either side, thick-glass cisterns percolated gurgling orange and purple liquids, and the simple smell of popcorn instantly vetoed the thousand odors of Annie's week.

Annie's Jujubes and box of popcorn lasted her through the colored cartoon and almost to the intermission of *Double or Nothing*. As she touched up her rouge in the dressing room, Annie looked in the mirror at the other women, evidently of a higher breed than she, for they were helped by uniformed attendants as they took off gloves and hats to apply eye makeup, then fog the air with powders and perfumes.

After the lights went up at the end of the feature film, a little man Annie mistook for a boy scurried onto the stage and was knocked off his feet by the curtain's heavy folds as they closed. This, she quickly surmised, was part of the entertainment. In a baritone voice out of proportion to his physique, the man announced the next night as Money Night.

"In case you weren't listening, I didn't say Saturday night was Monday night, I said Saturday night was Money Night. If Saturday night was Monday night, that would make Sunday Tuesday, right?"

The man went on with his routine as the two strolled up the plushly carpeted, sloping aisle, Harold explaining to Annie how Money Night worked.

"It's mainly to draw people who want something for nothing. You keep your ticket, which has a number on it, and if yours is one of the ten called, you get to go up and pick a paper bag off a clothesline stretched across the stage. Every bag is a guaranteed winner. Some hold a dollar or two. Some lucky suckers have escaped with twenty bucks. That's a week's wages to the working poor." Nevers paused. "Luck. That's the drug that'll get us through this economic depression."

Walking down the sidewalk, Annie took a final peek at the flashing neon facade of the Imperial Theater.

"That was swell, Harold. We'll have to do that again next week. Can we?"

"That? You don't want to go there again, doll. That's a fleapit."

"A fleapit?"

"A cheap movie house." Annie looked at him with surprise. "Next week, I'll take you downtown to the new Carrollton Theater or the Orpheum. If you were impressed by the Imperial, they'll knock your eyes out."

* * *

Saturday afternoon, Nevers and Annie picnicked in City Park. They sat on a bedspread by the large lagoon and watched snowball-eating children feed popcorn to the ducks and black swans.

When they finished eating, Nevers took Annie on a tour of the park. In several spots, they detoured around WPA workers digging new lagoons and sculpting statues in the art deco style. Annie admired the McFadden Mansion and could hardly believe the size of the park's pool with its cascading falls, central raft, and numerous high and low diving boards. What struck her dumb in her tracks, however, was the Peristyle, which resembled the Parthenon floating somehow on marshland. Half the size of a football field, with entrances guarded by marble lions, its fifteen-foot Corinthian columns supported the granite roof. Walking hand in hand with Harold on the cool cement floor, Annie felt for the first time in her life the massive weight of history. Gawking at the ceiling, she thrilled at the idea that it could tumble down and crush her—that in a thousand years she could be found like a citizen of Pompei in the arms of her lover.

"What in the world *is* this thing?" she asked, dodging a berserk girl on roller skates.

"This was just the beginning," Nevers replied. His voice echoed off the ceiling. "It was built at the turn of the century by an eccentric Gatsby-type fellow. He intended it as the entrance to his mansion. I guess he thought he was King Tut or something. Wanted to be remembered down through the ages." They paused to admire the scrolls at the columns' capitals. "Can you imagine what it must have cost just to transport the stones? If you ask me, Roosevelt ought to put those WPA boys to work finishing this thing. It'd be like the pyramids. It took a whole society hundreds of years to build those things. That's what's wrong with America. We lack a vision." He glanced at her. "Know what I mean? That's what wars are good for, to get all the people moving in the same direction."

Their skates sparking on cement, a rigmarole of screaming boys slid to the floor to avoid bowling down Annie and Harold. Abruptly, his mood changed.

"Disgusting," he said.

Clutching his arm, Annie said, "Oh, they're just playing."

"Not the boys. Children, I like. It's the parents." The two walked silently down the steps. "Breeders. That's all they are. Don't they have any better sense than to keep churning out kids? This is a depression. What kind of life can they give those children?"

Annie felt a low-grade anxiety well up in her chest. She had hoped Nevers would not be just a business partner, but would want to marry her, maybe even desperately, like in the movies.

"Don't you ever want children?"

Harold kicked a discarded cotton-candy stem. "Ah, I don't know. I feel like I want to do other things and they'd just get in the way." He glanced at Annie. "I suppose it comes from my being an orphan, you know?"

"I guess," she said unconvincingly.

They had wandered into a pack of children waiting with their mothers around a mangy-looking stuffed pony. A metallic clack drew Annie's attention to a large boxy camera atop a tripod. A swarthy, dwarf-like creature with round, gold-rimmed glasses parked on a Jimmy Durante nose emerged from beneath the black cloth.

Several children competed for his attention. "Me next, Mr. Wolfy! Me next!"

The man walked to a boy almost his size and looked at him gruffly. "*You*? You want I should crack my camera?" The other children laughed. Still deadpan, the photographer lifted a girl toddler and placed her on the pony. "Mama!" the photographer said as if the woman were deaf, "you stand behind the horse and hold the tot's leg, right? Don't let her fall."

Mr. Wolfgang Rosenweig was a Russian immigrant. For as long as Nevers had known him, the man had worn the same baggy white shirt and denim apron. The same felt hat had the same sweat stains, and he looked the same as ten years before. He had reached that age where he couldn't get any older. He was ancient.

As they watched Mr. Wolf's rough demeanor with the kids, Annie realized that he really was the way he acted. The fault lay in the children and their parents, who thought the man must be comical since he was short and old and talked funny. To them, he was like a freak in a raree show.

Annie got a glimpse of several sepia photographs and quickly forgot her gloom. She looked up at Harold.

With childlike anticipation, she said, "Let's have our picture taken, can we?"

Between waves of children, Nevers negotiated with Mr. Wolf, who couldn't get inspired to move his equipment the hundred yards to the Peristyle where Annie wanted the shot taken.

"Tell you what, Mr. Wolf," Harold said. "I'll pay you half a day's wages to move to the porch and take five pictures of us." Hands on his hips, Mr. Wolf eyed Nevers, his face hardening even more.

"Ten dollars," he said.

"Ten dollars! You don't make five in a day." Nevers faced down Mr. Wolf. "I'll give you three greenbacks and consider it highway robbery."

Mr. Wolf stared up at Nevers. His mouth opened and closed twice. "Deal," he said firmly.

At the Peristyle, the two posed by a column. While Mr. Wolf set up for the shot and polished his camera lens with a soiled handkerchief, Annie's eyes were riveted on the marble lions. In the final four shots, at Harold's insistence, Annie posed by herself with a lion. In the first, she petted the animal. The second was a profile shot of the two, nose to nose, Annie roaring in the face of the passive beast. The third showed her leaning back in mock horror with hands closed about her face. In the last, she leaned coquettishly against the creature, her arm around its mane.

As twilight shaded the grounds, Nevers drove Annie to Stock's Amusement Park, where they walked around looking at the lights and rides until thirst overcame them. At a hotdog-shaped booth, Annie drank a vanilla and Harold a chocolate soda. Between sips, Annie's eyes followed the Scenic Railway, a dilapidated roller coaster whose timbers creaked and popped when the carriages of screaming teenagers yanked around the sharp turns.

"Spare me that death," she said.

"Oh, no," Harold said. "It's really safe. Checked daily by inspectors with the latest equipment. All that noise is built in to heighten the thrill."

"Then why are they all screaming like that?"

"That's what you're supposed to do. It's part of the fun. Come on. Finish your soda and we'll buy some tickets."

While the attendant locked them in, Nevers said, "Now, don't forget to play the part. Scream a little so the kids won't think you're a fuddy-duddy."

As the chain cranked the line of coaches to the drop, the summit seemed much higher to Annie than it had from the ground. When the train plummeted from the peak of the scaffolding, she shrieked and, holding onto Harold's arm before the fall, gave up that bit of romance to secure her grip with both hands on the guardrail in front of her. At the next curve, Annie thought the carriage would careen off its tracks and end the young life she had so foolishly jeopardized. Finally, the train sped noisily into the landing and braked so fast that Annie felt the soda slosh against the front of her stomach. Nevers climbed out first, laughing as usual, though a bit rattled himself.

"Whoo, that was something," he confessed. "I haven't ridden one of those things in years." With an extended arm, he helped Annie out of the carriage. She quivered visibly. "Say, you look a little green around the gills."

"I don't feel so good," Annie admitted, holding her stomach.

"Let's get a Coke. That'll settle your tummy so we can come back and take *another* spin on the Scenic Railway."

Annie groaned and glared mock-angrily at Nevers.

As they sat on wrought-iron benches drinking their Cokes, Annie watched a group of hoodlums taking turns peering into a box while a boy in corduroy knickers cranked the handle.

"Turn slower," one of them complained.

"Hey, give it up," another said. "You've been looking twice as long as Smitty did."

Twenty minutes later, Annie revived enough to stroll around.

"What were those boys watching?" Annie started toward the stall of eyepieces. "Can we take a look?"

"You wouldn't be interested," Harold said, pulling her away from the booths. "Just some half-dressed ladies."

Annie raised her eyebrows. "A burlesque? I've never seen one. Can I take a peek, just to see what it's like?"

Nevers dropped a nickel in a slot, peered into the binocular eyepiece, and began cranking the handle. Annie slapped his arm. "Hey, I thought this was for me."

"Take it easy. I'm just making sure I'm turning at the right speed. Here." He cupped his hand around Annie's neck and pulled her toward the blinking light.

It was like spying on someone in their bedroom, Annie thought. The flickering blue light made the woman move jerkily about the room. She thought of Charlie Chaplin. A caption appeared.

"**AFTER A WONDERFUL EVENING AT THE OPERA**." The voluptuous woman, black-clad, paused before a looking glass. She clutched her bosom and sighed. She took off her earrings, placing them on the dresser, and began to unbutton her dress. The tapestry-like material fell around her ankles, revealing the woman's gartered legs and tightly corseted torso. As she stepped out of the dress, a man, undetected by the woman, opened the door on the far side of the frame.

Annie wondered if he was the man the woman had been thinking about while undressing. The woman sat on an upholstered bench and began unlacing her high-topped shoes. The man continued to watch, his eyes shining with lust. The woman held her leg out and rolled the stocking to the end of her pointed foot. Swiveling to place the little donut on the dresser, she saw the man and emitted what must have been an earsplitting scream. The man quickly entered the room and shut the door behind him. In exaggerated fashion, he rapidly moved his mouth.

"**YOU FOOL, DO YOU WANT THE NEIGHBORS TO HEAR?**" the caption read. He approached the woman, who was trying to cover the exposed tops of her breasts with her arms. The man grabbed her wrists and after a brief struggle managed to pry her arms outward.

"Turn slower," Annie said. "They're moving too fast."

Harold obeyed. "What's going on in there, anyway?"

"Shhh!" she said, then giggled, realizing there was no sound. "It's–. They're–. Oh, shush, I'll tell you later."

The villain forced the woman down on her bed. Up to this point, she had fended off his advances, but now, her bosom heaving wildly, she met the man's kiss and pulled him down on top of her. The blue light stopped flickering and stabbed Annie's eyes with an explosion of brilliant white.

"Ow!" she said, pulling back from the eyepiece. "Hey, that wasn't fair." Annie looked at Nevers. "Just when they–."

"Just when they what?" Nevers asked, grinning.

Annie turned towards the eyepiece. "It was–. Oh, you know *exactly* what happens in those things." She punched Harold lightly on his chest. "I bet. Don't you?" she said, looking up at him.

* * *

At the water's edge in front of the pier leading to Terra Incognita, his car still running, Nevers kissed Annie good night at eleven o'clock.

"I've got to run downtown and take care of some business," he said. Still in his arms, Annie pushed away to look at him. "Don't ask," he laughed. "I'll see you tomorrow at two for the ballgame, okay?" They had planned an outing to Heinemann Park to watch the Pelicans open a three-game series with the Lake Charles Lakers.

Nevers stepped out and walked around to Annie's door while she gathered the photographs from the glove compartment. When he opened the door, Annie stood up. Nevers embraced her and kissed her again.

"I love kissing you," he said. He kissed her hard. Annie felt the power of his arms around her. She clutched her purse and the photos between her breasts as Harold pressed his chest against her. He placed his palms on the tops of her shoulders and pushed her back on the car seat. Annie sat looking up at Nevers. He bent down, kissed her lightly on the cheek and, bringing his lips to her ear, whispered, "Say 'Kiss me.'" His stubble on her neck, the sound of his voice, the stale odor of cologne and sweat sent chills crawling up and down Annie's arms.

"Kiss me," she said. Nevers pushed her down on the seat. The photos spilled onto the floorboard. Harold lay on top of her, kissing her neck and face. "Kiss me," she said again as he worked the buttons on her blouse. Breathing heavily, she let her left arm fall in surrender. Her hand touched the photos. Nevers pulled her lingerie down and kissed her breasts. Annie gripped one of the photos. The pleasurable pain in her chest was more than she could bear without saying something. "My lion, aren't you?"

Harold continued kissing. "Hmm?"

"You're my lion." Nevers lifted himself off her. She dropped the photo and placed her hands behind his neck, drawing him down. "Kiss me some more." Harold nuzzled his face between her breasts.

"I love kissing you all over."

"My big lion."

Nevers growled, "I could tear you to pieces."

"I want you to. Tear me to pieces, big lion."

Abruptly, Harold said, "Can't!" He pushed himself out of the car. Annie put the back of her hand on her forehead. It was damp and hot. "Much as I'd like to, I can't."

Annie stood up and looked at her clothing in disarray. "What are you doing to me, Harold Nevers?"

"I don't know," he said, taking her in his arms again, "but we'll have to do more of it later, huh?"

Annie squeezed him tight. She never wanted to let him go.

7

July 1938

Just like the theater audience, the crowd at the ballpark was dressed to the nines.

Harold had greeted Annie at her bedroom door with a hatbox. He sat her down at the vanity bench facing the looking glass. Making Annie close her eyes, he rustled the gift from its box and placed the hat on her head.

"Open sesame."

Annie opened her eyes. On her head rested a green-felt honey hat, the satin sash encircling the crown tied in a small, tight bow.

"Simple but elegant," Nevers observed aristocratically.

"It's lovely," Annie said, "but you shouldn't have."

"Okay, then, give it back," Harold teased, grabbing for the brim.

Annie squealed and pressed the chapeau tightly to her head with both hands. She looked in the mirror again, swiveling her head from side to side.

"You're right," Nevers said. "Let's see." He stooped down and studied the angle of the hat. He twisted it to one side and dipped the brim over her forehead. "There."

"That's it," Annie agreed. She glanced back and forth from the hat to her dress's light-blue print. "I don't know. You think I should change?"

"Only if I get to watch."

Annie slapped his arm and sent him out of the room. As she stepped into a bright yellow sun dress sprinkled with small olive dots, she imagined Harold watching her. She thought of the woman in the burlesque. Who were the women that did such things? And why? Where did they come from? She imagined herself in the woman's place, with Nevers ogling her through the lusty eyes of the villain. After a while, she felt herself growing warm.

"Stop it," she chided in a loud whisper that unraveled into an impish snigger. She looked in the mirror, pleased at her other self.

"Mama, you'd never believe this," Annie said. She leaned over and touched up her rouge. "And you probably wouldn't want to see it."

* * *

They reached the ballpark in the third inning.

"Here!" a man called. "Over here!"

Annie grabbed Harold's arm and pointed to a man waving midway up the bleachers. As they settled in, Nevers made introductions.

"Annie Beatrice, Arkie Burk." The man reached for Annie's gloved hand.

"Pleased to meet you," she said.

"Likewise, I'm sure," the man returned.

"And Bliss Fulsom," Nevers said. A bleached blonde with black eyebrows extended a long, slender arm across Burk.

"Yours truly," she said pleasantly. Behind luscious lips painted bright red, she displayed a row of sleek teeth that resembled a small animal's.

Annie quickly ascertained that the sport on the diamond was secondary to the social event in the grandstand. Nevers ordered peanuts and Cokes for the four of them. He planted his bag of peanuts in the basket of a baseball glove on his right hand.

"For foul balls," he had explained to Annie when she saw the mitt on the dashboard. "It's good luck to catch a foul hit by the other team. Puts the hoodoo on 'em."

Nevers set the cold drink at his feet and pulled a silver hipflask of bourbon from his coat. Throughout the game, he doctored Arkie's Cokes but never took a drink himself. In the seventh inning, a man whistled beneath the stands and tugged at Harold's pantleg.

Nevers looked at Annie. "Alas, business calls me away, dear." Five minutes later, he returned. He picked up the glove marking his place and put it on. He leaned over to Arkie. "A hundred bucks."

"Not bad for half an inning's work," Arkie laughed. His speech was slurred.

"What's the score now?" Nevers asked.

"Four to three," Annie said. "We're winning."

"That depends on where your bets are laid," Arkie said.

Annie squeezed Harold's arm. "You have money on this game?"

"Not me, darling. I'm not a gambling man."

"Only the sure thing, right J.P.?" Nevers elbowed Arkie in the ribs. Annie could tell it hurt. Arkie corrected himself. "*Harold*, okay? Jeez, lighten up."

With two outs in the top of the ninth, the Lakers had a man on third. The Pelicans had increased their lead in the eighth with a solo homer. The score was 5 to 3. The crowd yelled for Bump, the Pelicans' pitcher, to brush back the batter, Simon Metcalf, the Lakers' cleanup man. The count was two and two. The next pitch was an inside fastball in the dirt. The runner on third scored on a passed ball.

"This is where it gets interesting," Harold said. "You should never get involved until the ninth inning."

The count was full. Metcalf waved his bat menacingly. The slow pitch curved to the outside corner and Metcalf stabbed at it, chipping it off the end of his bat. The ball shot directly at Annie, who screamed and leaned back as Nevers reached in front of her with his glove. The ball hit square in the palm of the mitt, spraying peanuts hulls into the air.

"Did you get it?" she asked, brushing the husks out of her hair and lap.

Harold laughed. "Nah. All I got was peanut butter."

"You silly man," Annie said.

Metcalf stepped out of the batter's box to compose himself. The catcher sent Bump a signal. Bump waved it off and called for another sign as Metcalf pounded the plate with his bat.

"All right," Annie said. "Catch it this time if it comes our way. Didn't you tell me that was good luck?"

Bump went into a gyrating windup to throw off the batter's timing.

"Fumble fingers," Annie said. "Mr. Fumble Fingers."

Nevers grabbed Annie by the arm and squeezed, nearly lifting her off the bleachers. A pain shot down her arm.

"Ow! You're hurting me, Harold!" The crowd roared to its feet as Metcalf connected with a loud crack.

"It's just a game!" Nevers yelled in Annie's ear. "You hear?" He shook her like a doll. "Don't criticize people when they're just trying to have fun, you hear?"

"Okay, okay." Nevers stood up and looked at the field. Annie rubbed her shoulder.

Metcalf had rounded first. Near the left field fence, Little Bobby Devers, who usually played shortstop, glanced over his shoulder at the ball, then in front of him at the fence. He leaped and stretched. He tumbled to the ground and bounded up, showing the umpire the ball protruding from the top of his glove. A snowcone catch. The crowd went wild. Metcalf kicked second base with disgust and glared out at Devers.

The crowd began vacating the stands.

"Don't we get to bat again?" Bliss whined to Arkie.

Arkie laughed. "And do what? Beat 'em six to four, or maybe eight to four? What would be the point?" Bliss was disappointed nevertheless.

In the car, Nevers acted like their spat hadn't occurred. At the pier, he apologized for having to leave so soon. He said he had to be in Houston by midnight and would be gone for a week. He lifted Annie's chin.

"Cheer up," he said. "Your first payday's next week. We'll go into the city and celebrate."

* * *

Monday was opening day for Terra Incognita. Annie greeted and seated the diners, fetched utensils and spices for Djurgis, ordered groceries, checked the customers out at the register, and balanced the books at day's end.

By Wednesday, Annie found enough free time to make diary entries for the previous week and write her mother to tell her of the restaurant's opening.

On Friday, two large parties of businessmen came in at noon, forcing Annie to serve as second-string cook while scrambling back and forth to the register. She was pulling a crab-stuffed snapper from the oven when Janice, one of the waitresses, called into the kitchen, "Register, Miss Annie." Annie set the platter down and rushed out of the swinging double doors right into Harold Nevers. Annie screeched and gave him a hug, then, remembering where she was, pulled him inside the kitchen.

"Sorry! I was in such a hurry, you're lucky I didn't flatten you." She reached up and kissed his cheek.

Looking over her head, Harold saw Djurgis taking pots off burners and putting skillets on, kicking cabinet doors shut, stirring condiments into various dishes, and generally performing a razzmatazz of motions that would have qualified him for a circus sideshow.

"I guess this means we're making millions," Harold said.

"Not millions," Annie smiled, "but more than I thought we'd make the first week."

Nevers looked around thoughtfully.

"What the hell," he said, shedding his jacket and rolling up his sleeves. "Let's knock this out so we can paint the town red tonight." Annie and Harold sweated together through the afternoon and set up Djurgis for the evening rush, then parted to get ready.

An hour and a half later, Nevers honked at the foot of the pier.

"Customers still coming in, I see," he observed as Annie flopped in the car seat with a sigh of relief.

"The parking lot's been full all day," she said. "How was *your* week? You haven't even told me."

"The usual," Harold began. He talked the few minutes to the turn-off onto Esplanade. "Here," he said, reaching into his jacket. He tossed a white envelope onto Annie's lap.

"What's this?"

"First payday, like I promised."

Annie felt her heart leap. The labor of setting up the restaurant, the excitement of going places with Nevers, had made her forget she was working for money.

"Open it. It won't bite you."

Annie slid her finger along the tab. Her eyes enlarged as she saw the bills. She counted five tens and ten fives.

"A hundred dollars! This is too much, Harold. Really. For a week's work?"

"Two weeks," Nevers corrected her. "Including training."

"But–." Annie was speechless. "What do I owe you for room and board?"

"Your company."

"Seriously, Harold."

"Not a dime." Nevers laughed. "Look, if you think you're flush with a hundred bucks, wait until business starts rolling in on the weekdays, too. You'll take in so much dough, I'll wake up one morning to find you've skipped the state with the week's till."

Nevers parked at the Chevrolet lot near Canal and Rampart. As Annie stepped out the door Nevers had opened for her, he pointed down the long vista of Canal Street. "Now, let's see you spend some of that loot."

Annie was dumbfounded. In the twilight, several stores were just turning on their lights. The first word that came to her mind was *carnival*. In a single block, steady white lights spelled out the names of banks, hotels, pharmacies, department stores, and barbershops. Neon tubes winked red, purple, and green. On the Saenger and Loews State theaters, rows of light bulbs crawled around the marquees like incandescent centipedes. A streetcar rumbled around a curve, shooting blue sparks from the wires overhead.

Painted on the sides of buildings or hanging from canvas awnings shaped like umbrellas, advertisements competed for Annie's attention. Luzianne Coffee. White Owl Cigars. FOR RENT. Royal Crown. Pepto-Bismol. Drink Barq's Root Beer, It's Good. The red Pegasus of Mobilgas. Over the Chevrolet dealership, an octagonal clock two stories high told Annie it was eight-thirty and urged her in fifteen-foot script:

Drink Coca-Cola
Enjoy Cooling Refreshment

Annie wanted to read all the signs and peer into all the windows. As they walked the first block, Nevers had to steer her around drainage grills and manhole covers that might snag a heel and trip her.

Pausing every few minutes to watch a green streetcar pass, Annie marveled at each one as if it were a metal dinosaur trundling down the avenue. They strolled under the Loews State marquee. "Twenty Degrees Cooler Inside," the letters promised. She saw signs for Krauss, Walgreens, and Godchaux's. They crossed the street at Baronne. Nevers suggested stepping into Maison Blanche.

"What's that across the street?" she asked. "Katz and Bes–. How do you say that?"

"Katz and Besthoff," Nevers said.

The three-story structure announced its wares in fat gold letters on a green backdrop: Pharmacy and Millinery.

"They ought to simplify that," Annie suggested. "People don't like to shop at places they can't pronounce."

"I'll tell the owners you said that," Nevers offered.

"No, really. Like, why don't they just call it Katz?"

"And offend Mr. Besthoff? He'd never go for that, I'll wager."

"Well, then, how about a compromise, using their initials, maybe."

Nevers tried the suggestion. "K and B, K and B. Nah, sounds cheap. It would draw the wrong kind of customer. They'd have to change their whole image. Merchandise, too."

Annie looked at the billboard on top of the building. Beside the image of a ten-foot porcelain refrigerator was the word WESTINGHOUSE. Atop the sign, a circular thermometer, demarcated every ten degrees, was prepared for temperatures up to a hundred and twenty. Currently, the hand rested between eighty and ninety.

Annie stepped into the street and was yanked back to the curb by Nevers. A red van zoomed past. Reading the side of the vehicle, Annie realized she had almost been pressed by SWISS LAUNDRY.

Finally deciding on D. H. Holmes, Annie and Harold threaded the aisles between dozens of counters, searching for something to buy.

"I don't feel like I need anything," Annie said.

"Spend the money," Nevers encouraged. "That's what it's for. Tomorrow night, we're going to the Roosevelt to listen to a big band. Why don't you buy an evening gown?"

Thirty minutes later, Nevers regretted his suggestion. Annie had to stop and inspect every item she passed on her way to the back of the store. There, she stared up at the mezzanine, where a man played an organ that piped music to all three floors. Annie finally decided on an ankle-length cream gown with blue floral print, fitted bustline, and mutton sleeves.

Outside, she said, "I could probably use a new pair of shoes with my dress." Annie started for Imperial's.

"Not so fast," Harold said. "Look, there's Marks-Issacs just past Grunewald's Pianos."

Annie looked to where he pointed. She saw green neon tubes in the outline of a grand piano.

"Shoes are shoes, I suppose," Nevers said, "but at Marks-Isaacs they have a special gizmo to help you with the fit."

"Then Marks-Isaacs it is. Lead on."

Inside the store, Annie selected several pairs of shoes, and the attendant returned with a stack of boxes. Annie finally decided on a pair of gray suede half-heels with ankle straps. While the assistant reboxed the remainder, she said, "Would you like to see how they fit?"

"Oh, they feel fine."

Harold said, "But you'll miss all the fun if you don't actually *see* how they fit."

As the attendant disappeared with the boxes, a valet led Annie to a metal device and kneeled down. "Place your foot under here," he directed. The man flipped a switch on the side of the box. A low hum amplified to a buzz. "Look here." The man pointed to a dark glass covering her shoed foot. It took Annie a few seconds to interpret the image on the screen. She gasped and pulled her foot from the instrument.

"Can you believe that?" Annie said to Harold. "It's not dangerous, is it?"

"Harmless. Put the other foot in and let's have another look-see." Annie inserted her left foot. She and Nevers studied the screen. The bones of her foot, surrounded by the outline of the shoe, appeared in faint white against a dark gray background. She moved her foot to the side.

"Look," she exclaimed. "You can see the nails in the shoe."

Nevers glanced at the valet and winked.

"Think we can fit her in and take a look at the rest of them bones?"

Annie slapped Harold on the arm. "Let's see *your* feet."

Nevers placed his foot in the slot. "These bones shall rise again," he said.

Annie gazed into the X-ray machine. Pointing, she asked, "What's that?"

"I have steel toenails," Harold said.

Annie slapped him again. "Just one?"

"It's my lucky penny. Carry it with me wherever I go."

"Why is it lucky?"

"A few years back, I thought I'd lost every cent I owned, but when I got back to my flop on Magazine Street, I found it in my pocket. I was pretty down before, but that picked my spirits right up because I realized I had never been flat busted. Right then, I decided to hang on to it so I'd never be broke again. Worked, too."

The first sign Annie read as they stepped out of the store onto the banquette said, "Dentists. Open until 11 P.M."

"Amazing," she said. "Doesn't this city ever sleep?"

"You never know when you'll need to pull a gold tooth to pay a gambling debt."

"And I suppose you've got a gold tooth."

"Two." Nevers hooked the side of his mouth and bent down for Annie to look inside. The back two molars on the top left were in fact gold.

"I thought you didn't gamble."

"Don't. The gold teeth are an investment. There wasn't even anything wrong with them."

"You're a strange man, Harold Nevers."

"Smart, too," he replied, ushering her left onto Decatur. "We'll walk down to Jackson Square, then take a streetcar back to the parking lot. How's that sound?"

"Sounds good. My feet are killing me. I stood all day in–." A castrato voice interrupted her.

"Hey, Mr. Harold! Where you been?"

Annie looked down. A legless man on a board raised a cup to Nevers. In his other hand, he wielded a stick with rubber stoppers on both ends.

"Wendel! Long time no see. I think *you're* the one's been gone."

A swatch of disheveled hair the color of dried marsh grass sat on the man's head. His skin was rough and scaly, like he'd been too long at sea. Beneath a ratty beard, a scarred smile revealed three or four decaying teeth.

"You got me there, Mr. Harold. Had me a girlfriend in Morgan City for a while. Kicked me out after a month, though." The man lifted a short stump from the board and waggled it up and down. "Terrible thing is, I couldn't kick her back. Ha!"

He rattled a few coins in the cup.

"How 'bout you, miss? Spare some change for an old vet? I lost my legs for the good old U.S. of A. in the Great War, and look what I got in return. My own street corner. Ha!"

"You're breaking my heart, Wendel," Harold said, digging in his pocket. He dredged up a few coins and selected a fifty-cent piece. "Here's a walking lady," Nevers said, dropping it in the cup.

"Thanks, Mr. Harold. You always was the generous one. A walking lady for a legless man. Ha!" Wendel wedged the cup between his stumps, positioned the stick in both hands, and gripped the cement with one of the stoppers. The board reared in the front and twirled. Paddling on alternating sides with the stick, he shot down the banquette with a metallic sound.

Annie looked at Nevers quizzically.

"Roller skates." He laughed.

"You shouldn't laugh. That's very sad."

"He's a con man."

"That's an awful thing to say."

"The truth hurts. I knew him when he had legs. Couldn't you tell he was too young for a veteran? That's why he grows the beard. To look older. He lost his legs and half a hand in a dock accident at the Poydras Street Wharf. After that, the police hired him to act like a derelict, to be an informant, and, wouldn't you know it, he turned into a *real* derelict. I guess he got into the role too much. That's some tough luck, huh? They still use him, though."

"I didn't even notice the hand."

"You should be more observant."

At Jackson Square, Annie sat on a bench to rest. They watched people passing for a few minutes. She yawned and looked up at the clock on the St. Louis Cathedral steeple.

"Eleven-thirty! Where did the time go?"

Nevers said, "Imagine that. You couldn't even get a tooth pulled at this time of the night."

* * *

The vibration of the streetcar made Annie even sleepier. She leaned her head on the window. At Dauphine, Harold said, "One more block." Annie opened her eyes. She saw a man running on the sidewalk, shouting wordlessly. Ahead of him, Wendel paddled furiously, dodging left and right around the walkers, picking up speed, opening the gap between him and his pursuer.

The Chevrolet lot was lit up like a baseball field, insects swarming around every lamp. On the blacktop, large overturned waterbugs with devilish antennae flipped around with a clicking noise trying to right themselves.

"We're going to take this sleepy girl home now," Harold said as he opened the door for Annie.

"When do I get to see *your* house?"

"Have to go out of the way to do that."

"I'm sleepwalking now. Five more minutes won't kill me."

Nevers turned the ignition key and reached on the dash for a pack of cigarettes.

"Here," he said, "this'll jolt you awake."

"Thanks, I don't care for them."

"How do you know? Ever tried one?"

They drove a few blocks in silence. Annie's eyes were drawn to the lights that hurt them when she looked. She blinked. Her eyelids scratched like sandpaper. She glanced at Harold, then out the window, reaching her hand towards him in a gesture designed to retain her dignity while admitting desperation.

She sipped lightly on the first drags. Nevers permitted Annie her dignity by not speaking. They passed Chartres and Decatur.

At the next intersection, Harold said, "Tchoupitoulas."

Annie lifted her chin. "How's that spelled?"

"T-C-H . . . -O." Nevers looked around for a sign. "U-P-X-Y-Z or something like that," he laughed. "Last week, a cop on the night beat found a bum hugging a light pole, so he went up to him and gave him a poke with his billy club. Dead as a hammer." Harold took the cigarette from Annie and pulled at it. "Tried to jimmy him free, but he was stuck." He handed her the cigarette. "Rigor mortis had already set in." Nevers laughed. "Took two men to pry him loose. Then they couldn't find a street sign to spell Tchoupitoulas, so they dragged him to Front Street and wrote up the report there."

Annie gave up a tired grin. Her eyelids drooped like a lizard's.

Nevers turned left on Poydras and right on Commerce. He slowed and pointed. "There it is."

Annie looked at the house. She thought of the bed inside.

"Could a body fall asleep in there?"

"Yep, but not tonight," Harold said, easing his car away from the curb. "I have a bit of touching up to do before it's ready for company."

"Need to move the bodies?" Annie kidded.

Nevers laughed. "You can't be *that* tired if you can still joke."

Annie tossed the butt out the window. It made her feel worldly. She formulated the words in her mind and liked the way they sounded. "No, I'm all right, but I'll need another cigarette to get me home."

Annie awoke at eight o'clock the next morning. By noon, she was strolling down Basin with Harold. A clot of men were yelling where it intersected Iberville.

"Get out the sun! How you 'spect it to do in the shade, fool?" The men couldn't decide whether it was cooler with their hats on, shading their faces, or off, using them as fans.

The foolish man moved back enough for Annie to see four eggshell halves on the walk, the two yolks staring at a jaundiced sky.

"Two more minutes," said a man shouldering his coat. Annie and Harold paused. Thirty seconds later, a heavyset man swabbing his brow and face with a handkerchief while avoiding the cigar jammed in his mouth, said, "That's it! Told you it wouldn't take no ten minutes for them thangs to skin over. It's hot as a fryin' pan out here. Pay up and let's get in the shade. Damn fools."

Some of the streets they walked on were paved with bricks. Annie looked at the wrought-iron balconies. Pairs of faceless nuns glided by in black. Annie marveled at how cool they looked. She tried to imagine herself in their habits. Where were they going in the heat of the day? What would they do when they got there? How did they decide on such a life?

Around every corner, there was a cathedral or a movie house. Some of the cathedrals opened their doors temptingly, exposing cool interiors. The signs on the theaters competed with the churches. "Take in a matinee. Twenty degrees cooler inside. First feature 2:15." Annie looked across the street. Two thermometers disagreed at ninety-eight and ninety-five.

At St. Louis Cemetery Number 1, Nevers showed her the grave of Marie Laveau. During antebellum nights, the mulatta voodoo queen hypnotized her customers with a black snake named Zombi. She convinced more than one skeptic of her infernal powers by pretending to conjure secrets she had learned from them by day in her other guise as a hairdresser. After mothering twelve children, she lost six in the 1832 yellow fever epidemic.

"I guess her voodoo wasn't powerful enough to save *them*," Nevers remarked after telling the story.

Next, the amblers bought two lemonades from a street vendor and sat on an iron bench encircling an oak tree with a whitewashed trunk.

"Let's sit out the heat in that theater." Annie pointed. "How's it pronounced?"

"Like *low*. Loews State." Harold glanced at his watch. "Sounds good to me. We'll just make the matinee if we hurry."

When Annie walked into the lobby of the Loews State Theater, her mouth dropped open. She didn't know where to look first: up, at the massive chandelier, or down, at its luxuriant, baroque carpets, or all around, at the marble columns and curving staircase a queen might descend at any moment.

The interior of the movie palace looked like a cross between the Vatican and a millionaire's mansion at Christmas. The auditorium's plush seats and cool darkness revived Annie, and by the time *Jezebel* was over, she was ready to attack New Orleans again.

The two walked a block down Canal. Annie heard the sound of fire-crackers growing louder as they neared the intersection at University Place.

"Shoeshine boys," Harold replied to Annie's questioning frown. After they had crossed the street, Annie watched three boys working on their customers by the entrance of the Roosevelt Hotel. The lone black boy finished first and looked at Harold.

"Step right up, mister." Nevers had not intended to get his shoes polished, but the boy charmed his foot onto the sole-shaped platform of his box before he could say no.

"Yes sir, mistah, I sho is glad you stopped. I been watching you for fi-six days now. These the finest shoes on or *off* Canal, musta cost fifty dollah, huh?" The boy had already swabbed black paste onto the shoe.

"Whoa there, podnah," Harold said. "I like to get to know the man that handles my intimate articles of clothing. What's your name?"

Looking up, the boy rapidly worked the polish into Harold's shoe with a brush and never even grazed his socks.

"Name Daar-nell. Wha' chore name?" During the whole conversation, his name was the only word Darnell said slowly.

"Hapscomb," Nevers said. "But my friends call me Happy."

"Well, Mr. Happy, I sho is glad you stopped. These the finest shoes I seen in two-three months, ain't that so, Beanie Boy?"

The boy who had not yet acquired another customer glanced indifferently at Harold's shoes.

"I seen better," he said.

"Not this week, you hain't. And probbly not this year." The boy whipped a rag from his back pocket and began rubbing the shoe. "Don't pay him no mind, Mr. Happy. His mama say he constipated all the time's what make him so ornery." He released one end of the cloth. It popped across the shoe with a loud report and faster than Annie could see how he did it, he had the rag around the back of the shoe and buffed it a couple of times, then snapped it again and finished off by spitting on the top of the shoe and spanking it three or four times with the rag. "Hah!" he said and slapped the shoe off the stand while reaching for Harold's other foot. "Bet you never got a better shine than that, Mr. Happy, now, admit it."

Nevers laughed. "You got me there, Darnell. Until a year ago, I always did my own."

The boy looked up at Nevers with a puckered face, like he had just sucked on a lemon. "Rich man like you? Shoot, you don't fool old Daar-nell. You probbly just th'owed 'em away when they got dirty, huh, Mr. Happy?"

When the boy was done, Harold reached in his trousers and pulled out a handful of change. He flipped one nickel, then another high in the air towards Darnell, who snatched the first with his left hand, the second with his right.

Nevers was about to return the change to his trousers when he got an idea. He picked out a quarter and dumped the rest of the coins in his pocket.

"Say, Darnell, you feeling lucky today?"

The boy tiptoed and tried to look in Harold's hand.

"'Pends on what kinda odds you laying."

"Heads or tails. You win, you get my two bits. I win, I get my nickels back."

Darnell inspected the nickels lying in his palm. He licked his lips thoughtfully.

"You on, Mr. Happy."

Nevers flipped the quarter high in the air. "Call it before it lands."

"Heads!" Darnell shouted and skipped, clapping his hands once. The coin hit the pavement and rolled in a slow semicircle before falling.

"Hah!" Nevers said. "Tails." He retrieved the quarter and held his hand out for the boy's earnings. Darnell slapped the nickels into Harold's hand with a dejected look on his face.

"Can't win every time," Nevers said.

"Nawp. Sho cain't."

Harold pretended to walk away. Darnell returned to his shoeshine box.

"Darnell," Nevers called. The boy looked at him. "Catch." Harold pitched the quarter in a high arc towards him. Darnell caught the coin and examined it. "That makes us both winners," Nevers said. "I got your two nickels and you got my two bits."

The boy beamed.

"Thanks, Mr. Happy. You come back anytime, hear? I'll be on whichever's the shady side of the street. And don't confuse me with these other boys. You can tell me on account of my name's Daar-nell."

Annie and Harold rounded the corner onto Canal, where Nevers stopped her with his arm.

"Listen," he said. He crept to the corner of the building and leaned against it. Annie heard the rags popping.

"Yes sir, mistah, I sho is glad you stopped. I been watching yo shoes walk by here for fo-fi days now. Finest shoes I ever seed, musta cost you fifty dollah, huh? Look at these shoes, Beanie. Ain't they the finest you ever seed?"

Annie and Nevers laughed, and Darnell heard them. As they walked away, the boy's raised voice reached around the corner. "Except o' course for Mr. Happy Hapscomb's shoes. You know Mr. Happy? Well, you ought to. Fine man . . ."

"Yeah, that's real funny," Nevers said. "The only problem is that almost every man you see around here used to be one of those boys. They know every scam in the book. They could stick a dull knife in you and make you think it feels good. And they'll eat you alive unless you learn to think like them. Listen. How can I put this?" He thought for a few steps. "There's some places where the only sin is innocence. In New Orleans, goodness is dangerous. You practice it and you're likely to end up like Wendel." They walked for a bit in silence. "You see what I'm saying?"

✶ ✶ ✶

After supper at Antoine's, Harold took Annie to the Famous Door for some Dixieland jazz. The tempo was too snappy for her mood, and she complained of the smoke after fifteen minutes. The blues at the 500 Club didn't move her, either. She had never been sad enough to understand the music.

Nevers snapped his fingers. "I know what you'd like."

Half an hour later, they arrived at the Roosevelt Hotel. In the Blue Room, Annie saw a few older couples waltzing on the dance floor. They were surrounded by dozens of young people soaked with sweat seated on the sidelines, a prowling look in their eyes. Harold and Annie observed the young dancers, who looked like foxes scanning a flock of chickens for the weak one.

"Say, Harold," said a man with an ill-fitting suit.

"Weasel, my man! How's it cooking?"

"Copacetic. Can't complain. Cuttin' the rug with a chick or two. And you?"

"Nothing much. I'm not with it, but that's a zoot with a real reet pleat *you're* sporting."

Annie would have burst out laughing at the gibberish, but she didn't want to miss a single word. The waltz ended and the older dancers broke up and walked to their tables. The band leader spoke into the microphone. "This next number is for you young jitterbugs."

Lightbeams from three directions hit a large, mirror-faceted ball hanging from the ceiling, ricocheting multicolored splinters of light around the room. A screaming rush of bodies charged the parquet as the band hit the first notes.

A boy in a college sweater spun his girl away from him and jerked her arm so hard Annie felt the pain. The girl popped towards him, they touched palms, and he pushed her away as if he couldn't make up his mind whether he wanted her or not. Again she whipped towards him like a yo-yo. For a split second, Annie was embarrassed for the girl as she slipped and fell, but the boy sent her sliding under his legs and back again, where she rebounded three feet off the floor, twisted completely around in the air and fell into a half-split. Annie squealed with fear and delight as the boy grabbed his girl by her ponytail and pulled her to her feet.

She had heard about it on the radio, seen pictures in *Life* magazine, but she had never witnessed the dance in motion. It was something between a haywire ballet and a gypsy troupe's gymnastics. Shoulders shrugged, spines snaked, necks popped, arms flailed.

It was Swing.

A girl did a back flip over her partner's arm and showed her underwear to anyone who cared to look. Back to back, they locked arms, then the boy bowed and catapulted the girl over his head. She landed on both feet with a smack, bounced off the floor, spread her legs, and swung down on his hips, gripping him obscenely around the waist. Then she went limp and leaned back, her arms and hair touching the floor as he took large mechanical strides backwards to the beat of the music, whipping her back and forth, her hair mopping the dust and sweat off the wood.

Coming to herself, Annie realized she was clutching Harold's coat with both hands. His perfect teeth glowed. His eyes reflected the sparks from the mirrored globe.

"This is so–."

"Hep," Nevers said.

"Hep," Annie repeated softly as she gazed out across the floor. The man named Weasel slapped Harold on the back.

"Her first time, huh?"

"For everything," Nevers said with a wink. He jerked a thumb towards the band. "These cats can scoot some bitchin' scat, huh?"

"Can't understand a word they're saying."

"That's the whole point. Long as it's between a scream and a moan, it'll send the ickeys into the groove."

The men spiced up their conversation with the animated vocabulary: alligator, killer-diller, spank the skin, send me down. Annie could stand it no longer. She nearly yanked Harold's coat off his shoulder.

"What are you saying? I need to know!"

"I have no idea," he said.

"Liar!" she laughed. "Tell me."

"Look." Nevers pointed to a woman sitting a few feet away. Tilted back, her head lolled from side to side. Her eyes were closed and Annie could tell she was somewhere between drunkenness and ecstasy. "Listen to the music and watch her."

Annie began to mimic the woman's movements in miniature as she felt the rhythms. A clarinet came to the front of the tune and hit a few up-tempo notes, then squailed into a long caterwauling cry. The woman's mouth opened. She frowned and squinched her eyes tight. Her arms flopped to her sides and she moaned in pain.

"She's an ickey," Harold said. "You could watch her all night and she'll never move from her seat, just sit there and go through all those contortions. It's the damnedest thing. Some of them have to dance and some of them–. The music sends them into a kind of trance, like that." Harold nodded towards the woman. "And you'd better know the difference. You get in the way of a jitterbug—that's the kind with the heebie-jeebies—and you're likely to get trampled when he makes for the floor."

Annie shook her head in amazement. Nevers ordered a Coke for himself and a Jax draft for Annie. While drinking, they watched the ickeys and jitterbugs through a couple of numbers. Annie could feel the wooden floor pulsating like a giant heart as several tons of dancers jumped and swung and flung to the same beat.

"I'm outta here," Weasel called over his shoulder as two girls from the sidelines dragged him onto the floor. He began working one like a top and the other like a yo-yo.

"Enjoying yourself?" Nevers asked. Annie smiled at him and nodded.

"So which are you," she said, "a jitterbug or an ickey?"

"Well, I'd hate to think of myself as something called an ickey, but I guess I'm an ickey. I must be missing–."

"Harold!" a wildly drunken man shouted from the dance floor. He was throwing a girl around whose hair looked like Christmas tinsel. It was Arkie Burk.

"Arkansas!" Nevers called out. "I didn't know you were an alligator!"

"In sheep's clothing!" he hollered back before disappearing in a hurricane of arms, legs, and twirling skirts. After the number, Arkie retreated to the table. Streaming sweat, he flopped into a chair.

"Whew! Knock me out! I'm almost done anyway."

"Who's the canary you were slinging?"

"Never saw her in my life," Arkie said. "Hope I never see her again. She'll be the death of me, sure. I'm too old for this stuff." He looked lazily over at Annie and perked up. "Say! I know you." He closed one eye, tilted his head, and aimed at her with his hand in the shape of a pistol. "Annie something, Annie Beautiful or something like that."

"Annie Beatrice," she laughed.

"Annie." He slid back into the chair in a quasi-stupor. "Annie the blessed," he said as if from a dream. He closed his eyes and caught his breath. After a minute, Annie thought he had fallen asleep or passed out.

A voice from behind them said, "Picture, sir?"

In a split second, Arkie went from zero to a hundred.

"By golly! That's just the thing! What say, Harold? Let's make a memory."

Nevers reached in his pocket. "I guess I'm paying for this memory, right?"

Arkie stood up and tilted, waving Nevers away. He reached for his pocket and missed.

"To hell with that. Arkie Burk makes his own way in this world." He reached in his trousers and looked down at his hand working under the fabric. He turned the pocket inside out and gaped at Nevers, then at the dance floor. "That cheap, hustling, no good, two-bit–."

"Ah-ahn," Harold said. "A lady's present."

Arkie sobered slightly and stared at Annie.

"This city," he hissed. "This city," he said as if he were saying it all and it would all be understood. Nevers helped Arkie to a chair and arranged his suit good-naturedly.

"I'll be glad to drop the money," Harold said. "Better take a picture now 'cause you won't remember any of this in the morning."

The photographer licked the contact of a large bulb and plugged it into the camera's silver dish. Holding the camera in one hand, he peered through the viewfinder and motioned with his other.

"Closer together. Closer. That's it. Now, say Swiiing."

"Swiiiiing," the three said.

The bulb popped with a blinding flash.

8

July 1938

Annie studied the curled photograph on the dresser in Harold's bedroom. She was looking to her left at Nevers, who smiled into the camera. On her right, Arkie was gazing at her. She couldn't believe how beautiful she looked. She examined herself in the large mirror on the wall and smiled.

Nevers stepped from the bathroom, wiping his face with a towel. "That was *some* band, huh?"

"Hep," Annie laughed.

"That heat was something, too. How do they stand it?" Harold picked up a clock from the dresser. "Three o'clock!" He looked at Annie. "And you're not a pumpkin yet?" He draped the cloth around his neck.

Annie smiled and said nothing, content to watch him move around the room. It was the first time she had seen him without a tie. He picked up the jacket folded over a chair back and walked to the closet. When he opened the door, a baseball bat fell and bounced on the floor with a ringing noise followed by a clattering racket that frightened Annie.

"What's all that?" she asked.

"Baseball bats."

"I can see that. What are they for?"

"Hitting baseballs," Harold said.

"Mr. Clever."

"Remember Beekman's?" Annie frowned at him. "Beekman's on St. Charles."

"With the funny awning like a bonnet?"

"Right," he said, hanging the coat. "They give away a bat with every three-piece suit you buy."

Annie looked at the bats spilling from the closet like a logjam.

"How many suits you have in there?"

"I'm not sure," Nevers said, nudging the bats into the closet with his foot, "but I've got about twice as many suits as bats."

"Really?" She was impressed. "Why's that?"

"Well," he said, still herding the bats into the closet. "There's always a coupla two or three boys hanging around the front of Beekman's." Nevers gave the bats a shove and shut the door quickly. "I've given about half of them away." He looked at Annie, his palms out pleadingly, and shrugged his shoulders. "I mean, how can you resist the looks those poor kids give you when you come out the store?"

She walked to him with a smile. Grabbing both ends of the towel around his neck, she pulled his face down to hers and kissed him.

"You're such a sweet man. I didn't know they made lions as sweet as you."

"Me, I'm a kitty-cat," Harold said. He bared his perfect teeth. "Don't let the fangs fool you."

Annie kissed him fully, then walked him backwards to the lamp. In the mirror, she saw herself holding him. She reached under the shade and turned the switch.

"Meow," she said, pulling him onto the bed. Harold removed Annie's blouse and camisole. She helped him off with his shirt and undershirt. Nevers got up and headed for the bathroom.

"I have to see you," he said. "I thought angels glowed in the dark."

He pulled the copper-beaded string under the wall fixture. A slice of light cut across the room. Annie looked at his silhouette in the doorway. Playing her part in the dance, she stood up and released her skirt and slip. He walked towards her and pushed her lightly. She fell back onto the bed and closed her eyes. She could hear him unfastening his belt and sliding his pants off.

Afraid and excited as his weight turned her towards him, Annie glanced up. She closed her eyes again. She knew men grew larger when they were ready, but she had never seen a man completely undressed. She even knew they came in several sizes. "Small, medium, and too big," she had heard the ruder girls joke. She wondered if this was too big.

Nevers kissed her and touched her, making her ready. She kept her eyes closed, embarrassed that he could see her naked. He rolled on top of her and moved himself against her. She opened her eyes and looked up at him.

"Shouldn't we . . . do something? Before?"

He rolled off of her and blocked the light.

"That's—. How can I put this," he said. "At the Roosevelt tonight. Did you see anyone wearing earplugs?"

"Why, no," Annie said, trying to see his face, but it was like trying to look at the dark side of the moon. "Were there people wearing earplugs?"

"Now, why would they do that? They're there to listen to the music. You wouldn't want to watch a fireworks display with sunglasses on, would you?"

"I suppose not."

"Same thing here. Wearing one of those would be like stopping up your ears in the Blue Room. You'd miss half the pleasure."

Annie nodded doubtfully.

"It'll be all right," Harold assured her. "I'll be careful."

Nevers kissed and touched her again. Annie closed her eyes. Even though she wanted him and had imagined this moment for a long time, it was difficult. The sharp pain competed with her pleasure. Annie realized finally she'd have to forgo the pleasure and work through the pain toward a future enjoyment.

When it was over, Nevers went to the bathroom. Annie opened her eyes. In the dim light spraying from beneath the door, she saw dark spots on the sheet. They were larger than she had expected. Her heart drummed with fear. Then her embarrassment at the stains welled into tears. She wondered what to say when Harold returned. Maybe he would speak first and set her at ease. He would know what to say. He was a kind, good man who gave baseball bats to poor little boys.

* * *

A noise woke Annie in the dark. She reached beside her. Harold was not there. There was no light under the bathroom door. She stretched. A stinging pain reminded her they had made love. Shadows of leaves fluttered on the ceiling. Twisting towards the window, she saw the dark outline of a tree. Nevers had lowered the top sash of the double-hung window. The gently swaying branches lulled her to sleep.

It was late morning when Annie awoke. The closed windows on the two walls were covered with foil against the sunlight. She knew Harold stayed out most of the night and slept till noon. The foil was his way of creating his own night.

Tiny beams of light leaking from a few holes in the foil allowed Annie to see Nevers beside her. A sheet covered all but his left foot, which dangled over the edge of the bed. Annie had never seen him asleep. Hoping he would not awaken, she gazed at his face, its composure reminding her of a baby's slumber. She wondered when he had come in and why she hadn't stirred. Had he stepped out to run one of his mysterious errands, or merely gone to the kitchen for a glass of water? Soon she grew tired of lying in bed without someone to talk with.

Carefully, she reached over to Harold and pinched his nostrils shut. After a few seconds, his mouth opened with a gasping intake of air. Annie burst into laughter. Nevers smiled lazily and rolled towards her, the sheet moving enough to expose the top of his chest, where she saw a tattoo of flowing golden hair atop a pink forehead. Annie reached for the sheet. Nevers stopped her hand before she could unveil the rest of the tattoo.

"I want to see," Annie said.

Rubbing his thumb and forefinger together, Harold said, "How much?"

"To see a tattoo? That'll be the day. I'll just wait till you're sleeping and take a peek." She tugged on the sheet and Nevers let it slip from his hand.

It was an angel. Its yellow tresses waved across a light pink forehead and fell about its shoulders. From there, a powder-blue robe of many folds cascaded down Harold's chest, growing fainter in color and detail until it disappeared into normal skin where the angel's feet should have been. The lifelike angel was precisely done, but what struck Annie most were its mahogany-brown eyes gazing at her with a serene, otherworldly stare.

"When did you get this?" Annie touched the angel's hair and slid her fingers down to the crimson sash around its waist.

"A few years ago, from Franklin D. Roosevelt."

"Right," Annie said sarcastically. "You expect me to swallow that one?"

"Well, sort of." Nevers smiled. "I got it courtesy of a starving WPA artist."

"They pay those guys to make tattoos?"

"Indirectly. I saw this guy painting a mural inside the Royal Street police station, a Pony Express scene. I told him I liked it, and he said he was glad to get the work, but post office walls weren't his true calling.

'That so?' I said. 'What is?' 'Human flesh,' he said. 'Best canvas in the world.' Well, one thing led to another and by the next week I was sitting in a back room of the post office, no lie, feeling like a pin cushion."

"The angel," Annie said. "Is it male or female?"

Harold's mouth turned down as he looked at his chest.

"Good question. I don't think angels 'do it.'" Annie giggled. "So I guess they look like a doll between their legs." She laughed. "You know, kind of smooth and hairless."

Annie smacked Nevers on the chest.

"Hey! You can't hit an angel. What kind of a person are you?"

They bantered for a while, describing tattoos they had seen. Nevers told her about Omi, a muscular man with thick, black lines tattooed from his head to his feet in the Borneo style. He traveled around the country exhibiting his body at circuses and county fairs.

"His whole body was covered? That's taking it a bit too far, if you ask me. What would his mother think?"

"She's the one gave him the tattoo," Nevers replied.

"Liar," Annie said. She thrashed him so good he had to fall out of bed to escape her playful wrath. Annie tumbled after him, and he finally agreed to fix breakfast if she would spare his life.

While Nevers puttered around downstairs, Annie bathed and dressed.

Entering the kitchen, she said, "Not done yet? I'm starved."

Nevers pointed a two-pronged fork at her. "I had to take a time-out for First Aid because of you, so don't complain."

Annie gasped. "Did I really hurt you?"

"It's not me you hurt." He unbuttoned his shirt to reveal the angel's face. "Look at this." Annie stepped closer for a better view. With a fountain pen, Nevers had given the angel two black eyes. Annie burst out laughing at the absurdity. "Angel killer," Harold accused. Annie drew closer to embrace him. He raised the fork in defense. "Back!" Nevers stabbed at her.

"Don't!" she squealed. "You might slip and really cut me."

"Back!" he said, approaching with the fork. "Into the den. Entertain yourself while–." He glanced at the skillet. "Cripes, you're making me burn the bacon." He ran her out the door and into the den. "Now stay here till I call you."

In the sunlit room, the first item that drew Annie's attention was a triangular cabinet wedged into a corner. She noticed several shelves of small fossils and other unidentifiable curios. Beside a delicate quartz arrowhead with ornamental notches was something that resembled a stone jellyfish. In the midst of red, blue, and green crystals lay an amorphous, glassy gray object, a petrified plant of some sort, she guessed. On a shelf by itself sat a bony mass shaped like a frog with molars covering its back.

After puzzling over the objects, Annie looked around the room. On a coffee table lay several picture magazines, mostly *Life* and *Look*, and an annual called *U. S. Camera*, a collection of distinguished photographs from 1937. Annie flipped around in the book, then turned to survey the rest of the room.

Covering most of one wall was a painting of working men with exaggerated muscles, a black locomotive in the background. Against the opposite wall stood a weighty Zenith console radio whose facade resembled a church organ. Over it hung a number of silver dollars in a glass case.

Harold broke into her reverie. "Breakfast is served!"

Walking into the kitchen, Annie said, "After we eat, you'll have to tell me all about those curious thingies in the den. They're very interesting."

* * *

After breakfast under a mimosa swag on his sunporch, Nevers led Annie into the den. Pointing as if she were afraid it would leap at her, Annie asked, "What's this froggy thing here?"

"That," Harold said, "is commonly known as a froggy thing, but it's actually a fish. Well, it's not the whole fish. And it's not really a fish."

"*Now* I'm confused."

"It's a skull." Annie's eyebrows lifted. "The skull of a devilfish. That's another name for a manta ray. They're like big stingrays. I mean big." Nevers extended his arms. "This one had a wingspan of over ten feet. When you hook one, they leap out of the water like they could fly away."

"*You* caught this thing?"

"About five miles off the coast of Grand Isle." Harold turned it over again. "See these things that look like teeth?" Annie nodded. "Those are teeth."

"You don't say?"

"And see these things that look like horns?"

"Those are horns."

"Wrong. Those are what his muscles attach to. Sort of like this little knot on your shoulder." Nevers touched the bony process that kept the strap of Annie's sundress from slipping off her shoulder. "Interesting, huh?"

"Scary," Annie said. "I'm almost afraid to ask what *that* is." She pointed to the glassy gray object on the middle shelf.

"That's luck," Nevers said.

"Oh, so that's what it looks like." As she caught on to Harold's humor, Annie's personality was becoming like his.

Outside, they heard footsteps and glanced toward the door in time to see a shadow approaching. The creaking sound of the metal box announced the morning mail.

"More luck?" Annie said.

"Could be."

"What kind of luck is this?" She picked up the glassy stem.

Careful," Nevers said as he returned the skull to its frog-like stance. "If you live a hundred years, you'll never see another one of those."

"Let me guess," Annie said. "It's a petrified seahorse."

"Rarer than that. Although I confess I've never seen a petrified seahorse. This is a fulgurite. It's what you get when lightning strikes sand."

Annie inspected the object in her palm. "It heats it up and glassifies it, right?"

"Precisely. I found it while gigging on Pontchartrain Beach. I'll take you sometime. You wade in the water at night and spear flounder hidden in the sand."

"Right. Knowing my luck I'll spear one of those devilfish and it would carry me into the Gulf on its back."

The mailbox creaked again.

Annie said, "Harold Nevers, you're the luckiest man in the world."

Nevers turned toward the door. "Mailman probably found a letter he didn't deliver." He took the fulgurite from Annie and replaced it on the shelf. "These might be more to your liking." He stepped to the silver dollars set in purple felt bordered by a black frame.

"This is easy," Annie said. "Those are silver dollars."

Nevers held up a finger. "But not just any silver dollars. These were minted in New Orleans and they're uncirculated. Can you find which one's missing?"

After a minute, Annie said, "This one. There should be one here." Skipping 1893, the middle row ran from 1889 to 1894.

"Right. It's the rarest silver dollar struck in New Orleans. That one I've got with some others over here." Nevers walked to a rolltop desk and pulled open a drawer.

"Look at this one first." He handed Annie a coin enclosed in a plastic envelope. "It's an 1880 with the second 8 stamped on top of a 7."

Annie examined it with a magnifying glass Harold had given her.

"Oh, I see it," she said. "Is it valuable?"

"Not really. Just interesting." Next, Harold showed her an 1882 with the O mint mark stamped over an S, then a 1900-O with the O over a CC.

"For Carson City, right?" Annie said. "Boy, this is easy to see. That O really messed up the C's."

"Look at Liberty's cheek. See those scuff marks?" Annie noticed the minuscule abrasions. "Those are called bag marks. Even though the coins haven't been in circulation, they've rubbed against other coins in the canvas bags they're shipped to banks in. Now," Harold said. "Look at this one." He held a scrap of green velvet in his hand. He lifted a corner to reveal the coin. "This," he said, "is the rarest of the New Orleans mint marks. It's the 1893-0 that's missing from the wall display."

Annie looked at the coin in Nevers' hand. It had a deep mirror-like finish free of any flaw, even bag marks.

"How much did you pay for it?"

Nevers laughed. "That's how much it cost—not how much it's worth. There's a difference. Its cost can be measured, like four or five hundred dollars, or a million. But something's worth is intangible."

Annie scanned the shelf of curios.

"Which one do you like most?"

"The fulgurite. It's the luckiest find I ever made. It didn't cost me a thing, but I wouldn't take a thousand dollars for it." He looked at the coin resting in the velvet. "This cost me something. I won't say how much. Partly, I paid for its rarity, and partly for its beauty. But scarcity. What's that? You look at this coin and it looks pretty much like any other silver dollar. But its beauty. I've never seen anything like this."

He turned the coin over carefully on the cloth. Annie observed something in his eyes she had never seen. He was clearly inspired by its beauty.

"If you could only have one, the fulgurite thing or the silver dollar, which would you choose?"

Nevers chuckled. "For a beautiful girl, you sure ask hard questions."

He studied the matter for a while. Scrutinizing the coin, his face slowly changed, all mirth finally draining from it. He frowned at Annie.

"If I ever have to make that decision–." His eyes dropped to the silver dollar. "I'll make it."

His reaction made Annie feel like it could actually happen one day.

9

August 1938

Nevers was away on business for two weeks. The free time allowed Annie to catch up on her diary entries and write her mother. It was ironic, she thought, that her life was so much more interesting than her mother's, yet her mother wrote her five long letters for every short one she returned. It made Annie feel strange, too, to read "Dear Toni Jo," like she was two people or couldn't make up her mind which she wanted to be.

Her mother's version of Toni Jo was supposed to be interested in who had a baby in DeRidder or that her cousin Lou Ann's cow finally dropped a calf, putting the two scraps of news in the same paragraph as if they were of equal importance. While writing her mother, Annie pretended to care that Mr. Jamison's dog, Rustler, who liked to sleep in the road, finally died a natural death, when what she wanted to say was that it was a miracle he lived as long as he did without getting run over by a car.

When Harold was in town, it seemed Annie was always getting ready or following him around New Orleans. She slept little, smoked a lot, and ignored the finer details of restaurant management. His departure was almost a relief.

It didn't take long for the local hobos to discover that the woman running Terra Incognita was an easy touch. Transients solicited restaurants for leftover rolls and piecrusts, or private homes at the back door for sandwiches. They knocked politely and, hat in hand, offered their labor in exchange for food. Proud men out of work through no fault of their own, they rarely accepted free handouts. They all had some skill a resident or proprietor could make use of.

"Fix that broken pump?" one might ask, keeping the implied transaction unspoken.

"Sweep up for a cup of coffee and a biscuit?"

If they were turned down, they apologized for having bothered the owner. If offered work, they did the job first and ate later, then thanked their benefactor with genuine gratitude.

Terra Incognita, though, had no back door. It sat at the end of a short pier, so the homeless men waited until the walk cleared of customers, then crossed the gray boards to the entrance and knocked. It was a feeling Annie never got used to, opening the door anyone could walk through. She always found some little chore for the men, and eventually looked forward to what she called her "regulars," men who made a circuit around the city, doing odd jobs on particular days for certain people.

One Friday morning in mid-August, Annie heard a knock.

As she approached the door, she tried to think of something the man could do to earn a square meal. She would have him run to the corner market for a few heads of lettuce and a sack of red beans. She opened the door. The man's head was down, his hat still on. He leaned on the door jamb with one arm.

"Yes?" Annie said politely. "Can I help you?"

"You shore can, ma'am. What I need is a big kiss and a hug." Startled, Annie didn't know how to respond. "It's been a powerful long time since I had either the one or t'other."

Annie looked over her shoulder towards the kitchen, hoping Djurgis would come to her rescue.

"Boo!" the man said, taking off his hat. Annie jumped back.

It was Nevers.

As always on his sudden appearances at the restaurant, Harold helped Annie and Djurgis through lunch, then stole her for the next two days. By four o'clock, the two were struggling beneath a fan in his bedroom, trying to make up for the past two weeks. Still shy of Nevers looking at her bare body, Annie was thankful for the darkened room, which she had nicknamed The Cave. Afterwards, they lay in each other's arms dozing.

Annie awoke a few minutes or an hour later, she didn't know which. She heard Harold moving around downstairs. She smiled and closed her eyes. She felt the need to smoke, something she rarely did when Nevers was gone. He thought she looked sophisticated while smoking, and she did it mainly to please him.

Annie rolled over and reached inside the nightstand drawer. She felt several thick sheets of paper and pulled the top one out. Inspecting the photograph in the dark room, she made out Nevers with two other men. She stretched and turned the lamp switch. To Harold's left was a beaming fat man Annie immediately recognized as Huey Long. On his right was Mayor Maestri, a rich man who had won the New Orleans office after Long's assassination. When Maestri's contenders learned that Long's political machine was backing him, they dropped out of the race fearing for their political and personal lives.

Considerably younger than the men his arms encircled, Harold nonetheless seemed comfortable in their presence, as if they were old friends. Annie wondered whether Harold really knew them. She thought they might have had only incidental business and Huey Long, a master publicist, had the picture taken for self-promotional reasons. Whatever the occasion, Annie found something frightfully exciting about knowing a man associated with these public figures of dubious reputation. Maestri also owned the New Orleans Pelicans baseball team and, after three years as mayor, controlled a network of gambling and prostitution that snaked through the city.

Annie drew the other print from the drawer, then heard Nevers coming up the stairs. Quickly, she replaced the photos as she had found them and eased the drawer shut.

After supper at the 500 Club, Annie and Harold ambled down Bourbon Street. Two months in the city had aroused her curiosity about its darker side. When she playfully suggested they go to a burlesque show, Nevers said, "Those joints are just places where uptown people go to be properly shocked. If you're really interested in how the other half lives, I can take you to a spot where the real thing occurs. Burlesque strippers don't even really strip. They only make the men hungry enough to keep coming back for more of what they'll never get. It's an art, I'll give them that."

When Harold finished, an impish grin came across Annie's face.

"I want to be properly shocked," she said.

Annie walked down the banquette with her hand in the crook of Harold's arm. From both sides of the street, piano notes jangled to lure customers. Nevers pointed to a balcony. With metronomic regularity, a woman sitting on a trapeze swung suggestively in and out of a window just above a wrought-iron grille. Clad in a black corset and black garters-and-hose hemmed with red lace, she waved and smiled to the men and boys leering or jeering at her from below.

"Take it off!" a drunken man yelled. The effort momentarily upset his balance.

The woman spoke at intervals as she was visible: "Come on inside . . . if you want to see more."

Through the crowd of legs on the sidewalk came the sound of a trolley. It was Wendel, paddling towards them on his roller-skate board. A few feet away, he leaned back and scraped to a halt.

"Miss Annie! You want me to protect you from this lecherous old man?" He pointed at Nevers with his stick.

"No, I think I'm fine," she chuckled.

"They say," he continued, "there's sin lurking behind every curtain and door in these parts of our fair city, ready to ensnare the innocent."

"I don't think there's any harm in just looking," Annie responded.

Wendel squinted up at her. "Well, now," he said, "some say there is and some say no. Myself, I wouldn't know. I was born bad." He winked at Annie and shoved off down the banquette.

In a stuffy, smoke-filled room, Annie balanced herself on a tall barstool before a small round table. Its top barely accommodated the two required and exorbitantly priced highballs. Onstage, under a subdued spotlight, a man in a tuxedo said something no one could hear. He walked offstage and the lights dimmed. A drumroll was followed by a rimshot. From behind Annie, a beam of light trained on the right side of the proscenium. A red-stockinged leg split the heavy black curtains. Several men whistled. The leg tantalized them too long and they blurted impatient catcalls.

Finally, the dancer slunk to center stage in long strides, sliding her high heels along the floor. She peered teasingly at the crowd with gauchely painted eyes. She wore a short, tight skirt, a bodice, and elbow-length gloves, all red. Her fine black hair was pulled back extremely tight, giving her a severe look. Her full lips contrasted with an aquiline nose. Annie thought that somewhere beneath the makeup and circus trappings was a beautiful woman.

Suddenly, the woman's entire body snapped, and she stood on tiptoes, right hand on hip, left hand on her head, derrière thrust out at the men. Those near the stage pounded it with their fists, begging her to disrobe. Everyone was laughing and having a good time including, it appeared, the woman.

After a few more maneuvers designed to torment the men, she pranced offstage. Next came a woman in white, followed by one in green, then yellow, then blue. The entire number took about twenty minutes. When the last dancer disappeared through the thick drapery, a drumroll signaled the finale. From stage right, the women filed to the center of the platform. The men screamed uncontrollably as the dancers grabbed their upper garments as if to rip them off. Finally delivering, they all tore the lingerie down a seam of snaps to reveal their breasts. The audience gasped. Annie could not believe her eyes. All of the alluring, lithe women were men.

"No!" Annie said, turning to Nevers.

"I told you," Harold laughed as she clutched his arm. "This is where people go to be properly shocked."

Feeling both amused and slightly nauseous, Annie took a large gulp from her highball as the audience derided the entertainers.

—"Queers!"

—"Go home to mommy!"

—"She-boy!"

—"Campy bastards, I catch one of y'all out back, I'll beat the living hell outta ya!"

As the impersonators exited under a hail of wadded napkins and a couple of shoes, Annie lit a cigarette with trembling hands.

The next act was unmistakably comprised of women. Their ample breasts spilled over the tight tops of beige bodysuits made of crushed velvet. Each sported a fan and the tail of an animal: a rabbit, peacock, cat, and horse. After the routine, Nevers spoke to Annie. "Want to stay? It's just more of this kind of stuff, over and over."

Annie was glad to breathe the fresher air. The temperature had dropped, and a breeze greeted them at each intersection as they strolled towards Canal. Passing a dark alley, Annie heard something between a scream and a shout.

"What's that?"

"Sounds like someone calling for help," Harold said casually as they continued walking. Annie strained to see down the alley.

"Shouldn't you try to help them?"

"Why?" Nevers said indifferently. "Listen. Suppose I run down there. What do you think I'll find?"

"I don't know," Annie said.

"I'd probably run into a knife or a gun. These things happen all the time. You get a couple of punks who need a few easy bucks and they set you up like this, prey on your good nature." Annie looked at him and admitted to herself that he could be right. "That back there," Nevers said, tossing his head. "You know who that is? That's shoeshine boy—old Darnell—in ten years. In New Orleans, you either hustle or get lost in the shuffle. It's a depression."

* * *

Back in The Cave, after washing the smoky residue from her body, Annie lay alone in Harold's bed, listening to him talking on the phone downstairs. It was two in the morning. She had left the bathroom light on with the door ajar, the way Nevers liked it. She glanced at the drawer of the nightstand and wondered if she had time to pull out the photos. She decided against it and fell into a light sleep punctured occasionally by Harold's laughter.

Then she felt him nudge her gently. Speaking softly, he asked her to move over. She smelled cologne as his weight pushed onto the bed. He draped his arm over her hip and pulled her towards him. His low, husky voice penetrated her ear. "Want to make the beast with two backs?"

Annie wondered if it were a type of lovemaking she had not yet experienced.

"What's that?" she asked.

"Shakespeare." Nevers held his hands up in the wedge of light coming from the bathroom. He put them together, palm to palm, and made a short, clapping motion. "It's what he thought two people look like making love." Annie watched his hands working up and down. She smiled. Nevers put his hand behind Annie's head and whispered in her ear, "Are you my little beastie?"

The sound of his voice, the meaning of his words, the feel of his stubble on her face gave her chills. She reached around his neck with both hands.

"Yes. Are you my big lion?"

"I'm anything you want me to be," he said. "Beastie." Annie felt a sexual urgency rush through her hips as Nevers parted her legs with his knee and braced himself over her. He reached down and moved her chin up with his. He kissed her roughly on the neck and licked the flesh all the way to her ear. Gruffly, he demanded, "Give it to me, Beastie."

Annie felt like she was about to cry.

"Take it, big lion."

As he started moving inside her, she looked. They had made love many times, but each time she had to see him to believe he could be that big and fit inside her. She put her hands on his chest above her and looked between them into the piercing brown eyes of the angel.

An hour later, Annie awoke with the gentle pang that indicated it was time to relieve herself. Leaving the bathroom, she saw Nevers lying facedown on the bed. From the doorway, she discerned the unmistakable colors of a tattoo on his back. She moved out of the frame to let the light reach across the room. Annie stepped quietly so as not to awaken him. Her throat constricted as it did when she was frightened or saw something very beautiful.

It was a dragon. Of some sort. More beautiful and dangerous than any creature she had ever seen. A hybrid of sphinx and basilisk, of hippogriff and gargoyle and manticore, it looked evil in design yet somehow holy in effect, a beast selected from the draconian population slurking in a guttered Chinaman's opium-induced nightmare. Rising out of a sulfurous fog, it was covered with diamond-shaped scales of green and blue. The monster's incandescent white eyes were embossed with black pupils. Its mouth vomited red and yellow flames. At significant jointures, the skeletal structure of its batlike wings protruded daggerstyle—living icicles dripping with the gore of its latest victim. The quartz shards of its stegosaurean spine tapered into a segmented scorpion tail that serpentined down to the hills of his buttocks where it disappeared into the subterranean aperture of its cave-home. Every aspect of the illuminated dragon seemed to possess hieroglyphic meaning, as if the tattoo were a medieval manuscript indited by a slavering but skillful madman.

Mesmerized by the horror and beauty of the thing, Annie reached out to touch it.

* * *

The next morning, Nevers read his newspaper and sipped coffee while Annie moved around the kitchen fixing breakfast, at each turn sneaking inquisitive looks at him.

Finally, he dropped the paper with a rustle. "Good God," he laughed. "What is it?" He looked at his lap. "Is my fly open, or what?"

"Nothing," Annie said.

"Ooh, no," he said, rising and tossing his paper on the table. "You're not getting away with looks like that in *my* house." He slapped her on the backside. "I'll throw my beastie down the steps on her cute little fanny if she doesn't tell me." He put his arms around her waist and peered over her shoulder. The spatula lapped grease onto a pair of eggs staring at him out of the skillet.

"*You're* the beastie," Annie said.

Harold backed away as she transferred the eggs to his plate, between a slice of ham and a puddle of grits. Smiling, he took his seat at the table and waited for elaboration. Annie situated a fork and knife on the napkin beside his plate. Arms akimbo, she glared at the eggs. She reminded Nevers of a petulant child and he laughed. In a quick movement, Annie picked up the knife and stabbed the egg yolks maliciously several times.

"Hey! *Hey!*" Nevers held his hands up and leaned away from the knife. He looked at his plate. The bright yellow ooze was bleeding into his grits. "You know I don't like to mix my grits and eggs."

"Good. Serves you right for keeping secrets."

"Secrets? Will you tell me what the hell's bugging you?"

"That *thing*," she pointed with the knife. "That dragon on your back."

"Oh, that. I didn't know if you'd like it." He grinned up at her standing over him. "I got it in a drunken stupor right after the angel."

Nevers turned to his plate and began stemming the yolk-tide with a triangle of toast.

Annie turned to prepare her own breakfast. As she puttered about the chore, Nevers realized he would have no peace until he offered details.

"All right, sweet beastie," he said. Annie settled into her place. "The WPA guy who did the angel, he'd been to Burma. Learned how to make dragons from a tufuga tatau." Nevers laughed at the words. "Basically, that's a slant-eyed tattoo master. While working on the angel, he showed me a book of samples and I liked the dragons. I was drinking against the pain of the needle and told him to fix me up a good one when he was done with the angel. The next morning, I had a complete angel and a stenciled dragon. Now, how do you think I'd look with only the outline of a dragon? Hell, I *had* to follow through with the thing."

"Why'd you want it?"

"Oh, who knows why young punks do things like that? I guess I thought it would make me look tough. I haven't even seen it in over a year. Does it still look good?"

Annie pushed her eggs around with a fork, her smile spreading.

"Makes you look tough," she said to the eggs.

"Ah, so you like it."

"I never said I didn't like it."

"Then what was all the fuss about?"

"You didn't *tell* me," she said, looking at him challengingly. "You don't play fair. If I had a secret, I'd tell you."

"Then it wouldn't be a secret anymore."

Annie hated it when Nevers cornered her with his tricky logic. Her mouth closed, she let out a guttural squeal. She picked up her knife.

"Sometimes I could just kill you."

* * *

That afternoon, Annie and Harold picnicked at their favorite spot in City Park, a sunny expanse of grass surrounded by shady oaks near a small lagoon. While Nevers held the branches, Annie stepped into the small gap between an azalea bush and a gardenia shrub, smelling the rich fragrance of the waxy white flowers. She always smiled as she walked into the clearing that was protected from the view across the pond by willow trees and the broad leaves of chest-high elephant ears at the water's edge.

Nevers had brought his new camera and had already spent a roll, taking pictures of everything from the time Annie made the potato salad to the moment she popped the checkered cloth beneath the trees. Then he took some photographs of Annie in traditional movie-star poses.

Nevers had recently talked her into wearing shorts on their picnics. "If they're good enough for Garbo and Harlow, they're good enough for you." Too modest to wear shorts in public, Annie compromised by putting them on beneath a skirt and dropping the skirt in their secluded bower. Today, Annie wore powder-blue shorts with cuffs and a pink, close-fitting knit top with spaghetti straps. She felt very sensual as Nevers observed her through the camera, directing her into the positions he wanted.

"Straighten your left leg and point your foot. Now, raise your other leg. Lean on your left arm." When she misunderstood his directions and fell into an ungainly posture, Harold set the camera down and, with mock impatience, rearranged her limbs.

After half a dozen frames, Nevers said, "Pull one of those straps off your shoulder." The camera clicked. "Lean towards me. Put your arms closer together. Cleavage."

He took the photograph.

"Now roll up your shorts." He checked the settings on the camera as she furled the hems. "One more time," he said, indicating with a motion of his hand that he wanted her to roll the shorts higher. "Lie on your stomach and lift your legs. That's it. Try crossing your feet at the ankles. Good. Now, look at me."

Annie gazed into the eye of the camera. Nevers could tell she was aroused. He took several more shots, then paused to reload. That done, he glanced at Annie sitting up clutching her legs, her chin on one knee.

"Don't move," Harold said. "Tilt your head that way." He pointed. "A little more. Little more. Stop." He pushed the button. "Turn sideways. Right." He lifted his head from the camera. "Let's see. Sit up on your calves. Good. You look beautiful. Push out." Annie moved her arm out toward the camera. Nevers laughed. "No," he said. "These." He pointed to his chest and thrust it out. Annie laughed as she mimicked him with an exaggerated movement, then drew her breasts back in.

"That's it. No, you had it. You look great." He took two shots. He lowered the camera and stared at her. "You look sooo . . . delicious." He continued to stare.

"Well," she said. "You gonna take a picture of me or slobber on me?"

"Slobbering sounds good."

"Take a picture."

"Any chance I could get you to shed that hardware?" He pointed. Annie knew he was referring to her brassiere. "You have a beautiful figure. Why make it look frumpy with a suffocating wrap like that?" Harold turned comic. "*Try Formfit. You'll like the youthful, perky uplifted lines it will give you.*" He paused. "And so will I!" He laughed. "Look, just take the underthing off and we'll shoot a picture."

"I don't know," Annie said demurely. A small pain of excitement pinched her heart.

"Who's gonna see 'em? I develop them myself."

Annie turned away from Nevers. She felt her face flush and grow hot. She worked underneath the blouse until she was free and stuffed the lingerie into the picnic basket. Turning toward Nevers, she felt her breasts tighten with excitement. She heard the shutter trip. Harold advanced the film and took another shot.

"Pull the material against you." Annie did as he commanded. "You know," Nevers said, "you'd look great as a blonde." Her eyes looked sleepy. "Push out some more."

Annie looked down at her breast. The camera caught her as her mouth parted in a barely audible gasp.

10

September 1938

Appearing suddenly, as if from nowhere, Harold usually surprised Annie when he came into town. This time Annie surprised him. He had called the restaurant to have her meet him at Galatoire's at seven that Friday evening. She walked in and past Nevers to see if he would recognize her. He glanced at her, admiringly, she thought, but didn't acknowledge her. Her hair was as white as Mae West's. The new cut and color altered the appearance of her face so that Annie herself could hardly believe the change when she had looked at her reflection the first time.

For the weekend, Nevers had scheduled a fishing trip to Grand Isle. Saturday morning, the two met Burk and his girl at the grassy airstrip west of City Park. Eddie Agnelly stored their gear in the cargo bin and helped them into the cabin of his new air yacht, a biplane built on a single pontoon shaped like a gigantic shoe.

Nevers made the introductions. "This is Nausica." The slender woman wore tight, lime-green slacks and a hot-pink blouse. Her hair was clown-red. "And you remember Arkie Burk, Annie."

"Whoa!" Burk exclaimed. "I didn't even recognize you, Annie."

"Who did you *expect* Harold to be with?" Annie quipped in mock jealousy. She extended her hand to Arkie's girlfriend. "I'm pleased to meet you, Nausica. That's such an interesting name."

* * *

After landing and storing a two days' supply of food in their separate bungalows, the men met on the screened porch of Harold's place and rigged four fishing rods with artificial lures. On Annie's rod, Nevers tied an orange shrimp with gold glitter embedded in the hard plastic. Two treble hooks dangled menacingly from the bait, which reminded her of an amputated finger.

"They actually bite that thing?"

"Just wait," Harold said.

The four made their way down to the water. Stepping across the high-tide line of driftwood and seashells, Annie flushed a killdeer that skittered from them with a wing jutting from its side.

"Oh, look," she said. "It's crippled. Harold, can we catch it and doctor it up?"

Nevers laughed. "You'll never catch that bird, because it ain't hurt. She's just trying to lure you away from her eggs." He walked along the tide-line until he found the nest. "See?"

They all inspected the eggs, three of them, disguised in what appeared to be a tiny brush pile.

"Well, what do you think about that?" Annie said.

Annie hesitated when Nevers kicked off his shoes and waded into the rolling surf, expecting her to follow. After some cajoling, the men finally convinced the women to come into the salt with their sneakers on.

Annie tested the water near shore. "Aren't there crabs and things on the bottom?"

A little more daring, Nausica was already knee-deep in the Gulf. The waves patting her legs, Annie walked hurriedly out to Nausica and grabbed her arm.

"Don't hang on to me, honey," Nausica said. "I step on a crab, and they'll have to ship me back from Dee-troit, 'cause that's where I'll land when I come down."

Holding hands, the two waded out near Burk and Nevers, who were already working their baits in the waist-deep swells. The girls followed their men as they broke in opposite directions up the shoreline.

Harold said to Arkie, "Holler if you get into a school, Arkansas."

"I ain't telling you nothin'," he yelled over his shoulder.

Nevers coached Annie on how to cast the rod, then let her practice.

Annie eyed Harold suspiciously. "They don't have those devilfish things in here, do they?"

"Oh, I forgot to tell you what to do if you step on one."

"Harold!" Annie whined.

Nevers laughed. "I'll guarantee you there's not a devilfish within five miles of Grand Isle."

Nevers watched and tutored her. "Reel a bit faster. When you feel something, set the hook hard."

Ten minutes later, Annie had lost her concentration. She felt a jolt at the end of her rod and forgot to jerk.

"I think I had one, Harold."

"Pay attention," he said. "We might be coming into a school."

He cast a segmented minnow where she had the strike. The lure plopped on the surface. He twitched it once, making it wobble like a wounded mullet. The surface shattered in a foamy explosion.

"That's him," Nevers shouted. The fish leaped two feet and somersaulted, shaking its head to throw the hooks. "Speckled trout!"

Annie saw the red and white plug in its gaping yellow mouth. Nevers landed the fish by grabbing it tightly behind the head.

"Come see," he called to Annie. He handed her his rod, then put the catch on a nylon stringer. Nevers admired the fish. Hundreds of black dots were highlighted by a silver background. "Three pounds, I'd say." Nevers turned the fish in the sunlight.

"Look at his back," Annie said. "It's purple."

"Yeah, they're pretty. Look at these traps." He showed her the fish's teeth.

"They're like rattlesnake fangs."

"Quick, cast out that way again. I think it's a school."

Annie cast and let the artificial shrimp sink to the bottom, then jerked-and-reeled twice. When she lifted the rod the second time, she felt a dull tug. Nevers was watching her rodtip as he tied the stringer to his belt.

"Jerk!"

The fish almost pulled the rod from Annie's hands. She drove the handle into her stomach and held on as the drag screamed and payed out twenty feet of line.

"That's a good one," Nevers said. The fish ran toward the beach, then up the shore. The drag began squealing again. "Bigger'n I thought." Nevers touched her rod and lifted it. "Hold the tip higher."

A few minutes later, the fish torpedoed into the shallows. Annie saw a single black spot on its tail, like an eclipsed sun. She had served the fish hundreds of times.

"It's a redfish," she squealed with delight.

"Sure is. Five pounds, at least."

Nevers grabbed the line and walked backwards, dragging the fish ashore. It lifted its tail once, then lay still, working its mouth and pectoral fins.

"My arms," Annie said, massaging her muscles.

Harold drove the big needle through the underside of the fish's jaw. "Fun?" Annie opened her mouth and lolled her tongue out. "Ready to go after 'em again?"

"Ready. But I hope I don't catch another one that big."

"A real fisherman would never say that." Harold approached Annie with the needle.

"You're not tying that thing on *me*."

"You catch 'em, you drag 'em." He began tying. "You clean 'em, too."

"No way. I'll cook him, but I won't clean him."

An hour later, Nevers whistled shrilly to get Arkie's attention and waved them in. Onshore, the party inspected their catch on the sand. Annie's stringer held the big redfish, fourteen specks, and a sand trout. Burk's had one red and three specks. Nausica had five specks.

Nevers spat on his lone speckled trout.

"Beginner's luck," he said.

At the bungalow, they held their stringers up to Harold's camera.

"All right," he called. "One, two, three, lift!"

Annie struggled with the hanging weight. A week later, when she saw the photograph, it wasn't the strain on her face or the sunburned cheeks that made her look like an exotic stranger. It was the white hair.

* * *

While the men cleaned the fish, the women cooked baked beans and French fries.

"That's such an interesting name," Annie said to Nausica for the third time that day.

"It's not my real name," Nausica said as she peeled a potato with a paring knife.

"Is that right?" Annie was on the verge of telling her that Annie was not her real name, either. "Where'd you get it?"

"That's a long story, honey. I'll tell you sometime when they're not around." She gestured toward the men with her knife.

After supper, the couples retired to their separate cabins. Although the hot part of the day was past, the onshore breeze had not yet begun, and the moderate heat was stifling. Nevers had planned a floundering trip after dark and suggested everyone rest until then.

Heavy with the greasy food, Annie and Harold swung tranquilly in their separate hammocks on the porch, talking and dozing. Facing each other, his feet at her head, they pulled at the hammocks, rocking them back and forth in an erratic, unsynchronized movement. Annie imagined she was being sloshed about in a small boat on the ocean and fell into a deep sleep.

She awoke an hour later. It was darker and cooler.

Nevers reached over and pulled her hammock towards him. Something about the way he did it made her know what it meant. Annie looked at the cabin where Burk and Nausica were staying.

"We'll bake inside," Annie said.

Harold nodded toward the beach. "You have a whole ocean to cool off in."

The bed frame was fitted with a single, firm mattress. Nevers had left the doors open, and a breeze blew from the porch through the bungalow and out the open window of the bedroom.

In the shadows of the dying day, they shed their clothes in the bungalow. Blood pounded in Annie's throat and surged through her hips. Harold stepped to her and held her close. She felt the anxiety in her chest that always made her think she would burst out crying. She felt him rise between her legs and whispered, "Ah, god."

As her legs began to quiver, Harold lifted her and set her down on the bed. Her arms fell back on the mattress. It felt something like surrender. Nevers entered her, and she moaned at the pleasurable pain he still caused because of his size, which had made her bleed the third and fourth times they had been together, until she began to think she was a renewable virgin. Beads of sweat streamed down her face and fell onto the sheet in audible thumps. Harold told her how beautiful she was, how sweet to surprise him with her white hair.

Annie listened, his voice mesmerizing her, making her feel limp and drowsy.

"Do you love me?" he said.

Her eyelids opened lazily. "You know I do."

"Will you do anything for me?"

It was a game they played. He asked questions and she answered.

"Yes. Anything."

Saying the word thrilled her. The word and the tone of his voice suggested things she had never imagined, things she knew Harold would know and would teach her. Until now, he had never taken the game farther.

"Do you love it?"

She looked up at him. He was watching himself slide in and out of her. As always, she was shocked at something that large moving easily inside her. She gasped and let her head fall back.

"Yes," she said.

"Say it."

"I love it."

"Say it bad," Nevers said. "Tell me bad words."

Annie felt his excitement. He was moving more passionately. Her breath came faster. Aroused and puzzled, she glanced up.

"I don't understand."

"Say–. Say it." He closed his eyes and stopped moving. He held his breath, then exhaled. "Say–." He looked down at her. "Say 'Fuck me.'"

Annie's head turned to the side. It felt like her heart had been stabbed with a hot icicle. She felt desired and desirous, and at the same time demeaned.

"I–."

Nevers lifted himself and pushed inside her hard.

"Beautiful Annie." She gazed into his eyes. "My sweet Beatrice." Although he had given her the name, he used it only in bed and it always triggered something deep inside her. "My beautiful, sweet Beatrice. Say bad things to me." He drew most of his length out of her.

What she felt came out sounding like "Nguh."

"Are you my sweet little bad girl?"

"For you," she said.

"Say bad words for Harold." He moved in and out of her.

She imagined saying the words. "Just–."

She struggled but could not bring herself to say them. Nevers increased her hunger for him by refusing his entire length. She looked down at him moving inside her.

"God, Harold." She fell back. "Just do it," she said in a voice near crying. "Do it."

"Are you my sweet bad little girl?"

"Yes. Only for you."

"Say 'Please.' Say 'Please do it to me.'"

She put her heels low on his back and pulled him down with her arms.

"Do it, Harold. Do it to me. Do it." He drove inside her and loved her vigorously as she repeated the words over and over.

Annie's throat filled with the painful swelling just before crying. As they reached the end, she couldn't tell if it was tears or sweat trickling into her ears.

* * *

Half an hour later, Harold whistled out the window to Arkie. In a few minutes, Burk and Nausica approached the porch where Annie watched Nevers lighting a gas lantern.

"Got your lantern?" Harold asked.

Burk lifted a lantern.

"Gig and stringer?"

Burk thrust a two-pronged spear forward like a movie Indian, then patted his trousers.

"Beautiful woman?"

Burk pointed to Nausica.

"Well, then," Harold said. "I guess we're ready."

In contrast to the afternoon's waves crawling ashore, Annie saw the glassy smooth water licking the beach in the light of a three-quarter moon. The atmosphere should have been quiet, but it gave off a background noise like someone making an incessant hushing sound. Annie wondered where it came from.

At the water's edge, Nevers suggested the pairs go in opposite directions, work the shore for an hour, then turn around and meet back at the bungalows.

"What are we looking for?" Annie said.

"Eyes," Nevers said. "Look for eyes." He scanned the lantern back and forth. "If it's just settled, a flounder looks like a big brown arrowhead sitting on the bottom."

After a few minutes, Harold whispered loudly, "There's one!"

Annie looked around in the small arena of yellow light.

"Where?"

"Right there." Nevers used the gig as a pointer. "Look, there's his head, and you can barely see his body." He outlined the flounder's shape with the gig.

Annie slapped his arm. "You're lying."

"I'm *not* lying. And we better stick him before he spooks." He handed her the gig and guided it over a spot in the light. "Now, push down hard and hold on tight."

Annie thrust the gig into the sand. Nothing happened.

"Did I miss him?"

"No, you got him. You probably stuck him in the spine and paralyzed him." Nevers clutched the shaft of the gig near the water. "Here." He handed her the lantern and slid his other hand into the water. "Walk to the shore."

When she reached the water's edge, Annie turned around.

"Okay," Harold said. "Here I come."

Pinning the flat fish against the gig with his hand, he lifted it out of the water and ran towards the light. On shore, he drove the gig into the sand and stepped on a dark brown flounder a foot and a half long.

"That beats all I ever saw," Annie said. "I speared that thing without even seeing it?"

"Just another one of nature's liars. Like that killdeer."

"Or those fishing lures."

Nevers laughed. "That's right. You have to meet nature on her own terms." After stringing the fish, Nevers removed his foot. The flounder flapped around on the beach with a sound that reminded Annie of a tickled dog's foot rapidly patting the floor. When it stopped, Nevers stooped down and gripped the flounder firmly. "See?" He turned the fish over, exposing its white bottom. "They're like people. They all have a dark side and a light side."

Annie thought for a moment. "Everyone?"

"Everyone," he said.

"Even you?"

Nevers glanced up at her. "Even you."

After gigging their fourth flounder, he pumped the lantern's piston and the mantles flared more brightly. Then Nevers had Annie retrieve a pack of Luckies from his shirt pocket and light one. He looked at the stars.

"Scorpio," he said, pointing.

"Where?"

Nevers stepped behind her. He took a drag on the cigarette and flicked off the ash.

"Watch." Using the glowing tip, he traced the pattern of the constellation. "There's his claws. And these two stars form his back. And here's his tail." The red cone slid down the tail and made a quick loop.

"Yes," Annie said. "I see it!" She made little jumps like a child. Nevers stepped around to her front.

"Want a pull?" Harold put the cigarette to her lips. The cone brightened as she drew the smoke into her lungs.

As they slowly waded, Nevers hummed his favorite spiritual, "Rock of Ages." The melancholy tune made Annie sad. Finally, she spoke to break the lonely mood the melody had evoked in her.

"You believe that about everybody having two sides?"

"Absolutely," Nevers said. "You think you know yourself?" He lifted the lantern to her face, then resumed scanning the bottom. He took Annie's silence to mean that she thought she did. "You dream a lot?"

"Some."

"All right," Nevers said. "Let's say you dream about your mother and . . . someone else."

"I had a dream about Djurgis the other night. He was pulling a dish out of the oven, but instead of spaghetti, it was a mop on the plate." Annie laughed.

"In the dream," Nevers said, "did you know what he was going to say before he said it?"

Annie thought for a moment. "I don't think so."

"Well, you *should* know," Nevers said. "After all, the whole thing's coming out of your head, right? Djurgis wasn't really there, and you composed the dream, like a play, so *you* have to be the one giving him his words."

Annie frowned. "That's right," she said.

"So you don't really know yourself," Nevers concluded.

They walked quietly for a while. Annie was both amused and mildly disturbed by what Nevers had said. She was trying to think of another dream when something powerful and swift slid from beneath her foot.

She let out a squeal, then a hysterical laugh as she realized she had stepped on a flounder they had not seen.

The two followed the shoreline as it curved south toward the ocean. They gigged several flounder and came to a cut flowing from a marsh.

"Too deep to walk across," Harold said. He examined the stars. "Better head back. They'll be waiting for us."

Nevers turned a knob on the lantern, and the mantles changed from white to yellow. The two began the trek back. Annie looked at the stars, then the ocean, then the slope of beach as it climbed to a grassy terrain. It occurred to her that she had no idea where she was and a small fear pressed on her chest. She looked at Harold in the feeble light and saw him as the man who had brought her so far in just a few months. Yet there he was, walking along as if nothing unusual had happened. With his right trouser leg above his knee and the left fallen almost to his ankle, he looked like an ordinary man doing something the lower classes enjoyed.

But she knew there was nothing ordinary about this man, not his name or his chest or his back, and certainly not his thoughts. And she knew him. It made her feel special and safe.

Nevers paused to light a cigarette. Annie's thoughts wandered back and forth over the time she had spent in New Orleans, thinking of what he had taught her and of his many oddities. The tattoos. His mysterious business dealings. The people he knew, high and low. Huey Long. Wendel. Shoeshine boys and men who flew airplanes. Strange objects he collected. Putting ketchup on his eggs. And he didn't drink.

"Why don't you drink?" Annie asked. "You never told me why."

"I did," Harold said calmly. Annie looked at him. She could tell he loved where he was and what he was doing, like there was nowhere else he'd rather be. But he always seemed like that, no matter where he was. The world was like a big playground to him, she thought.

"I know. You said you like having your wits about you, but you *never* drink. I haven't met anybody in New Orleans who *never* drinks. At least not yet."

Harold walked along as if she had said nothing. He finished his cigarette and flicked the butt into the ocean.

"You may not believe this." He looked at her. "But I knew Huey Long."

Annie's heart bolted. She wondered if he knew she had seen the photograph.

"I wasn't involved in politics, but I ran with some of the people around Long. Gambled with them. Sometimes I won a lot. Other times I'd lose a little. All in all, I made enough jack to keep me in fine clothes, and that was important. These were powerful men and they had big businesses. When they needed someone, they'd give me a call. I was beginning to think I was really something. Drinking, smoking cigars. So I gambled a little, drank a little, worked a little. Gambled some more, drank some more, worked less, drank more—you get the picture."

Annie nodded.

"I started drinking all the time. Beer mostly, then booze—but expensive stuff, not hooch. I looked pretty rough sometimes, but I always fixed up for a card game. This one night, I was drinking pretty heavy at a poker game. On the way from the restroom, I overheard a man called Skinny Tompkins say, 'I'll clean that drunken sumbitch out if he ever comes back.' This was a guy I thought was my friend. Gave me work several times. Good work. I decided I'd show him who he was dealing with and sat down intending to bust him. I lost a couple of small pots, then won a big one and let myself get cornered into a bluff. Instead of folding like a sane—and sober—person, I kept throwing chips down. On the last round of bets, I tossed in everything I had. Skinny turned up three eights and a pair of aces. I shoved my cards into the deck without showing. Trying to salvage some pride, I pushed my chair back and stood up too quickly. I tripped on the chair and fell to the floor on all fours. I was mad and sick. And embarrassed. It was all I could do to keep from throwing up before I reached the front door."

Annie said, "So you went home and . . ."

"Drank some more." Nevers chuckled. "And the more I drank, the more I realized I was just a young punk trying to run with the wolves. The next morning I woke up lying in my own vomit. I looked in the mirror and didn't know whoever was staring back at me. I got in the bathtub with all my clothes on and cursed myself. 'You spongy sot, lousy sousing son-of-a-bitching boozehound.' On and on like that for God knows how long." Harold looked at Annie. "Get the picture?"

She nodded.

"I decided right there I'd never touch another drop. Course, I was sick for a week. If you dance, you gotta pay the band. To top it off, I didn't have a penny to my name. Well, I had that one penny I told you about, the one I keep in my shoe?"

Annie nodded, remembering the X-ray machine.

"When I came out of it, I was mad as hell. Mad at myself for getting that way, and mad at Skinny Tompkins and those other leeches that sucked Huey Long's blood. I laid low for a month to get my strength back and plot my revenge. One afternoon, I rang up Skinny to ask if a game was going down that weekend. I slurred my voice a bit and he was friendly as could be, a wolf slobbering over easy prey. The whole evening, I drank tea out of an Old Forester bottle and acted drunker and drunker. I won a few medium pots and took a couple of small losses. Finally I drew the hand I'd been waiting for—Oh, I forgot to tell you. Arkie floated me a couple hundred bucks to get in the game. Anyway, I drew . . . what was it? Three kings, I remember that. And I believe it was a pair of sevens or nines. I was playing sloppy, like an overconfident drunk will do. I threw chips all over the table. I could see it in their eyes. They thought they were going to shear me till I bled. Come time to show, three of them were still in and there must have been two thousand dollars on the table. I raked the hoard of chips toward me and said in the crispest voice they ever heard, 'Gentlemen, I believe I'll call it a night.'" Nevers burst out laughing. "That's when I went into business for myself. Nothing like being flat broke to make a man feel like an entrepreneur."

At the bungalow, the couples compared their hauls. Nevers and Annie had twelve flounder. Burk and Nausica boasted over fifteen flounder and a redfish. After Nausica and Annie had visited the outhouse with a lantern, everyone gathered for photographs.

Annie saw the light in Burk's cabin wink out sometime after three o'clock. She was on top of Nevers, her hand on his mouth in an attempt to keep the other couple from hearing his passionate words. Half an hour later, they too were asleep and didn't awaken until mid-morning.

Eddie Agnelly was due to arrive at three that afternoon, so the vacationers ate lunch and fished for an hour, releasing their catch after bragging about their skill in landing the big ones.

On his first pass, Agnelly flew over and dipped a wing at the four as they waited by the make-shift landing strip on a stretch of beach with hard, packed sand. The pilot circled and approached from the east, heading into a southwest wind. Annie watched the plane drop for the landing. It seemed to point seaward, even though it glided straight along the runway. Just before its wheels touched down, Agnelly gunned the engine. The plane straightened. Its tires ricocheted off the wet sand, then rolled along the beach, spewing grit.

After the men loaded the gear, and the girls had boarded, Nevers and Burk turned the plane around by its tail, then climbed in. Agnelly taxied down the narrow strip and in a skillful maneuver spun the plane around into the wind at the end of the runway. In a minute, they were airborne. In an hour, they were at Jimmy Wedell's flying field west of City Park.

* * *

At ten that evening, Annie and Harold were making love in The Cave. There were times when the two embraced tenderly, lovingly. At other times, Nevers took her ferociously and was done in less than a minute. Her lion or her lamb, Annie liked it both ways.

She could hear Nevers in the bathroom, whistling "Rock of Ages." As usual, the subdued light had illumined their endeavors. Annie imagined watching the two of them from across the room. A tired arousal moved inside her breast and then yielded to her desire for a cigarette just as Nevers eclipsed the doorway.

A towel around his waist, he said, "Going downstairs. Back in a sec."

Annie reached for the pack of Luckies. The cigarette between her lips, she struck the last match. Damp from the trip, it fizzled.

She opened the drawer of the nightstand to search for another box. Scrabbling around, she noticed that the photographs were gone. She moved a watch on a fob, a single cufflink, a letter opener with a fish handle, then hit something heavy and cold. She removed the envelope obstructing her view and saw a small revolver with H&R embossed on its black grip. Annie opened the yellowed envelope and peered inside. It held a single-column newspaper clipping. "Nilson Boy Misses Pass, Keeps Going." She tilted the strip toward the light.

> At Saturday afternoon's game in T. R. Williams Memorial Stadium, local boy Harry Nilson, distraught over a pass he missed on a crucial play, ran out of the stadium and has not been

seen since.

His parents are offering a $100 reward for information regarding his exact whereabouts.

Young Nilson, a senior second-stringer, was called for duty when star running back Rex "Streak" Fordham injured his ankle in the fourth quarter.

Nilson's number was called for an end-zone pass, which he seemed to have snared, then fumbled. He exited the stadium as the whistle signaled the end of the contest.

The Diablos lost the game 7 to 6.

Not until the final paragraph did Annie realize that the article was about Harold Nevers. The low-grade depression she had been feeling for weeks welled up inside her. A series of thoughts fell into place very fast. A strangled sound came from her throat. Harold Nevers was not an orphan, and he had never been a sports star. He had been an ordinary boy crushed by a silly game.

The man whose bed she shared, who was he? Annie looked at the doorway leading to the stairwell and spoke her real name for the first time in four months.

"My name is Toni Jo Henry. I grew up in DeRidder, Louisiana. I'm twenty years old."

Harold Nevers, or Harry Nilson, had lied to her. Several times. She was angry, worried. Intrigued. How could she confront the man who had done so much for her, given her a job and money and an interesting life?—the man who even now was coming up the stairs to lie in bed with her.

11

October 1938

Annie tried to lose herself in work. In the evenings, she dressed up and took a streetcar to the shopping district on Canal Street. Occasionally, she ran into Bliss or Nausica and visited with them briefly. They always seemed to be having a good time, a great time, in fact, and always with a different man. She wondered how they could do it.

Nevers came into town as he always did, without warning, like a tornado. Each time after he had gone, Annie felt like a survivor surveying the devastation. This time, Nevers took her to the 500 Club. Men Annie had seen many times, and a few she had never seen, slapped Harold on the back as if they had known him all their lives. Some kept their eyes on Annie as they talked to Nevers. Once, a hefty man tiptoed to raise his head above the crowd and yelled at Nevers, "J.P.! Over here!" The man waved his arm. Harold grabbed Annie's arm and ducked into the crowd.

"This way," he said. "That's somebody I don't want to see."

"Why's he calling you J.P.?"

"It's a long story. I'll tell you sometime."

They walked out the back door into a cool drizzle. Shoppers were huddled under awnings to wait out the rain. Nevers pushed his way through the crowd. At the corner of Dauphine and Canal, Wendel called from their feet.

"Wet night!" he said from beneath a battered umbrella. "That you, Miss Annie?" She smiled at the outcast, who hugged a wine bottle to his chest. "Say," he said. "I saw a pretty picture of you the other day."

"Oh? Did Harold show it to you?"

Annie looked up at Nevers just in time to see his face darken with rage. Stepping forward swiftly, he kicked the derelict viciously in the chest and knocked him off his board. The grimacing man lay on his side, clutching his stomach with one hand, reaching for the rolling bottle with the other. He emitted a strained groan, then a forced laugh.

"I probably deserved that one," he said. "Now, if you'll just turn me rightside up, Cap'n, I'll be getting out of your way."

"Harold," Annie said in a pleading voice.

"Come on," he said, grabbing her roughly. Stepping around the fallen man, he pulled Annie down the walk as she gazed over her shoulder sympathetically.

* * *

When Annie awoke the next morning, Harold's car was gone. After a light breakfast, she walked around downstairs, meddling with the endlessly fascinating curios. Upstairs, there were two or three closed rooms she had not explored. She climbed the stairs and tested the door next to The Cave. It was locked. Across the hall, she put her hand on a bulky varnished-iron doorknob and turned. Dim light filtered through the curtains. Chairs, couches, and chests covered with spider webs populated the room, which smelled of dust and cedar and mothballs. She closed the door, making sure the bolt shot securely into the strike plate. At the end of the hall was a narrow door, a closet, she guessed.

She turned the faceted-glass knob. It was jammed. She gripped the knob firmly with both hands and twisted. The bolt popped from its home and the door sprung open. On the multi-tiered shelves lining the small room sat basins, shallow boxes, and large dark bottles. Annie pushed the light switch. A deep red glow suffused the cubicle. Although she had never seen one, she recognized the closet as a makeshift darkroom.

Above her head, Annie noticed a short-order wheel like the one in the Time-Out Cafe. She pulled a ticket from its clip. It was in Harold's style but written in an unreadable shorthand or code. Only the numbers were clear: 10, 25, 15, 10. Annie peered behind the door. Several shallow boxes were stacked up to the doorknob. She gripped the top three and stepped into the hall. She lifted the lid of the top box.

Annie immediately recognized the woman in the photo as Bliss. She was wearing tights and a bodysuit and sported a peacock tail similar to the one in the burlesque Nevers had taken her to.

Annie thumbed through a number of sheets and found Nausica looking at her. She was squeezed into a low-cut bodice, the nipple of her left breast half exposed.

Annie opened the second box. A young woman in ordinary clothes struck a suggestive pose in a secluded bower.

Toni Jo Henry wouldn't do anything like that, she reasoned, not in a million years, so the woman in the picture must have been Annie Beatrice. Both of the women inside her seemed to split apart, then come back together. Spilling the sheets across the floor, she fell to her knees with an anguished cry and wept uncontrollably into her hands.

When she came to herself, Annie gathered the sheets from the floor. The box contained photographs of Annie in four poses. The copies of each set numbered 10, 25, 15, and 10. While returning the pictures to their box, Annie caught a glimpse of her reflection in the windowpane. In tear-matted disarray around her swollen eyes was the lank, yellow-white hair of a dead woman.

* * *

When Annie returned that afternoon, Harold's car was parked on the street. She burst into the den.

"Where are you!"

"Upstairs! Come on up!"

"I'll never step another foot in that bedroom."

"What?" Nevers appeared in the doorway at the head of the stairs. His face lathered, he held his arms up like a surgeon, a straight razor in one hand. "I can't understand a word–." Nevers looked down at Annie. "What the hell happened to you?"

Annie's hair was no longer white. She had tried to dye it black because she wanted the color as far away from white-blonde as she could get it.

"Come down here."

"What's going on?"

"Get! Down! Here!" At each word, she stomped her foot in a childish tantrum.

Nevers descended the stairs.

Annie demanded, "What are you trying to do to me?"

"Nothing," Nevers pleaded. "What's going on?"

Annie rushed at him and began pummeling him with her fists.

"Don't lie to me. Don't lie! Don't lie! Don't lie!"

As she continued to strike him, he lifted the razor out of her way. Finally exhausted, she broke down crying and slid down his chest, collapsing onto the first stair step.

"Don't move," Nevers said. "I'll be right back." He ran upstairs and returned without the shaving cream on his face. He sat next to Annie at the foot of the stairs, waiting for her sobbing to subside. She looked up at Nevers, wiping her face with the palm of her hand. A smear of diluted black dye trickled down her neck. Not wanting her eyes to meet his, she focused on the kite-shaped scar on his nose.

"You know I'd never do anything to hurt you," he said.

"Liar!" she screamed. "You–." She raised a red fist and drew it to her breast. "Liar. Nausica and Bliss. They're–. Aren't they? They're prostitutes."

Nevers let out a growl that sounded relieved for himself and hurt for her.

"Ah, Annie, I thought you knew." He put his arm on her shoulder. "Come see."

"Don't touch me!" She withdrew into a compact ball. "Those pictures upstairs. What are those pictures for?"

"So that's it. You don't give a damn whether your friends are call girls. You just don't want your picture next to theirs."

"They're not my girlfriends."

"You like them well enough when we're out."

"I didn't know them."

"You *did* know them," Nevers said. "You just can't stand the fact that you like a couple of tarts. Well now you know. They're just like anybody else. Some you like, and some you don't."

"They're *not* like anybody else. What do you do with those pictures?"

Nevers thought for a moment. "I sell them, all right? I sell them."

"To who?"

"Anybody willing to pay."

"Why? And why me?"

"Business. It's just a business."

"You do it for money? Is that what you're always hauling around in those big tied-up bundles?"

"You think I do it for fun? Of course it's for money."

"With *my* pictures?"

"It was the first time. I give you my word."

"Your *word?*" Annie let out a snort that was half laugh and half cry of despair.

"Annie."

"Toni Jo! My name is Toni Jo!"

"Listen," Nevers said. "There's nothing wrong with those photographs. And there's men who pay good money to look at pretty girls." Nevers picked at a splinter on the step. "You remember at your mother's? When I said you could make three times what you were making at the Two-Rat Cafe? I was right, wasn't I? Haven't I paid you well?" Pouting, Annie shrugged her shoulders like a child defeated in an argument. "And you remember I said you could earn five times that in a year? Well, here's your chance. Let me sell your pictures, and I'll give you twenty percent of what they make."

"No!"

"Why not? Give me one good reason you shouldn't make money off your looks."

She glared at him threateningly. "It would make me a—a floozy."

An exasperated sound burst from Harold's throat. "Goddammit, Annie, don't you see? If you look at it that way, *everything* is prostitution. You work in my restaurant, and I pay you for your services. Is that prostitution?"

"I'm not selling my body. It's not the same. Knowing some old letch is staring at my pictures like–. I don't know. It's not the same."

"What do you think models do?" Nevers argued. "The Chesterfield girl, you think she's a prostitute?" Annie expelled a short laugh at the comparison. "If you're not a prostitute in your heart, Annie, you'll never be a prostitute—not if you sell your body a dozen times a night. Nobody can make you something you're not already. You plant a bean, you get beans. You never plant a rose and grow a weed."

Annie felt helpless under his words. Everything he said seemed both reasonable and repulsive to her. She exploded up the stairs. "Come here!" she shouted.

In his room, she held the yellowed envelope. Pulling out the newspaper clipping, she said, "What's this?" Harold's response was not what she expected. He slapped her.

"What are you doing in my private things?" He grabbed her and shook her. "Never! You hear me? Never dig in my private things. Just because you sleep in my bed doesn't mean you shouldn't act like a guest in my house." He shook her again. "You understand?"

Annie nodded, broken but still defiant.

"I should know," she began weakly. "Don't I have the right to know who you are?"

Nevers pushed her and she fell on the mattress. He sat on the bed and ran his fingers through his hair. For the first time since Annie had known him, he seemed to be struggling with himself.

"All right," he said at last, looking at her. "You want to know who I am? I'll tell you. My real name is Harry Nilson. I wasn't any goddamned super sports star, either. I guess you figured that out. I worked my ass off. I worked harder than anybody else, and I was only average. Can you beat that?" Nevers looked at her challengingly. "Well, I didn't like that and I didn't accept it. If I couldn't be a winner one way, I'd figure out another way. A couple of times a quarter, I replaced Streak Fordham so he could get a breather, and I did all right. I wasn't a bum, it's just that Streak was born with some kind of inhuman panther blood in him. Streak and I got to be buddies, and he told me around midseason how we could make some extra money working together."

Nevers stooped down and picked the clipping off the floor. He looked at it and shook his head.

"I thought he meant at a regular job, so I was shocked when he told me he'd been collecting ten to fifty bucks a game, shaving points to get a certain spread for a bookie. Don't get me wrong. This wasn't big-time gambling, just local yokels, businessmen, and riffraff trying to make a dime on someone else's talent. Sometimes in the middle of a game, the bets would change and Streak would have to play harder or goldbrick to adjust the new spread."

Nevers took the envelope from Annie and slipped the clipping inside.

"At *that*, game," Nevers said, slapping the envelope on the nightstand, "the opposing team was better than the oddsmakers predicted. Before the game, the bookie told Streak to keep the score within three points either way. You see, winning and losing get turned around sometimes when you gamble. You can bet a certain team will lose by two or three or five points, and if they do, you *win*. So you can win by losing. You following me?"

Annie twitched her head to the side, indicating she understood him but was still mad.

"All right. That particular afternoon, winning meant staying within three points of the other team. Whether we beat them or were beaten by them, Streak was in thick clover as long as the difference wasn't more than three points. Then he hurt his ankle, some quick bets were taken in the stands, and the bookie sent a runner down on the field. I was standing on the sideline when I felt someone shove a slip of paper in my hand. It was my new orders. It read, 'SCORE $50.'"

Nevers looked at Annie.

"All I had to do was score, and I could earn two weeks' wages. Everything about that last possession was just like I told you at your mother's that night. Whatever direction I faked first, that's where I went last. In the huddle, I told the quarterback if he dialed my number for a pass, I could run that son of a bitch to the state line. Remember me telling you that part?"

Annie nodded.

"Everything was perfect until we lined up. I scanned the stands for my girlfriend. She was older than me, twenty or twenty-one, best looking thing in three counties. I thought I was really something taking her around. Then a couple of guys said they'd seen her with an older man in Tyler. They were doing some roughnecking that summer and came back to Kilgore one weekend. I didn't believe them because she wasn't that type, so I told them it must have been a girl who looked like her.

"So there we were, lining up for the last play of the game. I was about to be the hero and win fifty bucks to boot. I looked into the stands for my girl, and what do you suppose I saw?" Annie shrugged her shoulders. "My girl kissing the bookie. That greasy son of a bitch wasn't good enough to kiss my dog and here was my girl smooching on him. Suddenly, it all fell into place. She played for money just like I was playing for money. Winning and losing had nothing to do with it."

"She was a—?"

Nevers nodded.

"Hell, and I really liked the girl. Now, try to imagine a young kid seeing that. I was furious and hurt. Finally, I composed myself and let the quarterback know I was ready. I'd fix that punk bookie. I came off the line like a madman. I faked right, feinted left, and stayed left. At the goal line, I glanced over my shoulder and saw the football coming down big as a watermelon. A spastic could have caught that ball. And I did. I held it for a split second, just long enough for that bookie to know what I had done. Then I dropped it."

Annie thought about the story.

"Your name. That doesn't explain why you changed your name."

Nevers chuckled.

"I changed my name for the same reason I left town. I said these were small-time gamblers. But that doesn't mean they were any less serious than the big boys. Getting lost wasn't enough. I changed my name because–. You never know. A year, five years. You see someone asking about you and the next thing you know, bam! You wake up rubbing your head with all your money gone. It happens."

"You left your parents just like that?" Annie snapped her fingers. "How could you do that?"

Nevers sighed.

"It's all like a big chess game. To explain one move, you have to go back twenty or thirty moves, *on both sides*. I created an entire new life. The preacher taught me that. T. Van Mahorn, *puh!* At least one of the things he said was true, though. You can be born again and again. The bad news is that when you recreate yourself, you have to destroy something. Each new birth is also a suicide." He shook his head. "Creation and destruction are like Siamese twins. There's no getting around it."

Annie looked at Nevers with tears in her eyes. She felt like holding him and relieving his pain. In a way, even with parents, he was still an orphan. Then she thought of the photographs, of Bliss and Nausica, his shady friends and secret trips, Huey Long and all the rest of his schemes.

"Harold, I want to believe you. Believe me, I do. But after all those . . ." She almost said *lies*. "How do I know what you're telling me *now* is the truth?"

Nevers became irritated at the endless questions.

"It's the truth because I *said* it's the truth," he snapped.

Annie almost hated herself for making him angry. She looked at his face: the kite-scar, one of his cheeks smooth, the other dark with stubble, a pat of shaving cream on his left earlobe.

"Why didn't you tell me the real story in the first place?"

"I told you what you needed to hear. Don't think about who you are now. Picture yourself back then. You *wanted* me to be your rescuer. You think you would have left your old life to follow a loser? You needed a sure thing, Annie, someone to change your life. I was doing you a favor by spicing up the story. If you ask ten people who know me to tell you who I am, each one will tell you something different. I'm whatever they want me to be. Look at yourself. You're an entirely different person from the girl who got out of my car four months ago."

Annie knew what he said was true. She had thought many times about her life back home and wondered how she had survived the boredom.

"And about those pictures," Nevers said. "There's no reason to be ashamed of making your life more comfortable by taking advantage of your beauty. You give somebody pleasure, and they'll pay you well for it. There's nothing wrong with that."

Nevers looked at her. Annie reached up and pinched the foam off his ear.

"So," he continued, "whether you like it or not, I'm using those shots and I'm going to pay you for them. It could mean an extra two hundred dollars a month. And once your face gets around–. Let me put it this way. Certain men are willing to pay extra to see just a little more. And there's nothing wrong–."

"Never," Toni Jo said. "Not even if I have to eat garbage to stay alive."

* * *

After Annie calmed down, Nevers suggested taking Monday off so they could get away from New Orleans to relax. He had told her several times of Waveland, near Bay St. Louis, Mississippi. She made him promise it wouldn't be like their other trips. Annie said she never saw anybody who could turn play into work like he did. Nevers agreed.

In an hour, they were parked on the gravel lot of the White Kitchen in Slidell. Nevers ordered fried chicken, Jax beer, and a Coke and had them delivered on a tray that fit on the driver's window. It made Annie feel they were just like regular folks.

They arrived at Waveland by six that evening and settled into their hotel room. Nevers said he was going fishing and she could come along and crab off the seawall if she wanted. Annie said she was plenty happy where she was.

Nevers came in after dark. He said he kept two redfish and five speckled trout, but had given them to an old colored man who had fished all afternoon and caught only one croaker. Nevers said he knew that wasn't true because three tails were sticking out the top of his bucket, but he gave him the fish anyway.

The next day, Nevers woke Annie at ten with a Coke and plate lunch of corned-beef sandwiches, chips, and kosher pickle. That afternoon, while sitting in a lounge chair by the ocean, she read all of the hotel's *Look* and *Collier's* magazines while Nevers ran around visiting. No matter where they went, people knew him. She remembered at one time being impressed by his popularity. Now, watching him scurry from one gathering to the next only made her tired.

That evening, Annie stood in the lobby idly looking around while Nevers checked out at the front desk. When she glanced down, Nevers was signing the check. She noticed it was October 30, the day before Halloween. As he wrote his last name, she inspected his first name. It looked like he spelled the word "Herald." She checked the hotel register, which lay open in front of her. There, too, was the name "Herald."

The discovery gave Annie a sinking feeling in her stomach. This was the man who adjusted his past according to his needs, yet even his fictitious name was not spelled the way she had thought. It made her feel again that she didn't really know the man she had spent half a year with. She walked outside and waited in the car for the next surprise.

* * *

At the restaurant on Tuesday, Annie heard people talking about it all day long. On the eve of Halloween, a clever young man named Orson Welles presented a new rendition of the old H. G. Wells fantasy, *The War of the Worlds*. Over the CBS band, Welles and his Mercury Theatre group broadcast the radio play as a series of realistic news bulletins that interrupted a weather forecast. A university astronomer in Chicago reported seeing a series of explosions on the planet Mars and speculated about their origin.

Listeners were then returned to "a tune that never loses favor, the popular *Star Dust*."

Several news flashes came in, then an interview with a Princeton professor. Eyewitness reports flooded in. Martians had landed at Grover's Mill, New Jersey, in large silver cylinders. More spacecraft joined them. Soon a legion of aliens attacked and defeated the New Jersey State Militia. New York City was being destroyed by heat-rays.

As word spread that Martians had launched a general assault on the nation, people fleeing metropolitan centers caused huge traffic jams. Some without radio saw the panic and thought the country was being invaded by Hitler's Nazis. Normal power outages convinced local citizens of their doom. In the aftermath of the realistic account, newspapers reported several suicides of people who left notes saying they would rather die by their own gun than by a Martian death-ray.

Throughout the day, Annie marveled that such disastrous results could ensue from a story someone had made up for entertainment. To Annie, it seemed like the whole world was going crazy.

12

November–December 1938

Herald was as kind to Annie as ever, and she felt defenseless in her love for him. He had good looks and money and class. He was intriguing and mysterious and cast a spell over everyone he met. There was a kind of power about him that made her forgive his faults both large and small.

"There's nothing to it," he told her. "All you have to do is go out with the man."

"Don't you even care about me?" Annie countered for the third time. They sat in Herald's front room discussing the transaction.

"Of course, I care. This doesn't change a thing between you and me, Annie. I'm trying to give you a freedom very few people have, especially in these times. Contrary to what you think, money doesn't put a curse on everything it touches."

"So I go out with him and . . ."

"Have a good time."

"And he gives me fifty dollars."

"No. I give you the fifty dollars."

"Why you?"

"Because it's crass the other way."

Annie mentally walked herself through an evening with a stranger.

"What if I don't like him?"

"You still have to be with him for the evening. That's what they're paying for, a pretty girl to escort around. It makes them look good. And feel good."

"And that's it. He picks me up and takes me home, and that's it?"

"He doesn't even pick you up. You meet him at a restaurant. It's the easiest money you'll ever make. Hell, there's people in this country who sweat a month from dawn till dark for that kind of jack. If you take advantage of your looks, you're sitting on a gold mine. Don't be a fool, Annie. Try it just once, and I promise you'll like it, but if you don't, you'll never have to do it again."

The two sat quietly in the room. Annie observed dust motes spinning in a shaft of sunlight.

"I've got a friend in the lumber business who comes into town every few weeks. He's a nice fellow and he won't pressure you. In fact, you know him. That'll make the first time easy."

Annie looked at Nevers apprehensively. There weren't many men she had met in New Orleans she wanted to spend an evening with.

"Here," Herald said, pulling a snapshot from the inside of his coat.

Annie saw a balding man in his mid-thirties striking a pose against a column in front of City Hall. He wore a two-tone pullover sweater and baggy gabardine slacks.

"Why, that's Arkie Burk," she exclaimed.

"See," Nevers said. "Totally harmless."

"Does he know I'll be his . . ."

"Friend. They're called friends. You're working this up in your imagination into something it's not. And, no, he doesn't know he'll be with you."

"Can I have a couple of days to think about it?"

Nevers shook his head from side to side as if he couldn't believe anyone would reject such an offer.

"Take a week. Take a year. The world's not going to stop spinning if Annie Beatrice turns down a gold mine."

* * *

What Annie wanted to do was talk with Nausica about the arrangement. She rang her up that evening and asked if they could meet at Solari's lunch counter the next day.

Annie saw Nausica first but, before calling out, inspected her as if she had never seen the woman. Nausica wore open-toed high heels and a dark green dress with a costume necklace of pearl-colored beads the size of golf balls. Annie ordered a hamburger and Coke. The bill was fifteen cents. Nausica chided her with good humor.

"Honey, you ought to live a little. I know Herald's paying you more than that."

Annie smiled weakly. "That's what I wanted to talk to you about. I've got more money saved up than I know what to do with and yet . . . Herald wants me to make more."

Nausica sobered instantly. "This sounds serious."

Annie explained the arrangement outlined by Nevers.

Nausica nodded. "See a picture show, have a nice meal. What's the big deal? Listen." Through a straw, Nausica vacuumed up the small pool at the bottom of her soda. She licked her top lip and looked at Annie. "What you want to watch out for is the hundred-dollar deal." Nausica slapped Annie's thigh. "For fifty bucks, they want a fun night on the town. For a C-note, they want it to wind up in bed."

Annie closed her eyes and leaned forward as if she had a stomachache.

"I knew it," she said.

Nausica put her arm around Annie's shoulder. "Now, honey. It ain't as bad as all that. You don't have to do anything you don't want to."

Annie straightened herself and sighed. "What do you think I should do?"

"I think you'd be a fool not to take some rich man's fifty bucks." Nausica fished a compact from her purse and touched up her lipstick. "He ain't gonna miss it, and he gets a pretty girl on his arm." Nausica grabbed Annie's hand affectionately. "Just be careful, you hear?"

Annie hesitated before asking the next question. "Have you–. Don't be offended, Nessie, but have you ever made a hundred dollars?"

Nausica laughed. She threw the compact and lipstick into her purse and snapped it shut. "Lots of times." Nausica eyed her curiously. "I thought you knew. My, my. I knew you were green, but I didn't think you were *that* green."

When Annie finished her lunch, Nausica took her leave by repeating her earlier caution. "Just be careful, honey, you hear? Tootle-loo."

* * *

Arkie Burk didn't treat the matter so casually. Annie Beatrice was the last person he expected to see at the corner table-for-two at Antoine's. At first, Arkie didn't recognize her because the lights were low and her hair was black-brown. It was an uneasy moment for them both.

"Waiter," he nervously called. "Drinks over here. A Scotch and soda and–." He pointed to Annie.

"Bourbon and Seven," she said.

The waiter placed menus before them.

"Annie, I had no idea I'd be seeing you here. I swear to you. I feel so awful."

Annie emitted a feeble laugh to ease the tension.

"You look nice," she said.

Burk glanced down. He wore a navy blue wide-lapeled suit with gray pinstripes and a burgundy tie sprinkled with light yellow dots. He placed his elbow on the table and planted his forehead on the heel of his palm.

"Good Lord, Annie." He shook his head. "Don't you realize where you are?"

Annie tried to cheer him up.

"Antoine's. Don't you know where *you* are?"

"Annie, Annie, Annie." Burk expelled a half-laugh. "Tuh!" He skipped his chair closer to hers. In a voice pregnant with dark meaning, he said, "You ever heard of the demimonde?"

Annie thought for a moment.

"Is that like the Café du Monde?"

Burk was taken aback by the utter innocence of her reply. After staring at her briefly, he burst out laughing. Recovered, he tried to explain in words delicate enough not to offend her.

"The demimonde is the middle world. It's somewhere between respectable society and the underworld. You see what I'm getting at?"

Annie gazed at him blankly.

"Look." He put one hand above his head, salute-fashion. "Up here, you've got the legal business world. Down here," he made the same motion near the tabletop with his other hand, "you've got the underworld, men who deal in illegal goods and services—unlicensed liquor, gambling, numbers, rigging horse races, that sort of thing."

Annie helped him out. "And prostitution."

Burk bent over as if he had been punched.

"Right," he said. "Now, the demimonde, the middle world, is here." He made a gesture midway between where his two hands had been. "The businesses aren't exactly illegal, they're just not—what's the word?—respectable, I guess. And the women who go out with men of the demimonde are called demimondaines. And this here," he pointed back and forth from himself to her, "is one of those things."

"In other words, I'm a demi–."

"Mondaine. Demimondaine." Burk nodded.

"But Herald said all I had to do was go out with . . . whoever. You."

"I know, Annie," Burk said. "But–."

He was interrupted by the waiter setting their drinks down.

"Can I take your order?"

"Give us a few minutes."

"No problem, Mr. Burk."

"Next he'll be disappointed if you don't do the other thing."

"But it's not that way with me and Herald."

Burk was growing impatient with her naïveté.

"Annie. I know what you're thinking. 'It won't happen to me.'" He reached across the table, gripped her arm firmly, and shook her. "Annie, listen to me. Don't kid yourself. You don't know Herald like I do. I've known him for years. He seems like a nice guy, and he can show everybody a good time, but he's kind of a shady character. You need to watch out for Herald. He's dangerous. Nausica, Bliss, Lilly. You know them?"

"I know Nessie and Bliss."

"Well, they used to be where you are."

"Meaning?"

"They were Herald's girlfriends at one time."

A pang of jealousy constricted Annie's heart and she closed her eyes. "Something told me that, but I didn't want to admit it, so I kept pushing it to the back of my mind."

"I thought you were different, Annie. I really did. When I saw Herald with you, I said, 'He's finally got a real girlfriend. This gal is something special.'" Burk shook his head. "I don't know. Maybe he's got a problem. It's like he goes around with these beautiful young women for a while and then gets tired of them."

The waiter spoke from behind him. "Ready to order?"

Burk twitched. "Uh, yeah," he said, opening the menu. "Give us a number five and a number . . . eight. Five and eight, okay?"

"Very good, Mr. Burk." The waiter took the menus.

"Now where was I?" Burk rubbed his chin. "He was with Nausica a year, then discarded her. Maybe they start looking too old."

"I can believe that," Annie said. "I look in the mirror after a weekend with him and my face seems like it's aged five years."

"And, you're not going to like this." Burk looked at Annie.

"Tell me. I've heard it all in the last few weeks."

"You've seen his odd little collections at his house?"

Annie nodded.

"It's the same with women. It's like he collects them and then . . ."

"And then?"

"And then he farms them out."

"You mean, like Bliss and Nessie?"

Burk nodded. "They're still his in a way."

"He pays them to go out with men," Annie said flatly.

"He's the middle man, the finder. They need him to locate the better class of men. The men give him an order, and he fills it. Blonde, brunette. Tall, short. Slender, buxom. He's a favor broker, made-to-order experiences, you know. That sort of thing."

Annie nodded up and down in understanding, then side to side in a rejection of what she understood.

"Not me," she said. "Not even this anymore. Not now that I see the way it works."

"Be careful, Annie. You've got to be real careful."

* * *

Over the telephone, Annie said to Nausica, "You didn't tell me the whole story."

After a long silence, Nausica said, "It would take a lifetime to explain how I got to this point. Can you meet me at the St. Regis tomorrow at noon?"

"On Royal?"

"Yeah. You can take the Desire streetcar right to the doorstep. But listen."

"Yes?"

"Don't go inside."

"I'll be there."

Annie didn't question her. She knew Nausica would have a good reason for asking her not to go inside.

* * *

Annie was surprised to see Nausica in casual clothes.

"I don't work *every* day, honey. Shoot, sometimes I work only one or two nights a week. This business has its advantages, too. It ain't all bad, you know. If it was, you think there'd be so many of us?" Nausica slapped Annie and laughed, then cased her over from head to foot. "But I can tell it ain't for you."

They milled about in the crowd gathered for the next streetcar. Nausica talked while striking a match.

"You think Herald's out of town, right?"

"That's what he told me."

Nausica's cheeks collapsed as she drew on the cigarette and squinted one eye against a plume of smoke.

"Rule number one," she said. "Never believe what he tells you. Understand?"

"I'm beginning to," Annie said.

"And you don't have to do something he asks just because you think he'll be disappointed. He'll get over it and he'll like you just as much. Let's get out of this sun."

The two walked to a nearby awning. Nausica continued to talk while scanning the street.

"Let me tell you how a man treats you that you've done a favor for. Herald tell you he'd seen the blue devils?" Annie frowned. "The d.t.'s, from too much booze. Hallucinations. Rats and snakes."

"He told me. Is it true? You said don't believe what he says."

"This one's true. I was with him. He was a barker at a joint I was dancing at a few years back. I stayed at his flat once or twice when I needed to flop. I found him lying on the street in front of his place. Somebody had rolled him, took everything he had except his underwear. And, honey, if you'd seen *them*, you'd know why they hadn't taken those. You never seen anything till you seen a man screaming about roaches all over him and there ain't nothing there. He was down to skin and bones, yellow as baby poo. Poisoned with alcohol and begging me to get him another drink."

"Did you?"

"Nope. I did it for his own good. Handcuffed him in the bed and sat up with him like a sick child. Turned his head when he puked so he wouldn't drown."

Annie's sympathy for the man she loved came out in a moan of pain. Her eyes teared up and she blinked and looked around to regain her composure. Nausica touched her on the arm.

"I know, honey. I was there. He begged me for three days and all I'd give him was water. And why? Because I loved him. Ha! Had to hold the glass for him his hands were shaking so bad. Then I gave him juices. Then soft food. Just like a newborn baby."

Nausica suddenly dipped her head down and gripped Annie's arm. "Turn this way. He's coming down the walk." Nevers pushed through the doors of the St. Regis cafeteria. "Let's sit tight for a while."

"Did he go back to drinking?" Annie asked.

"Nope. When he was in the d.t.'s, he cursed me. When he was dry, he thanked me. Said he was all washed up and I saved him." Nausica laughed. "You know who Nausica is? She's the gal that saved Ulysses when he washed up naked on the beach after a shipwreck or something. I never read it. Herald told me about. Said I was just like Nausica, so that's what he named me. Ha! I guess that makes him Ulysses."

"Sounds like a happy ending," Annie said.

"Until he got well." Nausica shook her head. "Best I can figure, he couldn't stand owing somebody for the rest of his life. Whatever he wanted me to be, that's what I became. When my face started showing the wear, he traded me in for a newer model. His savior, then his slave, I guess."

"But not now," Annie offered.

Nausica laughed. "No. Now I do it because it's the fastest way to make a wad of cash. Believe it or not, you hook up with the right men, it ain't so bad." She pulled Annie's arm. "Here's what we been waiting for." She drew Annie to the window. "Watch this."

The two observed Nevers as a waitress walked by him. He sneezed. The waitress stopped and said something to him with a smile.

"That look familiar?"

Annie recalled how Nevers had gotten her attention that first day in the Time-Out Cafe. She leaned her head against the brick and bit her lip. Nausica was about to speak.

"Stop," Annie said firmly. "Just give me a minute to take it in." She pulled a handkerchief from her purse and daubed at her eyes. She took a deep breath and exhaled. "It hurts, Nessie. How can I love him and hate him at the same time?"

"It's just one of those things, honey. He's got something you need."
She twirled her cigarette in a small circle. "Psychology, you know."

Annie looked at her with desperation. Her eyes were bloodshot.

Nausica resumed, "Not *want*, honey. *Need*. I loved him once, too,
and look what it got me. The silver lining around this cloud is that he
helped me get over him." She mused for a moment. "Like I helped him
get over the booze. You got to hate it to beat it. Well, after taking so much
from him, I learned to hate him." Nausica watched Nevers talking to the
laughing waitress. "You'd be surprised how easy it is if you put your mind
to it."

Annie finally broke into full-blown sobbing. "I don't know if I can
do it, Nessie. I guess I'll try to get along with him without doing all those
other things."

"You can't do it little by little, honey. You got to rip yourself away all
at once if you expect to survive at all."

Annie imagined herself walking out on Nevers. She would leave
him and go back home. She had more money than she ever thought she
would need to attend college and become a teacher, a life that now held
no attraction for her. She put her head on Nausica's shoulder and cried.

* * *

The following week, when Nevers pretended to have come back in
town, he called several times asking for Annie to go with him to a movie
or out to dinner. Making excuses related to work, she knew that Nevers
knew the alibis couldn't have been true. It was December and business
had slowed by half.

Nevers would be dropping by on payday, so Annie steeled herself
against his presence by reviewing the numerous deceptions he had
practiced on her, his meanness and disregard for her feelings. When he
arrived, he was as handsome as ever, but she deflected his embrace when
he stepped into the kitchen of Terra Incognita.

He apologized for offending her, then said she was taking offense
where none was intended. He tried to win a smile from her with a comical
quip. Annie held her ground. Nevers coughed and pulled his coat around
his throat.

"You should close that window when the wind's blowing from the north," he said. "Might catch a cold."

Annie eyed him suspiciously, wondering if the cough were a variation on the sneeze, a play for sympathy. He talked with her for several more minutes, the full burden of the conversation falling to him. Finally, he gave up.

"Well," he said. "I guess we're having our first fight." She was silent. "Listen, Annie, I know Arkie didn't get fresh with you. That's not the way it works. When men ask for a pretty girl on their arm, that's all they expect. There's nothing wrong with it." He looked at her, hoping to engage her in the argument. Finally, he turned and walked to the door. He coughed once and cleared his throat. "Think about it and you'll see I'm right." Pushing through the door, he called over his shoulder. "Phone me when you thaw out, hear?"

Annie tried to put him out of her mind. She wrote her mother for the first time in a month. She still hadn't disclosed the extent of her romance with Nevers, and now she was glad.

She went out with Nausica several times. Trying to divert her affections from Herald, she devised new ways to help the constant stream of drifters who knocked at her door asking for work when what they wanted was food.

Twice, Arkie dropped by to see how she was faring. She tried to imagine what it would be like to kiss him. His face wasn't as handsome as Herald's. It was more round and his receding hairlines had retreated even farther in the short time she had known him. But that wasn't it. He was pleasant enough. There just wasn't any spark there.

For a week, Annie was fine. Then she ran out of diversions. She was lying to herself and she knew it. Boredom was no ally. She rang Herald's house several times that Friday. Then she called his favorite haunts and left messages. Saturday morning, she awoke with him standing over her. He sat on the bed and held her hand without speaking. The familiar odor of his cologne was comforting. He looked almost contrite. Maybe he was right about the escorts, she thought. Nausica's warning politely intruded on her reverie. She would be careful, she said to herself.

Nevers coughed. She knew immediately it could not have been counterfeited. It was a shallow cough from the bottom of his throat, but it sounded rougher than a week ago.

She spoke softly. "You been taking care of yourself?"

"Me? Don't worry about me. How are *you* doing?"

"Same," Annie said. She looked at the scar on his nose, then into his eyes. "Missing you." Nevers lifted his head in half a nod, then turned and coughed. Annie sat up in bed. "Say."

"It's nothing," Nevers said, reaching into his coat and producing a bottle of cough syrup. He unscrewed the cap and lifted the bottle. "Cheers." He took a long swallow. "I'll be better in no time."

Annie tasted the cough syrup the whole time they were making love.

* * *

Annie spent the three days before Christmas with her mother. They worked puzzles and listened to the radio. On the morning she left, her Aunt Fay prepared a holiday meal for her and her mother. When Herald picked her up at the train station that evening, he presented her with three new dresses, four hats, two purses, a pair of gloves, and a bottle of perfume. She spent Christmas Eve at his house.

On Christmas morning, the two lay in bed listening to the radio. The weatherman forecast temperatures in the mid-eighties by noon. Throwing the sheets off, Nevers walked to the window and peeled down a corner of foil.

"Did you hear Santa Claus coming down the chimney last night?"

"Santa Claus was in bed with me last night," Annie said. "He was too tired from giving me all those presents the night before and had to rest awhile."

"Couldn't have been," Herald said. He coughed.

"Will you get off that floor in your bare feet. You'll never get over that cold if you run around half naked."

Nevers chuckled. "Worst that could happen to me today is I could die of a heat stroke."

Annie giggled. "Get back in bed."

"Get *out* of bed," Herald said. "And come see what Santa brought to good little girls."

Annie leapt out of bed and ran to the window. Squinting her eyes against the bright sun, she saw a new Plymouth convertible, powder blue, parked on the street. Now she knew why Nevers had been making her practice driving his Packard until they got into city traffic. She admired the automobile, then gazed into his twinkling eyes and hugged him.

"You do love me," she said.
"Like nobody else," he promised.

13

January–March 1939

Three weeks into the new year, Annie discovered she was pregnant. After crying through long arguments, she found herself in the elevator at the back of the Maison Blanche building, rising with a nauseous feeling in her stomach. Nevers held her as she concentrated on holding her illness down. They had an appointment with a doctor he knew.

For days, a single, forceful statement had been ringing in her head: "You will not be a breeder." After Nevers had tired of reasoning with Annie, he simply shouted the line at her over and over until one of his coughing fits gave her respite from the onslaught of cruelty.

In February, Mayor Maestri began his annual Roach Roundup. A few weeks before Mardi Gras each year, the mayor made a show of exterminating the city's human vermin so tourists would come to Carnival. Locked behind bars for the duration of the festival were all suspected racketeers, pickpockets, pimps, thieves, and miscellaneous miscreants. Maestri's men easily located most of the prostitutes, since it was largely through his auspices they operated. The Mayor bragged of his deed in the headlines of *The Times-Picayune*: "NEW ORLEANS GIVES UP CRIME FOR LENT!"

After a short period of bed rest, Annie returned to her normal routine of weekday work and Saturday nights on the town with Herald. Nevers had been especially kind to Annie for a month, and the details of the abortion grew dimmer every day. While having drinks one evening at the Roosevelt Hotel, he said to her casually, "I want you to meet someone."

"Sure," Annie said.

With two fingers, Nevers signaled the man over.

"Frank Webster, this is Annie Beatrice. Annie, Mr. Webster's a banker, one of the most powerful in the city."

Annie extended her gloved hand. "Pleased to meet you, Mr. Webster."

The man dislodged a black cigar from the corner of his mouth and smiled as he took her hand. The two incisors on the upper right side of his mouth were partially gold. Even as Webster spoke to Nevers about his cough, he continued staring at Annie.

"Better take care of that cough, you hear?"

"It's nothing. Just getting over a bout with the flu. Those things seem to linger forever."

"They do," Webster said. "That they do."

Until later that night, Annie thought Webster was just another of Herald's mysterious friends in high places.

"Annie," Nevers said to her after making love.

"Mmm?" Annie turned to him. The light from the bathroom put half his face in darkness.

"Are you my sweet Beastie?"

She touched his face. "You know I am. Are you my big lion?"

Nevers laughed. "Will you do your big lion a little favor?"

"Only a little one."

"I'd like you to go out with Frank Webster."

Annie went limp on the bed. "Herald, please," she said, her heart sinking. "I thought we had been through all that."

"I thought we had, too. And I thought it was settled. All he wants to do is look good at a Mardi Gras ball, and he said he likes the way you carry yourself."

"Herald, you're breaking my heart. I *love* you, don't you understand that? I don't want to go out with anyone else."

"If you love me, then do this for me. Webster's a good fellow. He gave me some work when I was younger and helped me get back on my feet."

"And you owe him."

"Something like that."

"You owe him *me*? Did you see the way he was staring at me? He looked like he was about to gobble me up."

Nevers laughed. "He's harmless. I give you my word."

Annie lay in bed for a long while. She thought going out with Webster one time might be easier than dealing with Herald's snubbing coldness for a week. She was almost asleep when Nevers coughed several times and reached for the bottle of syrup that now had its own place on his nightstand.

"When's this ball supposed to take place?"
Nevers took a long pull at the cough syrup and replaced the cap.
"Next Saturday night."

* * *

That Saturday afternoon, Annie and Herald attended a parade downtown. While walking her back to a stop on the St. Charles streetcar route, he told her where the banker would meet her and what to wear. At the stop, he spoke casually, as if he had forgotten to wear dark blue instead of black.

"Oh, and Annie."

"Hm?" She was searching down the line for the streetcar.

"Webster likes his women a little trashy, but they're all locked up at the moment, so if you don't mind, I'd like for you to tart up a bit for him."

Annie's throat constricted, making it difficult for her to speak. Finally, she managed a single, anguished word.

"Why?"

"There you go again," Nevers said good-naturedly. He slapped the back of one hand into the palm of the other. "Listen. It's like this. Some men like their women to look flashy. It makes them feel rich. Some like them plain. It makes them feel secure. Anyway, it's a Mardi Gras ball. There'll be people in such outlandish costumes, you'll look like the only normal person in the crowd."

"I hate this, Herald." The wind made the tear on her cheek feel icy. The streetcar appeared around a distant corner.

"Look," Nevers said impatiently, trying to squeeze her arm firmly through her heavy coat. "We can talk about this more later. Right now, I've got to meet someone. I'll pick you up at noon tomorrow. By then, you'll see how silly you were about this whole thing." Nevers started to move away. "And you'll be fifty dollars richer."

As he disappeared, Annie heard him coughing uncontrollably. She wondered if he were meeting another girl, maybe the waitress from the St. Regis cafeteria. Trying not to make a spectacle of her grief, she swallowed hard as the streetcar came on with the sound of an approaching migraine.

* * *

Annie sat on her vanity bench that evening, staring at the mirror. She had put on her usual makeup, then added extra eyeliner, shadow, and rouge. She had just circled her lips a second time to make them fuller. Holding the gold cylinder in her hand, Annie knew she had still not achieved the look Nevers had ordered. "Tart up a bit." The line had broken her spirit.

Annie finally realized Nausica was right. Herald Nevers wielded a kind of power over her. She was helplessly in love with him and would do almost anything for him. "Almost," she reminded herself. Hoping he would never ask more of her than tonight, she picked up the compact for the third time and added more rouge.

That night, Frank Webster introduced his beauty to all his friends. Some wore elaborate costumes. Others dressed in hats and tails, their bejeweled women showing off expensive gowns. Politicians, businessmen, socialites—they were all nice to Annie. Webster, too, was as well-mannered as a prom date. Somehow, though, Annie felt invisible, like she mattered to no one talking with her. Certainly, they meant nothing to her. She merely went through the motions in order to reach the other side of the evening and be with Nevers the following day.

Early the next afternoon, hung over from bracing herself with so many drinks the previous night, Annie studied her natural face in the looking glass. Compared to the mask she had taken off in the small hours of the morning, it seemed washed out. She was to meet Nevers at his house that afternoon. He had called and said he was too sick to pick her up. As she topped off her outfit with one of the Christmas hats and looked in the mirror, she noticed she had put on more makeup than usual, but it was too late to tone it down.

Annie was glad to have her own automobile. Without having to exchange pleasantries with streetcar passengers, she could let her thoughts unspool as they pleased. After stepping up from waitress to manager, she had come to realize how much she detested being cheerful for people she otherwise had no reason to smile at.

She knocked on Herald's door several times before a stranger's voice from upstairs commanded her to enter. The man at the head of the stairs was Herald, but Annie had never seen him like this. He talked in a raspy croak, and he was in a bad mood, clearly irritated by the vocal debility.

"How'd it go?" he asked, conserving his words. The effort of speaking visibly strained him. Nevers, leaning on the banister, stared at her with baggy eyes.

"Better than I expected," Annie said. She was careful to tell him what he wanted to hear.

"Good." He turned and shuffled into the bedroom. In the half light, Annie saw several spent cough-syrup bottles lying on their sides on the night table.

"Are you all right, Herald?" Annie touched him on the sleeve of his robe. He slung her arm away. His lips encrusted with pink and white, he sat on the bed and drained the last standing bottle. She stepped to the bathroom for a washcloth. There were two empty bottles in the trash can and another half-full on the back of the toilet. Viscous drops of red liquid spotted the sink and floor. Some of them looked like blood.

Returning with the damp cloth, Annie asked Nevers if he wanted her to call a doctor. An angry wave of his hand told her what he thought of the idea. Annie felt the muscles clench all over her body. She didn't want to say anything to upset him again. She put the cloth on the bedside table where he could reach it. She sat on the far end of the bed and waited. Nevers picked up the facecloth and worked it across his mouth, then flopped it on the nightstand. His head turned as his eyes scanned the room. They fell briefly on Annie, then moved towards the bathroom. He reminded her of a sleepwalker. Without looking at her, Nevers spoke in a raw whisper.

"The banker wants a hundred-dollar night and I need the money." With almost no light of recognition in them, Nevers turned his vacant, emotionless eyes on Annie.

"Ante up, Annie. It's time to Annie-up."

Annie's heart hammered with fear. She would never do what he wanted, but if she didn't, he would reject her. She knew that.

In a grieving voice, she said, "Herald, you're killing me. Don't you realize that? I can't do that, and I can't live without you."

Nevers had no intentions of arguing with her. His voice was almost gone.

"Ten times your old salary." He swallowed. "That's what I said a year ago." He coughed. "Well. Here you are."

Annie leaned her face into her hands and sobbed.

"Please, don't do this to me. You know I won't do it."

Nevers hated the girl for her weakness. He looked at her with disgust. "You think this is the worst I can do to you?" He paused as if concocting an especially potent dose of venom. "You sniveling little wench, I've only brought you half way."

Annie's sobbing transformed to a long wail of pain.

"I won't do it," she cried. "I won't do it."

Annie ran from the bedroom, down the stairs, and out the door onto the sunlit lawn.

* * *

"Have you talked with him?" she sobbed into the phone.

"Yes," Burk said. "He's sick."

"He's more than sick. He looks like death."

"Annie, don't you understand what's happened?"

Annie was trying to blow her nose. "Dno," she said.

"He fell off the wagon. He's gotten addicted to the alcohol in the cough syrup."

"Oh, God," Annie said. It had never occurred to her. "What can we do to help him?"

"*We* can't do anything," Burk said. "*You* need to do several things."

"Tell me." She was willing to do anything to help Nevers.

"First, *you* need to stop drinking. You're not helping yourself by staying half drunk most of the time."

Annie interrupted him. "I can't stand it otherwise."

"Listen to me," Burk said. "The second thing you need to do is leave New Orleans as fast as you can. Tonight, if possible."

"I can't do that, Arkie. Herald needs me. I've got the restaurant–."

Burk lost his patience. "To hell with the restaurant! Don't you understand? Herald is sick. He's going down, Annie. And he'll bring you down with him if you don't clear out. You can't help him at this point. You need to save yourself."

14

April 1939

Burk promised Annie he would check on Nevers. From Herald's house, Burk drove straight to Terra Incognita.

"Can you take care of things for a minute, Djurgis?"

The chef lifted his spatula. "Jes, Miss Annie. Sure ting."

Annie and Burk stepped out onto the walk skirting the lake side of the restaurant. To the east, men at Pontchartrain Beach were working in a last flurry before its grand opening the next day.

"It's worse than I thought," Arkie said, gazing out over the choppy water. "He won't even admit he's hooked again. He just keeps buying those idiotic bottles of cough syrup." He turned and faced Annie. "He's near the bottom. It won't be pretty when he hits."

* * *

Annie's days were filled with pandemonium for a week after the Pontchartrain Amusement Park opened. The restaurant teemed with tourist traffic. In a single day, receipts increased tenfold. Terra Incognita was no longer unknown territory.

Annie called Herald several times during the week to share with him the success of his business venture. Because of his voice, Annie assumed, Nevers didn't answer the phone. By Friday, she worried that he was unable to answer it. Anticipating the flood of new customers, Annie had hired five new waitresses, an assistant chef, and a full-time cashier. Friday, she turned the reins over to the evening crew and drove to Herald's.

From the curb, Annie observed the house. The second-story windows were dark. On the front porch by the door sat three grocery bags of empty cough syrup bottles. A dog had gotten into one and scattered its contents across the boards.

Annie was about to knock when she noticed the door ajar. She heard a fluttering sound at her feet and glanced down. A large cockroach working its way out of the neck of a bottle finally freed itself. It stopped and casually cleaned one feeler, then the other. Then, as if late for an important appointment, it scurried across the threshold into the house.

Annie shivered and clenched her fists. After her chill subsided, she stepped into the front room and hit the light switch. The roach was nowhere in sight. Focusing on the foot of the stairs, she passed through the room quickly.

Something, it suddenly struck her, wasn't quite right. The room was too tidy. She stopped and pivoted. The walls were bare. The painting and the silver dollar collection. Annie knew instantly that Nevers had sold them to slake his addiction.

Upstairs, she heard a cooing babble coming from Herald's bathroom, a burbling version of "Rock of Ages." Through the nearly closed door, she saw his bare leg on the white tile. The bedroom was dark except for a slash of light cutting across the room. On the bedside table next to a fifth of Old Crow—he had finally reached that point—sat two small pink horseshoes.

Annie stepped to the nightstand to inspect the objects. She turned one over. They were Herald Nevers' perfect teeth. She drew her hands to her breasts and closed her eyes. He wore dentures and she never knew it.

Annie's eyes opened onto the false teeth. They appeared broken. Looking more closely, she noticed two empty molar sockets. Nevers had extracted the gold teeth. A child-like sob came from the bathroom.

Annie knew it was time to turn and face the truth at last.

In the bright cubicle, Nevers sat on the floor in his underwear, one leg straight out, a knee clutched to his chest. Head down, he was staring at an object on the floor.

"Herald," Annie called tenderly.

The man looked up. Annie was startled at the darkness of his face. Stubble covered his cheeks like a black mask. The room smelled acridly of vomit. Nevers propped himself on thin arms, and his lips worked around a caved-in mouth. He stared at her out of swollen, fiery eyes, then returned his gaze to the floor.

"Tarnished," he mumbled.

"What?" Annie said. "I couldn't make out what you said."

"Tarnished." He plucked a medallion from the floor and held it up.

His arm wavered. Annie took the silver dollar from his trembling fingers. Herald's lips bubbled out a whimpering cry. "Eighteen ninety-three O. Rarest one. Tarnished." He shook his head at the floor, then looked up in amazement. "And do you know why? Hm?" He pointed at her accusingly. "You know why? No. You don't know, do you? Well, I'll tell you why." He lost track of his thoughts. "You know why?"

Annie shook her head at the pitiful man.

"Well, I'll tell you why." He pounded his fist weakly on the floor once. "I looked at it." He lifted his eyes. "All I did was look at it. And you know what happened?"

"No," she said softly. "What happened?"

"Tarnished." He swung his arm at the whole world. "And you know why? Hmm?"

"No, why?"

"Breaved." He licked his lips and spoke more carefully. "Breathed on it." He looked at her with sad anger. "Ain't that sumpin? Uncircalated and I breaved on it and tarnished it. The most beautiful coin I ever saw." His eyes welled over with tears. "Most beautiful thing I ever saw."

"Come on," Annie said, reaching down for him. "Let me help you to bed."

His arm looked as if it were being hoisted by a pulley. The dead weight of the man was unmoved.

"Help me," Annie said. "I can't get you up by myself."

Nevers pushed with his other hand on the floor. He got to one knee. His throat made a heaving sound and he turned toward the toilet, then lifted a finger.

"False alarm," he said. "False alarm."

Annie escorted him to the bed and returned to the bathroom for a washcloth. Nevers was holding the Old Crow when she reached the bedside. She tried to take the bottle from him. He waved her away.

"Gotta have it," he said bluntly. "Die if I don't."

"Herald." Annie called as if to someone down a well. "Do you know what's happened to you?"

He drank from the bottle and replaced it carefully on the nightstand.

"Had some bad luck."

"No," she said with firm calm.

"Yes. Had some bad luck. Thought I'd rally, but having a little trouble."

"It's not bad luck," Annie said. "You're on a bender."

He shot her an angry look.

"I know that. I know it, _____." He gazed at her vacantly. "What's your name?" He made a soundless snapping motion with his fingers. "Annie! You don't have to tell me that." He looked at her to make sure. "Right?"

"Yes," she confirmed. "Do you know where you are?"

Nevers looked around the room. "Hum." He rubbed his face with both hands and glanced around for something lost. His eyes lighting on the dentures, he picked them up and worked them into his mouth. Then he tested them. "Home. Home." He looked at Annie. "Home."

"I'm here to help you, Herald. Listen to me. You can always start over. Remember? That's what you told me. No matter how bad things get, you can start a new life."

Nevers laughed. "You can't help me." He glared at her defiantly. "Only God can help me," he said. "Only God." He pointed to the bottle. "You know what you're dealing with? You can't beat that stuff by yourself." He looked at her. "I lied to you. I didn't beat it on my own the first time. I had to ask God to help me."

"I understand," Annie said.

Nevers wagged his finger at her. "No. You don't. Not till you been there." Nevers looked at the bottle. "But not this time. I don't want God's help. I won't *let* God help me. I hate God because I *need* God. Otherwise, it's All a big Nothing." Nevers swallowed a belch and held an uplifted finger to Annie. "T. Van Mahorn." They both looked at the bottle. "T. Van Mahorn, some-nov-a-bitch."

Annie handed him the facecloth. Nevers wiped his mouth and threw the rag on the nightstand. "You know who I am?"

"You're someone I love who's hurting."

He waved her answer away. "I'm nothing," he said. "A punk." He said it as if it were the last thing he would ever need to say. He eased himself back on the bed and lay down, covering his eyes with a forearm. He chuckled. "Only when you become nothing can you become anything." He lifted his spare arm. "T. Van Mahorn." The arm fell exhausted onto the bed. "Son of a bitch."

Annie touched his arm. "You can do it again, Herald."

"A punk," Nevers said. "The tragedy of a punk who could have been a hero." In a motion quick with insight, his arm moved to reveal his eyes. He looked at Annie. "You think I'm a bad man, don't you?" He shook his head. "No. No one can judge me till they walk in my shoes."

Nevers replaced the arm over his eyes.

"If there had only been a war in my time. It's much easier to fight evil when it's coming at you head on." He peered at Annie from beneath his arm. "You know that? Much easier than to make a good life on your own. I mean, what do you do? Without a war, you can do anything you want. But it's hard. No focus." He rested his arm over his eyes again. For a long while, he didn't move. Annie thought he had fallen into an alcoholic sleep. "Punk!" he blurted.

"Herald." Annie touched his arm. "Let me help you. I can get you a doctor. We can take you to a hospital and help you dry out."

The words stirred his wrath. Nevers hated himself for his weakness, hated Annie for her kindness. He sat up, flinging imaginary sheets from his legs.

"Don't you understand?" he spat. He pointed at her. "Don't you understand who I am? I make nice girls into hookers. That's my job. Bliss, Nausica, Angelica. I gave them their names. I made them what they are." Nevers wiped his mouth with a phantom sleeve. "Whores. You, too, Annie. Annie Beatrice. Hah! You're nothing but a spittoon for my pecker snot."

Annie struck him on the chest with a fist.

"No!" she said. He fell to the bed like a loosely stuffed scarecrow. Annie hit him repeatedly. "That's not true. You know that's not true. We had something more than that."

Nevers defended himself against the onslaught. When she tired of striking him, he said in a voice that sounded utterly sober, "Go away. Leave me alone. Go!"

Annie fled the room sobbing.

And went straight to Burk. He nodded as she described the scene. She said they had to get Herald to a hospital.

"Fine," he said angrily. "But that's only half of it. You've got to kill him off in your head before he brings you down. The way he treats you won't change just because he climbs back on the wagon. He'll drag you through the muck just like he did Nessic. I know. I saw it. I was there."

Annie knew he was right.

"I love him," she said as if stating a fact that would end all arguments about this or any other topic.

"You do understand, don't you?" Burk said. "You're addicted to him just like he's hooked on the booze."

"I know it," she said with resignation.

"I can get you through this if you'll let me, Annie. But I'll have to show you some things you won't like." Burk looked out the window of his hotel room. "But if you can live through it, you'll come out in the clear." His look asked her if she had the strength for it.

"I'll try," Annie said weakly.

* * *

The next day, Burk had a doctor friend take Nevers to the hospital. Annie and Burk watched from down the street. Nevers went screaming and kicking as two black orderlies manhandled him down the steps into a waiting car.

"It won't work," he yelled. "I'll go back to my booze like a dog to its vomit. T. Van Mahorn son of a bitch!"

When the car disappeared, they entered the house. Burk stepped into the bedroom ahead of Annie. He scanned all around the room with a pointing finger.

"Notice anything unusual?"

"No. Looks the same to me."

Burk walked to the door and looked down the hall. "Come here." He waved her to the threshold. "You know what's in this next room?"

Annie shook her head.

"You won't like it," Burk said. He slapped the wall button of the bedroom, sending it into darkness. He grabbed the locked knob and jerked the door hard toward its hinges, away from the jamb where the bolt was lodged in the strike plate. The house shuddered. The second time he pulled, the door popped open. He extended his hand, indicating that Annie should enter first.

In the darkened room, she noticed four barstools situated under a countertop jutting from the left wall. To her right was a crisply made bed. Beside it, on a small wet bar, were liquor bottles and downturned glasses on a clean white towel.

"Sit down," Burk said. Annie approached the near chair, checking the floor for roaches. She looked back at Burk. "Sit on the stool and don't move."

Annie put her foot on the lowest rung and hoisted herself onto the tall perch. The toe of her shoe hit a heavy canister with a brassy sound. In front of her was an ashtray full of butts. She pushed it aside with the back of her hand.

Burk's voice called to Annie. "Ready!?"

"For what?"

Burk turned on the bathroom light in the next room. Herald's bedroom became visible on the wall in front of her. Annie reached out like a person in darkness, unsure of where the wall began. Her fingers collided with the cold, smooth surface. She saw Burk's figure in the bathroom doorway. In a few moments, he was standing beside her.

It finally hit home. Annie was on the other side of a large mirror. Against her will and without her knowledge, she had been made into a kind of prostitute. Men had paid to watch her make love with Herald Nevers, men sitting in the very chair she was in.

She folded her arms on the bar and rested her forehead on the wood. Her lips were trembling like those of a small child about to cry. The muscles in her legs and arms quivered weakly.

"I think I'm going to throw up," she said.

With his foot, Burk scooted a spittoon into view. Annie leaned over and retched into the receptacle. Beneath the counter, she saw three more of the brass cuspidors. As soon as their purpose became clear, Annie refused the image. She would not allow it to develop and stay in her mind. After she had recovered and washed her face, Annie questioned Burk.

"Have *you*, Arkie? Have you ever watched him with a woman?"

Burk turned his head down. "Yes," he said.

Annie didn't want to ask him the next question, but she needed to know the answer.

"Me?" She looked away from him.

He said nothing.

"Me? Tell me." She glared directly at him.

"I didn't think I would ever know you like this. At the time, you were just another–. Believe me, Annie, I would never have done it if I knew I was . . ."

"What? Knew you were what?"

"Going to fall in love with you."

* * *

That night, for the first time in her life, Annie drank herself unconscious.

The next day, she called Nausica.

"Yes," Nausica admitted. "I've been on the bedroom side of that mirror when I didn't know about it. And then later, when I did know."

"For God's sake, Nessie, why?"

Her voice was flat and controlled. "It pays better when you know. You can exaggerate, and the men on the other side don't know you're aware of them. That's the turn-on for them, seeing an innocent young girl in an act of passion."

"Explain it to me, Nessie. I'm trying to understand."

Nausica did the best she could.

"It's men," she concluded. "They like to watch."

Annie drank herself to sleep that afternoon.

When she roused in the early evening, she was in the back seat of Arkie Burk's car. She sat up and looked over the seat. They were driving into the dying sun.

15

April 1939–January 1940

"You're addicted to him, that's why! I had to tear you from him just like we forced him from his drink. Now, get in the front seat so we can talk like two human beings."

Annie remained in the back. She glared at the passing scenery. A hawk on top of a telephone pole searched the ground for its next prey. Billboards advertised Burma shave, Chesterfield, Hiram Walker gin, Chevrolet.

"Morgan City 8 miles," one sign informed her.

A painted board misspelled supreme love: "God Forgivs."

There would be railroad crossings, Annie thought. Ferries. Drawbridges. When the car stopped, she would run.

Burk intercepted her thoughts.

"You try to run at a crossing and I'll chase you down and *tie* you in the back." He looked in the rearview mirror. "Hear?" They drove in silence for a while. "Annie?"

"Toni Jo! My name is Toni Jo Henry. Don't ever call me Annie again. You got that?"

"Good deal." Arkie smiled, knowing she had taken the first step toward healing herself.

Three miles later, Burk slowed for a swing bridge. Two cars were idling behind the yellow line.

Burk adjusted the mirror for a better view of Toni Jo.

"Gonna look funny, a pretty girl in the back seat of my car."

Her arms crossed, she had slid against the door at the far side of Burk. When their eyes met, she scowled and looked out the window. The car began braking.

"Turn your head," Toni Jo commanded. Her dress rustled as she clambered over the seat and landed in disarray. The car stopped. Burk turned the key off and lifted the clutch. He stared straight ahead. Out of the corner of his eye, he saw Toni Jo put her hand on the door handle.

When the crossing gate lifted five minutes later, she had still not spoken. Burk started the car and eased ahead.

"It was the only way, Annie—Toni Jo. You understand that, don't you? Toni Jo?"

"You can't watch me forever. The first chance I get, I'll head for New Orleans."

"And I'll come get you and bring you back. I won't let him do this to you."

"He's sick," she said defensively.

"Sicker than you think. It goes deeper than booze."

Toni Jo touched her lips. They were shriveled with dryness. Instinctively, she reached beside her.

"My purse."

"In the trunk," Burk said. "I threw what I could into a couple of suitcases. That's enough for anything you'll be doing in Lake Charles. It ain't New Orleans."

Toni Jo wrenched the mirror towards her and peered into it.

"God," she said, touching her hair. Her eyeliner had spread into two black eyes. She punched the button on the glove compartment. It slapped down, and she rifled through some papers searching for a Kleenex. Thrusting her fingers to the back, she felt the cool heft of a pistol barrel. She glanced at Burk.

"Here," he said, pulling a handkerchief from his shirt pocket.

She began to work on her face. "Did you even check on him?"

"Yes," Burk said. "He'll be sick for a few days."

"And then?"

"I don't know. He's a big boy. He can take care of himself."

* * *

Burk and Toni Jo sat on a blanket at the beach, puffs of cotton-candy clouds painted childlike on a too-blue sky. Three small sailboats scudded across Lake Charles. The only impressive object on the skyline was the Jean Lafitte bridge spanning the Calcasieu River.

"When you find yourself missing him, think about what he did to you. I don't want to be mean, Toni Jo, but the guy was a creep."

"You ran around with him," she returned.

"For kicks. But he was dangerous, and I knew it. I didn't plan to set up housekeeping with him."

On their outings, Burk and Toni Jo waded at the beach. They talked about Nevers, who he was and wasn't, what he did and why, how she could have been attracted to him and when she'd get over him.

"He's still here." She hit her chest lightly with a loose fist. "I have dreams about him, nightmares. And when I wake up, I feel sick because I'm dead-certain I'd go with him if he suddenly reappeared."

"You can beat it, Toni. I know you can." A week after the drive to Lake Charles, for simplicity, Burk had dropped Toni Jo's middle name.

Toni Jo looked at the man who had rescued her.

"I know I can, but that doesn't make it hurt any less. Believe me. Maybe if I could have hurt him. But I couldn't have. He was so pathetic." She stooped and picked up a yellow plastic shovel floating near the shore. "If he had been well, I think it would've been easier. I needed to slap him or shame him. Something. You know what I'm trying to say?"

"You needed revenge. But it wouldn't have worked. He wouldn't have been ashamed. Christ, he had the sweetest angel I've ever seen and he thought he could turn her–."

"You're the sweetheart." Toni Jo hugged his arm.

Burk raked his fingers through her hair. She was letting it grow. By May, she had a tonsure of burnished brown hair that met the black-brown like a muddy riptide.

Burk leaned over and kissed her on the cheek, then tried to move to her lips.

She turned away. "Arkie, don't. It's–. I can't. Not right now. I feel like I could never kiss another man. It's like he took the heart right out of me." Toni Jo looked at the kind man. "Maybe later, when I'm over this. I'll try, okay? That's all I can promise. You won't be mad if I can't, will you?"

Burk gazed into her eyes and shook his head.

"No."

* * *

Upon their arrival in Lake Charles, Toni Jo had stayed at Burk's house on Hodges until she found a room in a boarding house on Bilbo. While Burk was at his lumberyard, Toni Jo window-shopped. They ate at seafood restaurants that seemed like lame imitations of those in New Orleans. They watched the Lake Charles Lakers play a preseason game. Toni Jo couldn't get interested.

Sitting in a booth on Saturday at MaryAnn's, a small, unpretentious diner a notch above the Two-Rat Cafe in DeRidder, Burk could see her languishing.

"Maybe if you went back to work," he suggested. "You could probably get a job here at MaryAnn's."

"Nah," she said, looking around. "I need a change of scenery. Something different."

Burk nodded. "I told you the pace would be slower in Lake Charles."

A burst of air chuckled from her lips.

"Yeah, but you didn't tell me it had *no* pace."

"Hey, it beats what came with the Big City."

"I know." Toni Jo leaned her head on his shoulders. "I know, Arkie. It's not your fault. It feels like the life went right out of me."

One thing Toni Jo did enjoy was driving up the Jean Lafitte bridge, then under the lacy steel canopy at its apex. The guardrails were decorated with crossed pirate pistols. She meant to count them some day. At the top, she slowed to take in the view of the Calcasieu River. It made her feel free and clean. In early evening, the refineries lit up like Christmas. Millions of blackbirds in undulating lines reaching to both horizons returned to their roosts after feeding all day in the rice fields. The sunset made her feel like she was on top of the world.

Almost every night, Toni Jo dreamed about the bridge. As she drove west, the grade became steeper and steeper until, near the pinnacle, cars lost their purchase and tumbled backwards. She wondered how the engineers could have been so dumb. Sometimes, the front wheels of her car would lift off the cement and she would awaken as the car began to fall. In other dreams, she reached the top only to discover that the bridge ended and she would awaken as her car plunged into nothingness.

Burk suggested Toni Jo visit her mother for a month.

"Maybe that will help. Get you grounded, you know?"

She was back within a week.

"Believe it or not, it's worse than here," she said.

One Sunday in early June, they watched a matinee feature of Laurel and Hardy in *Flying Deuces* at the Paramount Theatre. Toni Jo laughed twice. After the movie, the couple drove under the bridge and walked along the shore almost a mile towards town. "COLORED BEACH." The sign suggested they go no farther, but there was a commotion up ahead. As they neared the crowd clustered around a squad car, Toni Jo heard a dark woman wailing.

On the grassy sand lay a black man, his hands raised against an invisible attacker. A lean deputy in a khaki uniform directed the scene. Standing a full head above everyone else, he moved like a marionette, as if his joints had too much play in them from wear.

"Who's that?" Toni Jo asked.

"Sheriff's son," Burk replied. "Just a kid out of college and he's already his old man's number-one deputy."

The deputy's eye caught the lighter skin of the new spectators. He looked up.

"Arkie," he said nodding, officially serious.

"Slim," Burk returned. "What's the story?"

"Drowning. Second one this week. Shouldn't go in over their heads." He winked at Arkie, who chuckled at the private joke.

The deputy signaled to the attendants with his pencil. They grabbed the dead man's stiff arms and lugged him to the ambulance like a heavy suitcase.

* * *

Friday, Burk went to New Orleans on business. Toni Jo had asked to travel with him. Burk said it wasn't a good idea. Three months away from the city wasn't enough time to get over Nevers.

When Toni Jo shifted her attention from herself to Burk, a question sprang from her lips. "Do you plan to see Bliss?" The emotion surprised her. She was jealous.

"Yes." Toni Jo's face clouded with anger. "Of course not, Toni. Can't you tell when I'm joking by now?"

Sunday at sunset, Burk dropped by Toni Jo's room. He honked at the curb and she flew down the stairs.

Thirty minutes later, she sat before a pillaged banana split at the Borden's ice-cream parlor on Ryan.

"Well," Toni Jo said, "are you going to tell me, or do I have to ask?"

"No, I didn't see him."

"Did you look?"

"Yes."

"How hard?"

"He wasn't there, okay? I looked. The restaurant has a new owner and a new name. He vanished."

* * *

Toni Jo took a job at Muller's department store. The elevator had especially intrigued her. The operator, a wizened little man wearing an ill-fitting monkey suit, rarely looked at his passengers. He would hear a command, "Third floor," and turn the gray handle that reminded Toni Jo of the lever on a Coke machine. There were no indicators on the panel, yet the man, sometimes without observing the light between levels, stopped the booth precisely even with the floor each time. It was a job she could appreciate.

She lived mechanically through the scorching, humid summer and the long slide into autumn. A refreshing cool front in mid-October made the heat more oppressive than ever. As the Canadian fronts descended more frequently and lingered, the Louisiana countryside turned brown. Tallow trees died into arterial red and child-crayon yellow. Large sycamore leaves made wistful sounds as they rustled on their branches or children shuffled through windblown piles of them in the streets.

Toni Jo had nothing else to do and doubted she would find anyone better, so she married Arkie Burk in November. It was a loving but passion-less marriage. They discussed children. She didn't know if Burk knew about her abortion. She thought having a child might even the score.

It was a life.

Around Christmas, men began to compliment her. She wondered if marriage suited her so well that it created a noticeable change in her appearance.

"Have we met?" a young man would ask as she worked the elevator at Muller's.

In department store windows, she saw the reflections of men turning for a second look at her.

"I know I've seen you somewhere before."

"Aren't you Burton's daughter? No? Sorry, didn't mean to intrude."

They shook their heads and moved on.

* * *

In the Charleston Hotel's Cypress Room, Burk threw a New Year's Eve party for the office workers at Lake Area Lumber. For the first time in a year, Toni Jo Burk was happy.

In mid-January, Arkie made a week-long business trip to Houston. After work one evening, Toni Jo was searching for something to read on the shelves of their sitting room. With two hands, she pulled down a large, hardback copy of *Gone With the Wind*.

Since the novel had won Margaret Mitchell the Pulitzer Prize in 1937, people had been squawking about the impending movie. First, there had been the big fuss over who would play Scarlett. Then endless delays on the set. Finally, the picture was released. The critics said it was the greatest movie ever made. It would probably take another month to arrive in Lake Charles. Toni Jo decided that reading the novel would enhance her enjoyment of the film. She didn't want to leave a gap on the shelf and reached up to close the breach.

A novel caught on something behind it. Toni Jo pulled down several books to remove the obstruction. They were magazines. She counted as she retrieved them. Two, three, four. Attractive young women smiled at her from the covers. *Free Spirit. New Orleans Girls. Amour. C'est Bon.* She backed up. On the cover of *New Orleans Girls*, the woman smiling at her—it was Bliss.

Toni Jo set the bulky novel on the edge of a lower shelf and flipped pages until she located Bliss. In most of the photos, she wore bathing suits or sheer clothing that revealed the shape of her breasts. In a few, the bottoms of her breasts were exposed. Toni Jo read the captions at the head of Bliss's pictorial.

"Priscilla, a night clerk at the Hotel du Monde, formerly a London meter maid who ventured to America seeking her fortune as an actress. Has done some modeling. Does she look familiar? Give yourself a point. She's one of the Chesterfield girls."

Toni Jo smiled at the ridiculous lines. She turned to another girl and read, "Darlene, a college girl who likes fast cars, football games, and cool autumn nights with her boyfriends."

Toni Jo studied the face of the girl who would so freely reveal her looseness. A little on the pudgy side, Toni Jo thought. Probably couldn't get a man any other way. Amused, she turned to the next poseur.

"Jessica is a school teacher who likes to grade exams in her panties—

and nothing else! Watch out, Jessie, don't let the principal find out!"

Toni Jo laughed.

"Who writes these things?" she wondered aloud.

She looked at the next picture. It was a weak photograph. The light background blended into the woman's white hair. In the center of the print, slightly out of focus, Toni Jo's own face rose to meet her.

When she finished ripping the magazine apart and throwing it about the room in a screaming frenzy, she started on the others, then worked through two shelves, furiously casting books behind her, knocking over lamps and breaking a vase of artificial flowers. In the calm after her rage, she picked through the torn and crumpled pages littered across the floor, searching for parts of her body or face. With perverse curiosity, she decided she wanted to study each snapshot and read the captions to find out more about herself.

In most of the pictures, she was in the poses struck for Nevers at the picnic in City Park. In others, someone had doctored the negatives to remove the pondside background. In those, she sat on a beach at sunset. One cup of her bathing suit had slipped to show the dark half-moon of a nipple on a breast so voluptuous it looked ridiculously out of proportion to her slender head.

At the bottom of the page was the name of the magazine. *Amour.* Toni Jo thought she could find her face on other bodies in other magazines, but her stomach wasn't up to it.

As she gathered the sheets to throw them in the garbage, the process came together in her imagination. Nevers couldn't talk her into posing nude, so he put her face on other women's bodies.

Suddenly, Toni Jo knew the rest of her life would be easy. She now hated Herald Nevers.

16

February 14, 1940

Burk swore he had forgotten about the magazines. Before Nevers fell apart and was hospitalized, Arkie had bought the bundle from him because Bliss was featured in one, but now he no longer cared for her. He asked Toni Jo to forgive him.

For three days, Toni Jo slept in the spare bedroom. She didn't make love to Arkie for over a week. At least he's human, she thought. He had asked her forgiveness. That was more than Nevers had ever done.

One afternoon, Burk came home early and carried a dress box into the sitting room where his wife was reading.

"I brought you something."

"I see that."

"Don't you want to open it?"

"No thanks," she said, looking pleasantly at her husband. "I don't have to. Nothing in that box will change the way I feel about you." She smiled. "I just needed some time to get over those pictures."

It was the first time Toni Jo saw tears in her husband's eyes.

Arkie wanted to do something special for his wife for restoring their old harmony. He had seen her lugging the ponderous novel from room to room for over a week and suggested they drive to Houston for a gala opening of *Gone With the Wind*.

By a happy accident, the newly reconciled husband and wife were to see the movie on Valentine's Day. That Wednesday afternoon, Toni Jo put on her new dress and presented herself to Arkie. As they held each other tightly, Toni Jo looked at their image in the dresser mirror.

Ecstatically, she said, "It feels like a new beginning. For everything. Arkie, I'm so happy I could die in your arms."

Her husband laughed. "And leave me behind? I couldn't bear it."

"Let's go. I can't wait to see what everybody's been raving about for two years."

* * *

Three hours later, they sat in the Presidio Theatre waiting for curtain rise. Just before the scene everyone had been talking about, Toni Jo whispered in Arkie's ear.

"This is it."

Clark Gable said to Vivian Leigh, "Frankly, my dear, I don't give a damn." The audience gasped and Toni Jo giggled. How could they be so shocked, she wondered. But when the audience cried as Scarlett vowed against a blazing sunset never to go hungry again, she wept with them, profusely, into the second handkerchief Arkie had supplied her.

When the lights went up, the women felt foolish but justified in their happy grief for the maverick woman of the New South. The men cleared their throats and tried not to look at anyone as they casually touched their eyes.

For the first hour of the drive home, Toni Jo excitedly reviewed the movie's scenes, jumping back and forth in the movie's time, confusing actors with characters, speaking of Scarlett O'Hara, Clark Gable, Ashley Wilkes, and Olivia de Havilland.

As they drove through Liberty, Toni Jo said, "Wouldn't it have been grand to live back then, Arkie?" She didn't expect her husband to reply and didn't allow him the opportunity as she went on to talk about the burning-of-Atlanta scene, wondering how they had made it so realistic, "and those poor horses, you know *they* weren't acting, they were really afraid of the fire, do you think that's cruel, Arkie," and she didn't give him a chance to answer that question, either.

Toni Jo tensely recounted the scene where Scarlett shoots a Yankee deserter, then imitated Butterfly McQueen's squeaky voice saying, "I don't know nothing 'bout birthing babies."

By the time Arkie reached Beaumont, the emotional ups and downs of Scarlett and Rhett's story finally took their toll on his wife's nerves and she wound down to a happily fatigued mood. Slowly, Toni Jo slumped in the seat and fell asleep ten miles from Orange, leaving Arkie alone with his thoughts and the humming of tires on blacktop.

Arkie Burk could hardly believe his good fortune. While he watched sporadic lightning fulminating in the northeast, he took an inventory of

– 164 –

his life. He had a successful business, a beautiful wife, and would have children in no time. What more could a man want? The Germans were kicking up a stir in Europe, but that was a world away, and when Hitler went too far, they'd spank him back to the hinterlands in a minute. The country was finally climbing out of the Great Depression, and those boys in Washington were making sure it would never happen again. Earlier in the decade, J. Edgar Hoover's G-men had taken care of public enemies like Capone, Dillinger, Pretty Boy Floyd, and Baby Face Nelson, and the New Deal would take care of this problem. They weren't so dumb after all.

Burk caught himself smiling into the night and laughed at himself. He checked his wife to see if he had disturbed her slumber. She looked like a dark-haired angel. The lightning crackled across the sky like a spider web.

On the Texas side of the Sabine River, a lone man stood with a thumb in the air, holding his hat down against the wind. Burk had picked up speed to charge the steep bridge when his headlights revealed the hitchhiker. He let up on the accelerator and moved his foot toward the brake, then put it back on the accelerator. Suddenly, he felt sorry for the drifter about to get soaked. He had never been so content, and his happiness transformed into a feeling of generosity and compassion. He braked hard and passed the hitchhiker, then eased back until he came even with the man, who climbed into the back seat.

Burk stayed in second gear to the top of the bridge, where he shifted into third as he crossed the state line. He was going seventy when the car hit level ground with a bump, then settled into a dreamy float just as a pregnant cloud's water broke.

Burk adjusted the rearview mirror.

"You're a lucky man if I ever saw one."

"Guess so," the hitchhiker said as he took off his hat and ran his fingers through thinning hair. "Thanks for the ride."

"Don't mention it. I'm just going to Lake Charles."

"That's fine," the stranger said. "Much obliged."

"From around here?"

"Hereabouts."

When the lightning flashed, Arkie glanced in the mirror. The man didn't look too clean, but he was friendly enough. He had a week's growth of whiskers about to call itself a beard, and despite a gaunt face, his eyes seemed alert.

"Smoke?"

"Thanks, no."

"Don't feel obliged to talk," Arkie said. "Some don't like to. I can respect that."

The man nodded. "Thanks. I'm a man of few words."

Burk drove silently for fifteen minutes.

Toni Jo stretched and yawned. She gazed at her husband and smiled. "Are we getting close yet? I have to pee."

"Shh," Burk said, signaling over his shoulder with his thumb. "We got company."

Toni Jo peered over the back seat.

"Oh, sorry. No offense."

"Don't mention it," the stranger said.

She looked at Burk, who explained, "He's a man of few words."

"Oh." Toni Jo turned the radio on and skimmed around for a station. Even though the storm was behind them now, each lightning flash sparked through the speaker. She stopped at a song she liked, "Address Unknown," by The Ink Spots, then grew irritated at the bad reception. Finally she turned the radio off. She leaned back and rested her head. A sign read, "Lake Charles 5 mi." Toni Jo closed her eyes and resigned herself to the wait. She had almost drifted off when the stranger drew her back with a song. Toni Jo's eyes lifted in horror.

He was humming "Rock of Ages."

Her heart pounded. She locked her head straight forward, telling herself it couldn't be him. A lump of anxiety rose in her throat.

She swallowed and tried to think what the stranger had looked like. Scruffy beard, thinning hair, skinny. It couldn't be him. The stranger continued to hum, distracting her thoughts. The tone was familiar, with a difference.

Toni Jo looked at the glove box. She convinced herself it was him. They were approaching Lake Charles. She would have to do something fast.

"Arkie, take this road up here on the right." Her voice trembled.

"Toni, we're almost there. Can't you wait?"

"Take it!" she screamed.

The stranger quit humming. Burk knew something was dreadfully wrong. It had been nearly a year since he had seen his wife in such a state. He turned onto the shell road.

"Where?" he said.

Toni Jo scanned until she saw a drive leading into a rice field. "There! Stop by that tractor."

The car halted and she leapt from her door. Arkie had barely shut his when she clutched him by the shirt.

"It's him. The hitchhiker. It's Herald."

"Herald?" Burk squinted at the dark windows. "Don't be absurd, Baby. It couldn't–."

"Listen to me!" She yanked his shirt with the strength of a man. "I *know* him. I'm telling you, it's him." In a loud whisper, Toni Jo said, "Do something!"

"First, we've got to find out if it's him. What do you want me to do?"

"Kill him! I want you to kill the lousy bastard." It was the first time Burk had ever heard his wife curse.

"Don't be ridiculous," he said.

"Get him out here so we can look at him," Toni Jo ordered. Burk opened his door. He reached in and pulled the keys from the ignition.

"Say, buddy, sorry for the trouble, but would you mind stepping out for a minute? It seems we got a little problem."

The stranger opened his door and stepped into the night.

"Come around here," Burk directed him. "Okay, stop there."

The stranger stood in the floodlight of the car's far beam. A fine mist drifted in the yellow cone. The man was stooped and haggard, his hair much thinner than it had seemed inside the car. His suit was clean but ill-fitting.

Burk spoke quietly to Toni Jo. "It's too short for him. And his hair was thicker than that."

"I don't care. It's him. Tell him to take off his shirt. He's got tattoos."

Burk answered softly in a high pitch. "Are you out of your mind? He's just an old bum."

"Herald," she accused. "Take off your shirt!"

The man looked across the light. He glanced down at his shirt and back at the woman. Leaving his coat on, he unbuttoned the shirt.

"Open it!" Toni Jo called.

The stranger flared one side of the shirt out. Toni Jo squinted across the lights. His chest was dark and sickly looking.

Toni Jo glanced up at her husband. "I don't care," she said. "It's him. I know it's him."

"Toni, come to your senses."

Her anger revived. "Come here!" she commanded the stranger. The man moved through the light. "It's you, isn't it?"

"Ma'am–."

"Don't ma'am me, you bastard con man. Open your shirt." The stranger looked down. He opened his shirt and looked at Toni Jo. His chest was crisscrossed with ridges of scars.

Burk winced. "Toni, there's no tattoo there."

"You idiot! He took it off." She glared at the stranger. "Not this time, you swine. You're tricky, but not this time. Take off your coat. *And* your shirt."

The man pulled them off simultaneously. The coat dropped to the muddy ground. One side of the shirt remained in his trousers.

"Turn around!"

The man stared at her placidly, as if he would never harm a soul, then pivoted slowly, moving one foot, then the other, deliberately, like an old man. His back was a field of swollen scars.

"Why did you take them off?"

The stranger turned around and gazed calmly into Toni Jo's eyes.

"Because it was an abomination in the sight of the Lord."

"What–? What do you think I am, an idiot?"

"Herald," Burk said, "is it really you?"

Without moving his head, the man shifted his eyes to Burk. "Much obliged for the ride, Arkie. I'll be moving along now." He stooped to gather his coat.

"No!" Toni Jo said. "You're not getting away this time. Stay right there."

Careful to avoid him, she walked around the back of the car and opened her door. She popped the glove compartment, reached past the papers, and grabbed the pistol by its barrel.

When she reached Burk, she held the grip towards him.

"Here. Kill him."

"Hey–. Watch–. Give me that thing. Are you out of your mind?" He took the gun from her.

"Yes, I'm out of my mind. I want you to kill the slimy bastard for what he did to me. Now!"

Burk pointed the revolver away from his body at the ground. He realized his wife was too disturbed to reason with.

"Don't be a fool, Toni. Get in the car."

She shook her head. "He's not getting away. Not this time."

"And I'm not shooting him, so get ahold of yourself." He reached for her. She tried to evade his grasp.

"Let go!" she yelled.

He gripped her tighter and pleaded, "Let's talk, okay? Let's just talk."

Toni Jo was breathing hard. She seemed to calm down. "Okay, what do you want to talk about?"

"Let me just ask him a few questions." He looked at Herald Nevers. "Okay?" She nodded. "Herald, what are you doing here? How'd you get like that?" Burk pointed at the scars with the pistol.

Nevers looked at his chest. "I erased them with a soldering iron."

Arkie's head jerked and he whispered, "God." Nevers smiled. "What you did to Toni was wrong. You know that." Arkie's words were part question, part accusation.

"Yes. I've asked God's forgiveness."

Toni Jo stepped forward. "He's conning you, don't you see that?"

Burk held Toni Jo back with his arm and glared at her. "Let me handle this, all right?" He looked at Nevers. "That right, Herald? This a con job?"

"No con job," he said. "It's the truth. Jesus is the Truth. He saved me from myself."

"Liar!" Toni Jo said.

Burk held her back. "All right, Toni, just hold on. Let's move away and talk about this awhile."

"He'll run off," she said. "He's conning you just long enough to get a jump. You turn around, he'll be gone in a flash."

"All right," Burk said. "Let me think a minute."

Lightning flashed feebly in the south.

"We can tie his hands while we talk. Okay? Will that suit you?"

"No! He'll run. Make him take his clothes off, then tie him to the car."

"Toni–."

"Make him!"

Arkie glanced from Nevers to Toni Jo and back to Nevers. "Herald," he said. It was half plea, half command.

Nevers bent over and unlaced his shoes. He pulled one off. Balancing on one leg, he pulled the sock off and put it in the shoe, then stepped carefully into the cold mire. He took off the other shoe and sock, then unfastened his belt and trousers. Nevers looked at Burk and Toni Jo. He turned around and let the trousers fall to his ankles.

"Pick them up and put them in the trunk," Toni Jo said to Arkie. She kept an eye on the naked man while Burk did her bidding and returned with a rope. "Tie him up," she ordered.

His back to Toni Jo, Nevers spoke for the first time of his own accord. "I'm not the same man you knew, Annie. I'm a new man."

She went into a frenzy. "Liar! You're exactly the same. And my name is Toni Jo, you bastard. Annie was your whore."

The man turned.

In the fog-clouded lights, his heavy genitals looked out of proportion to the rest of his emaciated body. Burk was enraged at this man who had been with his wife. He felt diminished in her eyes. Humiliated.

Seeing the naked man who had let others watch while he used his equipment on her, Toni Jo lost her senses.

"You maggot, slime, shit, goddamn bastard shit sonofabitch sliming whoremaker!" She turned on her husband. "Kill him! Kill him now!"

Burk raised the gun and pointed it at Herald Nevers' chest. He pulled the hammer back and held his breath.

"Don't do this, Arkie," Nevers said. "I'm not worth it."

Toni Jo moved towards her husband.

"He's a con man, Arkie. Don't let him fool you. Shoot him." Burk continued to aim at Nevers. Toni Jo lost her patience. "Kill him. If you love me, kill him. Do it."

Do it—the phrase reminded her of what Nevers had tried to make her say. It triggered a savage vengeance in her.

"Do it!" she screamed. "Do it!" She reached for the pistol. It fired.

Shocked, afraid he had hit Nevers, Burk loosened his hold on the pistol. Toni Jo wrenched it from his hand. She aimed the heavy piece at the man's bare chest.

"This is the only thing you ever deserved," she said.

"Annie," Nevers said.

"Toni Jo! Goddamn you, my name is Toni Jo Henry."

"Toni Jo, don't do this. You're a better person than this. Don't let me do this to you."

Toni Jo wanted Nevers to fear her, but he was calm. For a moment, she thought his conversion might be real. It was an irony she could not tolerate, that he was forgiven and free.

"Down!" she yelled. "Get down on your knees."

"Toni," Burk said.

She turned the pistol on her husband. "Stay back, or I swear to God I'll shoot you, too."

"Toni," he repeated.

"Toni Jo! Can't anybody get that right? My name is Toni! Jo! Henry!"

Burk moved back a step. His wife was obviously deranged.

Toni Jo swung the pistol back to Nevers and trained it on his chest.

"Get down in the mud," she commanded.

Nevers knelt down.

Toni Jo stared at him. "Herald Nevers," she began. Then wildly in her mind—*No, not Herald. Not Harold, or even Harry Nilson. Not anymore. He was right that time when he was drunk and said he was nothing.*

Toni Jo forced herself to walk slowly towards him, as if she were sneaking up on an especially large cockroach for a disgusting but necessary extermination.

The man, naked, kneeled before her in the misty yellow light.

When she reached him, she pressed the snub-nosed .38 against his forehead and pulled the trigger, spattering his last thoughts, gray and warm, onto her face and dress.

The man fell back in the mud with a wet slap.

Burk screamed, "Jesus God, Toni Jo!"

PART TWO

For history records the patterns of men's lives, they say:
who slept with whom and with what results,
who fought and who won,
who lived to lie about it afterwards.

Ralph Ellison, *Invisible Man*

17

February 14, 1940–January 1941

Burk looked at the naked man lying in the mud, curls of steam rising from his limp body in the chill night air. Nevers' left hand was raised above his head as if he had a question for the teacher and would patiently hold it there until she called on him. Toni Jo stood over Nevers, aiming the pistol at his chest.

"Good God, look what you've done, Toni."

"Is he dead? Or should I shoot him again?"

Burk lunged at his wife. He grabbed the pistol and wedged a finger between the hammer and its home. Toni Jo released the gun and expelled a long-held breath.

"Finally," she said. "I can live."

"No, Toni. This can't happen. We've got to get him to a hospital."

"Are you out of your mind? That man," she pointed to Nevers, "that *animal* raped your wife's innocence, and you want to bring him to a hospital?" She glared at her husband. "You do that, and I'll leave you in a split second. No, I'll kill you. I swear to God, I'll kill you."

They looked at the body as if leaving the decision to Nevers. His right arm, flung outward, drew slowly toward his side.

"He's alive!" Burk said. "We've got to get him to a hospital."

Burk put the pistol on the hood and stooped next to the body. He swiveled Herald's face toward the car lights. A thick stream of blood issued from a neat hole low on his forehead. His one open eye wandered aimlessly about.

"He's dead!" Toni Jo yelled. "He's just twitching like a frogleg in hot grease. Roach bastard son of a bitch! Leave him!" Toni Jo screamed. "What would you tell them when we got there?"

Burk dragged Herald's body to the car.

"Stop! I *want* the son of a bitch dead! Can't you see that?"

Burk stared at his wife as if he couldn't believe he was married to someone who would say such a thing.

"Help me, Toni. Please."

He propped his friend's muddy feet on the running board and climbed in the back seat. He began to pull the man in without his wife's help. The labor was difficult until the torso reached the seat. Then, the mire acting as a lubricant, the body slid easily into the car. Only the head and arms protruded from the doorway. Crouching, Burk made his way to Herald's head. For support, he put his hand on the dying man's chest. He was about to step out of the car when Toni Jo appeared.

She pushed the pistol into the car.

"Toni!"

The gun's muzzle spat blue and yellow fire. Burk felt the hot powder sting his cheek. The concussion deafened and confused him. His hand went numb. He inspected it under the dome light. The slug had taken a bite from the outside of his index finger. A dark oval seemed to be painted on the scarred chest of Herald Nevers.

"There! He's dead. Now let's get rid of him."

"Oh God, oh God," Burk said. "This is terrible."

"This is *not* terrible," Toni Jo corrected him. "This is exactly what the bastard deserved. Now let's dump him and go."

Burk whimpered with fright. "We can't."

"Why not?" Toni Jo glanced around. "Let's throw him in that rice canal."

"Too many people know him," Burk argued. "With scars like that, on his chest and back, someone'll recognize him."

Intent on the problem, neither husband nor wife noticed the car coming up the road. It halted at the entrance to the field. The driver rolled down his window and called out.

"Say, bub, need some help?"

Burk yanked Herald's arms into the back seat.

"No!" he yelled from inside the car. He stepped out, planting one foot on the ground while holding Herald's head inside with his left thigh. He wondered if the man could see their clothes smeared with mud and blood. "Just–. Just having a family quarrel."

"Sorry," the stranger said. "Didn't mean to intrude. But you might cut your lights so's you won't run your batt'ry down."

"Thanks," Burk said. "I'll do that."

The car started easing away.

"Arkie?" the voice called. "Is that you?"

Burk froze.

"Arkansas?"

Toni Jo whispered fiercely, "Say something!"

"Johnny C.?" Burk's voice was noticeably weak.

"Yeah, it's me. Sure I can't help you?"

"No! We got it under control." He tried to laugh. "I'll have her in line in no time."

"Well," the man said. "I live just up the road on the right if you need me, hear? And you might oughta cut them lights out before you kill your batt'ry."

"Will do," Burk said. Toni Jo quickly leaned in the window and pushed the light switch. "Thanks!" Burk called.

"You bet," his friend said, pulling away.

Toni Jo and Arkie stood quietly in the dark. Burk moved away from the car. Herald's head hit the door frame with a heavy waterlogged sound.

Burk spoke first. "What are we going to do now?"

"They can't link us if they never find the body."

"Look at the car," Burk said. "It's covered with mud. And blood. It'll never come clean."

"You can sell the car," Toni Jo said. "In Texas. You sell it to someone cheap enough, they'll be glad to shut their trap."

"It's not that easy," Burk countered. "People knew Herald. I don't care what he looks like now. Somebody'll notice he's gone."

"So?"

"They'll check into his things."

"And?" Burk was silent. "And?" Toni Jo repeated.

Burk spoke suddenly, with anger. "And I've been in touch with him, all right? Christ, he was my friend. What was I supposed to do, ditch him because he got drunk? He was my friend."

Toni Jo stared at the darkened figure of her husband.

"You son of a bitch," she whispered. She thought for a while. "Big deal," she finally said. "So I know another son of a bitch. Let's dump the body and get back to town so I can get the hell out of your life as fast as I can."

"It's not that easy," Burk said.

"The hell it ain't."

"I've written him a couple of checks. Several checks. For almost a year. They're sure to question me." Burk surveyed the car. "It'll never work."

Toni Jo clutched his shirt. "You coward. Don't you do this to me." She shook him like a doll. "Straighten up, you hear me? We can fix this." Toni Jo could see that Burk was in shock. "Get him out of the car," she ordered.

Burk moved mechanically. As he tugged at one of Herald's muddy arms, his hands slipped. Cupping one hand under Herald's armpit and gripping his hair with the other, he slid the body onto the ground and came away with a hank of snarled hair stuck to his muddy palm.

Toni Jo called from nearby. "Over here!"

Burk soon realized he couldn't pull the dead weight of the slippery corpse through the claylike muck. He reached into the car and turned on the headlights to search for the rope. After making a few turns around the corpse's hands, he began to drag Nevers toward his wife's voice. The rope slipped off the mud-slick hands. Fearing another car, Burk tied the rope around his friend's neck and dragged him onto the levee.

"Here!" Toni Jo called.

When Burk appeared, she grabbed the rope and helped him pull Nevers down the narrow cow path on top of the levee. Fifty yards later, she said, "Stop!"

Burk put his hands on his knees to catch his breath. They had stopped before a pump house. Toni Jo lifted the dead man's arms and slung him to the side of the levee. The corpse hit with a slap and slowly slid down the embankment, its limbs moving like a troubled sleeper's, then halted in a contorted position.

Winded, Toni Jo tried to conserve her words.

"In the pipe," she said. She started down the levee and slipped to her knees, coming to rest against the corpse. In fear, disgust, and anger, she hit Nevers on the chest. "Goddamn you, Arkie, get down here and let's get this over. I don't plan to spend the rest of my life in jail for this piece of shit."

At the base of the levee, they looked into the maw of an irrigation pipe.

"I don't know," Burk said.

"He's *got* to fit," Toni Jo said. "We'll *make* him fit if we have to cut the bastard into pieces."

Burk scooped mud into the pipe for lubrication, then shoved his old friend in headfirst. The task done, he built a mound over the feet at the opening of the pipe, thinking the ploy might give them a few extra days.

Climbing the levee's steep grade, they both fell several times. At the car, they began to scrape the mud from their clothing.

"What the hell difference does it make?" Burk said in exasperation. "Get in."

He turned off the headlights and reached for the ignition. The key was gone. Burk pounded the steering wheel, spattering mud in his eye.

"Got-*dammit!*" he said. Then he remembered. The keys were still in the trunk lock. Careful not to get mud on the key's teeth, he retrieved it and slid into the seat.

He inserted the key and turned. The engine groaned heavily three times, as if laughing at him. His heart racing, Burk released the key. Neither husband nor wife said anything for five minutes.

Burk tried the key again. The engine laughed slowly, then more quickly, and the machine fired to life.

Fifteen minutes later, they were inside the city lights. Toni Jo's tension finally burst into hysterical laughter.

"Pigs!" she cried. "We look like we've been in a pig-chasing contest!"

Burk turned into the driveway. As Toni Jo entered their house, he stepped behind the car to lower the garage door. Gripping the handle, he scanned up and down the dark block. "I guess we got the pig," he said.

Toni Jo shed her mud dress in the bathroom. She was about to put it in the tub and rinse it when her anger returned. She called to her husband.

"Get this out of my sight," she commanded.

"But it's your–." Burk's heart sank when he saw the dress. "What should I do with it?"

"I don't care. Throw it in the garbage."

* * *

The next morning, Toni Jo took a taxi to the depot, where a locomotive was cooking in the station while its passengers, disembarking or boarding, said hello or goodbye to their lives. Ten minutes later, after a two-year absence and somewhat changed, Toni Jo was on her way home.

Gazing out the club car window, she realized she was seeing the most boring terrain in America. But if the flat pastures and repetitive farms dulled the senses, at least they held no jack-in-the-box surprises that popped up to grab you by the throat.

Mrs. Henry knew immediately that something was troubling her daughter. While reading newspapers and listening to the radio all day, Toni Jo smoked cigarettes one after another. Toni Jo explained she was merely upset by the failure of her marriage. Just that day, her mother had heard about the marriage for the first time.

When Mrs. Henry suggested she find work to take her mind off the problem, Toni Jo stared at her incomprehensibly, weighing the enormity of her recent deed against the fluff of waitressing.

"Good idea," she said.

At the Time-Out Cafe, Big Jake, his hands dusted with flour, hugged Toni Jo with the sides of his forearms.

If it hadn't been for the fact that C.T. had lost a hand at the mill and added himself to the wounded veterans' peacetime occupation of the barbershop, Toni Jo would have sworn that time had stood still and waited for her return. It was Friday. The following Monday, she would resume her old identity and dream again of becoming a teacher.

Two mornings later, unkempt from a restless night's sleep, Toni Jo took her place at the same kitchen table where she had spilt milk as a toddler in a high chair. Her mother glanced up from the Sunday paper.

"What's gotten into people?" she asked her daughter.

"I don't know," Toni Jo replied. "You tell me."

Her mother slapped the paper with the back of her hand. "This poor fellow. Minding his own business and this man picks him up hitchhiking and shoots him for no reason."

Toni Jo tore the paper from her mother's hands. Near the top of the front page, her husband peered out at the world with a bewildered look on his face. The caption identified the murderer as Horace Finnon Burk. Toni Jo had seen his full name only one other time—on their wedding license.

She sat down and rested her forehead on her folded arms.

"Good Lord, honey, what's the matter? Do you know this man?"

Without looking up, Toni Jo rolled her head from side to side, trying to negate all she had done and everything done to her in the past two years. It didn't work. She lifted her head and looked at her mother.

"He's my husband," she said.

With surprising calm, her mother asked, "Which one—the killer or the hitchhiker?"

For the first time, Toni Jo gave her mother a detailed account of her latter days in New Orleans, of Herald's alcoholic binge and her rescue by the man she had known as Arkie.

While her mother nervously prepared breakfast, Toni Jo read the article.

Late yesterday evening, two boys, sons of Johnny Calderona, were hunting rabbits atop a rice canal levee on their father's land. Walking in freezing temperatures, they noticed several icicles hanging from the mouth of an irrigation pipe and broke off one of the larger stalactites.

Doing so, they uncovered the bare toes of a man stuffed inside the pipe. They ran to their father, who drove to the site and tried without success to pull the corpse from the conduit, because it had either frozen or swollen into place.

The older Calderona then primed the water pump, thinking to thaw the ice and flush the body from its resting place. The plan worked, but also flensed the skin from the chest and back of the victim who, it turns out, was naked. He was emasculated as well.

Mr. Calderona recalled seeing an acquaintance at the location several nights previous and called local lumberman Horace Burk to see if he had noticed any suspicious activity in the area. Calderona reported his surprise when Burk broke down and confessed to murdering the hapless man.

The drifter remains unidentified, and the murderer has given no motive for his actions. Deputy Sheriff Lambert Deer is in charge of the ongoing investigation.

The odor of frying eggs and link sausages made Toni Jo queasy. Abruptly, she left the table, saying she was going for a walk. She returned an hour later to tell her mother she was leaving for Lake Charles.

"To file for divorce?" her mother asked.

"No," Toni Jo said. "To confess to the murder. Arkie didn't do it. I did."

* * *

Toni Jo had no idea how to go about turning herself in and went straight to the courthouse, as if she might be tried, convicted, and sentenced immediately. By mid-afternoon, after some confusion, she was locked in the Calcasieu Parish Jail.

For the next year, Toni Jo's home would be a second-floor corner cell facing west over the body of water that gave its name to the city of Lake Charles. The only female inmate, she was accorded privileges no others enjoyed.

Michael Prudhomme, her court-appointed attorney, visited Toni Jo daily for the first few weeks of her incarceration. Only a little taller than Toni Jo, he was a recent graduate of the Law School at LSU, where as an undergraduate he played shortstop on the baseball team. He had a ready smile and dark gentle eyes that reminded Toni Jo of a raccoon's. His gold-rim glasses constantly needed readjusting on a pug nose and too-small ears. At twenty-five, only four years his client's senior, he looked too young to be holding someone's life in his manicured hands.

When Toni Jo met Prudhomme the first time, she was depressed. Sheriff Abraham Deer had recently notified her that for the duration of her jail term she would be unable to see Burk. They would be allowed to exchange letters, although these would be subject to the perusal of defense and prosecuting attorneys of both parties so no collusion of stories might be transacted. After her confession, Toni Jo became irritated, then angry, at Arkie's insistence on his sole guilt. She did not want his blood, too, on her conscience.

A black trustee led Prudhomme to the cell and opened it from an array of keys representing more freedom than he had ever dreamed of while on the outside. Prudhomme's large white teeth smiled at Toni Jo, and his eyes twinkled like those of a chess devotee about to sit across from a master. He took a seat in the chair opposite her bed.

"Well," he said, pulling a yellow legal pad from his briefcase. "Toni Jo Henry Burk," he read. "Is that all of it?" He emitted a high-noted half-laugh.

Instantly, Toni Jo realized that her advocate might quickly become annoying and intended to set him in his place. She put a nearly spent cigarette to her lips and inhaled deeply. She sized him up and began dressing him down, her words expelling smoke from her mouth and nostrils.

"Look, Mr. Boy Lawyer, I'm the one who killed Herald Nevers, or whatever name he was going by when I rearranged his thinking, and I can live with the consequences. What I can't live with is the fact that my husband is taking the blame for what I've done. So what I want you to do is get the real killer, me, convicted and get him off the hook. Can you do that?"

Prudhomme pushed his glasses up his bridgeless nose and giggled nervously. "Mrs. Burk–."

"Call me Toni Jo."

"Well, Mrs. Burk, professional decorum–."

"Call me Toni Jo or you can leave this tank right now. It's crowded enough with just me in here."

Prudhomme sobered slightly.

"As you say, then." He looked at the documents in his file. "My duty, uh, Toni Jo, is to"—he flipped his hand as if to toss her the truth—"my duty, since you've confessed, is not to try to get you off the hook, as they say, but to make sure none of your constitutional rights are violated."

"What you're telling me is that you can't help my husband."

"Yes. Right. Precisely. Your trial and his trial are two separate entities. You will both be convicted or acquitted by a jury, not by your attorneys."

"Both convicted. How can we both be convicted if only one of us pulled the trigger?"

Prudhomme's smirk returned.

"One of the idiosyncrasies of our adversarial system, Mrs. ah,—Toni Jo."

He matched the fingertips of his left and right hands and made spider-on-the-mirror motions.

Toni Jo stared at the man. "Can I testify at his trial?"

"Purely a procedural matter," Prudhomme said. "If you're called, you can testify. If not, you can't."

"Not even if I want to?"

"Not even if you want to."

* * *

The two trials were to take place simultaneously. Toni Jo would track the progress of her husband's trial in *The American Courier*, the daily newspaper of Lake Charles. Her first court appearance was scheduled for April 10, the day after Burk's. Being called "the prettiest murder defendant in these parts in our time," Toni Jo received most of the coverage, with a photograph accompanying nearly every article. After Burk's face initially appeared with the bewildered look, it was never featured again.

When Toni Jo's cell wasn't sticky hot, it was stale from inadequate ventilation. She occupied her time by watching the traffic below, fishermen or sailboats on the water, and the noxious yellow fumes rising from refinery stacks across the river. Twice, she saw lightning strike the reticulated steel canopy crowning the Jean Lafitte Bridge as bug-like cars scurried up and down its eastern slope.

At night while lying on a thin, lumpy mattress whose buttons pinched her when she moved, Toni Jo studied the sounds and smells that carried across the water: a shift whistle, tugboat horns, the metallic crashing of machinery, release valves blowing, and occasional explosions followed by the penetrating tang of chlorine or the stench of burning sulfur. Several times that summer, she awakened to a layer of fine coke dust covering her cell. Through all of this, the odor of creosote and salt water permeated her days. In early spring, a light fur of pale green mold grew on the cement-block walls. Summer flies pestered her from morning to night.

The Fourteenth Judicial District Court for Calcasieu Parish was jammed with spectators wanting a peek at the attractive defendant the *Courier* had depicted as a gun-toting moll. Women popped their fans and men suffered silently as sweat poured down their backs, gluing white shirts to wet skin. Judge Page's courtroom reeked with the competitive odor of a gymnasium.

After jury selection, District Attorney Davis Avario moved the Court to allow Richard Palmer, a lawyer from Harris County, Texas, to prosecute the case. Palmer, a former district attorney in Houston, graduated first in his class from the University of Texas. Once a tall blond youth from a moneyed Austin family, he was now entering his fifties with most of his hair. The wrinkles and rough texture of age had imbued his face with a handsome dignity missing from his undergraduate good looks. The crow's feet surrounding his small green eyes seemed to have been wrought from smiling at everything having gone his way. Despite a small fan blowing directly on him, Palmer had already doffed his coat and rolled up his sleeves. When he rose from his chair, a sheet of paper stuck to his forearm. He peeled it off thoughtfully and began.

"Ladies and gentlemen of the jury." He looked at them with a winning smile. "It's hot." A few of the members smiled and shifted in their seats. Palmer's face sobered. "But not as hot as the barrel of this pistol, Exhibit A, on that cold night of February fourteenth. Valentine's Day. Don't you find it ironic, good citizens, that on the day we set aside to celebrate romantic love, the defendant's heart was seething with hatred toward a fellow human being in need of help? As we begin these proceedings, I'd like to remind you of a few things you will find instrumental in arriving at a just decision. First, we should all be careful not to make a parody of this trial. It has already received its share of sensational newspaper coverage. So remember this. We are not trying the defendant for her youth. Nor is she on trial for her beauty. We are trying her because she murdered in cold blood a Houston businessman, as well as a husband and father of two, named J. P. Carroway."

Toni Jo reeled with dizziness. The man she had seen through several incarnations was not done yet. She loved him as Harold Nevers, was intrigued by him as Harry Nilson, and grew suspicious of him as Herald Nevers, then, thinking to extinguish all his possible identities, killed him as a transient faking a religious conversion. Now, to play one last trick on Toni Jo, he had been resurrected as someone called J. P. Carroway. Having had occasional misgivings about her deed before this point, Toni Jo was now glad she had annihilated every person embodied in the man she last knew as Herald Nevers. Her attention returned to the voice of the prosecutor.

". . . the murder of Joseph Paul Carroway. A third thing I would ask you to do is put out of your mind the fact that another defendant is being tried for the same murder. That fact is irrelevant. Both of their fingerprints were lifted from the murder weapon. The pertinent question is what happened in those hours that no one can tell us about except Toni Jo and Horace Burk, a husband and wife who might have had any number of reasons to dispense with a tire salesman having car trouble on a wintry night—then, when their crime was uncovered, to confuse the issue by mutually confessing to be the lone trigger man."

Palmer turned to face Toni Jo. "Or woman. Each spouse insists on his or her lone guilt. Perhaps they are thinking this ploy will enable each of them to elude justice. I caution you, therefore, not to aid and abet them in a miscarriage of justice. I will close my opening statement by asking you to look through superficial appearances and into the heart of the accused and read the dark inscription there. Then, on a conclusion that follows from circumstantial and physical evidence, base your decision on unchanging moral principles."

Throughout the prosecutor's presentation, Prudhomme had been scribbling notes on a yellow pad and consulting Vincent Levine, a seasoned lawyer Prudhomme had asked to assist him. Prudhomme's hands shook as he stood and tidied the papers before him. At the jury railing, he scanned the two tiers of jurors.

"Gentle ladies and men of the jury, the attorney representing the state has suggested that your judgment of my client not be based on her youth and beauty, but on her deed. Mr. Palmer is a seasoned advocate. He knows, by asking you *not* to consider Toni Jo's youth and beauty, that he is calling attention to those very qualities in her. Thus, when you come to make your decision, you will discover a prejudice *against* her implanted in your reasoning by reverse psychology and may find yourself compensating in the opposite direction of your thoughts as they will have been formulated over the two or three weeks of this trial. So I would ask you to follow my adversary's advice and base your decision on the evidence, and *only* the evidence. Remember, too, that we are not trying this young woman because Joseph P. Carroway had a wife and children. We are trying her for an action she does not even deny. Her very honesty betrays the fundamental goodness of her soul. Likewise, I would ask you to follow Mr. Palmer's advice about not looking at Toni Jo's exterior, but into her heart, a heart originally innocent but later vilely corrupted, as you will see, by a man who deceived her in every way imaginable. Thus, in the case at hand, there are several extenuating circumstances. What I will suggest now, and prove to you later, is that the multiple aliases of Mr. Carroway so confused my client that she questioned her own identity as a good and decent person, and on that night, her reason muddled, in a moment of passion, she committed an unpremeditated act and lashed out at the cause of her internal conflict.

"I will conclude with two points. My adversary has asked you to distrust your spontaneous emotions. Going against my colleague on this matter, I would ask you instead to *feel*—feel for the brutalized virtue of my client, feel and thereby understand and, understanding, render a compassionate verdict. Second, ladies and gentlemen, while we are not trying Toni Jo based on her youth and beauty, neither are we trying her based on Mr. Palmer's facile use of language nor on his expertise in the finer aspects of courtroom disputation. In summary, *don't* be, as Mr. Palmer directed you to be, dispassionately objective. Instead, project yourself into the heart and mind of my client and you will see that if you had been in her place, you might have acted exactly the same and would hope for compassion and leniency, too. For mercy is an indispensable component of justice. Without it, we become unfeeling abstractions of the State. Mr. Palmer spoke of moral principles. Let me close by reminding you of the highest moral principle, of treating others as you would like to be treated in similar circumstances."

Over the next days, Toni Jo's interest waxed and waned as the two attorneys contended with each other, matching reason with reason, outbursts of feeling with logical calm, parrying with legal subtleties, then thrusting with guarded evidence at opportune moments. Details of the trial spread by newspaper, radio, and first-hand accounts. Letters from all over the parish began pouring in as the trial progressed, some castigating Toni Jo for her misspent life, most supporting her in her tribulations and suggesting she repent and ask God's forgiveness for her deed.

The American Courier granted Arkie Burk's trial only a fraction of the coverage his wife's was given. As Toni Jo read the newspapers in her cell, the impressionistic reportage riveted the scenes in her mind.

"She took the gun from you, you say. Did you try to wrest it from her?"

"No. She threatened to shoot me."

The sarcastic expressions on some of the jurors' faces indicated their doubt.

"The terrible irony, members of the jury, is that my client is accused of a crime he tried to prevent. In fact, he *confesses* to a crime he didn't commit in order to protect someone he loves, despite the fact that he saw a terrible side of the human heart on that cold Valentine's night."

"The fact that the accused did not actually pull the trigger is utterly beside the point. After the bullet was transferred from its home in the gun to the head of the victim, *by whoever pulled the trigger*, Horace Finnon Burk helped to hide the body. The tracks at the scene of the crime irrefutably demonstrate that. The fact that *he* picked up the hitchhiker, that *his* gun was used, that blood is in *his* car, that *his* rope was still around the victim's neck—all of this suggests that he is more than an accessory, that he is the principal if not sole perpetrator of the misdeed."

In the middle of the third week, Toni Jo was called to the stand in her own trial. She wore a light print cotton dress and sandals.

"Mrs. Burk," the prosecutor began. "Both you and your husband have confessed to murdering Mr. Joseph P. Carroway. Although, hypothetically, both of you could be lying, it's more likely that only one of you is lying. But despite all of these little spousal games you and your husband are playing, there is ample precedent for convicting both of you for the murder of J. Paul Carroway. Now, just for the record, Mrs. Burk, did Joe Carroway ever try to kill you?"

Toni Jo thought for a moment.

"I believe, in some ways, he did. He tried to kill my spirit–."

"Excuse me, Mrs. Burk, I hate to interrupt your provocative answer, but I don't think anyone has ever been convicted for killing someone else's spirit. Let me ask you this, then. You have stated in your deposition that you met Carroway in a diner where you worked. Did he force you to go with him to New Orleans?"

"No."

"Did he make you any false promises?"

Toni Jo thought about how long it would take to give an adequate answer to the question and decided her comments wouldn't matter anyhow.

"No."

"Did he pay you well?"

As the questioning proceeded, Toni Jo developed the urge to advance the prosecutor's cause.

"Very well," she replied.

"Why did you kill him?"

"Because I couldn't have lived with myself if I hadn't."

* * *

Closing arguments were scheduled for the last Monday in April.

Friday night, through the jailhouse grapevine, Toni Jo got word of the outcome of her husband's trial. After deliberating a little over thirty minutes, the jury had found Horace Burk guilty and sentenced him to die by hanging one year to the day after he did not murder J. P. Carroway.

Monday morning, prosecutor Richard Palmer delivered his final statement in a three-piece suit and never broke a sweat.

"Good citizens of the jury, there is no reason for me to prolong this trial with a lengthy address. The facts you have been presented over the past three weeks are incontrovertible. Mrs. Burk even admits her guilt. I would remind you, though, that we are trying Toni Jo Burk for her deed on the night of February fourteenth. We are not trying Mr. Joseph Paul Carroway for his personal shortcomings pointed out by opposing counsel. We simply cannot live in a society that allows a person to murder a man merely because she doesn't like the way he conducts his private life."

Pretending thirst, the prosecutor walked to his table and drank from a glass. Returning to the jury with the tumbler and a bottle of ink, he balanced the two containers on the rail. After dipping a fountain pen in the ink, he held it over the glass. A black bulbous drop fell into the water. In a few seconds, it swirled into a dark cloud, contaminating the entire vessel.

"A parable, if you will, ladies and gentlemen. Evil," Palmer said, pointing to the bottle of ink, "and Good," pointing to the glass of water. "It takes only a very little evil, just a single drop, to spoil much good. In the instant it takes to pull a trigger, Toni Jo Burk stained not just the life of Joe Carroway, but the lives of his dear wife, now a widow, and his now fatherless daughters. And if you do not find her guilty, you will have let her poison the very fabric of our society, which is founded on fairness and, as you well know, life, liberty, and the pursuit of happiness." The attorney paused. "It is now up to you to restore order to our society by delivering a fair judgment for her crime."

Toni Jo's attorney knew the jury had made up its mind long ago concerning the guilt of his client. The best Prudhomme could hope for was to convince the panel to return a verdict of manslaughter, for which Toni Jo might receive a sentence of ten years and serve as few as five.

Prudhomme, too, brought a glass of water and an inkwell before the jury. Pointing to the tumbler, he said, "Ladies and gentlemen, this pure water represents the life of Toni Jo Henry before she met Mr. J. P. Carroway. And this," he said, pointing to the inkwell, "represents the heart of J. Carroway."

Prudhomme picked up the jar of ink and poured its entire contents into the glass of water. He stared the jury down.

"Now, I ask you. What chance did this innocent young girl have against such darkness?" Barely able to contain his indignation, he glared at each panel member. "Your job, ladies and gentlemen, is *not* to restore order to our society by delivering an uncompromising verdict. If it were in your power, your duty would be to restore the life of Toni Jo Henry Burk to its original, pristine condition. But since you cannot do that, I would ask you—I beg you—to temper your judgment with compassion. For you see, Toni Jo Burk did not murder J. P. Carroway. No, friends, I believe that you have been sorely misled these past few weeks. The man my client dispensed with on that cold February night was someone calling himself Harold Nevers. And if we argue that Harold Nevers did not exist, well, then, where is her crime?

"Arguing this way, you might say, is trickery. But this trial comes down to identity—the identity of a woman as it was besmirched, and the *several* identities of a man whose name, as far as we have taken this case, is Joseph Paul Carroway. But I wonder, if we delved even further into his past, if we might not come up with other aliases and other families? And what about the identity of our nation? Mr. Palmer has invoked its very nature by reminding us that it is founded on certain principles. But the most paramount of those principles is the right to defend ourselves when no one else will defend us against our oppressors. I'm sure you remember from school the opening paragraph of the Declaration of Independence.

"All right, then. Toni Jo Burk found herself not only defenseless, but abandoned by all the usual means of justice, and took the law into her own hands. Moreover, I would argue that, by turning herself in to save her husband, she has *redeemed* herself. Taking all of these things into account, then—first, that Carroway most foully wronged a good woman; second, that you cannot restore her innocence; third, that she killed someone who never existed; fourth, that she acted in self-defense when no one else would help her; fifth, that she acted in a moment of passion without malice aforethought—taking all of these unusual and mitigating circumstances into account, then, I would ask you in the name of justice and decency to deliver a fair verdict by finding Toni Jo Burk guilty of a lesser included offense: at the very least, Murder in the Second Degree, or, if you can find the goodness in your *own* hearts, manslaughter."

As the defense attorney returned to his table, he saw spectators in the gallery and standing along the walls make slitting motions at their throats and heard cries of "Hang her! Hang the murderer!"

For every hour the jury was out, Prudhomme's hope grew by degrees. Six and a half hours later, the jury foreman stood to deliver the verdict.

The courtroom fell silent.

Judge Page spoke. "Ladies and gentlemen of the jury, have you reached a verdict?" The jury foreman, Wilfred Fontenot, indicated they had.

The judge directed Fontenot to hand deliver the jury's decision to the bailiff, who handed it to the judge. Judge Page studied the sheet, then asked the jurors if the document represented their collective judgment. Mr. Fontenot's last function as foreman was to acknowledge that it was.

Judge Page turned to the defendant and instructed Toni Jo Burk to stand. Toni Jo, Prudhomme, and Levine rose simultaneously.

"Mrs. Toni Jo Burk, the jury unanimously finds you guilty of Murder in the First Degree. Having been found guilty of murder with malice aforethought, the statutes of this state direct me to condemn the convicted to death. Accordingly, you are hereby remanded to the custody of the Department of Corrections pending execution by hanging. May God have mercy on your soul.

"Ladies and gentlemen of the jury, that concludes this trial. Thank you for fulfilling your duties. Justice has been served."

Judge Page's gavel rapped the bench with the finality of a pistol shot.

Immediately after the judge dismissed his court, Michael Prudhomme filed a motion for a new trial based on two grounds: First, he claimed that the crowd's slitting motions and cries for blood had a prejudicial effect on the jurors. Secondly, the prosecuting attorney, Richard Palmer, was neither qualified before the Louisiana bar nor an elector of the parish or state.

After reading newspaper accounts of Prudhomme's emotional plea for leniency, people from all over Louisiana flooded the jail and district attorney's office with letters supporting the beautiful murderess. Toni Jo was baffled by the contradictory reactions of the courtroom spectators and the general populace. A week later, thousands of letters nationwide augmented the hundreds written by Louisianans.

* * *

Toni Jo had to wait through a long, torrid summer for her retrial. Westerly breezes skimming off the lake kept her tolerably comfortable through mid-July. Occasionally, she saw Deputy Sheriff Lambert Deer escorting new inmates to their cells or liberating them to the outside world. Toni Jo felt she might suffocate before reaching her second trial.

Without warning, the Deputy appeared one afternoon. She observed him midway down the corridor, his khaki shirt sweat-stained at the armpits. Toni Jo hoped the plan she had been rehearsing would work. She stepped to the window and looked directly at the sun as it dropped beneath the dark anvil of a thunderhead. It made her sneeze twice. If Nevers could do it, she figured, so could she. Deer glanced toward her cell.

"Bless you," he said. He ambled down the cement passage dividing the chambers. The Deputy, taller and younger than she had remembered him, paused before her door. He tipped his hat up, exposing a crease on his forehead. "Mrs. Burk. Anything I can do for you?"

"No," she said, "but I thank you kindly for asking."

Deer looked around her cubicle, then at his boots. "Well, you holler if you're disaccommodated in any way and I'll see what I can do."

"Thanks."

Deer touched his hat. "Afternoon, then. I'll be getting along." He turned and took a few steps.

"There is one thing," Toni Jo said as if the thought had just rushed into her mind. Deer pivoted.

"Yes ma'am?"

"No, on second thought, I guess that wouldn't be fair. To the others, I mean."

Deer looked at her calmly. "Well, come on out with it or I'll never know."

Toni Jo looked directly into his eyes with a doleful expression. She made her statement sound like a doubtful question.

"I don't suppose there's any way for you to get me a fan?"

Deer walked back to her cell. He looked at the high, barred window, then at the rumpled sheet on her mattress that indicated Toni Jo had been standing on it to intercept refreshing breezes.

"I'll see what I can do," he said. "No promises."

Toni Jo exhaled loudly, exaggerating the relief she already felt.

"You'd be a life saver if you could do that. Really."

Deer turned to go about his business. "Remember, no promises."

"Fine. I understand," Toni Jo said. "By the way." Deer stopped in his tracks. "Can you make it the oscillating type?"

Deer shook his head and chuckled. As he walked away, Toni Jo heard him speak to both of them. "Watch out, Slim. Next thing you know, she'll want air conditioning."

* * *

Two days later, Deer showed up with a fan. He opened the barred door, placed the fan on the cement, and pushed it towards Toni Jo like he was feeding a wild dog that might turn on him.

"Put it together myself from two busted fans at my Daddy's house." He pronounced it "Deddy"—my Deddy's house. Toni Jo found it charming that a man of law would refer to the Sheriff, his father, a man nicknamed "Mule," in this way.

"Oh, thank you so much." Toni Jo made sure to overreact. She reached down and lifted the heavy metal appliance, then broke into coquettish laughter.

"What now?" Deer said.

"Do I have to turn the blades myself?" Deer didn't understand. "No outlet," she said.

Deer wasn't amused. He felt thwarted in his good Samaritan role.

That afternoon, he returned with an adapter to screw into the light socket on the ceiling of Toni Jo's cell. After installing the gadget, Deer stepped down from the chair, worked the fan's plug into its female companion, and turned the lever on the base of the stand. The motor made a struggling hum, but the blades did not move. Refusing to believe his bad luck, he advanced the lever to "High" and gave the blades an encouraging spin. The black petals of the metal flower slowly rotated until the motor gained full speed.

Deer swabbed his face with a handkerchief and, for a few moments, blocked the breeze with his body.

"Hey," Toni Jo began teasingly.

"Ahn!" Deer said. "I deserve it." He was a man of few words. And Toni Jo was beginning to like him—at the same time that Arkie Burk was starting to grate on her nerves. Since their verdicts in April, he had written her numerous letters apologizing for the mess he had made of her life. It gave Toni Jo the eerie feeling that her husband had not told her everything he knew about Nevers, or himself. And she did not want to know. She wanted to forget. What good would it do now to know anything else about Nevers? Or Burk. Toni Jo rarely responded to his letters. She was working on another plan.

The fan got her to the end of September, when her second trial began and the humid days were relieved by northern fronts that grew cooler and stayed longer as the trial progressed. Two days before Halloween, after a virtual rerun of her first trial, Toni Jo was convicted and sentenced to die the following October.

Finally, it hit her. By this time next year, there would be no Toni Jo Henry. She would be dead. A poem from high school came to her mind:

> No motion has she now, no force;
> She neither hears nor sees;
> Rolled round in earth's diurnal course,
> With rocks, and stones, and trees.

For a day and a night, Toni Jo despaired. There was no point in making new diary entries. The succession of days was like watching a Movietone reel of herself doing nothing, again and again and again. Toni Jo ate little and slept fifteen hours a day.

Near Thanksgiving, she was awakened by the merry sound of the trustee's keys. A priest appeared at her cell door. The holy man had a small red nose pressed into a pleasant, doughy face. Santa Claus without a beard, Toni Jo thought cynically. Avoiding the topic of her death, Father Jacob talked about change. As if by magic, he said, one could turn the direction of one's life around. Or, if not one's life, then one's thoughts, one's disposition.

Toni Jo thought Father Jacob was a coward, not directly saying what he meant—that since she had no future life to turn around, she should adjust her attitude about her past life and prepare for the afterlife.

The priest did most of the talking on their visits. Having no other appointments, Toni Jo decided she would while away her time by antagonizing the man. She contradicted whatever sugarcoated view of life he tried to make her swallow: through adversity, we build strength of character; no matter what we've done, God can forgive us—that sort of thing.

She didn't need God's forgiveness, she said, for evening an unsettled score with a man who had wrecked her life. Father Jacob said only God had the right to take a life, that vengeance was His and His alone, that no man was so bad he couldn't be redeemed. Toni Jo reminded the priest that he hadn't known Harold Nevers.

At length, frustrated, the priest asked Toni Jo what she thought man's job on this earth was. On that and related subjects, she had done some thinking in the past few months.

"Nothing," she replied without hesitation.

"Then what do you believe in? You must believe in something."

By example and anecdote, Nevers had taught Toni Jo the answer to that one. She just hadn't been listening.

"I believe in the evil core of the human heart."

All cheer drained from the face of the good priest. He stared at her for a long while, like a checkmated opponent looking for an escape when the only way out is off the board.

On the verge of tears, he said, "I implore you in the name of Christ our Lord to consider you might be wrong."

Toni Jo stared at him without emotion. Father Jacob knew he was losing her. He had brought her a Bible on his last visit, but he could see the book had not moved.

"Please," he said, "keep an open mind. Don't despair. Read from God's Word and search with an open heart for its messages."

Toni Jo was growing weary of the priest's company and hurried Father Jacob from her presence with the promise to do as he asked if he would not return for a month.

In the meantime, Deputy Sheriff Slim Deer surprised her with a Christmas present, a Philco 355T radio in a walnut cabinet. Toni Jo divided her time among the radio, the Bible, and magazines. She especially enjoyed the Photocrime section in *Look*: "How good a detective would you make? Try to solve this short mystery with the clue pictures on this page."

Toni Jo dialed past news and farm quotes in favor of variety shows— featuring Jack Benny, Burns and Allen, Glenn Miller, Edgar Bergen and Charlie McCarthy, and Bing Crosby,—or serial stories with Amos 'n' Andy or the Lone Ranger. Toni Jo recalled laughing at Charlie McCarthy on Sunday evenings with her mother. Now she wondered why anyone older than six would be amused by a ventriloquist talking to a dummy on the radio.

But she loved Orson Welles as The Shadow, asking the imponderable question, "Who knows what evil lurks in the hearts of men?"

Each time, Toni Jo's sarcastic response was, "*I* know."

Her favorite songs were "Angel in Disguise," "Fools Rush In," and "Where Do I Go From You?" The routine lifted Toni Jo's depression and dissipated her anger.

A week into the new year of 1941, Father Jacob reappeared. After the small courtesies of reacquaintance, he asked if Toni Jo had changed her mind about her place in God's world.

"Somewhat," she said. The priest lifted his eyebrows in hope. "I said the human heart is rotten at its core." Toni Jo was almost ashamed at having baited the man who only meant her well. "I can't say that I've read your Bible from cover to cover, but I have read around trying to cut to the good parts. I was raised Methodist, you know, so I've read a good bit of this already. Anyway, after reading a lot of the stories, I've decided that life is a tug of war between good and evil. Take Job, for instance. Here he is, minding his own business, when one day God and the devil get into it and use him as taffy. Now, does that sound fair to you?"

Father Jacob stared at her blankly.

"Or take Jonah or Abraham or any number of those guys."

The cleric tried to subdue his wince at the reference to the holy patriarchs as guys.

"What did they ever do to deserve what they got? I mean, God asks Abraham to kill his son? How cruel can you get? So I've decided that if there is a God, He treats us like wishbones. He and the devil take a pull, and one or the other comes up with the big end, but we're the losers every time. So this is what I've decided." The priest looked at her expectantly. "No good, no evil," she said. "The only way to win is to make life neutral."

Father Jacob was both impressed and troubled by Toni Jo's naive theology. It was so wrongheaded that he puzzled over where to begin untangling her misconceptions.

Toni Jo interrupted his thoughts. "One thing I did find interesting, though."

"Yes?"

"If life is like a big riddle and you get to go to heaven if you solve it, then there's a way out for everybody."

The priest smiled at the familiar goodness of her logic.

"This guy Job had the right idea. If you're a good person, you can only do what you think is right and hope for the best. I even marked it."

Toni Jo opened the Bible using the built-in scarlet ribbon. "Here it is. 'Though He slay me, yet will I trust Him, but I will maintain my own ways before Him.' You want me to have faith in God, Father Jacob? *That's* faith, if you ask me."

Toni Jo launched into an amateurish exegesis.

"You see, the idea is that Job is a good man and here he is getting kicked around as if he had done something wrong. So he decides that if God's going to punish him for doing right, well then, to hell with Him—he'd just go on doing right."

Father Jacob flinched at the curse, and Toni Jo smiled.

"I don't mean to offend you, Father, but that's the way I see it."

Toni Jo was so unacquainted with the intolerance of orthodoxy that she assumed the priest would take her new philosophy with humor, even if he couldn't subscribe to it himself. He remained, however, insulted.

He spoke of repentance and change, citing numerous instances in both Testaments: Adam and Eve, Moses, the Ethiopian eunuch, the Israelites, Saul becoming Paul. Through the forgiving power of Jesus, he said, her free will, in conjunction with an act of faith, could override any bad thing done to her or by her.

When Father Jacob finished, Toni Jo knew she had been beaten with the heatless whip of doctrine—dogma the man had learned secondhand in a stuffy classroom of a seminary far removed from what she had seen of the world. She mustered a polite but firm reply.

"I'm sorry, Father, but I just don't see it that way. I can't repent a sin I never committed. Job said"—Toni Jo flipped a few pages—"'All the days of my appointed time will I wait, till my change come.' That's what I plan to do, Father: wait out my term until the time of my change from this world to the next. I'm not afraid. It's just a change."

For the first time, Father Jacob lost his patience and viewed Toni Jo as an obstinate child.

"You're wrong. And I hope God will have mercy on you. As for me, I pity you."

The priest's condescension touched a sore spot in Toni Jo, who had been demeaned too many times by Nevers.

"Save it for somebody else," Toni Jo said, rising. "A pity saved is a pity earned. Spend it on someone who needs it. I don't."

18

February–October 1941

Arkie Burk was scheduled to hang on February 13, 1941. Toni Jo was twenty-three years old. Even though it was her husband she had been reading about in the newspaper, she couldn't force herself to have any wifely feelings for him. She felt detached. The accounts, written by Cal Sonnier, seemed unreal.

During Toni Jo's trials, she had seen the reporter scampering up and down the marble steps of the courthouse trying to get a word with Toni Jo or her lawyers. The short Cajun had an eager expression enhanced by receding hairlines that gave him the look of someone running into a strong headwind.

Cal Sonnier knew his trade. In a series of daily articles leading up to Arkie Burk's deathwatch, he presented his researched facts on hanging. Sonnier's editor topped the articles with stark headlines: The Rope, The Ritual, The Condemned, The Death Debate. From the pieces, Toni Jo learned several things she wished she hadn't.

Twenty-four hours before a hanging, a new rope is stretched by suspending a heavy bag of sand from it. To prevent the rope from being sold by the inch as souvenirs, it is destroyed immediately after the execution.

Eight in the morning is universal hanging time. The prisoner gets a final meal of his choice and a last wish, within reason. The night before his final day on earth, the man is transferred to a holding cell near the gallows. There, during equipment tests, he may hear the double-flap trapdoor being sprung, followed by the foreboding thud of a sandbag reaching the end of its drop.

Minutes before his time has run out, the condemned

is led to the execution room, where a white hood is placed over his head. Some say this keeps him from being alarmed by the forbidding scaffold. Others claim it prevents witnesses from having nightmares of the man's face before, during, or after the drop. The intense strain on the hanging man's face caused by the tightening noose was in ancient times termed *risus sardonicus*, a sardonic or mocking grin.

. . .

After the convict is helped up the steps, his ankles are bound together and his wrists tied behind his back to keep him from grasping the platform as he falls. Two assistants then pick up their charge and place him on the trapdoor. Some faint and must be revived before being killed, for the State requires the convicted to be conscious of the retributive act.

Depending on the inmate's weight and the strength of his neck, determined by muscle tone and girth, the drop necessary to separate the man from his life usually measures between eight and seventeen feet. An experienced hangman, educated by trial-and-error, does the estimate by dead reckoning. Slow strangulation occurs if the drop is too short. Too long, and the result is decapitation.

. . .

The time and cause of death have been hotly debated for centuries.

Experts in one camp aver that although breathing stops in seconds, death does not claim its prize until the heart stops beating, sometimes for fifteen minutes or more. Those who say hanging is cruel and unusual punishment, and therefore unconstitutional, explain that the victim does not die immediately. Instead, after the tearing of muscles and skin, the veins near the neck's surface are blocked by the tightening noose, while the deeper arteries continue pumping blood to the brain, inducing a severe headache. Heart and respiratory rates slow until stoppage, at which time death occurs. Some doctors avow that a good knock on the head would be more humane than this medieval garotting.

Another camp argues instantaneous death based on the fact that the second cervical vertebra fractures at the end of the drop. A small battalion within this camp believes it's the knot of the rope that injures the *medulla oblongata*, thus terminating life and all sensation immediately after the spinal cord is separated from the brain.

———

Warden J. Michael White set Arkie Burk's execution for February thirteenth. He wasn't up to reading his name in cockamamie headlines designed to sell papers: **ST. VALENTINE'S DAY EXECUTION: Man Loses Head Over Wife's Ex-lover**, that sort of thing. No-siree, he would have no part of it.

Arkie's last request was for a conjugal visit with his wife. After some exchanges between the warden and the lawyers of the two inmates, the visit was granted based on precedent. Toni Jo was informed of the matter only after the legal rigmarole.

She said no. Emphatically.

And she had many reasons, one of which was that she was repulsed by the idea that someone she had made love to one day, would be a corpse the next.

What Burk got instead of his final wish was a ten-minute phone conversation with his wife.

They talked eight minutes. Burk said he tried to save Toni Jo's life and couldn't understand why she threw it away. In the end, he cried while she maintained a stoical silence. Toni Jo could not, for the life of her, figure out what to say or how to feel.

* * *

The entire cell block was dead quiet on the day of her husband's execution. She tried to imagine the procedure. Arkie was led from his cell. The noose was slipped over his head. He dropped. Quickly or not, he died. They took him away. Someone buried him. He was now in an oblong box underground. Cool and dark.

None of it had a reality she could grasp.

By the end of the week, the letters began coming in. Men from all parts of the country professed love for her. Some of the letter-writers tried to convert her. Many claimed to be relatives. Almost all of the men mentioned her beauty. Was the death of a beautiful woman so disturbing? What if she had been ugly?

After a few days, she read only the addresses. Occasionally, a friend from DeRidder would write. Those letters were simple and direct. No twists of the heart or mind to wrestle with.

She propped an unopened letter from Mrs. Henry on top of the radio. Toni Jo wasn't sure she could stand reading about the anguish she had caused her mother.

It took Slim Deer two weeks to muster the courage to face Toni Jo and offer his condolences. He might not have seen her even then if he hadn't heard the reports—awful screams in the night reverberating down the corridor, ringing the metal bars. In recurring nightmares, the hangman's rope was dragging Toni Jo forward like a calf to the slaughter.

She had never heard Deer raise his voice. Sometimes he spoke so quietly she had to lean forward to hear him. Near the end of February, she was awakened at noon from one of her coma-like sleeps by his angry words.

"Don't you have any sense of common decency! Don't you have any sense, period!"

These were not questions. He was dressing someone down for an error in judgment. It took Toni Jo a few moments to figure out that he was mad at a subordinate for letting Sonnier's articles on hanging reach her cell.

After Deer composed himself, he appeared around the corner of the cell block. He looked glum, like he was the one who would never see another New Year. Or Christmas. Or Thanksgiving. Toni Jo had to speak first. Otherwise, he might have stood till sundown watching his hands twirl the sweat-stained hat.

"I'd like to say I'm okay," she began. "But it's different when you're looking down the calendar. It's like a slide you can't stop yourself from slipping down."

"It's my fault," Deer said. "I should have been more careful about watching what came into your cell."

"No, it's all right." She tried to help him. "I'm fine. It's just that . . ."

Deer looked at her for the first time. Anxiety had drawn her face. "I'm afraid, Mr. Deer." She paused to fight back the tears. "Somehow I never thought Arkie would die. Now he's dead and my turn's next. It feels very strange to look at the squares of October and know that one of those will be blank, and then the next one, and the next one. Like that, forever."

Deer turned his gaze from her. It hurt him to see her like an animal about to be slaughtered. Unlike animals, she could see it coming.

"You have to help me, Mr. Deer." It was not a plea. It sounded like a statement of fact, like "The earth is round." Everybody knows that. He *had* to help her.

Deer's head jerked to the left in half of a No. "There's nothing I can do."

"You can," Toni Jo said. She spoke frantically. "Make me comfortable. This cell is getting to me. I dream they're putting the noose around my neck and then I'm falling and just before I hit I know I'm falling too fast and too far. I'm afraid my neck won't be strong enough. I have no one. My mother's no help. She's worse than I am about this."

"I don't know. I'll see what I can do."

Toni Jo reached through the bars and held his arm. It was thinner than she thought it would be, but wiry with strength.

"Come back at supper," she said. She opened her mouth to speak again, as if she had a plan, then realized she had nothing else to say. Only a feeling of urgency. "Please."

"I'll see what I can do."

Deer's voice sounded like a promise with the life beaten out of it.

* * *

But he did come back. And Toni Jo had done a lot of thinking in the meantime. To Deer most of it sounded desperate. This time, he visited inside her cell, the wall blocking them from the other inmates' view.

"You know the D.A.," she said. "He could get me released if he wanted. All we have to do is present new evidence that Arkie acted alone. And Arkie's dead. He can't contradict a thing. He said he'd been in touch with . . . Herald." She hated saying his name. "Arkie had exchanged letters with him, so all we have to do is find one of those letters. Then we could prove that Arkie killed him out of jealousy, that I had nothing to do with it, and then I'm free."

Deer stared blankly at the young woman, ghost pale with auburn-brown hair. Her innocence about everything was so stupendous he hardly knew where to begin. He opened his hands to her as if to show he had no tricks, no magic trumpet he could blow to bring down the walls of her Jericho.

He shook his head. "I don't know," he said. "I just don't know. I want to help you, but I can't see . . . any way."

"Try," Toni Jo pleaded.

After a long silence, Deer spoke. "I've done some thinking, too. It's nothing like what you have in mind, but it might make your time a little easier. There's a ground-floor room. It's bigger than this one. And cooler. With better accommodations. An easier view of the lake. It's the only room down there."

"That sounds nice," she said. "I appreciate your concern. But would you also try the other thing? Promise?"

"I promise, but there's something else about the room you should know before you decide to move." Deer looked at Toni Jo to gauge her reaction to his next statement.

Toni Jo looked at him. What could be worse than where she was?

"It's the solitary confinement room." Deer bowed his head in shame. "It's also the death row cell." Toni Jo's heart leaped. "It's where they spend the last night. They're allowed some visitors: family, close friends, clergy." Their eyes locked for the first time in all his visits.

"I'll take it," Toni Jo finally said, as if she had been offered the last and worst room in a roach-infested motel. "Might as well get used to it."

Grim humor. Deer had seen it happen before. The first stage on the road to acceptance of the condemned man's death.

Chief Deputy Slim Deer didn't want the transfer to look suspicious. He waited a week and had two deputies escort Toni Jo downstairs. The room had obvious improvements. A new paint job. Curtains, of all things, on the barred window. A dresser and a swivel chair.

"I hope you like it," Deer said two days later. He was careful not to come by too soon after the relocation. "You'll be more comfortable writing at the desk." He had noticed that she kept a journal of some sort.

They talked for twenty minutes.

"I got to get back. I'm on duty."

Her next comment held him a while longer. "You know what I miss? Aside from freedom, I mean."

"No," he said. "What?"

"Birds." Deer had expected something profound. His head went up, then slowly down, as if someone were pulling strings attached to his wooden head.

* * *

The bird was unpretentious. A blue parakeet. "He'll keep you company when I'm not here," Deer said.

After trying out Parakeety and then Keety, Toni Jo settled on Peety: too long, too cute, just right. She had time to fine tune her life. Nothing but time.

March, April. Deer visited when he could. Began to bring her things. It pleased him to add cheer to the monotony of her daily routine. Candy. Trinkets. Flowers. They learned how to laugh together. Deer had consulted Levine and Prudhomme. Had been working on Davis Avario. The D.A. couldn't come up with anything, Deer told her. Toni Jo took the news with surprising calm.

May. Deer asked her to dye her hair. Brought it up casually.

"No," Toni Jo said. Her reaction alarmed him. When he pressed for explanations, she stubbornly held her ground and offered no reasons. Deer finally had to reveal what he had intended as a surprise.

"It's part of a disguise," he said. Toni Jo frowned. "A date," Deer said. "You've been telling me how much you wish you could see a movie. Well, this is it. Next Wednesday. A matinee of *The Great Lie*, with Bette Davis. The kids are all in school. I asked Mr. Randolph—he owns the Paramount—what his slackest day was and he said Wednesday, no question."

Toni Jo couldn't believe what she was hearing. The sheriff's son planned to take her, a death-row convict, to a movie in broad daylight. It was preposterous, like the plot of a Laurel and Hardy skit.

Tuesday, she was a blonde again.

Wednesday, wearing a headscarf and sunglasses, she walked out of the lockup with Deer, who wore plain clothes.

In jail. Out of jail.

Dying. Alive.

She felt light enough to fly.

"Two," Deer said into the opening of the glass column as he pushed a dollar down into the silver bowl.

"The only two, Mr. Deer," the woman returned with a wink.

Toni Jo feared being discovered. Her heart ricocheted around her ribcage. A smiling usher greeted them in the lobby.

"Help you find a seat?"

Deer laughed and gave the boy a dime.

"No, I think we can manage it."

Toni Jo, who in the last months had eaten little and slept a lot, devoured everything in sight. The heavy odor of buttered popcorn almost knocked her down. She had to have some. And a large Coke. Chocolate kisses. A Mars bar. Orange slices. Jujubes.

They started in the center of the theater and moved four times. Up, back, left side, right side. The freedom of movement was almost more than Toni Jo could handle, as if she would miss something if she didn't see the screen from every angle.

Deer finally settled her down. "Easy, easy," he whispered redundantly in the empty auditorium. "It's not like we can't do this again."

Toni Jo smiled in the dark. After finishing her popcorn, she wiped her hand and slipped it into Deer's. It was like holding hands with a statue. He was actually afraid of her. She was amused. A deputy sheriff. It was too cute, really.

An hour into the movie, Toni Jo had to let out some of the Coke. She hadn't had a soft drink in over a year. She had taken in twice her fill, the squirrel anticipating a long winter.

Knowing he would decipher the code, she whispered into her date's ear. "Will you excuse me?"

Deer sprung into action. "Sure, sure." He stood and held her elbow as she stepped toward the aisle.

In the restroom, Toni Jo looked at herself in the mirror. She touched up her little bit of makeup. The outing was so impossibly wonderful that she only then realized there were no attendants. The Paramount couldn't compete with the New Orleans movie houses. She recalled their names. The Orpheum, Loews State, Imperial, New Carrollton. They were like palaces. As she picked at the side of her mouth with a tissue, her heart bolted and her eyes suddenly looked directly into her own eyes.

She could walk out of the restroom and onto the street. Who would expect to see her walking down the city sidewalks like a rich young wife on a shopping spree? She popped her purse open and put on the sunglasses. Her hands fumbled nervously with the scarf. She had to take it down and retie it.

Then she was out the restroom, heaving open the heavy glass entrance doors before the usher could reach her.

Her heels clacked madly on the sidewalk. She was free. Escaped.

Where should she go? She barely had time to formulate the thought when a voice called from behind her.

"Going to a fire?"

It was Deer.

She wanted to cry, to sob. Her throat felt like a bladder needing relief. She halted. Deer caught up with Toni Jo and walked around to face her. She couldn't bear to look at him. She buried her face in his chest and cried, partly out of shame before the man who had trusted her. And partly because, for a few moments, she was not going to be hung by the neck until she was dead, dead, dead.

Deer held Toni Jo until her shuddering subsided. All right, she thought. Now we know each other.

He knew what *she* was capable of—had known, it suddenly hit her, what she would do even before she herself had seen the opportunity. And she knew *him* better now. He was smarter than she had given him credit for being, and craftier.

"I'll never try that again," Toni Jo said, looking into his kind face. "I promise."

"I know," Deer said.

"Can you forgive me? Will you take me to another movie?"

"I forgave you even before I asked you to the movie. I knew you would try it. Once. If not here, then somewhere else. As for another movie, we haven't even finished watching this one."

Hand in hand, they turned and made their solitary way back to the theater.

"But we can't make ourselves too visible. Probably wouldn't be a good idea to do the same thing twice. How about a picnic next time?"

"That would be wonderful," Toni Jo said.

In a matter of two minutes, she felt like she had died and been born again.

* * *

June, 1941.

Toni Jo and Deer looked like any young lovers. From a distance, anonymous. A blanket picnic in Locke Park, cattycorner from the red-brick Convent of Hearts to the west and Joseph's Drive-In to the south. Deer's picnic basket was empty.

"Some picnic," Toni Jo teased.

But Deer had a plan. They walked to Joseph's and filled it with burgers in wax paper and fries in red baskets.

It was so simple. A picnic on a quilt under the open sky, and children playing near watchful mothers. Nothing like what Nevers had shown her—glitz and bustle. It took Nevers and jail to make Toni Jo appreciate a little outing.

Their fingertips explored each other's hands while they talked. Deer kissed her, nervously, for the first time. Toni Jo thought: pity, sympathy.

Love? It was not what *she* felt, but it was nice. Better than the massive nothing closing in on her inexorably with each heartbeat.

Emboldened, Deer spoke of his ambitions. He would become sheriff one day, when his father stepped down. Then, after being sheriff a couple of terms, he would run for mayor.

With the Deer name, Toni Jo assured him, he could do anything he wanted.

He fell silent. He plucked grass blades and tore them lengthwise along their spine. Deer told Toni Jo he wished she could see his accomplishments. They were quiet for a while. Their eyes tracked a solitary ant trying to figure out how it was going to lift a French fry shipwrecked on the ocean of blanket.

Deer stood and helped Toni Jo up. They walked to a swing and he pushed her wordlessly. Back and forth, slowly. Then he stopped pushing. Toni Jo looked over her shoulder, letting the pendulum run down.

Deer moved closer to her, put both of his hands on her left shoulder and whispered in her ear.

"I–." His voice choked. He tried again. "I want to marry you."

Toni Jo closed her eyes. She thought, *This just can't be happening.* She admired Deer, even held a deep affection for him. He had done so much for her. She placed one of her hands over his.

"What would be the point? How could it ever work?"

She saw the months laid out like dominoes. They would have a private ceremony in the jail. Only one other person would have to know. The honeymoon was bound to be disastrous. She smiled at that. They would take a few short excursions from her cell. Then October would be there like a . . . what? Something big. She couldn't think of anything that big. Death. Maybe it wasn't size, but darkness going in one direction, or all directions, forever.

Deer slid one hand from under hers and held her hand between his.

She liked Deer. He had taken care of her. Who *wouldn't* want to marry him? But she didn't see the point. She had been with Nevers without a marriage. Anything was possible, he had taught her. She looked around. A few cars glided down Ryan Street. One of them pulled into the Borden's ice-cream parlor and gave birth to more children than she could count. It felt like she had drifted above the trees like a hot-air balloon and was watching the two of them from a distance. She could see them doing this again and again, for life. Till death do us part. A short life, whose dead-end was just down the road a piece. A long life would be better. A life sentence.

There! The stab in her heart, like the day her escape had fallen in her lap, too good to be true. She took a deep breath and calmed herself down. Then, in a casual challenge:

"If you can get me life, I'll marry you"—spoken as an impossibility, like saying, "If I were a millionaire, this is what I would buy."

* * *

Deer talked to everyone he knew. Consulted the best lawyers in town. Asked his father for help. The only advice he got from him was to stay away from the woman.

"She can ruin your career, your life. Be careful. You mess with mud, you get muddy."

Toni Jo anxiously awaited Deer's next visit. If the worst came, she wanted another plan, and if that didn't work, another and another. Anything, any change at all from the slope her life was running down like a freight train with failed brakes was better than riding out the trip without trying.

"Then let's be together while we can," she said after the bad news. "The marriage isn't important. I'm sorry, but it just didn't mean as much to me as it did to you. I hope you can see it from my point of view." She shrugged. "What difference would it make?"

They talked for a while, made plans for a trip at the end of June to his house on a hundred-acre tract next to his father's land. Then she dropped Plan B on him.

"I've been thinking, Slim." She hated the name. It made him sound like a cartoon sheriff, but she didn't want to hurt his feelings by telling him. "It's not so much my death as the *way* I'll die that bothers me. Is there any way, do you think, to get the way I'll be executed to–. How do I say this? From hanging to the electric chair?"

Deer stared at her in disbelief. He pulled at his top lip, a habit he engaged in while thinking. The judge determined the week of the execution, but the warden could choose the day and time as long as he let the condemned man know a week ahead so he could prepare.

Warden White said he would look into the matter to see if it was possible.

He did. It was.

Toni Jo felt a terrible burden lift from her. Choosing the method by which she would die was somehow like getting a new life.

On the last day of June, they celebrated on Slim Deer's farm. They rode horses. They fished with cane poles in a square cattle pond. The big red bluegills floated in the water on a nylon stringer. They would fry them in the early evening and eat them on the porch. Toni Jo hooked a bass. It was big and green and broke her line when it jumped. When Deer lifted the stringer, a thick, squat water moccasin held onto a bream. It had mangled the lower part of the fish's body and wouldn't let go. Toni Jo screeching with laughter and fear, Deer grabbed the black snake quickly by the tail and popped its head off.

Deer cleaned the fish by a horse trough, then cooked them over a butane tank on the screened-in veranda of his ranch house. Toni Jo watched and bantered from a porch swing while June bugs thumped against the screen with a familiar, domestic sound.

After supper, she took a long bath. In the jail, there were only showers. She felt clean as they kissed on Deer's couch while listening to the radio. Evening smells wafted in through an open window: cattle, cut grass, and after-shave. Toni Jo desired him for the first time. Dinah Shore sang "I'm Through With Love," reminding her.

It was too good to be true, she cautioned herself. Don't count on anything. It could all come to a halt tomorrow, and then there would only be the long days to fill until the last one was cut short.

His caresses progressed. He asked permission. Toni Jo wondered if he had ever been with a woman. A tall, lean country bumpkin too good for his own good. But she really did feel something for him. Who wouldn't?

In a very roundabout way, he asked, or rather hinted—Could they, would she like to . . . not now, but maybe the next time she came over?

"Why not now?" Toni Jo said.

Shocked, Deer lifted his head and dropped it, the marionette.

When they reached his bedroom, he turned the light on, then off. They talked in the dark between cool sheets. Eventually, he got around to it, said he was worried about . . . you know. Toni Jo had to think for a while.

"Oh," she said. She thought, He's afraid of getting me pregnant and can't even bring himself to say the word. The smile died on her face as she thought of Nevers. Ripped a pregnancy from her without even pretending concern. She followed her thought as it played itself out. What difference would it make if she did get pregnant? After all, if she did—. The knife stabbed her heart again. Plan C or D, or whatever she was on. She had lost count. She breathed hard. Deer mistook it for arousal.

"Why wait till next time?" she said into the dark.

"Well," Deer began, "I thought . . ." No matter what he was thinking, he couldn't say it.

Toni Jo took up the slack.

"There's nothing to worry about." She spoke carefully, like an apprentice laying down his first bricks. "Me and Arkie tried. We wanted children. After a while, I went to the doctor. He said it would be very difficult for me to have children. Maybe if he operated, but even then he wasn't sure. He said I had a tilted uterus."

Deer tried to process this. He was too embarrassed to ask. Tilted uterus. Lady problems. Private stuff. Things he knew nothing about and didn't want to know. It was enough to know that she wouldn't get pregnant.

So they finally got around to making love.

July, August. Several times.

In mid-July, late in the afternoon, Toni Jo heard yells coming from the floor above her, then stomping. The inmates were enraged. She heard the bars being pummeled by fists, then felt the vibrations. She wondered if the outburst were over the food. Maybe the heat. She remembered what it was like up there. The riot, or whatever it was, lasted half an hour.

That evening, Deer came by after his shift. Toni Jo asked about the ruckus. The deputies had been tuned in to the Yankees' game, with the inmates straining to listen, when Joe DiMaggio's 56-game hitting streak came to an end. Some of the men sided with Joe D., while others hated the Yankees. An argument ensued. The convicts would go to bed supperless.

Toni Jo shook her head in disbelief. Death row had changed her perspective. Who would care how many times Joltin' Joe or anyone else hit a baseball?

* * *

September, 1941.
The honeymoon, such as it was, was over.
The warden, perfunctorily, informed her of the date. October 13, 11:01 P.M.
A Monday. Less than a month away.
Deer made sure all reading material was screened before it went to Toni Jo's cell. He did not want any news of the electric chair reaching her.
He had to follow other procedures, too. By the book.
Toni Jo's new *Life* and *Look* and *Saturday Evening Post* magazines fell apart in her hands. She asked Deer about it.
"Just something we have to do." Evasive. Toni Jo asked again. Deer tugged at his top lip. "We have to take the staples out. It's required."
Toni Jo still didn't understand and waited. She had to press for a reply. "Why?"
"They've been known to be used–. Some men on death row have used the staples to commit suicide. Slit their wrists with them."
"Good Lord," Toni Jo said. It would never have occurred to her. "What would be the point? They're going to die anyway."
Deer thought for a moment
"Some of them just can't stand the thought of hanging, or whatever. Some want to do it themselves. Like cheating the system. Who knows what they're thinking?"

* * *

The earth turned and it was September 23, the autumnal equinox, when days and nights were of equal length no matter where in the world you were. Toni Jo's life was in the balance.
The earth turned a few more times and it was October 1. Deer was

not taking it well. Once while visiting, he cried when The Ink Spots came through Toni Jo's radio: "I don't want to set the woooorld on fi-yer, I just want to start . . . a flame in your heart." He had avoided the word as long as possible, but finally confessed that he loved her.

Saturday, the eleventh of October. Toni Jo's deathwatch would start the next day, and then Deer would know her for only twenty-four hours more. He came by at noon on Saturday to ask what she wanted for her last meal.

Officially, the job was the warden's, but he had asked permission to fulfill the duty.

Something was wrong. Toni Jo was cheerful. It broke his heart to see it. Deer had heard of such things. A kind of ecstatic surrender to fate. He hoped she wouldn't fall over the edge into lunacy. He didn't think he could bear watching her go to pieces.

"It's okay," Toni Jo said when he expressed concern. "Really."

"It's awful," he said. "I hate . . ." Deer thought about what he hated. "Everything." He looked at Toni Jo through watery eyes. "What's wrong with the world?" he demanded. "That man deserved to die. He was scum."

Toni Jo touched his arm.

"I have a surprise for you." She had a serene, beatific smile on her face as she looked at him. "My luck is finally changing."

Deer became afraid of her as she slipped into someone else. Insanity. It was worse than he imagined it might be because she was cheerful.

"I won't be executed on October thirteenth."

Deer held her like a child shielding an abused doll.

"It's okay," he said. "I won't leave you. I'll be right there with you."

Toni Jo pushed him away. She was someone else. Her face wore a cruel smile. Something unthinkably mean possessed her.

"The state can't kill an innocent unborn," she said. "And I'm carrying one."

It took Deer a few seconds to process what she had said. She came at him again.

"I figure I'm three months along. That gives me till next April or May. By then I'll think of something else to delay the date again. I might not be able to keep it up forever, but I'll be goddamned if I'm gonna sit here and let them light me up without a fight."

Deer couldn't believe what he was hearing. He had never heard her speak like this. It was like watching a beautiful bride turn into a demon. He stared at her with an expression of terror on his face, unable to speak, almost in a swoon.

Toni Jo looked at him with derision. Even now, she cared about him, but he looked pathetic and weak. Something deep inside her rose up and wanted to hurt him again.

"Well, what did you expect from someone who has nothing to lose?" Deer looked at her while pulling painfully at his top lip. "Mr. Deputy Sheriff," she said. "Mr. Boy Scout's honor." Anything to hurt him.

And he took it. Blow after blow.

19

October 1941–November 28, 1942

Chief Deputy Slim Deer, a Catholic, was wrenched in two directions by Toni Jo's being with child. It was important that no one find out about the pregnancy. Or, later, about the baby. His career would be destroyed, the family name dragged through the mire. Yet he knew he had an obligation to the mother. And the child. Although he had been tricked, he was responsible. He understood that.

* * *

The execution of Toni Jo Henry, set for October 13, 1941, had been delayed, then rescheduled for November of 1942. Inexplicably, everyone in Lake Charles now used Toni Jo's maiden name.

Cal Sonnier reported the mysterious stay, about which he could gather not one shred of factual information. The citizens of Lake Charles went wild. The rumor mill had a bumper crop to grind, and it worked at full capacity night and day.

One rumor said the young woman cheated justice by suicide; another, that she had made a daring escape with outside help. Toni Jo and a tall stranger almost reached the Texas line before being stopped for speeding. One rumor that fell like a quail hit with a tight pattern of bird-shot was that Governor Sam Jones, formerly a Lake Charles attorney, had exercised his power of clemency at the last minute and Toni Jo was now on her way to the home of relatives in Tennessee.

What really happened was that Deputy Sheriff Slim Deer made a confession to Father Jacob, who, in sworn confidence not to reveal his source, expedited the information to Warden White, who called Angola to tell the warden there that he could postpone transportation of Little Sizzler, the portable electric chair, the following day. From Baton Rouge, Warden Donaldson said he would have to track down the chair on its current route around the state and let the driver know he could skip Lake

Charles and go on to his next stop. New Iberia, he thought it was.

What also happened after Toni Jo cooled down was that she and Lambert Deer were pronounced man and wife in a very private late-night ceremony in her cell a week after the stay of execution.

For several restless nights, Deer had agonized over how he could fulfill his duty to mother and child while keeping the potentially ruinous affair from the public. Then he hit upon a plan. He again talked with Father Jacob, who swore himself to secrecy. The only hitch then was a witness. Father Jacob solved the apparently insurmountable problem in a flash.

Sister Mary Catherine.

No one was more devoted to her order. At seventy, she had been a Sister of the Incarnate Word for over half a century, serving first as a nurse at St. Patrick's Hospital, then as a teacher at the Convent of Hearts. She had been forced into retirement because of failing eyesight and made a vow of silence to last until her death. That was the witness at their wedding: a purblind nun committed to a lifetime of silence.

* * *

Deer could hardly have been called a model husband. After the ceremony in late October, he ignored his bride for a week. Toni Jo had time to think about the events of the past month. In a few days, she had gone from deathrow convict to wife and mother-to-be. She reviewed her life. It was hard to believe that in three years a small-town waitress had become a restauranteur, demimondaine, wife, and murderess known nationwide—then wife again, after executing a plot she would never have thought herself capable of hatching a short year ago.

Nevers. He was growing in her mind again. In troubled sleep, she often dreamed of him falling in the headlight beam with a wet splat—the bullet wound transferred by nightmarish necromancy to the head of the angel, now restored, on his chest. She turned to Arkie as he screamed, commanded him to drag the body to the rice canal. Then she heard Nevers laugh and saw his corpse rising in the vapor. She shot him five more times. He thrust his hand into her stomach. Delivered a bloody child and threw it on the ground.

Toni Jo would awaken, panting, sweating, crying. Holding, guarding her womb.

It was then she knew that the child born of her own cunning would serve as atonement for the abortion performed against her will.

* * *

Desirous and shy, autumn descended like a tentative lover trying to make a confident move. Returning upriver from the Gulf, redfish and speckled trout swam into the lake, tracking hordes of white shrimp migrating into the marshes and bays to spawn. The fishermen with their rods, the shrimpers with trawls, spread out over the waters to worship and prey.

Toni Jo slept and awoke, felt her baby growing inside her. Ate every meal and thereby fed the unborn child and came to feel blessed with new life.

November, the early days of December. The sky cool and gray as a wet newspaper.

December 7, 1941.

The Japanese attacked Pearl Harbor. Deer rushed down the cell block to tell Toni Jo. Two minutes later, he returned. It was a radio hoax, like *The War of the Worlds.*

Five minutes later, confirmation. It was true. There had been an invasion, but not from outer space. The world had gone crazy. The world was at war with itself.

* * *

Winter camped on the city for two weeks in January, then wrestled with spring through February and March. Deer visited his wife regularly, but was distracted by war news. And his father had been hospitalized. Diabetes. Doctors fought for and finally gained control over the disease while Slim Deer waited and worried and watched for the next bit of life-changing news.

Amidst all the commotion, in the tranquility of her cell, Toni Jo had formulated a plan. She would have to be taken to St. Patrick's Hospital for the delivery. There, after her child was born, she would pretend weakness, anemia, something—and while no one was looking, escape in the middle of the night.

But before the offspring of her now-devious mind could reach full term, it died in utero.

* * *

On the twenty-fifth of April, 1942, a nameless baby was born in the deathrow cell of the Calcasieu Parish Jail. Dr. Silvers, a retired obstetrician, attended with an old nun from the Convent of Hearts, once a midwife at St. Patrick's. Silvers had only a remote curiosity about how the female inmate came to be in a family way. He was old. He had seen it all. When his old friend Abe Deer had asked him to lend his services in a peculiar case, Ben Silvers didn't even ask for explanations.

The nun had worked with Dr. Silvers before, but Sheriff Abraham Deer explained to him before she arrived that her failing sight and recent vow of silence might cause complications. Silvers told Deer not to worry. Even in the early days, Sister Mary Catherine had worked quietly and, since he did most of the work himself, he doubted even a difficult labor would require assistance.

The patient was sedated, the delivery accomplished, and Toni Jo awoke from the gelatinous haze of twilight sleep.

Slim Deer and Silvers stood as she came around. When she asked for her baby, Dr. Silvers gave her a sedative from a prepared hypodermic and informed her it had been taken to a foster home. Toni Jo lifted herself on one elbow. In a rage, she shrieked at Deer, accusing him of betrayal. A pain flared up from her insides, stopping the words. She glared at her husband.

Deer composed himself. Looking at her calmly, he said, "What did you expect from someone who had everything to lose?" They were the cruelest words he would ever speak.

Toni Jo tried to stay focused on him, wanted to burn holes in him with her eyes. Finally, exhausted, she slumped to the mattress in a feverish swoon.

* * *

A week after Toni Jo had been relieved of her child, she fell into a profound depression, grieving at the absence, the overwhelming emptiness. She had wanted to take care of the infant. She needed to know something about her baby. Anything. Her present state of mind was unbearable.

Deer still cared for his wife, probably even loved her, but he could not allow his indiscretion to be broadcast to his future constituency.

He explained to Toni Jo that the child was now a charge of the orphanage on the grounds of the Convent of Hearts. Neither it nor its eventual foster parents were ever to know its true parentage. This concealment was necessary, Deer said, because the stigma attached to being a murderer's child could lead to its abuse by the heartless. Sister Mary Catherine would effect the transaction.

Toni Jo listened intently, anger, grief, and understanding mixing in her chest like a bad drink.

"Why couldn't I keep my baby until . . ."

"It wouldn't work," Deer said. "There was no sense in y'all becoming attached." He looked at her with compassion. "I hope you understand."

She knew he was right. Her emotions subsided into a mellow sadness. She glanced up at Deer, who had chosen to remain standing in her cell.

"Was it a boy or a girl?"

Deer gazed at her vacantly and shook his head.

"It–. I don't know. I never looked," he said, his eyes filling with water. He swallowed hard before resuming. "Either way, I wasn't sure I could bear the knowing."

* * *

The cool walls of her dark corner cell kept Toni Jo comfortable through June. Once, after pulling the fan from under her bed and then plugging it in, she received a shock that left her arm with a deep, dull ache. She inspected the wire exposed through the frayed cord. For the first time, her execution by electricity became an immediate reality, and she was afraid. Deer had told her the procedure would be completely painless. It was the latest and most humane method of executing justice. She hoped he was right.

But in case he wasn't, she saw no harm in trying again to break her engagement with Death. After working through her initial anger at Deer and the postpartum depression caused by the rift from her baby, Toni Jo had come to see that in the long run Deer was probably right in doing what he had done. Always civil, sometimes openly friendly towards him, Toni Jo attempted a reconciliation with her husband.

Deer saw through the ruse. He would not fall into that trap again, he said.

The summer had given Toni Jo little to record in her diaries. She would have been writing the same entry, day after day. She began mailing some of her things home, but decided to keep the diaries from her mother, whom she hadn't allowed to visit for almost half a year, telling her it would only make it harder on her after she was gone.

In September and October, Toni Jo "Annie Beatrice" Henry Burk Deer reread her life. She had written only on the front of the diary pages and began on the backs to flesh out the gaps with details, writing a retrospective commentary on her stupidity and the cruelty or kindness of others: What she could have done if she had only known. Who she didn't like. Who and what she would miss. A Gulf breeze rushing into her face on Grand Isle. It hadn't been all bad.

Looking back on it, her life read like a mystery she now had the key to. She could fan through the next pages, a hundred or so days, and see the conclusion. There was something comforting about it all, knowing your life like a movie unreeled on the projection-room floor. There. You could point to it. The last frame. **THE END.** November 28, 1942. Toni Jo would have a chance to prepare herself, to prearrange—arrange and rearrange—her thoughts like headstones in a well-planned cemetery.

The electric chair began pulling her towards it like a magnetic lover.

* * *

November 1, 1942.

The last month of her life. As Toni Jo's deadline approached, the daily paper, delivered with her noon meal, reached her with short columns cut out, then longer, and finally whole sections excised. Those would be Cal Sonnier's articles. Deer, she knew, was having someone screen the material before it reached her. Occasionally, she ran across the last few paragraphs of a jump story on a later page that a careless censor had missed.

During the last week of her life, most of the front pages were missing. The rest was war news. The major advertising tactic was patriotic appeal: Simoniz Wax—"Needed for the Defense of Every Car's Beauty." Pall Mall—"In cigarettes, as in naval patrol planes, it's modern design that makes the big difference." Harvey's Barber Stropper—"Makes any blade a WHISKER BLITZER."

Meanwhile, on her radio, Bing Crosby was dreaming of a white Christmas.

On November 23, the Monday before her execution the coming Saturday, Toni Jo found an intact article buried on a back page. It told of Cal Sonnier's attempt, through legal channels, to secure a female witness for the execution: "If Louisiana is going to consign a female convict to the electric chair for the first time, it should also have its first female witness. It's only fair."

It was the first time Toni Jo Henry knew she was about to make history.

The Wednesday edition of *The American Courier* lay on her tray, heavy and sad. The paper would not run the next day, Thanksgiving, so this was a gala issue.

Toni Jo scanned the movies newly arrived for the weekend. Fred Astaire and Rita Hayworth in *You Were Never Lovelier*. The ad looked romantic, but there was something about a man dancing that she never liked. Too prissy.

Road To Morocco, with Bing Crosby, Bob Hope, and Dorothy Lamour. A smiling camel peeked over the shoulders of the male stars. Toni Jo smiled, too.

Ginger Rogers and Cary Grant in *Once Upon a Honeymoon*. It was some kind of war movie. If she had the chance, this is the one she would see:

TOGETHER FOR THE FIRST TIME.
"He kissed her all over the map."
"She finished the man who started the war."

Toni Jo wondered if the teasers referred to the characters' actions in the film or to off-screen intrigues between Ginger and Grant. She asked Deer if he could take her to the movie. He said the holiday crowds would be large, and they couldn't risk being seen.

Toni Jo wasn't much disappointed when he said no. She hadn't thought it likely.

"Well," she said. "I guess this is it, then. We'll never see each other again. At least, not in this life." She tried to laugh.

Deer was silent for a time. In his mind, he played out a quick scenario. He would escape with Toni Jo and make a life elsewhere. But all of his meaning was in Lake Charles. He had never known anything else.

"I–," he began. "As chief deputy, I have to supervise the . . ." He couldn't bring himself to say the word.

Toni Jo helped him. "The execution."

Deer nodded.

"Well, then," his wife said. "I guess I'll see you there." The statement struck her as amusing, like saying to a friend, I'll see you at the ballgame tonight.

* * *

Thanksgiving Day gave Toni Jo only one reason to be grateful. The traditional time for electric chair executions was Thursday, but hers had to be postponed until Saturday because of the holiday. On Friday, she thought: I could have been dead yesterday. *By this time Sunday, I will have been dead twenty-four hours.*

Her deathwatch started at noon on Friday, November 27. When asked about her last meal, all she requested was a Coca-Cola, in a small bottle so cold that frost would coat the green glass.

* * *

At 8 A.M., Toni Jo was awakened, then reminded they were shooting for 11:01.

Breakfast at 8:30.

At 9, a barber entered her cell with Warden White and a deputy. She had not been told about this. The barber cropped her hair close with a pair of scissors, then plugged in his shears and began to shave her.

"Is everyone shaved before an execution?" she wanted to know.

The deputy glanced at the warden, then back to Toni Jo.

"No," he said. Red-faced and heavyset, he looked more frightened than Toni Jo. His pants fit badly and he was constantly hiking them up.

"Why not?" she asked.

The deputy looked at Warden White, who nodded a go-ahead. Toni Jo thought the deputy looked a mite slow-witted, but she quickly surmised that he was in charge of the chair.

"No need to shave someone about to be hung, but with the electric chair–." He paused. "Ma'am, a bald head reduces resistance to electricity. And minimizes singeing and burning, which leaves a bad smell." He hitched his pants up and looked at his feet. "Plus, you wouldn't want a fire in the jail."

When the men had departed, Toni Jo picked up a mirror. She didn't want to look, but she did. Her head resembled an egg with a face painted on. After being shorn of her identity, dying didn't seem so bad.

At 10, Deputy Red-Face returned with a set of clothes and asked her to put them on. She slipped into the baggy outfit. It had no buttons or zippers. She didn't have to ask. The metal would heat up. Burn her body.

Wryly, she thought, *Wouldn't want that to happen.*

She had one hour to live. What do you do in your final hour?

Toni Jo Henry turned on her radio.

At 10:30, she was told the execution would be delayed. A technical problem. The wires were too short to reach her cell. She would have to be executed in the corridor.

"Thank you for telling me," she said.

"Oh!" she exclaimed as the red-faced deputy ambled down the hall after hitching his pants up. She had almost forgotten. "Can I have my Coke?"

While waiting, Toni Jo picked up her diary and wrote,

November 28, 1942.
On the last day of my life,

She never finished the entry.

Her soft drink arrived at 10:45. She held the bottle in her hand. It was cold and damp. Had probably been covered with frost when the deputy retrieved it. She watched the tiny silver bubbles swimming up through the coffee-colored liquid along the neck. She tipped the soda up and drank deeply. The carbonation burned her throat, the sweet pain squeezing tears from her eyes. She looked at the bottle. There was something eminently sad about the familiar shape. Like a friend. The last pleasant thing she would ever see.

At 11, she was called from her cell to be weighed and photographed. She thought, *They weren't this interested in me while I was living.* When she reached the documentation room, she thought, *It's 11:02. I should already have been dead, but I'm still alive. I can see and hear and taste and touch and smell.*

Back in her cell by 11:15.

Clattering in the hallway of the cell block. She imagined the scene. Assistants setting up the chair. Directions whispered intently. Hurry. Be quiet.

The chair was tested at 11:30. The copper electrode connections were buffed clean of verdigris deposits, then moistened for better conduction.

The generator started with a low growl that reached a high wail, like the squall of a wildcat. She heard a living, dull thud as enormous electricity coursed through the wires. Her radio speaker crackled in response, her cell vibrated with the pure violence done to the innocent air. Then silence for fifteen minutes.

She had finished her Coke and was listening to a song she had never heard. Happy, upbeat. Her mouth, she suddenly realized, was dry. She reached for her purse and extracted a slice of gum. She chewed the wad in unison to the snappy rhythm of the song.

"Toni Jo?" Her heart jolted. She glanced up. Deputy Red-Face was looking at her through the barred square in the door. "It's time."

"Can I finish listening to this new song? It's so with it. It's called 'Jingle Jangle Jingle,' by Glenn Miller. Do you know it?"

The man turned his ear toward the cell and listened.

> I got spurs . . . that jingle jangle jingle
> As I go riii—ding merrily along.
> And they sing, oh, ain't you glad you're single,
> And that sooong . . . ain't so very far from wrong.

"Can't say as I do." He listened a moment longer. "You really must come along now."

Toni Jo turned the knob on her Philco and the song faded.

As if by magic, the door opened invitingly.

Down the short corridor, she saw a conglomeration of people standing around like they had been served bad hors d'oeuvres at a garden party. Coming in from the window, the drone of an electric motor provided background music.

For some inexplicable reason, an advertising slogan popped into Toni Jo's head:

Drink Coca-Cola

◆

Enjoy Cooling Refreshment

The crowd parted as if she were the guest of honor. Thick black cables coiled from a window down to a high-backed chair with black straps flopped about like tentacles.

A large book was open on a podium. A Bible, she thought. She was stopped while each of the guests signed the book. It was a register. One after another, she watched them write in the log and politely step around each other in the crowded hallway. Two doctors, the sheriff, and two deputies—one, her husband. Then Cal Sonnier and her attorneys, Levine and Prudhomme, who nodded at her with glum courtesy. Then Judge Page, District Attorney Avario, and Father Jacob.

Seeing the twelfth witness, almost a whole woman, she thought, *So Sonnier got his wish.*

Supported on either side, the sightless nun was led to the podium, a pen put in her hand, her hand placed on the page. All she had to do was write *Sister Mary Catherine.*

The woman who had attended Toni Jo's wedding and childbirth would blindly witness her death.

After the signing, everyone turned to the condemned as if she were a bride coming up the aisle. She reached the chair, turned, and sat. She reached up to flip her hair, a nervous, feminine gesture, and found she had none left. The chair was made of heavy, dark oak and reminded her of a throne. Someone, a man with children perhaps, had made the chair especially for this purpose, put the care of his hands into the wood, and still it was uncomfortable. As the belts were hastily secured, she had time to think, *No one would have wanted to sit in something like this for very long anyway.*

The whirring of the dynamo grew louder.

Then it seemed as if everyone had a question for her.

Father Jacob: "Would you like extreme unction?"

She frowned at him.

"The last rites," he said.

"Oh." She thought for a moment. "No. Thank you all the same."

They started at her ankles. The right pantleg of her uniform was raised and pinned beneath her knee with a strap, exposing her slender calf.

Something was wrong. Deputy Sheriff Slim Deer wasn't able to finish his task with the buckle. A choked sob escaped from his mouth as he stood from his stooped position, hurried down the corridor, and disappeared around the corner. Sheriff Mule Deer was left to complete his son's job.

Toni Jo was furious. Abandoned again. Herald Nevers.

That son-of-a-bitching swine.

Someone shook her arm. They had buckled down her waist and were working on her wrists and forearms. She felt like she was being strapped in for a roller coaster ride. The Zephyr. She chewed her gum frantically. Her heart pounded with primitive terror as her forehead was pressed against the chairback and strapped down.

"–your effects?" she heard.

"What?" she said.

"What would you like us to do with your effects?" Sheriff Abraham Deer posed the question. She looked at the faces looking at hers.

"It doesn't matter." She came to the face of Sister Mary Catherine, bordered by the black and white wimple, her eyes focused on eternity, and remembered the baby in her care. "Could–?" she began.

"Yes?" Sheriff Deer said. "What is it?"

Toni Jo reached to point at the holy Sister and found her arm constrained. She looked at it strapped tightly to the arm of the chair.

"My things," she said. "Could you keep them?" She was looking at the nun, who was unaware she was being spoken to.

"Sister?" Father Jacob said.

The nun serenely tilted her head toward the priest.

"Will you keep her personal effects?"

The Sister gave a barely detectable nod.

Cal Sonnier wrote furiously on a narrow pad as the electrode at the end of a black cable was attached to Toni Jo's exposed right leg just above the ankle strap. Next, a cap resembling a metal bowl was placed on her head and then connected to the second cable, which dangled menacingly above the chair.

Sheriff Deer turned to his red-faced deputy.

"The time?"

He looked at his watch.

"Twelve minutes after noon."

Sheriff Deer reached towards the mouth of his charge.

"Please," he said. Toni Jo was chewing her gum wildly. "Open," the sheriff said.

Toni Jo finally understood. She opened her mouth and the gum was taken from her tongue.

Sheriff Deer looked at her. His eyes were gray-blue and steady. "Do you have any final statements?"

She tried to shake her head no. Then, an afterthought, "Give my baby a good home."

All the witnesses thought she was demented. All but three.

A heavy dark-brown leather mask was fitted against Toni Jo's face and secured to the chair with laces. There was an opening for her nose. She could see light through the aperture. The barn-like smell of leather and decay filled her nostrils.

"Are we ready?"

She recognized the sheriff's voice.

She didn't know how much time she had.

She tried quickly to think of her life.

Her mind raced from her earliest memory, her mother's face and the fragrance of baby powder, forward until it hit up against the man who had brought her here.

"*Everything!*" she shouted unexpectedly, surprising even herself. "You took everything from me!" She felt her neck muscles straining against the strap on her forehead. "I'm not done with you yet, Herald Nevers. I'm coming to get you, you son of a bitch!"

The red-faced deputy yelled outside the window, trying to make his voice heard above the angry whine of the dynamo.

"Pull the lever! Pull the switch, for God's sake!"

The man in the back of the truck looked at a dial, then, cupping his hands around his mouth, faced the window. "We're below threshold!" he bellowed as the motor was winding to the high-pitched wail before the squall of deadly energy.

Toni Jo struggled in the chair as if she wanted to rip the straps off and get to Nevers.

"Pull it!" the deputy screamed again, competing with the engine. "For God's sake, man, do it!"

Do it—the phrase triggered the sickening memory of what Nevers had made her say in bed.

"Yes!" she screamed. A manic frenzy possessed her. "Pull it. I want to get at him as fast as I can. Do it! Do it!" She laughed a hideous laugh. "I'm coming for you. I'm going to get you, you son of a bitch. Here I come! I'm

PART THREE

The evil that men do lives after them;
The good is oft interred with their bones.

Shakespeare, *Julius Caesar*

20

1953–1961

I saw Sheriff Lambert Deer for the first time when I was ten years old. He wore a khaki uniform pressed into knife-like creases, a gold badge shining impressively over his heart. He had come to the Episcopal Girls' School to talk about traffic safety, and I sat on the front row, close enough to watch sweat droplets appear over his top lip like a mustache of glistening beads. Later, when I was thirteen or fourteen, Mother told me at supper one evening why Sheriff (by then, Mayor) Deer campaigned for traffic safety. In 1947, his bride of less than a year had been killed by a drunk driver while carrying his first child. I was touched by the fact that he had remained a childless widower ever since.

Never imagining I would know him personally one day, I heard about him now and again—in newspapers, on the radio, or from girls who moaned and mock-swooned over his uniformed good looks. My younger brother, Bobby, who had recently joined Junior Deputies, came home one afternoon yammering about the Sheriff letting him shoot his pistol. I hated admitting to myself that I was actually jealous. After that, I searched out the Sheriff's pictures in newspapers to cut them out and paste in my scrapbook. I didn't think it was any big deal back then. Lots of my girlfriends did stuff like that.

"They used to call him Slim," Mother said when he was running for mayor in 1954. She saw me sprawled on the den floor gawking at his picture in the paper. It was hard to believe he had ever been skinny. Now he was built like a heavyweight boxer. In bold black letters that seemed to hover and shimmy over an orange background, his campaign signs confidently taunted the electorate:

VOTE
Sheriff Lambert A. "Lamb" Deer
for Mayor
IS THERE ANY OTHER CHOICE?

Throughout the day, big white cars draped with patriotic banners drove slowly around the neighborhoods blaring slogans from their rooftop bullhorns. These images came back to me years later. But first I put the Mayor, my real-life idol, aside for a while, replacing him with reproductions of signed movie-star photographs and then real boys, pimpled and shyly eager, who took me to school dances or met me at "make-out" parties in friends' garages.

In 1959, near the beginning of my senior year at LaGrange High School, my father ran for a seat on the City Council. Quite unnaturally, he won. I say unnaturally because Dad was the quietest man I ever knew: passive, yet concerned; a bookkeeper for PPG; the last man you'd imagine running for public office. The main image I have of Daddy is him reading the newspaper in a beat-up armchair he rarely stirred from after his long days at work. When Bobby and I, or my older sister Maureen and I, went to Daddy, expecting him to settle our childish arguments, he listened carefully, waited a few seconds, then spoke deliberately. Daddy even mowed the grass slowly, moving methodically across the lawn as if chewing the cud himself. He was the tortoise to lay your money on—if he ever entered the race.

It was strange to see our name on the political advertisements: William "Billy Bird" Bienvenu. In red, white, and blue, with stars above and below his name. On weekends, he canvassed the neighborhoods with at least one member of his family. I would stand still as Daddy introduced himself and spoke a few words about his views. Then, when he introduced me, I would step forward with a smile, feeling like a Sunday-school girl showing off her new dress, bashful and proud. My father never seemed very crafty to me, but it was obvious he knew all the tricks that mattered. Three months later, we had a public servant in the family.

Which was good and bad. Before, I had been neither particularly reserved nor outgoing. Now, I was visible. A mark. Previously, I could sit inconspicuously in class and take notes, looking ignorant but interested. Now, my government and history teachers called on me with questions whose answers I hadn't a clue about. Walking down the halls, on the beach, at ball games, people I didn't know cast furtive glances my way and whispered to friends and spouses behind their hands. Sometimes, I heard them.

"That's Billy Bird's daughter."

"Maureen?"

"No, the younger one. Leigh I think's her name."

"Mmm-huh. He's a good man."

"Yep. The rest of that crowd, I wouldn't give you a wooden nickel for the whole bunch of 'em."

Just before my graduation, in May of 1960, Mr. Bork's history classes held a mock presidential election. Forty percent of the students at LaGrange were Catholic. After the ballots were tallied at sixth hour, Mr. Bork's voice came through the P.A. system during end-of-the-day announcements. His voice quavered with excitement when he said Kennedy had trounced Nixon by garnering eighty-five percent of the vote. That meant non-Catholics were willing to throw a few votes his way.

The mini-election was in fact a prognostication of the real thing. In the televised Nixon-Kennedy debates, Jack Kennedy was incredibly handsome. With his extemporaneous repartee, JFK beat the daylights out of the stodgy Nixon. People began to forget Kennedy was Catholic. All but the Catholics, who had waited a long time—forever, really—for this moment in history. In November, we had our first non-protestant President Elect. On a blustery January day, he ushered in a new era with confidence and caution:

> "We observe today not a victory of party but a celebration of freedom, symbolizing an end as well as a beginning, signifying renewal as well as change. For I have sworn before you and Almighty God the same solemn oath our forebears prescribed nearly a century and three-quarters ago.
>
> The world is very different now. For man holds in his mortal hands the power to abolish all forms of human poverty and all forms of human life . . .
>
> So let us begin anew, remembering on both sides that civility is not a sign of weakness, and sincerity is always

subject to proof. . . . Together let us explore the stars, conquer the deserts, eradicate disease, tap the ocean depths and encourage the arts and commerce . . .

All this will not be finished in the first one hundred days. Nor will it be finished in the first one thousand days, nor in the life of this Administration, nor even perhaps in our lifetime on this planet. But let us begin.

. . .

Finally, whether you are citizens of America or citizens of the world, ask of us here the same high standards of strength and sacrifice which we ask of you. With a good conscience our only sure reward, with history the final judge of our deeds, let us go forth. . . ."

* * *

The summer before the presidential election, I entered politics myself. Among the city's several departments, the least prestigious jobs were in Public Works. The least desirable position was file clerk. After graduation, through my father's influence, I became—wouldn't you know it—a file clerk in the Department of Public Works.

Here's what went through our office: anything having to do with garbage, water, public transit, or streets and drainage. An animal-control division was on the drawing board when I arrived and would be implemented by the time I switched departments a year later. But there's one division I failed to mention. Sewerage. How I hated that word! It sounded so nasty—so nasty and foul that I set about on a kind of personal crusade to clean up the word by changing it to "sewage," which, for whatever reason my girlish mind had conjured up, sounded more sanitary.

I had intended to keep the job for the summer only, but something larger than we are—chance or fate or God—has a way of redirecting our lives. "The best laid plans of mice and men," Mrs. Hennigan used to say. Maureen, who was barely a year older than me, had been at LSU for a full term when I graduated. In her letters, she told me of the campus and football games, sororities and fraternities, things that sounded interesting to watch, but the fact of the matter is that I never was much of a participator. Mo begged me to come to LSU and not waste my time at McNeese Junior College. "McNeese sits in the middle of an old cow pasture," she wrote. "*That* should tell you something." Mom found Mo's arguments convincing, and now that Daddy was "one of the little big shots," as she was fond of saying, she was positive they could work out a way for me to attend LSU. After all, Mother said, I was the real thinker in the family and deserved to go to the big university. Like people often do, Mother mistook my reticence for deep thinking.

Ha! If she only knew. She should have said I was the dreamer of the family. I had this idea that I would meet a graying doctor or lawyer (a bachelor, of course, someone who had waited half his life for the right woman, meaning me), and this distinguished gentleman would be irresistibly drawn to my beauty, plain though it was, and beg me to marry him over the protestations of my parents. Just exactly where I would meet this grizzled, latter-day Romeo I couldn't have said. But things always had a way of working out. Didn't they? Well, didn't they? That's what the romances I devoured by the dozen promised.

Now, you probably think I'm going to say that this best laid mouse-plan got squashed by the rat-trap of reality. But that's not what happened at all. What happened was even more romantic than my outlandish imagination could have fabricated.

21

1961–1962

I filed papers. Norlene, the office manager, or Natalie or Cheryl would give me a pile of dog-eared carbon copies and sit me in front of a gray cabinet, and I would file and file. When I was done, they'd give me more stacks and point me toward another cabinet. By five P.M., my hands were covered with ink, my face smudged by the day's war paint.

In just a few weeks, I became aware of the pecking order. Kind but businesslike, Norlene, a pixie with a high-pitched voice, was friends with Cheryl and Natalie, girls she had gone to school with, but not with Debbie, once a cheerleader at St. Marion Catholic. And nobody liked Gloria, who was oblivious to the girls' ire and delighted in everyone. None of this was immediately apparent. To an outsider, Norlene and Cheryl seemed to be arch-rivals bent on making each other's lives miserable. So you'd be shocked the first time you saw them laughing on their lunch hour at MaryAnn's Cafe. Their competitive fussing was in fact a secret code that drew them closer each time a barb struck home.

Although my first month on the job was mostly dull, I did see some advantages to staying put. For one thing, niftily-dressed men would occasionally pass through the office. Possibilities I could almost touch. All I had to do was actually meet one of the younger attorneys. Norlene and Cheryl's incessant chatter on this topic definitely had an encouraging effect on me. This was, after all, City Hall. Running errands up and down four flights of stairs, I saw most of the city's big wheels roll right by me during any given week, and the birdwatchers in the office educated me on the species that hadn't found nest mates.

When Mayor Deer passed through, I got a tragic feeling in my heart, like a man of his stature shouldn't have to soil himself by walking down the halls of the Department of Public Works. If anything, though, he treated us with extra kindness, as if he understood that someone had to do the dirty work. The Mayor always said a few words to each of the girls, and after the third or fourth time Norlene introduced us, he remembered my name.

"Leigh Ann," he said with a smile and one squinty eye as he aimed at me down the barrel of his finger. "Right?"

"Yes, sir." What I wanted to say was, "Leigh. Just Leigh."

"I knew I'd finally get it," he said. "My brain's filled with so many trifles it doesn't have time for the really important stuff, like pretty girls." You could tell he really wasn't flirting. It was that superficial kind of talk important men engage in when they want you to know you're alright in their book. I felt foolish, looking over my shoulder and up at him from the swivel stool, a swatch of ink probably streaked across my face.

"Do you like your job?"

"Oh, yes sir," I said. "Very much." What was I supposed to say to the Mayor?—"No, I can't stand it?"

The Mayor turned to Norlene. "Is she a good worker?"

"The best," Norlene said. "We give her all the dirty work, and she just smiles and asks for more." The Mayor laughed. He and Norlene went way back.

"A regular Cinderella, huh?" He said this to Norlene while looking at me. It made me feel like a pet, something for the amusement of its owner.

"Looking for her Prince Charming," Norlene quipped.

"Well," Mayor Deer said, "I can tell you one thing." The Mayor looked around at all the women. "He ain't in here." Everyone laughed at his cleverness. He punched me on the shoulder. "Sister," he said. "I tell you what. You work hard here, and I'll see if I can move you to a more kicking department, hear?"

When I bragged to Bobby about the Mayor's attention, he gave me the most bored look he could muster. "Big rip," he said. Janice was lying in his arms on the sofa. He was a senior working hard on being coolly detached and couldn't afford his big sister bringing up the embarrassment of his former life as a Junior Deputy.

At the end of the summer, I decided to stay. College wasn't for me. Never was. I tried to convince myself that I based my decision on the money I was making, on the feeling of being a tiny cog in the great machinery that ran the municipality, and of course on the prospect that any day Prince Charming would sweep me off my feet and into a lakefront mansion where I would command a host of servants.

Looking back on that time, I think it was probably just plain old inertia that kept me where I was. A year passed, and still no dapper young attorney from a moneyed pedigree had married me. But at least the Mayor kept his promise. In the summer of 1961, I was appointed clerk's assistant in the Legal Department, which was composed of the City Attorney, two lawyers, and a support staff. James Hargrave, the City Attorney, looked like a ninety-year-old W. C. Fields, and the two younger lawyers were married and fat to boot, so there I was again, Cinderella without a beau to escort me to the ball.

The next year moved slowly and might have been unenduringly tedious if it hadn't been for the outbursts over President Kennedy's latest political stratagems or private escapades: the Bay of Pigs, Marilyn Monroe, and all that. I filled the endless days dreaming up and populating my own little Camelot, fancying myself a junior-auxiliary Jackie Kennedy who would be swept off her feet by . . . who else? It had to be the most improbable and therefore unattainable man I could imagine. Otherwise, the fantasy was worthless. Who but Mayor Deer?

I imagined how an ordinary comment from him would elicit an incredibly witty response from me. He would smile and give me a special look. Our eyes would lock and he would slowly approach and take me in his arms, drawing my sensuously parted lips to his. I spent many a day in romantic agony while anticipating the next arrival of our good Mayor. Generally, he showed up three or four times a week, each time cheerfully greeting me with an impersonal pat on the back, exclaiming, "Sister Leigh of the Pious Ink Blot!" or some similar condescension that would blow my cotton-candy kingdom to smithereens.

And so the days went, sliding from oppressive heat to biting cold without a transition. A month of winter, a short recess of spring, and then the heat again.

The summer of 1962. That's when I really started to live. Rumors of Mayor Deer running for governor sprouted into plans. Just when I knew all the municipal politicians by name, the faces of other important men began to plague me. Then the money started showing up. Millionaires I heard of daily but had never seen: Ralph "The Ghost" Rivers, T. H. Burden, and Martha White, a wrinkled old crone with clown makeup who made her zillion by purchasing every overworked piece of farmland and worthless marsh in Cameron and Calcasieu Parishes and striking oil on nearly every acre. Lord, it was like a convention that never stopped.

Then, mysteriously into this menagerie of millionaires and band of bigwigs floated another element. Priests. Fathers, Brothers, and a Monsignor circulated through the secular crowds that took care of the affairs of this world. Occasionally, I saw a priest with a cigar in his mouth, taking a light from a politician. Clergy, politicos, the old and new rich—I didn't want to know anything about the glue that held this dubious brotherhood together. It was exciting, though, the hustle and bustle, the feel of being caught up in a relentless mass moving toward the future with purpose. In October of 1962, Mayor Deer asked me to be part of his campaign. He asked me in front of everybody, in that way of his, like he was talking to one of the boys and there was no answer but yes. This was the moment I had been waiting two years for. My heart was jumping against my ribcage like a bullfrog in a shoebox. I looked up at him and delivered the incredibly witty response that would launch our romance.

"Me?" I said.

A struck-dumb look came over his face. He glanced around the office and burst out laughing.

"Yes," he said. "You."

I was red as a tomato. Down a long tunnel, I heard myself say, like an idiotic schoolgirl, "Why, what can *I* do?"

The Mayor laughed again and looked around.

"Why, anything you want to, Little Bit. Except, of course, run for governor. That's my job, see?" The voice he used was somewhere between that of a comedian and a cartoon villain.

I could barely contain myself for the rest of the day. I felt . . . something. Special. Important in a small way. A dust mote blown about by the winds of destiny. A foot soldier in the battle for higher ground. Leigh Ann Bienvenu, modern-day Joan of Arc.

"Anything I wanted to" turned out to be stuffing envelopes and making phone calls. The job was neither fascinating nor glamorous, but I consoled myself with the fact that I was a part of Mayor Deer's campaign and thus he would *have* to talk with me sometime.

Inside a week, I was lodged in my post at campaign headquarters across the street, next door to Immaculate Conception Church. From my second-floor desk, I could look out the window and see City Hall, the jail, and the Courthouse guarded by the greening statue of a Confederate soldier and a silvered cannon from the first World War.

Priests, politicians, and millionaires promenaded across the streets, stopping in little clots under the massive, drooping limbs of the live oaks, then scurrying on with some priceless morsel to communicate to the next ant in the hill.

* * *

It was bound to happen. Scandal. No self-respecting Louisiana political campaign could run its course without one. November, 1962. The serious, get-down-to-brass-tacks part of the gubernatorial race had begun. On the front page of the November 28 *American Courier*, the headlines announced:

TWENTIETH ANNIVERSARY!
Toni Jo Henry Execution
Citizens Recall Rumors

The execution was legendary. Lake Charles held the distinction of executing the only woman ever to sit in Louisiana's electric chair. After twenty years, gossip about the woman still abounded. Some said Toni Jo Henry had served as the jail's prostitute to get privileges ranging from cigarettes to excursions outside the lockup. Others said she had serviced only Sheriff Abraham "Mule" Deer and that was enough to get her all the special favors she wanted. None of the citizens quoted in the article was mentioned by name. Beside the headline was a photograph of the stylish young murderess reading under a fan at the desk in her cell, a caged parakeet barely visible in the upper right corner.

Naturally, as such things go, the old Sheriff's son was left to answer for his father. Mayor Deer was outraged. At a strategy meeting, he said someone was trying to sabotage his political career. He offered five hundred dollars to the person who could expose the people responsible for the libelous comments.

I had heard about Toni Jo Henry for most of my life. Suddenly, however, her life enlarged in significance as it became capable, to my surprise, of affecting mine. It was a week before I could look up the original accounts of the execution. I had been working till nine each night and falling exhausted on my bed by eleven so I could be at work for seven the next day. I wasn't after the five hundred dollars. I only wanted my curiosity satisfied about the matter that upset Louisiana's next governor.

At the Parish Library, I asked Mrs. Harrison where the old newspapers were. She tilted her head down until her glasses, attached to a necklace, slid off her nose.

"I'm afraid we dispose of newspapers after a month."

"Oh," I said with great disappointment. "I really need to look up some things from . . . around the war time."

She inspected me for a moment. "Well," she said, "the only thing I can tell you is to go to the morgue."

"The morgue?"

Mrs. Harrison emitted a weak laugh, realizing her mistake at assuming too much on my part.

"That's what they call the room at the *Courier* where all the back issues are stored."

I put my hand on my chest and sighed with relief.

At the *Courier*, a cub reporter met me and said he'd have to ask his boss if I could enter the morgue. He disappeared behind a maze of partitions and reappeared, much older, a minute later.

"I'm Cal Sonnier," the familiar-looking man said, holding out his hand. "City Editor. And I have the pleasure of meeting—?"

"Leigh Bienvenu," I said, taking his hand. "From the Mayor's campaign headquarters."

"A lamb in a den of wolves. You'd better be careful."

His black and gray eyebrows arched, and I knew then who he reminded me of. With his high forehead and bushy mustache, he was a perfect blend of Charlie Chaplin, Edgar Allan Poe, and Adolf Hitler. Taking his comment as a joke, I laughed and asked about seeing the morgue. We had to walk single file down the aisles between the rows of bookcases.

"Here," he said, stopping before a shelf housing large binders of dried leather. "What year were you looking for?"

"Nineteen Forty-Two," I said, my heart pounding. "November."

Sonnier pressed his glasses to his nose and squinted up and down the stacks until he spied the volume he wanted. He pulled it and ushered me back to the newsroom with a toss of his head. Sonnier dropped the folio on the nearest desk. A small explosion sent paper flakes and dust devils whirling into the sunlight. "Holler if you need anything else, hear?"

"I will," I said.

On the maroon cover, the month and year were impressed in gold lettering. As I pulled the heavy chair to the desk, a feeling of reverence came over me. Then a feeling of dread. I had a premonition that I would find something I didn't want to find. I knew the date Toni Jo Henry was executed: November 28, 1942. I decided to sneak up on the red-letter day as if I had been catapulted back in time and was a reader during the week before the murderess's appointment with justice. At first, my curiosity sidetracked me through clothing ads and comic strips. I'd never heard of Mandrake or Mickey Finn. The first relevant article I came across was dated November 21.

A delicious thrill crawled through my body as I read the headline:

DEATH BY ELECTROCUTION
A History

For the next seven newspaper days, Calvin Sonnier (it felt strange knowing an older version of this same man) examined the execution from every angle: What Is It Like? Is It Right? Chance of Executing an Innocent Man? Why the Autopsy?

Sonnier presented conflicting "expert" opinions. He began the series with general information, then, as the death day approached, served up the more grisly details. After the switch is thrown, the current shoots into the head, travels through the brain, neck, and heart, then violates the other organs, "some of which explode," the electricity coming to ground through the ankle.

I had thought the killer was shot with high voltage for a few seconds and that was it. In fact, the deadly charge is delivered in two doses. It was like reading a prescription.

Shot one, administered for fifty-seven seconds, was comprised of a 60-cycle alternating current of 2,000 volts at 4 to 8 amperes. (I had no idea what all this meant, but the results were quite clear.) Attending physicians say the subject is immediately struck unconscious, justifying the process as humane. Instant death is achieved via destruction of the brain, which occurs with such speed that the nervous system can't react quickly enough for the condemned to feel pain.

The visual report of an execution was more unsettling. After the first jolt, the body jerks, lunges against restraining straps, and stiffens. Deep, rapid breathing ensues. This fact made me suspicious about "instant death." A spiral of smoke rises from the head, then a crackling noise is heard, followed by the odor of burning flesh. The hands turn red, then white, and the neck cords stand out.

After dose one, the current is cut off for three seconds. The body slowly relaxes. Just when it looks rested from a mighty labor, the second shot, also fifty-seven seconds, brings the corpse to life again in a series of twitches. After the second dose, the skin looks sunburned because it has reached 140 degrees Fahrenheit. The body is left alone for three minutes to cool off so the coroner can handle it. The autopsy reveals second degree burns at the electrode on the right leg and a pinkish froth similar to beach foam coming from the mouth. If the current was miscalculated, the brain is baked hard. During their investigation, coroners calloused by years of gruesome deaths joke that it's not the volts that get you, it's the amps.

What I read next would already have occurred if I had been there in 1942. I turned to the evening edition of November 28. At the top of the page were three photographs: Toni Jo Henry smoking in her cell, a dozen witnesses standing around the empty electric chair, and a sheet-covered corpse being lifted into the ambulance on a gurney.

The headline screamed, TONI JO PAYS SUPREME PENALTY. The article itself was surprisingly sketchy. Pushed to the far right-hand side of the page, it was headed "Henry is Silent, Calm to the End" and subheaded "State Exacts Life for St. Valentine's Slaying of Ex-Lover."

The narrative described Toni Jo's bride-like walk to the chair. She was strapped in. The generator whined until it sounded like an angry wildcat and someone unseen pulled a switch. Two minutes later, a physician checked Toni Jo's heartbeat and said to the Warden, "Toni Jo Henry has expired." Then the Warden said to the Judge, as if he hadn't heard, "Your Honor, the Court's order has been fulfilled." Sonnier then backtracked and related other oddments of the scene: Toni Jo's last meal, a Coke; the execution was delayed because the generator wires were too short to reach her cell; one of the eyewitnesses was a nearly blind nun; and the final statement of the condemned—"Give my baby a good home," a comment Sonnier interpreted as the distracted ramblings of a brain under extreme duress.

That was all.

I felt a lump in my throat, then realized my face was moist with tears.

As I reached into my purse for a Kleenex, my eyes fell on the three photos capping the page. Toni Jo looked so peaceful in her cell, gazing out at the camera with the eyes of a deer about to be slain.

Deer. The word reminded me of the Mayor. I looked at the other photo. There he was, barely recognizable. Much thinner. With an exhausted, worried look on his face. I jumped from person to person to see if I knew any of the others. Another deputy, two doctors, Sonnier with hair, the nun, a priest, and assorted other people. The priest. He looked familiar. The caption said Father Jacob. Yes, his face suddenly came true. Add a little putty, a few cracks, some gray hair—and there he was. Monsignor LeBlanc.

It slowly dawned on me that every important man in the city was connected to every other. But I needed a guide to show me the intersections related to the case at hand. In the City Room, Sonnier sat working deliberately, immune to the haste swirling around him, his desk as orderly as a tea set. I rapped gently on the metal frame of his partition.

"Excuse me, Mr. Sonnier, but I was wondering if you would answer a few questions. I'll only take a minute of your time." Barely moving his head, Sonnier peered at me over his reading glasses and returned his eyes to the pad before him. After a minute, he put his pencil down and swiveled toward me. He looked at me with eyes, sleepy and glazed, that years ago had seen their last surprise.

"Now what's this matter of urgency?" His eyes locked on me calmly, like a lion looking disdainfully on prey too small or stupid to be worth pursuing. Nervous, reluctant to infringe on his time, I threw my question at him as if he knew what I had been reading for the last hour.

"What's this about taking care of my baby?" Another man would have looked at me with utter bewilderment. Sonnier merely tilted his head an imperceptible distance backward, a gesture that said, "What kind of fool am I dealing with now who thinks I want to take care of her baby?" He waited for the next development. "Toni Jo Henry, I mean. I've been reading about her execution."

Sonnier's head moved forward a bit. "Well, why didn't you say so? That's something I know a thing or two about." With his hand, he made a subtle gesture. "Have a seat." I sat in the chair and placed my purse on the floor. "Someone's always trying to dig that poor woman up. They ought to let her rest in peace." He looked at me indifferently. "What's *your* angle?"

"I work for Mayor Deer. There've been some rumors floating around that his father and Toni Jo Henry. . . ." I returned his stare. I was telling more than I needed to. "I wasn't around then. I just wanted to see what I could see." Sonnier wasn't going to help me out. "For myself, you know. I was just curious." His smug demeanor was starting to irritate me. Deciding to play his game, I stared at him and waited for a reply. After an uncomfortably long while, he spoke.

"Curiosity. That's what killed the cat, you know."

I held my tongue, pretending to deliberate, then gave what appeared to be a measured response.

"So I'm told."

The part of Sonnier's mouth visible through his mustache grew the smallest of grins.

"Fair enough," he said. "Now what's this about me taking care of your baby?"

"Not mine," I said. "Toni Jo Henry's. At her execution, you wrote that she said, 'Take care of my baby. Give him a good home.' Something like that."

Sonnier put a hand on his chin. "Sounds vaguely familiar. Yes, seems like–. You have to understand, Miss . . ."

"Bienvenu."

"Bienvenu. That was twenty years ago and I'm not in the habit of rereading my own material. I'm not that vain."

"At the execution it came time for last words, and Miss Henry said she wanted her baby taken care of. I'd be grateful for anything you can remember about that. In the article, you seemed to think Miss Henry was talking out of her head. Because of the stress and all."

Sonnier's eyes looked past me, about twenty years past me. After an extended pause, he broke out of his trance and spoke.

"Nineteen forty-two, right?" I nodded. "I came onto the newspaper in '41 as a comma chaser, a copy editor. I had just moved up to reporter and needed a scoop. Jim Mead—he's the editor now, you know. Back then, he occupied the chair I sit in now." Sonnier slapped the armrests. "Well, not the same chair, but you get the idea. City Editor. He was a gatekeeper. He could let a story through or quash it without explanation. A week after the execution, I wrote a piece suggesting that the original execution date was postponed because of some illicit carrying-on between the Sheriff and Toni Jo. Possibly even a baby. Ah, there's your baby," Sonnier said with mild surprise. "Funny, I had almost forgotten about that." Sonnier was lost in thought for a bit. "The article never saw light. Mead spiked it. He was right to can it, but I didn't think so then. Journalism is about facts, not speculation. What do you think? It doesn't seem likely that the baby could have been snuck out without somebody seeing him, or hearing him. Babies do cry, don't they?"

I shrugged my shoulders. "He?"

Sonnier looked at me. "He, she. Whatever. Those kinds of secrets have a tendency to rear up sooner or later and bite you on the ass." Sonnier again lost himself in thought. Then, out of nowhere, he said, "Sorry. No offense."

"You knew her?" I said.

"Toni Jo? Some. Interviewed her two or three times."

"What was she like?"

Sonnier looked at me.

"Now that's a different matter," he said, as if I had broken the rules. "That's not facts."

I held my ground by saying nothing. Sonnier rested his head on his thumb and gazed at the floor. A couple of minutes passed. He looked up at me, a red circle in the middle of his forehead.

"There was charity in her voice," he said, "like every word was a gift you'd never expected." He shook his head. His level, emotionless eyes filled with water that never spilled.

22

December 1962–June 1963

A week trickled by before I saw the Mayor again. He was cheerful, walking confidently, looking taller than six feet two. Everybody loved him and he knew it. He passed me twice before I got his attention.

"Mayor Deer?" He pivoted towards me on his boot heel.

"Lamb," he said. "Lamb, Little Bit. Call me Lamb."

I wondered at his innocence and hated to speak, knowing my words would spoil his party.

"Under one condition," I finally said.

"What's that?"

"Call me Leigh, not Little Bit."

A startled look appeared on his face. He laughed.

"Anything you say." He looked at me as if truly seeing me for the first time. "Now what was it you wanted?"

"I need to talk with you in private." The other workers had been eddying around us, the men slapping him on the back as they steered by. He put his hand on my shoulder and, after ushering me to a corner of the room, leaned over.

"Now, what's so important it calls for a confidential congress?"

I tried to look into his eyes, but couldn't hold mine still. After several false starts, I looked squarely at him and just came out with it.

"The scandal about the baby. There's something to it, isn't there?" Deer's face lost all expression. He held me with his eyes for a few seconds, then checked his watch.

In a calm voice, he said, "How would you like to have lunch with the next governor?"

* * *

It was a late lunch and MaryAnn's was sparsely populated. The Mayor called to Bert Bataglia, the owner-chef, for two burgers and two Cokes.

We took seats at a corner booth to wait for the order. Lamb spoke as if he were talking to an invalid.

"How did you find this thing out?"

Only then did I wonder if I were doing the right thing. I hung my head, feeling personally responsible for the baby.

"The newspapers. I went to the *Courier* and looked up the articles on Toni Jo Henry's execution."

"The newpapers couldn't have told you anything."

"Intuition, then," I said. "In the article, Toni Jo said something about making sure her baby had a good home. Sonnier explained the comment as the ramblings of a woman under extreme duress."

"And?"

"And I don't believe that. It just didn't ring true, given everything else I read about her."

Deer looked at me for a while, inspected me. He nodded his head slowly. "All right," he said. "There was a baby. But I don't know whose it was. That's the honest to God truth."

"I was just worried," I told him. "It seemed so obvious to me, others are bound to know it, too. I was worried about what would happen if someone–." I couldn't bring myself to finish.

In a kind voice, not at all upset or nervous, he said, "It's important that you keep this to yourself."

"I will," I said.

* * *

As the gubernatorial race heated up, it looked like a free-for-all. The major contenders early on were ex-House member John J. McKeithen, former Governor Robert F. Kennon, and New Orleans mayor deLesseps Morrison.

Then it seemed as though every brother and cousin that Huey Long ever had decided to run. You'd think the Long dynasty would unite and crush everybody, but that's not what happened. Huey's widow and his son Russell sided with Gillis Long, but McKeithen won the endorsements of Earl Long's widow, Blanche, as well as Mrs. Jewell Long, widow of Congressman George Long, Earl and Huey's brother. Throw in Huey's sister Lucille Hunt and distant relative Speedy Long for good measure, *plus* eight others scrambling for their allegiance, and what you had was a problem in Long division.

Everybody's platform was built of identical planks: taxes, teachers' salaries, education, and racial segregation in public schools, which was supported by all the candidates but one, Lambert Deer. In a public forum, President Kennedy's Civil Rights program was chewed up and spat out repeatedly, causing Baton Rouge newswoman Margaret Dixon to write, "The main issue seemed to be who could hate Mr. Kennedy the most."

Mayor Deer should have been slaughtered in the melee, but he wasn't. While the wolves fought each other, he looked like he could very well make off with the carcass. It was only December, and the primaries were ten months away. Anything could happen.

Mayor Deer had a campaign manager and four campaign secretaries, one for each corner of the state. Reuben McInnis headed up southwest Louisiana. Aggressive and brash, he was just right for the job, but one day Mayor Deer appeared when Reuben was calling Kennedy a nigger lover. Deer fired him on the spot. The next day, to my utter astonishment, he asked me to replace McInnis as campaign secretary for southwest Louisiana. I told him I couldn't do it. He assured me I could. It was like painting by numbers, he said.

Two days before Christmas, the Mayor called me to his office by phone. An hour later, as soon as I could break away, he handed me an elongated box wrapped in red with a green and gold bow. It was a watch. I inspected the watch, trying to figure out what it meant. I didn't want to look at the Mayor. When I did, I saw someone I had never seen before: a handsome, middle-aged man with cool, powder-blue eyes and thin brown hair graying at the temples. The day after Christmas, I was at his house.

On New Year's Eve, he kissed me for the first time. Throughout January and February, we met clandestinely, though not frequently. Often, Lamb was very tired. Lamb. It's funny how easily he became Lamb to me. Now it was "the Mayor" or "Mayor Deer" that sounded alien. We saw each other ten and fifteen minutes at a time, whatever he could manage.

Between the publication of the newspaper article in November of 1962 and April of 1963, the "baby rumor" fluttered in and out of headquarters like a sick, confused bat that finally flopped to the floor, a harmless mouse with wings, panting weakly. Left unsubstantiated, the rumor had run its course and worn itself out. No one seemed to care one way or the other about the Mayor's father's one-time connection with a murderer's imaginary baby.

Quite naturally, since I felt closer to Lamb every day, the death of the rumor served only to pique my interest in it. In May, I called Sonnier, asking him to dredge up anything he could find from his personal files on Toni Jo's tenure at the parish jail. He said that might take a few days. The *Courier* had kept no such records that far back, and whatever had survived from his early days would be boxed in his attic. The next day, I spent my lunch hour in Sonnier's cubicle.

"I thought it would take a few days to locate," I quipped.

"I'm as interested in this as you are. I just don't have time to look through the stuff. Let me know what you find."

I dug gingerly through the box of yellowed pages, brushing off roach droppings with a Kleenex. I immediately recognized some of the articles in draft form.

"What does HFR mean?"

Sonnier looked up from his work. He never seemed in a hurry, but he was always busy.

"Hold For Release." He payed out only the information I asked for, rarely anything extra. The articles contained blue-penciled line-outs here and there, but nothing substantial was deleted. At the end of the hour, I had unearthed no startling discoveries.

"Would you mind terribly if I took these with me?"

"Terribly."

"I'll return them in two days, at the most," I pleaded.

"I didn't say you couldn't take them. I said I'd mind it terribly when you did."

"Oh," I said. "Then that means I can have them?"

"Not *have*," he said. "*Take*. Take and return. In two days," he said as I lifted the dusty box and prepared a hasty retreat before he changed his mind.

As I was leaving his door, he stopped me.

"Miss Bienville. I have only one requirement of you."

"Yes, sir. Anything."

"Find something."

"Oh," I smiled. "I will." I turned to go.

"And *tell* me what you find."

"I will." I stepped around the partition and halted.

"Mr. Sonnier," I said over the wall.

"Yes?"

"It's Miss Bienvenu, not Bienville." I waited for a few seconds. I heard the slow, purposeful scratching of his pencil on paper.

* * *

The most interesting items in the box were Sonnier's notes taken at the execution scene and his article that City Editor Jim Mead had canned. Scrawled in red over the typed manuscript were the words "Yellow Journalism." The spiked rejection was held together by a rusty paper clip. In the margins, Mead had tersely written words like "hearsay," "innuendo," and "fact?"

From the article, I could see Sonnier had been onto something, though he couldn't fill the gaps between his inferences with concrete evidence. Thinking an objective observer from twenty years' distance might see something he had been too close to to notice, I turned to Sonnier's personal notes. Using his own method of shorthand, Sonnier chronicled the movements of the dozen or so legal, clerical, and medical witnesses at the event: their names, functions, and placement around the chair—signing the register, taking position, cinching straps, connecting electrodes, the deadly command, the death-check, the body's removal.

His one blind spot was atmosphere. Rank, fact. Location, fact. Description, fact. Fact-fact-fact. To him, the participants weren't people. They were chess pieces. That's the trained reporter in him, I thought. Or the man in him. A woman might have seen with different eyes. I reread the sheets. The care with which Toni Jo's pantleg was pinned high so as not to touch the electrode and catch fire—a nice detail. It wouldn't have mattered if he hadn't recorded it.

"What's this?" I said aloud. *L. Deer kneels to secure TJ's arms with straps. He coughs. Stands. Tries to clear his throat. Hasty exit. Queasy young dpty. Short commands. Gum taken. Condemned is ready. Final statements? "Give my baby a good home." She begins to yell. Other officials shout. Chaos. Her life stops in mid-sentence.*

"Yell." "Shout." "Chaos." What had actually occurred was at odds with the official report of the execution: "Henry is Silent, Calm to the End." Something else was peculiar, though. Lambert Deer left the scene!

That's the crucial event Sonnier missed. Perhaps he was writing too fast to pay attention to what it meant. I couldn't prove it. But I knew it. That meant I knew something no one else knew, not even Sonnier, who saw but didn't have the eyes to really see. After jotting down Sonnier's words verbatim, I returned the box, asking his forgiveness for not finding anything consequential.

"There's a word for this," I said. "When you engage in fruitless research, what's it called?"

"Water hauling?" Sonnier suggested.

"Right," I said. "I made a water haul."

I next saw Lamb near the end of May. He had been at the capitol for a week. He phoned midday Friday, asking me to meet him at the Sheriff's Headquarters at five o'clock. I had neither the time nor the presumption to ask him why.

At five, I had been waiting for fifteen minutes on the east bank of the ship channel under the Jean Lafitte bridge.

In one unbroken motion, the Mayor stepped from his chauffeured car, took my arm, and sashayed me down the plank of an idling Coast Guard cutter whose deckhand had already freed its ropes. That's the way it was with Lamb: a call, quick instructions, an unusual setting. Instant romance.

We sat in deck chairs drinking Cokes atop the pilot house as the vessel made for the coast at midspeed. Lambert Deer was not a drinking man. We talked and laughed. Threw bread to argumentative seagulls.

Two hours later, we came into Calcasieu Pass at Cameron against an incoming tide, blackfolk precarious on the jetties, pointing their poles at the water as if casting a sure bet. The boat slowed in the current, cut its engines by half. We passed through the rocky straits into the open Gulf and stood, steadied by rails against the slow-rolling swells, in fading light the color of a trout's back. It was like nothing I had ever felt. Expansive and clean. Lambert Deer had a flair for the dramatic. He executed a long kiss.

We always had wonderful times when he came into town after being hauled around the state with his entourage of underlings, men and priests fueled by money and prayer.

The Coast Guard cutter bobbed in the current for a few minutes, turning slowly, like a compass needle, until, aimed for home, the throttle growled to life and shot us upriver into the growing darkness. In the yellow-lighted cabin, we talked of the future, the governor's mansion, ambition, opportunity, and change. A new day. At that moment, I lost all heart to spoil his visionary world with my soiled discovery. It had to be tonight, though. I promised myself.

* * *

Three hours later, in a porch swing on the veranda of his ranch house, June bugs thumping against the screen with a familiar, domestic sound, everything else having been said, I took the first step of a thousand-mile journey.

"I did some snooping while you were gone," I said into the darkness that reeked of cattle and after-shave.

"That right?" He was rocking the swing gently, toes wiggling beneath his socks. "And you found a dead rat in the cistern." We rocked three times before I answered.

"You always do when you go looking."

"Sometimes it's better not to look."

"Cal Sonnier loaned me his notes on the Henry execution." The swing stopped—one, two—then resumed.

"Interesting stuff?" he ventured.

"Sketchy," I said. "Sketchy, but revealing. Between the lines, you know." The swing moved as he nodded. "Sonnier attributed the Deputy Sheriff's retreat before the execution to his being green, a beginner at violent endings." I waited for a response and moved on. "But that didn't make sense. The drama of the scene begged for another interpretation. A young deputy would follow through, don't you think?"

"Why's that?"

"Out of duty, the necessity to learn," I said. "You know. Pride, fear of embarrassment. A dozen other reasons. No, a good deputy would never have left the scene."

"Unless?"

"Unless he were emotionally involved with the condemned." I waited a long while. He wasn't going to help me the rest of the way. I took a deep breath. "He would stay to see an ordinary prisoner executed, but not a woman he was having an affair with."

After a long while, he offered, "The mother of his child."

The swing stopped. The quiet, high-pitched whine of silence filled my ears.

"Something like that," I said.

Lamb stood up and walked through the yellow rectangle of light leading to his kitchen. I heard the sound of ice tumbling into a glass.

23

July–November 1, 1963

Throughout the summer, Lamb and I saw each other as time allowed. He was still mayor, with duties to catch up on when he returned from speech-making forays around the state. If we talked in the headquarters building, it always seemed as though Monsignor LeBlanc was watching us. It gave me the creeps, and finally I mentioned it to Lamb. We had been racing horses around his property and paused to let them catch their breath.

"I know," he said. "He's been poking around, telling me to be careful about appearances. He means well. He probably thinks of it as good moral advice instead of prying into something that's none of his business."

"I understand, but why does he look at me like that?" I stopped to secure a barrette that had shaken loose. "He acts like I'm raining on his birthday party."

Lamb sidled up next to me. He leaned over and kissed me on the cheek.

"Sorry," he said. "There's more. The fact is, he suggested we break away from each other." I glared at Lamb to show my anger at LeBlanc. Lamb tried to recover my lost favor. "Just until the election is over."

"I don't understand. Why does he hang around, anyway? What do you need him for?"

Restless to run again, his horse shook its head up and down and made a snuffling noise.

"He can pull a lot of Catholic votes my way." His horse walked ahead and I spurred mine to catch up. "Fact is, Leigh, I need him."

"And?"

"We'll just have to be more careful about appearances around headquarters."

* * *

We weren't careful enough. In late September, 1963, the first primary less than two months away, Monsignor LeBlanc took me aside and after a few pleasantries smoothly suggested Lamb's success in the race might be jeopardized if too many constituents discovered he was seeing a young girl.

"As far as I can tell," I warmly replied, "we're both adults."

"True," LeBlanc said, "but this is an election and voters are fickle. Take Kennedy. Now he may or may not be having liaisons with Marilyn Monroe, but come lever-pulling time next fall, you can bet your last silver dollar he's going to lose some votes over that deal, whether it's fact or fiction. You see, Leigh, just as much as realities, it's appearances that matter when you're in the public eye."

"*That's* a joke," I said. "The difference is that Kennedy's married, and I'm no movie star. Not by a long shot." Monsignor LeBlanc looked at me with solicitous calm for a few seconds. He was good at that particular expression. He had practiced it his entire life.

"Think about it," he said. "Will you, Leigh? It's important."

I nodded yes just to get rid of him.

* * *

For the next several weeks, Monsignor LeBlanc smiled congenially when our paths crossed. I didn't trust him. He was being kind to me because of some ulterior motive, buttering me up for the kill. In mid-October, LeBlanc approached me again. I knew something was up because his putty-skin looked moist, like he was nervous. He started casually.

"Leigh, your older sister—Maureen, isn't that her name? Did you know she was adopted?"

Furious, I spoke hotly to him. "That's not true. Why are you being mean to me?"

LeBlanc gestured for me to keep my voice down.

"It *is* true," he said.

I tried to whisper, but my words came out as hisses.

"Maureen and I look just alike. People are always saying so, and we both look like Mother. Our front teeth cross just like hers. If you think this *lie* has something to do with the election, why don't you come out and say it?"

"Leigh, I'm sorry. I didn't mean to upset you." He rubbed his hands together. "You're right, Leigh. There's more to this than I'm letting out. But I must *swear* you to secrecy. Believe me, Leigh. You must tell no one."

Now we were getting down to it. There was urgency in his voice, the kind you can't fake. I reminded myself that he was, after all, a priest.

"Okay, then. What is it?"

"No one, Leigh. Not your sister, not Lamb." His dark eyes locked on me soberly. "Leigh. Not anyone."

"All right," I said. "Just say it."

"Maureen is the daughter of Toni Jo Henry."

The floor dropped beneath me. "Oh, God." I closed my eyes. My stomach clenched, and I could feel blood racing through my body. When I opened my eyes, the periphery of the room went dark. "This is ridiculous," I said. "I don't believe you. Even if it's true, I'm not going to stop seeing Lamb. Even if it's true, no one has to know."

"If I know, there must be others who know."

"How do *you* know?" The Monsignor looked at me without replying. "How do you know?"

"Other people know, too. Take my word for it, Leigh. And they might use you to expose Deer at a crucial time in the campaign."

* * *

Toward the end of the second week in November, when the first primary was gathering steam, Monsignor LeBlanc said he wanted to confer with me after work. He was waiting for me on the sidewalk outside the door, mouthing an unlit cigar.

"Come with me." That was all he said as he turned. We walked around the block to the whitewashed brick convent, then up a narrow flight of stairs to a small, dim room. LeBlanc knocked gently on the partially open door and stepped into the room with a reverence I found refreshing. He shut the door behind us and waited a few moments.

"Leigh, I'd like you to meet someone very special. This is Sister Mary Catherine." The nun appeared to be fashioning rosaries out of thin leather strips, tying knots without looking at the artifacts. "She's, well, she's quite agéd. She taught at Sacred Heart Academy for more years than I've been alive." LeBlanc chuckled.

"I'm very pleased to meet you," I said. I stepped toward her and reached out my hand. In spite of her loose-fitting habit, I could tell she was a frail woman.

"Oh," the Monsignor interrupted. "I forgot to mention that Sister Mary Catherine took a vow of silence over twenty years ago. It's not mandatory in her order, but when her eyes began to fail, she decided to mute her voice as well."

The Sister had been writing on a notepad, which she handed me after LeBlanc's explanation. The words, though neatly shaped, flowed across the page heedless of the lines:

I am pleased to know you, but sorry to meet you under these circumstances.

Then, separated from the first message by a thick line, in a darker, more urgent hand,

You are not who you think you are.

I looked at the Monsignor blankly and shrugged my shoulders.

"Sister?" he said. The nun acted on his cue. Without moving from her chair, she reached for a small cedar box on the table by her bed and produced from it a black page filled with white type. LeBlanc took the sheet from her and relayed it to me. I read the document, my heart surging at my unfinished name: Leigh Ann _____. It was a birth certificate. My parents kept our birth certificates in a fireproof strongbox, and I had seen mine only a few times, but I noticed that this one had been altered.

"What does this mean?" I pointed to the word after "Father"— "Unknown."

"I thought it would be best if you saw it yourself."

"I don't understand. Is this genuine?"

"Yes. It's the original. You see, Leigh, like your sister, you're also adopted."

I felt sick to my stomach. I looked at the black sheet and mechanically read it again. Attending Physician: Dr. Silvers. I had never paid attention to that line. Now, I recognized him as the doctor at Toni Jo Henry's execution.

"And Bobby?" I said. "What about him?"

"No, he's your mother and father's real child. They thought they couldn't have children. They had Bobby only after adopting you and Maureen. A happy accident."

After recovering a bit, I said, "Then that explains why Mo and I are so close together in age. I had always wondered about that."

"Yes and no. Look at the date on the certificate."

"Nineteen forty-two." I thought I had been born in 1943. That meant I was twenty-one, not twenty. My head felt light. I pressed on my temples to try to focus. "This is all so confusing."

"When you were adopted as a one-year-old, a new birth certificate was drafted as if you had just been born when your parents adopted you."

"Can they do that? *Who* did that? Isn't that illegal?" Monsignor LeBlanc's face remained expressionless. I was actually older than my big sister. It was all too much to take in at once. Dizzy, I sat down on the mattress and held onto the metal bars at the foot of the bed. "What's this got to do with me and Lamb? Maureen's all the way across the state at LSU. You're being unfair to me."

I finally broke. I cried uncontrollably. Every new statement was a crushing weight. I had to lash out at something.

"None of this makes sense. I can still be with Lamb. No one ever has to know any of these things."

"Leigh, listen to me. I tried to keep you from seeing Lambert the best way I knew. I really did. But you wouldn't give in. And now you have to know everything." Monsignor LeBlanc took a deep breath. He pulled a soiled handkerchief from his pocket and swabbed his brow. "It's not Maureen, Leigh. Toni Jo Henry is *your* mother."

Like an electric shock, a scalding horror shot through my entire body. "Then–."

"You see now why you must stop seeing the Mayor."

Rapidly, I tried to put the sequence together. In jail, Toni Jo Henry had a child by Lamb Deer. It was a girl, who was put up for adoption, and I was that child.

That meant I had to be—. Sister Mary Catherine emitted a rusty sound, like an engine trying to start after a long winter of disuse. The old nun looked at me with dead-white eyes, her head shaking with age, and pointed at me with a gnarled finger. She swallowed and then croaked, "He's your *father!*"

My senses cleared in an instant.

"That's a lie! That's a God-damn lie!"

I had never used such words in my life. LeBlanc and the Sister stared at me, the nun with eyes that seemed to know a great deal more than they could see. Their silence was their reply, and I knew it meant they were telling the truth. The room began to tilt and slowly spin.

"I don't believe you," I said weakly. Still, they said nothing. I put my hand over my mouth. "I'm going to be sick."

Monsignor LeBlanc reached under the bed and produced a chamber pot. The muscles in my stomach contracted, but there was nothing for them to give up. I heaved several times. Finally, two clear, slippery ropes of sour bile drained from my mouth into the pail.

When I regained my composure, Sister Mary Catherine handed some books to Monsignor LeBlanc, who passed them to me. They were diaries, the last two years of Toni Jo Henry's life, verification of what he had revealed to me.

That night, I went straight to my room, telling Mother—my adoptive mother—that I was tired. She said I should eat something before retiring. I told her burgers had been ordered in at headquarters for the late workers.

As I read the diaries, I wouldn't let myself feel convinced that I was a part of all this, the daughter of a murderer, the only woman executed in Louisiana's electric chair. It was preposterous. I kept reminding myself that I had always been suspicious of Monsignor LeBlanc. He might be lying to me for reasons of his own.

I read about Toni Jo Henry's surrender and confession, the trials, Arkie Burk's hanging, Toni Jo's strategies to get her execution changed to electrocution. Then luring the man she called Slim, their excursions outside the jail, their first kiss. The story seemed completely unbelievable, but no one could make up something like this. I got nauseous when she wrote about kissing Slim, the Mayor, Lamb Deer, my love, my father.

After five minutes of giving up nothing but viscous strands of saliva, I returned to the entries. Toni Jo's anger at having her baby—me—stolen from her. Then, written after it had failed, a description of her postpartum escape plan.

In the early morning hours, I reached the last week of my real mother's life. Feeling light-headed, I went to the icebox and returned with a Coke. I looked at the next entry—November 21, 1942—then at my calendar. November 21, 1963. And I was 20. Chills broke out on my arms. No, I caught myself, I was 21. That would take some getting used to—one less year to live than I thought I had.

I knew the execution date without looking: November 28. She would have had seven more days to live. I paused to wonder what I would feel if I had only one more week to spend in this world. I read the last pages of my mother's life.

"Deathwatch." There was that word again. The last twenty-four hours. I wasn't even in the middle of the diary. It didn't seem right. There should have been more pages. Then I remembered that she was paying for a crime, giving her life for taking a life. I turned to a new page, the final entry:

November 28, 1942.
On the last day of my life,

This entry, the diaries, and her life ended in mid-sentence. I wondered what she had been about to write, and what had interrupted her.

Then I was done, and I had to come back to my own life. The horrible, horrible reality came upon me again. The idea that I had kissed my father disgusted me. I stood up. I had been sitting cross-legged on the bed for so long that my legs wobbled with weakness. I felt light-headed. Little worms of light swam in my vision, and I was forced to sit down again.

Even after all the terrible things I had read, a single event kept screaming for attention. I had kissed my father. I felt the gassy syrup of the Coke coming up and ran for the bathroom. The carbonated liquid burned my throat as it spilled into the bowl. The awful smell rose in my nostrils. I flushed the toilet and waited for the next wave of nausea.

After the water settled, I looked at my tired face, transparent on the slightly disturbed surface. Then it hit me. I was sick because I was pregnant.

24

November 22, 1963

Yes. That, too. My own father. As horror was added onto horror, I had to know more. For the first time, I went to Monsignor LeBlanc and asked for any information he could give me that I didn't already have. He said I knew everything of consequence, but if I wanted details Sister Mary Catherine could supply the remaining diaries. I was surprised by this, thinking Toni Jo Henry had kept them only while an inmate in Abraham Deer's jail.

I spent the rest of the day and the entire night reading the diaries, flipping back to reread passages that later entries shed new light on. Sunlight had been coming through my window for nearly an hour when Arkie Burk picked up a hitchhiker and Herald Nevers was finally dead. I felt a strange sense of satisfaction. I had been lost in thought for some time when Mother called me for breakfast. I told her I wasn't feeling well and wouldn't be going in to work.

I fell asleep and awoke at eleven, famished. I washed my face and stepped outside, surprised at how clean I felt, despite the truth that was growing inside me.

Even before walking to MaryAnn's for a burger and Coke, I knew what I was going to do. I had no idea what I would do tomorrow, but I knew that today I had to find my mother's grave.

I took a bus to Highland Cemetery after calling the caretaker for information regarding the burial place. The voice on the line said that every year three or four curiosity-seekers called about the grave, which was unmarked, as all murderers' resting places were, to prevent desecration of the headstones or vandalism by souvenir hunters. The best he could suggest was to look in the northwest corner, for maybe an empty plot between other tombstones.

I wandered around the sector methodically, trying to avoid the ground

I had already covered by weaving up and down the serpentine paths between the graves. After a futile search of an hour or so, I returned to town. When I stepped from the bus onto the curbside, I sensed a peculiar dread in the air. Down the block, people were huddled on streetcorners, looking up at radio speakers saying something that made their hands cover their mouths. It all sounded garbled to me until I walked closer and heard the voice, crackling with static, break through:

"The announcement is now official. At one P.M. Central Standard Time, President John F. Kennedy was pronounced dead at Parkland Memorial Hospital, after being struck on a Dallas street by an assassin's bullet. A man calling himself Lee Harvey Oswald is currently in police custody . . ."

25

December 1963

The world is very different now.

When I heard the news of the assassination, I dropped to my knees. For almost an hour, I was so stunned I forgot about my own problems. Here was a man who symbolized hope and charity for a whole generation, a whole country—a Catholic who opened doors for fellow Catholics, for Lamb Deer and others like him. And his life was snuffed out in a few seconds. The tragedy reminded me of how little my life was, and how utterly valuable.

As usual, we had our first freeze just after Thanksgiving. The leaves were dying, and yet there was something eerily beautiful about it all. Birth, death, renewal. I had a lot of thinking to do. The first gubernatorial primary was over and Mayor Deer was still in the race. I looked at my parents—I mean Mr. and Mrs. William Bienvenu—as if they were strangers. They were good people ignorant of the pain they caused by their pure innocence. My grief or tragedy or whatever I'm caught up in was caused by deception on the part of . . . how many? A half dozen people? More?

My parents obviously didn't know where their second daughter had come from. Or was I adopted before Maureen? I guess it's all futile speculation at this point. Still, it would be nice to walk up to *someone* and, with a mouthful of blame, let them have it.

I thought of killing myself. That would be the easiest way out. Or I could go somewhere and have the child, then give it up for adoption. I could try to have the baby removed. I had heard of it. I just never imagined I would be on the deciding end of something like that.

Should I let Lamb know?

Know what?

That I am pregnant?

That he is my father?

Let him know one, but not the other? Know that I have decided to have the child, hide the child, lose the child?

What would he do? Kill himself? Reject me?

Send me away so he can play governor?

Into the midst of my doubts and worries and wrestlings with my conscience floated another matter: Should I tell Maureen she's adopted? Was Mo, in fact, adopted? Or was that a ruse by Monsignor LeBlanc? I forgot to ask. Mo—my big sister who is younger than I am. My world could go in any of a hundred directions based on any of these decisions.

I know only that I will not choose to destroy the baby. I have an older, unborn half-sister that my real mother was forced to expel by a man she trusted and ended up dying for.

Then I was brought into the world as part of a plot so she could escape from a hospital with her life. Although I had no choice in it, everything surrounding my life has been wrong.

Up to this point. But I can clean the slate and start anew.

The worst part is that I still love him, Lamb Deer. And I *have* to see him one more time. I've been imagining the scene. I will reveal nothing to him. Not who I am, or who I know him to be, or what my condition is. I will surprise him by kissing him full on the mouth. I can see his face. His eyes will twinkle and he will say, "Well, Little Bit. What's that for?"

"That's because I love you," I will say. Then I will slap him on the face, hard. "And that's because I hate you." And then I will walk away and never see him again.

At least, that's the way I imagine it will be, if I have the guts to do it.

* * *

It is the first day of December, 1963, the day I start my life. From what I have been able to learn about Toni Jo Henry—when I call her that, I have to remind myself she's my mother—I must believe that she was a good woman. If anything, she was too good. One of the lessons she taught me is this: there's danger in trusting everyone. If you do, you're gullible and probably deserve what you get. So I don't want to trust everybody, but neither do I want to assume the worst of every person I meet. Somewhere between relentless suspicion and blind trust, then— that's the right place to live. Sincerity can always be subjected to proof.

While packing, I reviewed the case many times. Toni Jo Henry met someone who took advantage of her, and her system couldn't stand the shock of discovering the true nature of this man she loved. So my mother learned, and then practiced, a savage wisdom. But I will avoid that.

Well. There. Now I must *do* something, something that signals an end as well as a beginning. I look around my room one last time. I feel for the ticket in my coat pocket.

Now, carrying you—my daughter and half-sister, your father's daughter and grandchild—I, Leigh Ann Bienvenu, will go forth into the world and practice a wary goodness until I get it right, until it becomes a habit and I earn my only sure reward. Then I will write this all down and pass on to you, when you are nearly grown and need the lesson, as much of it as I think you can bear.

The Beginning

Norman German is a professor of English and fiction editor of *Louisiana Literature* at Southeastern Louisiana University. His short stories appear in literary and commercial magazines, including *Shenandoah*, *The Virginia Quarterly Review*, *Salt Water Sportsman*, and *Sport Fishing*.

His novel *No Other World* fictionalizes the life of Marie Thérèze, the ex-slave slaveholder who founded Melrose Plantation near Natchitoches, Louisiana.